Also by Samantha Chase

EXCLUSIVE
······· AND ·······
A TOUCH *of* HEAVEN

SAMANTHA CHASE

sourcebooks
casablanca

Published by Sourcebooks Casablanca, an imprint of Sourcebooks, Inc.
P.O. Box 4410, Naperville, Illinois 60567-4410
(630) 961-3900
Fax: (630) 961-2168
sourcebooks.com

Printed and bound in Canada.
MBP 10 9 8 7 6 5 4 3 2 1

For my mom: For always believing in me. For always encouraging me. For always being there with the advice I needed. But mostly, for simply being the best mom. Here's to the spa we often talk about and maybe someday will own. Love you!

Contents

EXCLUSIVE

Prologue

"Are you sure about this?"

He nodded. "I think it's time."

"I'm not so certain. Why her? Why now?"

He rolled his eyes because this wasn't up for debate and it wasn't as if they hadn't had this discussion before. "We've been over this before. The book sales have far surpassed anything I ever imagined, and with the movie deals coming in, I think it's time to start inching my way into public life." His words were met with a laugh.

"You have no idea how lucky you are. The fact that you've gone this long without anyone having a clue as to who you are, where you live—hell, no one even knows what you look like! Are you sure you want to give that up?"

He nodded. "It's time." Standing, he looked at the framed photo on his desk and smiled. "Believe it or not, I miss being a part of something…more."

"You can be a part of anything you want. No one has to know who you are or what you do for a living. For crying out loud, create an identity for yourself and go out and live a little more if that's what you want! I just think inviting a bunch of people—"

"Not a bunch," he cut off, "just one."

"You're seriously losing your mind, you know that, right? There is no way anyone is going to agree to that kind of condition. We can say that there can be no more than three—"

"No," he said more firmly. "One. She comes alone, or it doesn't happen."

"And then what will you do? Will you just forget about this entire thing? Go on living like this—cut off from the world? Is that what you want?"

Sitting back in his seat, he sighed. "She has to come. I know that in the end, she'll agree to the terms." He paused and looked across the room at his friend. "And besides, don't be such a drama queen. I'm not cut off from the world. I live a very fulfilling life and I do socialize."

"Going into town to food shop and waving to people on the dock when you take your boat out is not socializing."

"It is to me."

"Okay, fine," his friend said, obviously realizing it was pointless to argue. "I'll draw up the papers and make the connections and then…we'll see." He looked down at the papers in front of him. "These dates work for you?"

"I'm the one who picked them, so yes. They work for me."

"Okay, good. I wouldn't want to interfere with all of your waving and picking produce."

"Good one." He rose and held out his hand. "Thank you for handling this for me. Let me know the minute you hear back from her."

The door closed and he let himself relax and sit back down. He had never planned for his life to work out quite like this. Didn't think he'd live to see it end up like this. And yet here he was. For years he'd enjoyed the quiet, the solitude, and the freedom to blend into the background without anyone knowing exactly who he was. It had been novel at first, even a little fun. But now, he wanted more. For all of his accomplishments, there was still something missing.

He could buy anything in the world that he wanted. His success had afforded him that. But the one thing he wanted most, he couldn't buy. When the idea first hit him to do this, to allow himself to be "unmasked," he knew there were dozens of media outlets that would kill for the opportunity. He didn't want a media circus, and he didn't want to be looked at like someone who belonged in a freak show.

This was his life. He'd created it. He'd earned it. He'd nearly died to have it. It was time for the world to hear his story. He was fortunate enough that he had the power to choose who to tell it to.

If only she'd agree to come.

Chapter 1

A CUBICLE WAS A DEPRESSING PLACE.

There weren't enough photos of tropical getaways, mountain views, or favorite vacation spots that could possibly begin to make you forget you were crammed into a tiny square of space where the air was stale and that the sun always failed to reach. Taylor Scott reached out and straightened her postcard from Florida and frowned, wishing she were there—or anywhere— right now.

"So, tell me everything you know about Jonathan Wade."

Taylor knew it was the voice of her senior editor without looking up. "Excuse me?"

Sitting down on the corner of the cluttered desk with a dramatic sigh, Victoria Martin finger-combed her silvered hair behind one ear as she looked down at her youngest reporter. "We just received an exclusive invitation to interview Jonathan Wade! Can you believe it?"

Honestly, Taylor couldn't. "So...do you need me to pull up some file footage on him or something?"

Leaning forward, Victoria smiled like the Cheshire Cat. "He has requested that *you*, and only *you*, do the honors."

That got Taylor's attention. Her head snapped up as she pulled off her glasses. "*Me?*" she squeaked as she looked around to see if Victoria could be addressing one of her coworkers. They all appeared to be staring at their computers and listening to music as they went about their tasks. "Jonathan Wade wants *me* to interview him?"

"Exactly," Victoria said with a hint of exasperation. "Now, tell me everything you know about him." She straightened on her perch, crossed her arms over her chest, and waited for a response.

"I'm afraid I don't know much, Vic," Taylor stated as she made herself more comfortable in the squeaky leather chair. "He's a bestselling mystery writer. His books have been topping the *New York Times* bestseller list for over five years, they're loved and admired by men, women, and even teenagers. The movie adaptation of his first book, *Midnight's Obsession,* is due out in theaters early next year and is already gaining Oscar buzz. He's won several literary awards—which he never accepts in person—and he's a recluse."

"Recluse is putting it mildly, Taylor. No one even knows what the man looks like! There's no telling if he's young, old, married… Nothing. His agent and publisher have been most understanding about not putting his face on the book jackets." She flipped her hair over her shoulder and looked down at Taylor. "If it were me and I were his agent, I might have gone along with the whole thing in the beginning, but I don't know how they're able to keep it up—especially with the movie coming out!" She shook her head in disgust. "They claim it adds to the 'mystery of the mystery.' Whatever the hell that means."

Victoria was a brilliant editor and mentor, but irony just seemed to escape her at times. Taylor looked up at her expectantly. She'd known her boss long enough to know she wasn't done with this discussion.

Pushing a stack of papers aside, Victoria leaned forward again on Taylor's desk and narrowed her hazel eyes. "So how do you know him, Tay?"

"What? I don't! Why…? What would make you even think that?"

"You mean to tell me a world-famous reclusive author wants a relative newcomer to the field of journalism, who works for a little-known magazine, to get the exclusive interview of the century?" It wasn't like Victoria to be so sarcastic, but right now her voice very nearly dripped with it.

Taylor stared back and shrugged. "Look, believe what you want, but I have no idea who this man is. I don't have a clue why he wants me for this piece, but I guess I'll do it."

"Of course you will, Taylor. Don't be ridiculous," Victoria stated in her authoritative boss voice. "The concessions for the interview rights are a little demanding, but I guess when you are offering this kind of story—and it's exclusive to us—you can ask for whatever you want." Taylor arched a brow, intrigued. "He wants you to meet him up in Maine on his farm. According to the request he sent, it's in a place called Mechanic Falls. Ever heard of it?"

Taylor shook her head. "No." Sitting up straighter in her chair, she turned to her laptop and began furiously typing to get her search started.

"Anyway, his agent will be sending you directions once you sign a confidentiality agreement." Taylor's only response was to nod as she continued her online search. "He wants the interview done over a two-week period. You may take pictures, but you will have to be the photographer—no other staff is permitted to go with you."

Looking up from her screen, Taylor hesitated. "I don't know how much I like this, Vic." Uncertainty rang out in her voice. "For starters, I am certainly no photographer and—"

"This is the opportunity of a lifetime, Taylor. Don't think, just do!"

"Oh, sure, that's easy for you to say! You're not the one going off to some tiny town where no one knows where you are or who you're with! No one knows what he looks like, and yet I'm not supposed to think about it!" She stood abruptly and began to pace in her tiny square of office space. "I mean, honestly, I'm twenty-eight years old and work for *Newslink* magazine. I know what goes on in the world, and I know what kind of freaks are out there. How do we know this request is legit and not from some man who molests women or a crazed ax murderer or something?"

"Geez, Taylor, ease up on the drama, will you? Our legal people are hammering everything out to ensure your safety as well as Mr. Wade's privacy." Victoria stood and placed her hands on Taylor's shoulders. "You are a very lucky young woman, Taylor. This kind of story this early in your career could mean big things for your future." She released Taylor and walked toward her office, turning to look into the cubicle one last time. "It could be your ticket out of this tiny magazine and on to *Time* or *Newsweek*. Think about it."

Oh, Taylor would think about it, all right. In fact,

she had a feeling she wasn't going to be doing anything *but* thinking about it. Sinking back in her chair, Taylor rubbed at her temples. Just thinking about it now was giving her a headache. Sure, it was the opportunity of a lifetime for someone in her position, but at the same time, it was scary as hell to take that leap.

What if she wasn't up for the challenge? What if she wasn't as good a journalist as she thought she was? Could she honestly deal with that kind of criticism and rejection on such a grand scale? Because there was no doubt this story was going be seen and read internationally. This one story was going to put *Newslink*—and her—on the map. Would her career survive if her story was deemed horribly written? Would she end up working in a mail room somewhere and that would be the closest she came to working in an office ever again?

Headache.

Migraine.

Nausea.

Opening her desk drawer, she bypassed the Advil and grabbed the antacids. Popping several as if they were Pez, she chewed and contemplated all the ways this could go south for her. Her writing could be ripped apart, Jonathan Wade could be a boring or uncooperative subject, her camera could break and she'd have no pictures—on and on her mind spun with negative scenarios.

"Okay, stop it," she muttered as she reached for the Advil. Shaking off the negative thoughts, Taylor grabbed her pad and pen and began making notes on the town of Mechanic Falls—size: eleven square miles, population: thirty-two hundred per the last census, blah, blah, blah. It sounded like the perfect place for a recluse to live. Too bad she couldn't get information on the type of farm he owned or the size of it. Taking a chance, she went to the online white pages and typed in "Wade." No listings. Not surprising. *Like no one's ever thought of that one before*, she thought with disgust.

Discouraged, she tossed her pen down and put her head in her hands. There was the very real possibility Wade was a pen name. Authors did that all the time.

"Think, Taylor, think," she muttered to herself. A Google search proved to be another dead end, with nothing more than the barest of information—all of which she already had. Even by page ten in the search, she couldn't find one bit of new information. Standing, she stretched. "Clearly this is not the way to go." She walked over to the tiny kitchen area and got herself a glass of water before going back to her cubicle to pace. If anyone thought there was something wrong, they didn't mention it. Her coworkers were going about their days as if she wasn't even there—as if the fact that what could possibly be the story of the decade hadn't just been dropped into her lap.

Pulling out her chair, Taylor sat down and took a different approach. "His catalog," she said softly. "I've got to get my hands on all the books he's written. Maybe there's a clue in them as to who Jonathan Wade is." A quick search had her filling her e-reader with the dozen titles that were available. "Hmm, maybe audiobooks would be a better—and faster—way to go. Then I can listen to them while I take notes…" The idea had merit and left her excited that she'd be able to get so much done while doing her research. She was familiar with Wade's books—she'd even read a few—but for the most part, she didn't spend what little free time she had reading. Her work kept her so busy with research and writing that the last thing she wanted to do in her down-time was look at more words.

Living in New York City gave her so much to do to fill her time. She jogged, she biked—her favorite form of stress relief—and walking around the city left her with endless inspiration for stories to write. She was always able to get a good grip on her subjects before she sat down with them, to form the kind of questions that engaged her subjects, and they were impressed with her advance work. Taylor had a sinking feeling she was going to come off sounding like a babbling idiot to Jonathan Wade simply because she was walking in there blind. It made her pretty uncomfortable. She didn't like being at such a disadvantage.

Staring at her reading list, Taylor tried to form her first opinion of the author. An image of an older man— probably in his sixties—with graying hair and a serious expression popped into her mind and wouldn't budge. It fit. For the types of mysteries he wrote, Taylor thought he must have lived a fairly full life from which to get his ideas.

Standing again, she stretched her tired muscles—too much biking the day before—and headed down the wide hallway toward Victoria's office to find out when this mystery assignment was supposed to begin.

"You didn't mention when I'm expected up in Maine," she said as she breezed into her boss's office. Victoria was finishing a phone call and held up a hand for Taylor to give her a minute. Looking around the room, Taylor envisioned having a big office to herself someday. No more cubicles. This particular office wasn't her style—a lot of black lacquer and chrome, with no warm colors or comfortable, overstuffed furniture.

She was so lost in her observations she didn't notice Victoria's phone call had ended until she was standing directly in front of Taylor. "Well, he wanted you up there immediately, but I put him off for a few days so you'd have time to cram. You're expected on the farm Friday afternoon. I know it means working over the weekend, but I didn't think you'd mind. The top brass have agreed to fly you up to Maine—business class—and pay for a rental car, if you'd like."

Taylor was floored by the offer. The management of the little-known magazine was notoriously tight with money and expense accounts. That they were willing to splurge made her feel as if she was finally being taken seriously.

"I guess it would probably be for the best. I'm sure the drive up there would be wonderful, but I don't think my ratty old Jeep would make the trip."

"I thought you got rid of that? It costs more to park it than it's worth."

So true, Taylor thought. "I've got it parked at a friend's place on Long Island. When I go out to visit, it's nice to have a car of my own to drive."

"Honestly, Taylor, once this piece comes out, you can junk that vehicle and move up in the world! Buy a vehicle from this decade, for crying out loud!" Victoria was beginning to get excited about the whole thing. Taylor only wished she could match her enthusiasm.

"That remains to be seen," she stated levelly. "Do we have any kind of schedule yet? Have we gotten an outline of how this is all supposed to go?"

Victoria reached for a stack of papers on her desk before turning back and handing them to Taylor. "Legal is looking over the contracts, but this stuff here only pertains to you."

Taylor hesitantly took the papers. "What do you mean?"

Victoria gave a small shrug. "These cover things like how many hours a day you'll have access to Mr. Wade, your accommodations at the farm, and the parameters for the questions."

Taylor quickly scanned the documents. "Wait a minute," she said and homed in on one particular item. "It says here that for the first week I'm not going to have access to Wade at all." She looked up at Victoria in confusion. "What is the point of being there if I'm not going to be allowed to talk to him?"

"Yeah, I saw that too. He's out of the country doing research for his next book." She shrugged it off. "It looks like you'll be doing a lot of preliminary stuff with his assistant."

What little wind Taylor had in her sails over this assignment quickly left her. She collapsed into one of Victoria's uncomfortable chairs and sighed. "Well, that just sucks."

Taking pity on her, Victoria sat down beside her and took one of Taylor's hands in her own. "Look, I know it's not perfect, but you're looking at it the wrong way."

"Wrong way?" Taylor repeated with exasperation. "How can I be looking at it the wrong way? I'm expected to go to a place I've never heard of, to interview a person no one has ever seen, and to be away from home to work on an interview for two weeks when I'll only have access to my subject for one of them! I'm getting less and less comfortable with this interview the more I find out."

"I know it's not ideal—"

"That's an understatement."

"But the assistant could be a wealth of information."

"Or she could be there to blow smoke up my butt for seven days." Taylor wondered if maybe she would be able to bond with the woman over manicures and pedicures or chick flicks and ice cream...the types of situations where women normally got together to talk, relax, and generally gripe about life. That could totally work.

"He."

"What?" Taylor asked.

"He. Jonathan Wade's assistant is a man."

Great. There went her momentary splash of inspiration of having a little girl-time to fish for information. With her luck, the assistant was probably older than what she imagined Wade to be and was more like a stuffy, formal butler. She immediately began scanning the documents again for some sort of information on the assistant—something, anything!

"Michael James Greene Jr.," she read aloud. "Well, that doesn't tell me much."

"What were you expecting?" Victoria asked.

She shrugged. "I don't know. I just—" Stopping, a slow smile spread across Taylor's face.

"What? What are you smiling about?"

Another shrug. "I used to know a Mike Greene." She paused. "It was a long time ago and I haven't talked to him in years, but...what are the odds of it being the same guy?"

"Pretty slim. After all, it's a fairly common name."

"I suppose. Still, it's kind of a coincidence, don't you think?"

Victoria didn't seem fazed either way. "Wade's traveling and wants the prelim stuff done before he gets there."

Maybe now was the time to voice her concerns before negotiations went any further. "Look, Vic, I know you're super excited about this assignment, and I'm aware that it's a huge honor that Jonathan Wade has asked for me specifically, but—"

"No," Victoria interrupted. "There is no 'but' here. Yes, this is a little unconventional, and yes, it's a little weird to be going so far into the unknown, but think about all you stand to gain from this! You're getting the interview with the man everyone wants to interview! He could have gone to Katie Couric, he could have called Oprah...but he didn't. He wants *you* for this project! Can you honestly stand here and tell me you're going to walk away from that kind of opportunity? Do you really want to be known as the person who walked away from the chance of a lifetime?"

"Do you realize this could all backfire?" Taylor shot back. "This guy could be a total freak! His assistant could be a total freak! You're sending me to a farm in the middle of nowhere with two guys who no one knows! I think I have every right to be a little bit skittish about the whole thing. I want someone else with me. A photographer, a bodyguard...somebody!"

Taylor was growing more and more frantic with every word she said and clearly Victoria knew she needed to act quickly to get Taylor to calm down. "Okay, okay,

okay…" she soothed. "I see your point and I don't want you to worry about it. Let me talk with legal and with Wade's people and see what we can do, okay?"

Taylor was fairly shaking, but she agreed and stood on unsteady legs. "Okay. If it's all right with you, I'm going to head out of the office. Grab some fresh air and maybe something to eat. I've downloaded all of Wade's books so I can listen to them while I do my research and go about my day."

"That's very clever," Victoria said, speaking carefully so she wouldn't spook Taylor more than she already was.

"I wish I had my bike with me," Taylor said, more to herself than to her boss. "A good ride would go a long way to help me relax and come to grips with this assignment."

Inspiration struck. Victoria came up beside Taylor and put her arm around her. "Why don't you take the rest of the day off? Go home, grab your bike, and go for a ride. It will be good for you."

"But…?"

"Taylor, this is an important assignment and I've already gotten approval to let you know that if you need to work from home until you leave, that would be okay. Just check in and keep me posted on how it's going and how we can help. Okay?"

Nodding, Taylor considered the offer. "And you'll get someone to go with me?"

"As soon as you leave, I'll get on the phone to try to make it happen."

The fact that it was a long shot was left unspoken. "Sure. Okay." Taylor stepped away from Victoria. "Vic?" The older woman stopped to consider her. "I won't let you down. I know this is a big deal, and I'm just feeling a little overwhelmed by it all. But I promise to do my best to make the magazine proud."

———ᴧᴧᴧ———

As soon as Taylor stepped out of the building, she felt like she was able to breathe for the first time in an hour. Her day had started off relatively boring—as did most days—and never in her wildest dreams could she have imagined the turn of events that took place today.

Why her?

Why now?

All around her, people were walking and going about their business. Didn't they see she was spinning out of control? That the biggest celebrity interview was just dropped in her lap and rather than feeling privileged and honored, she wanted to run and hide? Obviously not, judging by the way no one even glanced in her direction.

Damn city.

Taylor didn't live far from the office, but today the short walk gave her time to think and plot and plan her strategy for this assignment. She felt so far out of her league and yet invigorated at the thought of this being the piece that helped her break out.

As she walked along the crowded streets, her mind raced with different angles to approach her subject—and then convinced herself they all sucked. She second-guessed everything she thought up, and by the time she was walking through the front door of her building, she was exhausted. She climbed the four floors to her apartment and quickly closed the door behind her before sinking to the floor.

What had she agreed to?

How was she going to make it work?

What if her story wasn't good?

On and on the questions swirled in her mind until her headache grew from dull pain to full-blown pounding.

Trying to push her depressing thoughts aside, Taylor wondered where the confident girl of eighteen had gone. She had started college with all the confidence in the world—she was going to win awards with her stories and be the darling of journalism. She almost snorted at that thought now. *Darling of journalism?*

After all her years of studying and writing and researching, she had some success in her career—yet still she felt inadequate. Maybe that was why this assignment was weighing like a boulder around her neck. Why would someone as gifted and sought-after as Jonathan Wade want her for such an anticipated piece? Surely all the major television networks as well as the mainstream news publications would be better suited for a man of his caliber.

Ah…that had to be it. Because of who he was and the life he'd led, maybe he still didn't want the glare of the media on him too strongly. A well-known journalist would bring a lot of publicity in their wake. Maybe Taylor was a safe entry back into the world without complete loss of privacy through overexposure. That had to be it.

Relaxing a bit, Taylor recalled what she did know about Jonathan Wade's writing.

All his books had a recurring theme—his hero-slash-detective was not quite the same caliber as James Bond, but was compelling and handsome just the same. He attracted women as Bond does, but Jonathan Wade's detective was constantly searching—no, aching—for the one woman who got away.

His description of this elusive woman struck a particular chord with Taylor. Maybe it was her own ego talking, but the woman's physical description almost fit her perfectly. From the blond hair and aquamarine eyes to the height…why, the woman in all the books even had a birthmark on the small of her back like Taylor did! It was an eerie coincidence.

Surely that's all it was, right? Honestly, Taylor wasn't conceited enough to believe she was the only blue-eyed blond on the planet with a birthmark, was she? Still, when she read or listened to his stories, she'd mentally placed herself there, in the arms of the hero. The woman of his fantasies.

How awesome would that be? If such a thing were even possible. As far as she knew, Taylor had never been anyone's fantasy—and she had the dating track record to show for it. So for a little while, as she prepared for her trip, she allowed herself to slip into the world Jonathan Wade had created and pretended there was at least someone out there who pined for her.

Too bad he was fictional.

What must that be like—to be the object of one man's fantasies? To know there was a man out there who was consumed with thoughts of you and who would move heaven and earth if he could, just to be with you. Did such a love even exist? It had never happened for her, and with thirty quickly approaching, she feared it never would.

Chapter 2

FRIDAY MORNING FOUND TAYLOR UP BEFORE DAWN TO catch a 9:00 a.m. flight out of LaGuardia up to Maine. Sleep had become a distant memory since accepting the assignment. She'd been listening to Wade's books almost nonstop and she was down to the final one. For days, she had listened while at her laptop until her eyes crossed just trying to find something—anything—about the man. It seemed as if he had appeared out of nowhere almost eight years ago. How was that possible? Bill collectors looking for her wayward mother seemed to find Taylor no matter where she moved, even when their last names were different! How could someone so popular be so hard to find?

Knowing it was finally time to get started had given Taylor her first glimpse of peace in days. Who knew, maybe she'd actually get some rest once she was up at the farm.

She glanced at herself in the mirror and earnestly began to pray for a full night's sleep once she arrived. Taylor had never been a woman to obsess about her appearance, but she began to worry about how Jonathan Wade—and his assistant—were going to react to seeing this clearly exhausted mess coming to stay in their home. Maybe she'd scare them and they'd ask to do the interview over the phone or via Skype!

Leaning closer to the mirror, Taylor came to the

conclusion that makeup would have to go a long way in hiding the shadows under her eyes. All her life she'd been told how blessed she was with her hair, her skin, all the things women placed in the hands of professionals to make them perfect. Her hair was naturally blond; the highlights in it caused her to receive envious looks from women in salons, but to Taylor they meant nothing. She wore it long, easily six inches past her shoulders, and straight. Ponytails were a favorite style because they required so little effort.

True, she had gotten it cut yesterday just to make it look a little neater and more polished, but as much as her stylist begged, Taylor refused to budge on shortening her long locks. And she'd even splurged on a manicure and pedicure—just because. And an eyebrow waxing. With one last swipe of the mascara wand, she cursed the fact that she hadn't gotten the facial or the massage. Maybe then she wouldn't look so damn tired. At the time, she'd thought it was the right decision—it was practical—and she prided herself on keeping her life as practical and uncomplicated as possible.

It was her life's motto. Her appearance, simple. Her little studio apartment six blocks from the office, simple. Too many complications made her crazy. She didn't date much because she valued her privacy and had experienced far too many crazy boyfriends who'd walked away after messy breakups. Was she lonely? Maybe. Did she miss the sex? Not as much as she would have thought. Still, it would be nice to find someone with common interests who she could spend some time with—occasionally—and just fill that tiny void in her life that needed to be filled.

Something she'd have to look at a little more closely when she got back from Maine.

———∼∼∼———

Sitting on the plane awaiting takeoff, Taylor let her mind linger on all the things she had packed for this assignment. In her habit of simplicity, she had made a list and only took what she deemed absolutely necessary. True, she had no real idea what one needed for life on a farm, but she figured no one was going to ask her to go out and feed chickens or milk cows.

At least she hoped they wouldn't.

Mentally cataloging the numerous pieces of equipment she'd packed—digital audio recorder, cameras, laptop, batteries, flash drives, and chargers—brought on the now-familiar headache she was beginning to associate with this assignment.

The only thing missing was the colleague Wade would not allow.

Her insecurity was starting to get the best of her and if she didn't get it under control right then, her work would most definitely suffer.

Taylor couldn't remember a time in her life when she didn't enjoy writing. As a grade-schooler, she wrote short stories; in high school, she worked on the school newspaper, and her friends used to marvel at the letters she'd write to them. By high school, she'd known her destiny was to be a journalist, and she'd even received a scholarship to Columbia University because of her talent.

A lot of good it was going to do her when she fell on her face before an international audience because she had a mental breakdown on a plane over this assignment.

Sighing at yet another depressing thought, she fought to focus on the audiobook that was playing. It was a ninety-minute flight up to Maine, and then it would be another hour's drive to the farm. Taylor needed to finish this audiobook and get her thoughts gathered so she was prepared to meet the man who had taken up her every waking moment for the last five days.

Or, rather, meet his assistant.

If all went as planned, she was confident that her knowledge of his work would carry her through the early parts of the interviews with Wade himself. As for the assistant, she was sure she was coming properly prepared for her time with him. She'd want a tour of the farm and to find out how long he'd worked for Wade, and then gauge how much information he'd be willing to give. She wouldn't jump into instant interviewer mode with him. No, Taylor figured she'd have to spend some time earning his trust without appearing overanxious.

Plus, someone in his position might have a lot of insight into Wade's private life. Things like his dating habits, his love life, and if this mysterious woman in his books was based on someone he had once loved and lost. Perhaps, if she presented it correctly, when Wade met her, he would be so impressed by her interactions with his assistant that he'd be ready and willing to open up about his private life.

She'd have to remember to play it cool. Be charming. Not look too anxious. She chanted that quietly to herself for a few minutes before glancing out at the clouds and finally allowing herself to relax and enjoy the voice on the recording.

—◊◊◊—

The flight was uneventful and Taylor's pleasure was prolonged by the fact that the car rental agency did, indeed, have a car waiting for her and she was checked in efficiently. Taking the keys from the rental agent with a smile, she was thrilled to see the sporty white SUV waiting for her.

"Thank you, *Newslink*," she said to herself as she climbed into the brand-new vehicle. "Mmm…new car smell and everything!" She was positively giddy. There was no other way to describe it. Starting the car—and it started on the first try!—she took a quick look around to get her bearings. She punched the farm's address into the GPS system and once it was ready, plugged in her iPod so she could finish listening to the conclusion of *Enveloping Darkness*, then pulled away from the parking lot.

The drive was beautiful and the sound of the masculine voice coming from the stereo kept her in a state of pure relaxation. If the man Jonathan Wade picked to read his books looked as good as he sounded, Taylor knew she would have found her perfect man.

Some authors did do their own readings, so for a minute, she allowed herself to imagine it was Jonathan Wade's voice coming through the speakers. If it was, talking with him for a week would certainly be no hardship! She'd resort to asking his favorite color and what he liked for breakfast if it meant keeping the conversation going.

The voice was deep and mesmerizing, almost like a caress, like he was speaking only to her. The voice didn't sound old, but then again, there was no guarantee Jonathan Wade actually was old. She slammed her hand on the steering wheel out of frustration and cursed— again—the fact that she had no bio to go on for this interview. If only she had a little more information in her pocket, she'd feel more prepared and at ease! How could a person be so popular in modern culture and yet have so little known about him? It was even more frustrating and intimidating to know that she was going to be responsible for presenting this mystery of a person to the world.

What if he didn't live up to what everyone was expecting? Or, more to the point, what if he didn't live up to what Taylor herself was expecting? Taylor scolded herself to relax already, and listened intently to the end of the book.

The sun was rising over the clear blue water. Marcus knew his time on the island was over. Had last night been a dream? Had he truly awakened in the night to the feel of skin so soft against his that it felt like silk? Were those her lips that had kissed him with the kind of tenderness he'd only ever felt with one person?

Remembering her touch, how her breath felt on his heated skin, had him aching to feel her again. Why was life so cruel as to keep taking this woman from the arms that wanted nothing more than to hold and protect her forever? She had been full of heat and life in those arms last night.

There was no evidence of her now. One day, however, there would be no questions. His answer would be standing in his embrace.

Sighing, Taylor thought this particular voice was

definitely one she would love to stir her awake in the night. If the man in question lived up to that sexy voice, there would be no way she'd sneak off in the night. Hell, he'd have to pry her off with a crowbar!

Feeling suddenly hot, she flipped on the AC, laughing at herself because it was October, in Maine, and the temperature outside the vehicle did not demand air-conditioning. It was her own wildly vivid imagination—and sexual dry spell—that was heating her up. Lord help her, she needed to gain her composure and be professional at all costs during this entire process in order for this piece to be a success. What on earth would she do if the man was attractive? If just his voice could make her this hot and bothered, she'd be a babbling idiot by the time the two weeks were up.

Shaking her head to break that train of thought and looking at the GPS to see how much farther she had to go, she was surprised to see she was just minutes from her destination. Feeling nervous and self-conscious, she did some deep-breathing exercises and practiced using her "professional" voice.

As if on cue, her cell phone rang and made her jump. Putting it on speaker, she said, "Hello?"

"Everything going okay?" It was Victoria.

Taylor couldn't help but smile. If she wasn't mistaken, her boss's voice sounded almost as nervous as her own. "Yes, boss, all is well. I'm driving a wonderful little SUV, the sun is shining, I'm only minutes away from the farm, and I feel ready to conquer the world!" *Liar, liar, liar!*

"You *are* going to conquer the world, my dear. You mark my words. Once this piece hits the stands, you are going to be the toast of the town and you can say I was the one who gave you your first big break."

"I'll remember that." Taylor chuckled.

"Good luck, Taylor. I'll expect to hear from you in a few days." And then she was gone and Taylor felt a little bit lighter than she had just moments ago. She could do this. There were people who had confidence in her and she owed it to them to have confidence in herself.

Feeling revived, she pressed down on the accelerator. What she had been dreading, she was now ready for: to reach Jonathan Wade's farm and to face her journalistic destiny.

She rolled her eyes. "Geez, dramatic much?"

She very nearly missed the entrance to the farm while she was laughing at herself. It was poorly marked by an undistinguished simple white mailbox. Then again, what was she expecting, a neon sign flashing *Home of Jonathan Wade*? Slamming the brakes hard, she put the vehicle in reverse and then pulled into the long dirt driveway that wound through a quarter mile of dense forest. When at last she was through the trees, she stopped the car.

The house was large, yet so simple and beautiful that it took her breath away. If Taylor could pick one house to live in, she knew this would be it. It was like something out of a magazine and yet like nothing she had ever seen before. All white with black trim, it was two stories, but she wouldn't have been surprised to find out there was a finished lower level for extra living space. If she had to define the style, she'd say it was a Victorian country farmhouse. If such a thing even existed.

There was a large wraparound porch with hanging

plants and flower baskets lining it, and she could imagine sitting outside on a warm summer night just watching the sunset—it was that perfect. Although she couldn't see from where she was parked, she just knew there would be seating areas and a porch swing up there waiting for someone to use them.

Off to the right of the house was a barn. Traditional in style but painted to complement the main house, it came off as an extension of the house rather than a utility building. Maybe it was in the landscaping, but to Taylor's mind, it all seemed too pretty, too perfect, to be what she normally considered a barn. Even though the house boasted a three-car garage on the side, to the left of it there was a detached two-story, two-car garage— also matching the house—and just beyond that was a large expanse of open land.

Taylor could only stare. All her life she'd lived in a big city or crowded suburbs. That was where all the action was, all the jobs, everything a person could need. The older she got, however, the more she found herself longing for peace and a little solitude. Wouldn't it be lovely to come out and sit on the porch swing after dinner and hear nothing except the sounds of nature?

"Get a grip!" she yelled at herself. A quick smack on the head brought her back to reality. "You're barely on the man's property for two minutes and you're fancying yourself living here and enjoying peaceful nights on the porch!"

Pulling up in front of the detached garage, she parked and emerged from the vehicle. Closing the door, Taylor stopped, stretched, and took in a breath of what had to be the most magnificent air she had ever inhaled. *So this is what nature's like?* she thought to herself. Upon closer inspection of the property, Taylor found the green of the trees looked brighter than she had ever seen; the changing colors of the leaves almost looked too perfect to be real. If she stood still long enough, she could hear the distinct sounds of different species of birds. At home, all she ever heard was the constant hum of traffic. But here, on this particular piece of land, Taylor felt as though she would be able to hear a leaf fall.

She could commune with nature later. She tried to decide if she should introduce herself before she unloaded her car or after. Stepping around to the rear of the SUV, she came up short when she noticed a man walking toward her. Taking a steadying breath, she pasted a wide smile on her face.

This is it.

He was a young man, maybe a few years older than she was. His brown hair looked sun-kissed and although it was a bit unkempt, it seemed to suit him. He was dressed for work on a farm—blue jeans, thermal Henley, down vest, and boots. He was taking off his work gloves as he approached, and Taylor couldn't help but notice how large those hands were, and when she looked up, she was greeted with eyes so dark blue they were almost black. When he stopped in front of her, he gave her the most endearing smile ever bestowed upon her.

She smiled back as she held out a hand to him. "Hi, I'm Taylor. Taylor Scott." He didn't say a word, but once he wrapped one of his large hands around hers and held it, her heart just about beat right out of her chest. It was big and warm and just rough enough against her softer skin that all kinds of erotic images began to play in her head. There was something oddly familiar about him, and Taylor figured she'd better find out exactly who he was before she did anything to embarrass herself. "Are you…Mr. Wade?" she asked casually.

He laughed, but rather than taking offense to his response, Taylor almost immediately relaxed. "Not hardly," he said. His eyes met hers and he knew the instant recognition hit Taylor.

"Oh my God!" she gasped. "Mike? You're—" She stopped as realization hit her. Michael James Greene Jr. She had been right! "I can't believe it's you!"

"Hey, Taylor," he said, his own posture relaxing a bit. "How are you?"

"I'm good. It's been a long time."

"Ten years," he said easily.

She nodded her head. "Wow, I didn't realize it had been that long. How have you been? What are you doing here? Wait! Are you…did you…" She cleared her throat and tried to calm her nerves. "Are you the reason I got this interview?"

Placing his other hand over the one he was already holding, he leaned in a little closer. "That's a lot of questions," he teased. "And we'll get to all of them—after we get you inside and settled into your room. Lunch is ready, and I figured we could talk and get caught up then if that's all right with you."

Taylor sent a silent prayer heavenward for her good fortune. At least with a familiar face around for the next two weeks she'd feel a little less overwhelmed and outnumbered. True, it had been ten years since they'd last seen one another, but for a short period of time, he had been a very important part of her life. It was going to be great not only to get this interview, but to get caught up on what Mike was doing with his life.

Other than working on Jonathan Wade's farm.

Before she knew it, he had her luggage out of the SUV and was closing the trunk. "We can get the rest later if you'd like," he said. Doing a quick tally in her head, she knew all that was left in the vehicle were some smaller bags with her equipment, but she wasn't going to need any of them right now. "Sounds good to me," she said and started to follow him toward the house.

He was just as attractive from behind as he was from the front. Mike hadn't been quite this built back when she knew him, and for just a moment she allowed herself simply to appreciate the sight of him. Yeah, he could definitely be an asset to her for the next two weeks. Everything that was female about her melted just a little bit merely remembering the touch of his hand on hers.

A low hum of appreciation escaped before she could stop it and Mike chose that exact moment to turn around and smile at her. *Oh my*. Between the hands, the smile, and…just him, Taylor had a feeling she was going to be a babbling idiot anyway.

It was going to be a long two weeks.

Chapter 3

THE DOOR OF THE GUEST ROOM CLOSED BEHIND HER—after she promised Mike she'd meet him downstairs in ten minutes. Taylor wanted to ask for longer but her stomach's growling had given her away. Sheer embarrassment had her practically closing the door in his face just so she could have a moment to recover.

The house—what she'd seen of it so far—was even more magnificent on the inside than the outside. She had only managed to see the two-story foyer and to catch a glimpse of the dining room to the left and the parlor to the right as she followed Mike up the stairs, but as she turned around and looked at the room that was going to be hers for the next two weeks, she felt like she had won the lottery.

The walls were painted the palest of pinks, and the entire back wall seemed to be dominated by the bed. The headboard was upholstered in a slightly deeper shade of pink and surrounded by an antique fireplace mantel that had been painted white. There was a mountain of pillows on the bed in varying shades of pink and white. As she stepped closer and ran a hand over them, she noticed all of the fabrics varied as well, with cottons and linen and satins and silks…it almost made her want to crawl in the bed right then and there.

On either side of the bed, over the petite nightstands, hung delicate crystal chandeliers. Her mind was spinning at the thought of sleeping in this room. Just standing in it made her feel like some sort of princess. She had never been a girlie-girl, but being here now, it kind of made her wish she was a little softer, a little more feminine.

"So not gonna happen." She sighed and moved her luggage over to the closet and went into the en suite to freshen up so she wouldn't be late for meeting Mike.

Mike.

Wow. She never would have seen that coming in a million years. For so long, Taylor had wondered what had become of him. Seeing him today was a shock to her system. They had met the summer after she had graduated high school. He was a friend of the boy she was dating. Mike had been older than they were, but her boyfriend always thought he was more mature than people their own age and, therefore, Mike was cool to be around.

And he was.

The three of them went everywhere together. It wasn't until summer was nearing its end that she realized Mike was there to act as a buffer between her and Eddie who, it turned out, had been cheating on her the entire time they were together. It hurt when she found out, not so much about Ed's cheating but how Mike had known and hadn't said anything. She had thought they were friends, but she was wrong. And then one day he just stopped coming around.

Tossing thoughts of that summer out of her mind for now, Taylor focused on making sure she looked all right before heading back down the stairs and joining Mike for lunch.

She took her time, going down the curved staircase slowly, pausing to notice the crown molding and the beautiful paintings on the wall. For such an impressive house, what stood out the most was that it looked as if it were meant to be lived in and not just for show. That little bit of information was something she was going to tuck away for her article, and it made her like and respect Jonathan Wade just a bit more.

Mike was waiting for her at the base of the stairs. "I was going to come up and get you," he said with an easy grin. "I didn't point you in any direction when I left you upstairs."

Taylor chuckled. "Believe me, after the way my stomach growled earlier, I would have found you."

"C'mon," he said, holding out a hand to her, "lunch is on the table."

Taylor looked at his hand and then at those intense blue eyes and wanted to melt right there on the stairs. Probably not the best way to get reacquainted. Daring to be bold, she put her hand in his and—fireworks. That was the only way to describe it. Her body fairly vibrated at the feel of his large hand wrapped around hers. Where earlier it was a casual handshake, this definitely felt more like an intimate caress, and if Taylor didn't get ahold of herself soon, she was going to do something completely inappropriate.

Like jump him.

Wordlessly—and praying he hadn't noticed her odd reaction to his touch—Taylor followed Mike into the kitchen and came to a stop. Mike turned around and looked at her curiously. "Taylor? Are you all right?"

"We're still in the house, right?" she asked as she stared at the room around her. It was Mike's turn to chuckle. "I mean, I didn't miss anything like us leaving and driving someplace else, right?" He still didn't comment, only stood there and watched her with an amused look on his face. "This is just beyond anything I've ever seen." She pulled her hand free, and while she missed the connection immediately, she was too busy touching all the surfaces and mentally making notes.

"It's just a kitchen, Taylor," Mike said, but his tone implied he knew it was more than that—like he wanted her to voice what it was that she was seeing.

"Oh, it's so much more than that," she said with awe. "This is…a dream. This is one of those kitchens even the laziest of cooks don't mind making a meal in."

"There are lazy cooks?"

Taylor looked over her shoulder at him and smiled, then raised her hand. "I enjoy cooking, but there are times when I don't want to put the effort in. But in this kitchen? I don't think I'd ever leave it. I think I'd stay in here and cook food for the next six months, and then still want to cook more!" She opened drawers and cabinets and the refrigerator and freezer and then marveled at the eight-burner gas stove. It was almost an orgasmic experience.

Luckily, she caught herself before she let out another moan. Pulling herself together, she turned and faced him with a sheepish smile. "Sorry. My entire apartment would fit in this kitchen. It's a little surreal."

Still amused, he said, "It is impressive, I'll give you that. Come on, I know you're hungry." He motioned toward the farm-style table that was set up next to a large bay window overlooking the yard. Taylor sat where Mike indicated and soon they were next to one another with a feast laid out before them.

"Is someone else joining us?" she asked as she practically sat on her hands to keep from reaching out and taking one of everything that was on the table.

"Nope. Just us."

"Seriously?" Her eyes went huge and when he nodded, she had to accept that after this, Mike would definitely know she was not soft and girlie. She was hungry and she was done waiting. "Then if it's all right with you, I'm going to help myself." And she reached out and took a couple of spoonfuls of tortellini salad and then helped herself to what looked to be a freshly baked ciabatta roll, right before getting a scoop of chicken salad. Sitting back for a minute, she scanned the table and speared some fruit from the fruit salad. When she eyed the platter of baked goods, she considered what was already on her plate and decided she'd still have room to sample them when she was done.

She had cut open the roll and was putting the chicken salad on it when she glanced at Mike. "The only thing I can say in my defense is that I didn't eat this morning." And then she picked up her sandwich and took a bite.

And moaned.

That was when Mike began to put food on his own plate. He had been having such a good time watching Taylor that he hadn't wanted to look away. But now that she was clearly starting to relax and enjoy her lunch, maybe he felt he could do the same.

With more than half of her food gone, Taylor decided to stop and breathe. *Very unladylike, but it was all so good!* To stop herself from continuing to gorge, she put her fork down and looked at Mike. "So, I have to tell you," she began, "seeing you today was a total shock. Was it just a weird coincidence or did you sort of help me get this assignment?" When Mike hesitated, Taylor rephrased her question. "Why don't you tell me how you came to be working up here in Maine? Last I saw you was when we both lived on Long Island."

He seemed to relax and wiped his hands on a cloth napkin before folding them on the table. "I've been up here for about six years now. I take care of the house and the property. It's peaceful here. I didn't think I'd enjoy the quiet so much. Now that I've been here and gotten settled, I can't imagine being anyplace else." He took a sip of the fresh iced tea before looking at her again. "What about you? Are you still actually on the Island or are you living in the city?"

She nodded. "In the city. I've got this tiny little studio apartment, but the rent is fairly reasonable and it's close to the newsroom. It's definitely a lot more crowded and louder than it ever was on the Island and there are times when it overwhelms me, but…I like it."

He wasn't so sure he believed her, but he left it alone for now. "And you've been with *Newslink* for, what? About three years now?"

She smiled at the fact that he seemed to know about her and had followed her career. "Yup. It's not glamorous by any stretch of the imagination, but it pays the bills."

"But is it your dream job? Is it where you see yourself in five years?" he asked, clearly interested in learning more about her.

"No, it is definitely not my dream job, but with the way journalism and trade papers are going, I feel lucky just to have a job in the field. I've gotten to meet a lot of interesting people and for the most part, it's a good job. I just want…more."

"In what way?"

She shrugged. "I want to write for a paper or a magazine everyone knows and respects. I want to have my work on page one instead of page seventeen." Leaning back in her seat, she closed her eyes briefly and allowed herself to admit out loud what she normally kept to herself. "I want to write more than fluff pieces, and I know it sounds crazy, like some sort of cliché, but I do want to write the great American novel." She opened her eyes and looked at him. "I know I probably shouldn't say that, especially here in the home of one of the greatest writers in the world, but there it is."

"There's nothing wrong with what you're saying, Taylor. I think it's great that you have a dream and if I know you, you'll find a way to make it happen."

"I enjoy interviewing people. I love talking to them and hearing about their lives and the stories they tell. Maybe I don't have to write novels, but maybe help people write their stories, their memoirs or biographies." She shook her head and waved a hand at him. "Don't mind me, clearly I still don't know what I want to be when I grow up."

"And still I say there's nothing wrong with that. Not everyone figures it out in their twenties."

"Thirty is approaching like a freight train," she said and then laughed. "I always thought by now I'd be doing something…more with my life. You know?"

He nodded. "I may be in my thirties, but this isn't the life I thought I'd have either."

"I think you're very lucky."

His eyes went wide. "Me? Why?"

"Look around you! You take care of this incredible place and you get to walk around in peace and quiet and breathe in the fresh air. I look at you and I'm envious. You're the first person I've ever met who looks… happy. I look at your face and I see a man who seems to have peace."

If she only knew, he thought. "Well, I am happy here. I get to make my own hours for the most part and the biggest demands are the ones I make on myself. I still don't know how it happened—I feel like it all sort of dropped in my lap."

"That's amazing. I can't imagine what it must be like to work for someone like Jonathan Wade. I'm really nervous about meeting him. I mean, I don't know anything about him other than his books and now I'm here for two weeks and I just wish…"

"You have nothing to be nervous about, Taylor," he reassured her as he placed one of his hands over hers. Their eyes met this time—he had felt it too. The connection. The spark. Clearing his throat, Mike did his best to act as if nothing happened. "Trust me. You're going to be fine."

Taylor wished she could believe him, but right now the only thing she could focus on was the touch of his hand on hers. She had to get over this. It was crazy. She'd held hands with dozens of guys and it wasn't such a big deal. Why it suddenly turned into one with Mike, she had no idea. Somewhere in the back of her mind, Taylor knew she needed to break the connection, but couldn't seem to do it. Instead, she decided to distract herself with talking about something safe.

"This house is amazing. That room I'm staying in is like something out of a fairy tale. It's made for a princess. Does Mr. Wade have a daughter?"

Mike smirked, and it was as if he knew she was fishing without knowing she was fishing. He shook his head. "No, Mr. Wade doesn't have any children."

"But…the room? It's far too beautiful to just be a guest room. I can't believe he'd go through so much and put so much effort into a room that probably never gets used."

"It doesn't get used a lot, but he entertains from time to time. The house was like a project. It was custom-built to a very specific set of—well, specifications, and it's been a work in progress ever since."

"Are there any parts of it that aren't done?"

"Every room has been done and is decorated and does get used, but every now and again they'll get a little facelift or a complete makeover."

"Wow," she said in amazement. "A facelift in my place is getting new slipcovers for the ratty old sofa I have." She chuckled. "It's the most comfortable sofa I've ever had, but it's ugly as sin. Every once in a while, I have to change the slipcover to make it look pretty again."

"Hey, if it's comfortable and it works for you, then more power to you." He liked this, this casual banter that seemed to encompass everything and nothing all at the same time. "So, tell me how you ended up in the city."

"It just made sense. I went to college at Columbia and I lived in the dorms. I interned all over town and made some good connections. By the time graduation rolled around, I knew I wanted to stay in the city. There wasn't too much waiting for me back home. My mom had moved in with her boyfriend and it just made more sense to stay where I was."

"At least you found a place you could afford. I hear the rents are crazy."

She nodded. "I'm subletting from someone, but it's not someplace I want to stay permanently."

"Where would you like to live?" At his question, she laughed and shook her head. "What? What's so funny?"

"I've been living in the city for so long that I never thought about living anyplace else. But once I got here? Suddenly, it was like my eyes were opened and it was very easy to start dreaming about living in the country."

"You could. There are definitely more places like this that are more affordable than what you'd find in the city."

"Yeah, but…work."

He squeezed her hand. "You're going to write a book, remember? You won't need to commute to an office."

"Right. And I'm going to get that six-figure advance to live on so I can make that happen. I wish."

"Stranger things have happened, Taylor. Trust me." They sat in companionable silence while they finished their lunches. Taylor, unable to stop, helped herself to a brownie and a cookie, and when Mike saw her eyeing a second cookie, he chuckled.

"What? What's so funny?"

"It's refreshing to sit with a woman who actually eats. And I mean something more substantial than a salad. I'm glad you're enjoying the food."

"Like I said earlier, I hadn't eaten breakfast, but in general, I do enjoy eating. I do a lot of biking and luckily I have a good metabolism, so it hasn't caught up with me yet."

"Biking, huh?" She nodded. "Well, there are some great biking trails nearby, but even just out on the roads around here, you won't find a lot of traffic to disturb you. We've got a couple of bikes out in the garage so feel free to use them while you're here."

"Seriously?"

"Sure. No one else is using them and it's not like you're going to be working all day, every day, for the next two weeks, right?"

"I hope not!" she said. Once she settled down, she would need to get started with her work. Clapping her hands together and rubbing them, she looked at Mike. "Okay, so I'm supposed to work all this week with Mr. Wade's assistant. Your name was on the paperwork and I know you manage stuff for him here on the farm, but I'm guessing there's probably someone else I'll be speaking with, right?"

Mike was confused for a moment, but instantly recovered. "Taylor, I'm Mr. Wade's assistant. I'm the one you're working with. There's no one else. Why would you think that?"

Her eyes went wide. "It's just…I mean, you said…"

"Yeah, I mean…I told you I manage the property and all. I just figured you would know that I—"

"Oh my gosh, I'm sorry!" she said hurriedly, and then put her hand over his. "I didn't put the two together. I just thought you were the guy who handled all the big stuff around here. You said you managed the property and it's quite expansive, so I didn't think you'd also have to take care of the business stuff, too." Her earlier image of an old stuffy butler came to mind and she broke out in another fit of laughter.

"Now what's so funny?" he asked, mildly amused himself.

"It's just…" she began and then started to laugh in earnest again. "All this time I've been trying to picture in my mind the people I'd be meeting here. And I guess I had Wade's assistant in my head as being a really old guy! Like in a suit…like a stuffy old butler!" She saw Mike wasn't laughing along with her and instantly sobered. "Sorry. I don't know why I thought it, but I did. I hope I didn't offend you."

He shook his head. "No, no—no offense taken. I forget that when you're as isolated as Wade is, people will form opinions and judge you simply because they don't have anything else to go on."

"I wasn't judging, Mike," she said a little defensively.

"No, I get that. But this is the first time I ever gave a thought to what people must think about this whole situation. Tell me the truth," he said as he leaned forward, "when you were offered this job, what were your first thoughts?"

"Seriously? I almost fainted. I couldn't believe I would get offered the opportunity to interview Jonathan Wade. I thought it had to be a mistake."

"Okay, but beyond the professional aspect of it, what did you picture in your mind when you were told you were coming up to the farm for two weeks?"

"I didn't want to do it," she said honestly. "I told my editor I wasn't comfortable with the whole thing, that I wanted to have at least an assistant with me."

"Why?"

Now she looked annoyed with him. "Are you for real? I'm a single woman being told I have to travel all the way to a remote farm to stay with a man nobody has ever seen and nobody knows anything about except for his body of work. And on top of that, I'll be working with his male assistant." She gave him a level stare. "What woman in her right mind would consider such a thing?"

"And yet you're here," he responded with a hint of sarcasm.

"Only because it was made very clear that if I didn't come, I'd pretty much be sealing my fate."

"Wait," he said as he sat up straighter, "that wasn't part of the deal. In no way was your job supposed to be used as a bargaining chip. You have to know that, Taylor. That wasn't something that was done on this end."

She held up a hand to calm him. "I know that, but you don't know my boss. She's seeing this interview as the thing that's going to put *Newslink* on the map."

"It will."

"Oh, I know. But if I didn't do it, it wasn't like they could send in another reporter to get the story. The contract was very specific that it had to be me." She paused and considered her next words as she met Mike's eyes. "Why?" she asked, her voice going a little softer. "Why me?"

Mike held her eyes, but he didn't answer right away. He couldn't. The time wasn't right. When he noticed Taylor was starting to squirm in her seat, he smiled. "I guess that's something you'll have to wait and ask Mr. Wade."

She sagged dejectedly in her seat. While she knew Mike was probably not at liberty to share the reasons why she was the one here, she had hoped that due to their former friendship he'd be willing to give her a hint.

Her disappointment was obvious and Mike knew he should do something to make it up to her. "Tell you what, how about we work off a little of this lunch by taking a tour of the farm? Would you like that?"

It wasn't quite what she was hoping for, but considering she was here because she had a job to do and part of it was doing research on her subject, Taylor supposed it would be wise to start learning about him—starting with his property.

This was the most bizarre assignment she had ever had, and nothing was going in the order she was used to working in. Going with the flow was one thing, but she felt like she was completely battling the tide here.

"Sure," she finally said. "That sounds great." She rose and began clearing the dishes.

"Taylor, what are you doing?" Mike asked, taking a plate out of her hands.

"Cleaning up, why?"

"You're a guest here. You don't have to do that."

She playfully pushed his hands away. "Oh, please. I'm nobody, and if I'm going to be here for two weeks, living in the house and all that, I'm perfectly capable of picking up after myself."

"Yeah, but—"

"Not another word. I don't expect to be catered to while I'm here. So let's get this cleaned up and then I'm just going to freshen up. Remind me to grab my camera and my recorder from the car, please."

For a moment, Mike could only stand back and stare. Ten years ago, he had known she was different—someone who was honorable and gracious and…special. She chatted about the plane ride as she cleaned and loaded the dishwasher and Mike found himself completely enthralled with her all over again.

Two weeks may not be long enough.

Chapter 4

MIKE WAS ALREADY WAITING FOR TAYLOR BY HER SUV when she came out. Within minutes, she had her equipment and Mike was taking her by the hand and leading her to the barn.

"We have several horses who live in here," Mike said easily. "There's been talk of expanding the barn and boarding horses, but it's never panned out. So, for now there are four of them and they're great for getting around on the property." Then an idea hit. "How about it, Taylor? Would you be willing to tour the property on horseback?"

A moment of pure panic hit her. *Horseback? What was he, crazy?* She was a city girl. She rode a bike, in cabs, on the subway—not horses. "Um…maybe not on my first day," she said and flushed with embarrassment.

"That's fine," he said with a chuckle, sensing her uneasiness. "I've got a truck to take us around, but I want you to promise me you'll try it at least once while you're here. You don't have to go all around the property, but at least try a short ride."

She took a deep breath and let it out slowly. "Okay. But only a short one."

"Deal." He showed her the stalls, the tack room, and the ring behind the barn where they exercised the horses, and even introduced her to some of the farmhands.

"How many other people work on the property?" she asked.

Mike thought for a second. "All in all, including in the house, I'd say there's about a dozen people."

"Including you?"

He nodded. "We've got a great staff here, and it's a real group effort to keep the grounds looking like they do."

"It's amazing," she agreed. "You can't even see it from the road. It's such a pleasant surprise when you finally get through the trees and see all of this."

"And this is just the beginning," he said with a broad grin and reached for her hand again. "C'mon. Let's head back over to the garage and I'll take you on the real tour."

Excitement bubbled up inside her as they walked quickly across the massive yard. A cool breeze was blowing and there wasn't a cloud in the sky, and Taylor had to remind herself that she was working. So far, she had spent the day catching up with a friend and eating delicious food. Now she was going to drive around without a care in the world.

Opening the garage door, Mike motioned toward the Jeep that was parked inside. It was topless and a lot newer than Taylor's, and she could only stop and stare at the beauty of it. Mike caught her expression and worried for a minute. "The Jeep makes it easier to get around on the property. Most of the paths are pretty rough and none of them are paved. I hope you don't mind."

"Mind? Are you kidding? I'm having total Jeep-envy right now!" She laughed as she climbed in and buckled her seat belt. She looked over at him excitedly. "I have a super-old Jeep back home, and although I hardly ever have the opportunity—or the need—to drive it, I just can't seem to let it go."

"I can understand that. I pretty much kill a lot of the

trucks we have because the paths are so rough, but at the same time, I kind of like driving them. So far the Jeep has held up the best."

She smiled and held on as he backed out of the garage. He noticed where her hands were and laughed. "You'll have a white-knuckled grip before too long," he teased. When they were fully out of the garage, he looked at her one last time. "You're sure you're okay with this? We don't have to do this today if you don't want to."

Taylor gave him a look. "I'm a lot tougher than you think. I can handle a little bit of four-wheeling," she said and straightened in her seat. "Bring it."

Mike threw the truck in gear and they took off. With the roof off it was difficult to talk much over the sound of the engine and the wind blowing, so Mike did his best to slow down or stop when they hit a point of interest. He hadn't lied when he said it would be a bumpy ride. The paths were clearly defined but definitely rugged, and some of the entrances weren't so clearly marked. More than once Taylor felt her heart thumping in her chest. Mike knew exactly what she was thinking and was having fun playing with her like this.

Over the course of the ride, he pointed out where the large vegetable garden was and talked of what they grew there and how some of what they had eaten for lunch had come from it. Next came the fishing pond—man-made and stocked because Wade loved to fish. As they came around a bend, Taylor noticed animals off in the distance.

"What kind of livestock does he have here?" she asked curiously.

"There are about a dozen head of cattle, maybe a half-dozen sheep, plus the horses."

Taylor was impressed. There wasn't much else to see that was so out of the ordinary, but the picturesque nature of the property as a whole kept her mesmerized. Mike continued to drive around—pointing out different types of birds and trees—making sure Taylor was able to get her photos and experience it all.

When they arrived back at the garage, Taylor was surprised that three hours had gone by. "Wow," she said as she climbed down. "That was the fastest three hours I've ever spent."

He had to agree. It had been a long time since he had taken the time to go through the property so thoroughly—even though he knew the importance of it. But it was also the chance to see it through someone else's eyes—Taylor's eyes—that had him feeling as if he was seeing it all for the first time. While he knew the place like the back of his hand, he had forgotten the simple joy in spotting a scarlet tanager or a red-winged blackbird. As he watched Taylor's response to seeing them, he remembered a time when it had been thrilling for him, too.

When had that stopped?

They were heading back toward the house when Taylor paused. "I'm sure you have stuff to do that doesn't include entertaining me. If it's all right with you, I'm going to go up to my room and start making some notes for the article—you know, talking about the things we saw today and whatnot—and then some questions for you for later. If you don't mind."

"I don't mind at all. That's what I'm here for."

She smiled at his words and didn't doubt his sincerity. "Still," she began, "I don't want to keep you from anything important."

"I'll let you know if that ever becomes a problem, okay?" He loved watching the play of emotions on her face as she relaxed. "What do you say we meet up for dinner in about two hours? Will that give you enough time to start your notes?" Taylor nodded and walked into the house while Mike stood and watched the door close.

As much as Mike was enjoying their time together, he definitely needed a little time alone to get his head on straight. He'd known seeing Taylor again was going to cause a little inner turmoil—she was the one he had wanted, but she'd belonged to his best friend. Now, all these years later, it was as if no time had passed at all. One look at her and he was ten years younger and they were connecting just as they had back then.

While getting caught up today had been great, Mike knew it was just a matter of time before the past came up in conversation. He had to brace himself for it, because it wasn't pretty. He had a feeling that even though he was ashamed of the things he had done, Taylor might not be so shocked. He was well aware of what people thought of him back then—and Taylor knew most of it—but he never wanted the ugly part of his life to touch her.

It was why he stayed away.

But she was here now. Granted, she was here to do a job and interview Jonathan Wade, but for this week, she was with him and only him. He intended to honor the terms of the contract and let her ask all the questions she wanted about the great author, but that didn't mean he wasn't going to make the most of their time together. There were so many things he wanted to show her, share with her, that he was itching to get started.

A week wasn't going to be enough. He knew when

his time was up and he had to hand her over to the subject of her assignment, he would be all but forgotten.

—–∿∿∿—–

Two hours later, Taylor found Mike in the kitchen. She adjusted her glasses and looked around the room. Normally she didn't wear her glasses around anyone, but she just didn't have the energy to deal with her contacts right now. She was ready to relax.

The aroma from whatever was cooking made her mouth water. She stood in the doorway and watched as he set the table and arranged a bouquet of fresh wildflowers in a vase, and couldn't help but smile. She had yet to see who the mystery chef was, because this was twice in one day that she had arrived and the food was already waiting for her. A girl could get used to this sort of thing.

As if sensing her presence, Mike turned and caught Taylor's eye. "Hey," he said as he straightened. "I was just going to come and get you. Everything's ready. I hope you're hungry."

"Clearly you don't know me all that well," she said with a chuckle. "I'm pretty much always hungry." She stepped up to the stove and lifted a lid, moaning with delight. "And all that stuff they say about the mountain air increasing your appetite? It's true."

Leaning against the counter, Mike considered her. "There's only one problem with that theory."

"What's that?"

"We're not in the mountains." He waited for that to register and then almost burst out laughing at her crestfallen expression.

"Oh."

"Not to worry," he said as he approached her. He leaned in close. "They say the same thing about country air."

"Oh—you!" She swatted at him playfully. They worked together to put dinner on the table—pork chops, mashed potatoes, sautéed green beans, and a salad. They sat down, and Taylor felt Mike's eyes on her. "What?"

"I don't remember you ever wearing glasses," he said simply, his chin resting on his hand as he looked at her face.

"Oh, well...I avoid wearing them in front of other people because I feel like they make me look like a dork, but after flying today and the drive around with the top down and then all the time on the computer, my contacts were killing me. It was either peel them out now or scratch the hell out of my eyes later." She heard him chuckle. "What's so funny about that?"

"You are like no other woman I've ever known, Taylor," he said honestly as he helped himself to a spoonful of mashed potatoes. Then he stopped and thought for a moment. "Then again, you've never been overly concerned about your appearance."

"Well, thanks a lot!" she snapped defensively and grabbed the bowl of potatoes from him.

"No, no!" he said quickly. "I didn't mean that in a bad way. It's good. More women should be like you." His voice softened. "I've always thought it was cool that you weren't the type of girl who was more concerned about what she looked like than anything else."

She blushed, at a loss for what to say.

"Of course, it does help that you were always beautiful, so you didn't need to worry about anything."

Her blush deepened and she stood up quickly. "Um…I'm going to grab some iced tea. Would you like some?" Mike shook his head and held up his glass of water, watching her walk across the room as he kicked himself. He had made her uncomfortable. That was the last thing he wanted to do. He rested his head in his hands and tried to come up with something witty to say to change the subject when he heard a crash and Taylor cried out.

Jumping up from his seat, he saw the broken glass on the floor and blood gushing from Taylor's finger. "Oh my God, Taylor! Are you all right?" He crouched down beside her and inspected her hand. Carefully, he helped her step over to the sink to get cleaned off. He kept his touch gentle as he ran her hand under cool water and then raised her fingers to inspect the damage. He was holding her from behind and it didn't take long for him to realize this position was so not helping him.

Taylor looked over her shoulder with wide eyes. "I…I don't think any glass got in. It's just a cut. I grabbed at the glass to try to clean it up and it just slipped." She looked over at the mess. "I can't believe I'm such a klutz. I'm so sorry!"

They were standing so close together that Taylor was having trouble focusing. Mike's thumb was running rhythmic circles over her wrist as the cool water washed over her hand. He checked one more time to make sure there weren't any pieces of glass in her skin before stepping back. "I'll get that cleaned up." He motioned to the broken glass. "There's a first aid kit in the pantry." His voice was a little gruff and he made quick work of moving away from her and getting the broken glass up off of the floor and wiping the area clean.

Once they were seated back at the table, Mike poured her another glass of tea and placed it in front of her. "I'm sorry about that," she said as heat crept up her cheeks again.

"Don't worry about it, Taylor. It was an accident and it isn't a big deal. C'mon, relax and let's enjoy our dinner."

She nodded, and found that "enjoy" would be an understatement. Just as lunch had been, dinner was absolutely delicious. She placed her fork and knife down and took a sip of her drink. "So, I'm curious," she began. "Food appears and yet I don't see anyone here. The staff must be super discreet."

He laughed and took a drink of his own beverage. "No, they're not."

"Sure they are. This is my second meal here and I haven't seen anyone. How is that possible if they're not being discreet?"

He put his elbows on the table and gave her his full attention—because he didn't want to miss her reaction. "You've seen the cook," he said easily.

"No, really, I—" And then it hit her. "You? You're the cook?"

His smile broadened. "Yes, ma'am."

"But…how? Why?" She slumped a little in her seat. "I don't get it."

He shrugged. "I enjoy cooking. And basically, there's only two people at the most here to cook for, so it was pointless to hire a cook to keep on staff. We need people to help with the property and the animals and to come in and clean the house, but cooking is something I don't mind doing. Actually, I give the housekeeper a shopping list and she gets everything I need and then I can cook."

She mimicked his pose and placed her cheek in her hand as she studied him. "Boy, you are just full of surprises today. If this is what our first day is like, I can't imagine what you've got in store for me tomorrow."

Again, he knew she was fishing and he figured talking about what he had planned for her was a fairly safe topic. "Well, besides being available to answer all the questions you come up with, I plan on showing you around town and some of the local hot spots."

"Are these places Wade frequents?" she asked as she cut into her dinner.

Mike nodded. "Can I ask a favor?"

"Anything," she said with a smile and then let out a little "mmm," at how good the food tasted.

"Would it be all right if we didn't talk about work tonight? I mean, I know that's why you're here, but I'd like to kick back and relax and just get reacquainted." He watched for her reaction and when she just stared at him—without blinking—he thought that once again he had put his foot in his mouth.

"So…you just want to talk about…life, and whatnot." It wasn't a question.

"If it's all right with you," he rushed to say. "We have an entire week to talk business and…well, I just thought it would be nice to hear what's been going on with you other than the basics we talked about earlier."

She considered his words for a minute before nodding. "Okay, but just know I'm going to want to know about you, too. And not just about your job. I'm probably going to ask what brought you here. I promise not to turn it in the direction of Wade and your work for him, okay?"

"Sounds fair to me." They continued to eat for a few minutes, then Mike broke the silence. "So, do you keep in touch with any of your old friends?"

Taylor shook her head, her long blond hair moving behind her. "Not really. Most of them have gotten married and moved away. Plus, after I moved to the city, it was hard to find the time—and the money—to go to the Island to hang out."

"I can imagine. It's still a shame, though. I know you had a lot of good friends who you were always with."

"Well, I did, but that summer was our last one together. Besides, with everyone getting ready to head off to college, once things went south with Eddie, I sort of stopped hanging out." Mike nodded at her words, but she dreaded the topic of his former best friend. "Do you still keep in touch with him?" There was only a slight tremor in her voice and she cursed it. Eddie was ancient history, but he had definitely done his share of damage to her ego.

Mike looked down at his plate and then pushed it away before folding his hands on the table, his smile sad. "We did for a while. He got married the summer after I met you. Did you know that?" Taylor nodded. "Anyway, he moved to Maryland and had a couple of kids in just as many years and then he split."

Feeling a little uncomfortable, Mike rose and walked over to the refrigerator and grabbed a beer before rejoining Taylor at the table.

"He moved up north for a while and moved in with his mom. We hung out a bit, and then he met wife number two, got married, and moved away."

"Where to?" Taylor couldn't help but ask.

"Back to Maryland. He said he wanted to be near his kids." He sighed. "Next time I heard from him, another year had passed. He'd had another kid and was living alone. His wife threw him out after finding him in bed with their babysitter."

"Some things never change." Taylor chuckled humorlessly. Eddie had been, she thought, the great love of her life. At eighteen, Taylor was in love with him and they had started planning their future together, only it wasn't meant to be. She had gone out of town with her mother for a long weekend toward the end of the summer. It was supposed to be a time for them to have a girls' weekend before Taylor left for college. She came home early to surprise him.

It was Taylor, however, who had been surprised.

She found Eddie in bed with one of her friends. Foolishly, she'd shown up at his house on a Saturday afternoon. They had been dating for so long that she was comfortable entering without knocking or ringing the bell. His parents weren't home and she had simply walked in and gone looking for him.

Big mistake.

Or maybe pure luck.

Either way, it had taken a long time to recover from that. If she were being honest with herself, she would say she still hadn't completely recovered from his betrayal. Maybe that was a reason she felt okay not being in a relationship: there was less chance of getting hurt that way.

It had been years after that incident before she let herself get involved with anyone. She had always been cautious where the male population was concerned. After being abandoned by her father, her mother had instilled in Taylor a fear of how easily her heart could be broken. Eddie was the first and last man she'd allowed herself to get close to.

Mike cleared his throat to regain Taylor's attention. "You okay?"

Embarrassed and feeling the heated blush flood her body—again!—she nodded. "Where's he at now?" Curiosity got the best of her.

Mike looked away, clearly uncomfortable with what he was going to say. "Ed was killed in a car accident about a year ago." His words were deep and low and full of emotion. Taylor reached out and put a hand over his for comfort.

"I'm so sorry, Mike. I know you guys were close."

"The thing is, Taylor, for a long time I thought we were. But now, I look back on all the years we knew each other, Ed and I, and realize that I never knew him at all."

"What do you mean?"

"For starters, there's you."

"Me?" she squeaked.

He nodded. "Eddie was crazy about you. He'd talk about you so damn much that the rest of us guys wanted to clobber him. It was always 'Taylor this' or 'Taylor that.'" Mike turned Taylor's hand in his. "I used to envy him for what he'd found with you. He was so confident of the future the two of you were planning. He wouldn't even introduce any of us to you until you had been dating for about six months. I guess he was afraid we'd hit on you or something," he said with a wink and was relieved when Taylor smiled.

"I didn't realize that," she said. "I mean, that he had waited to introduce us."

"I thought surely he was exaggerating where you were concerned, but after meeting you, I knew he hadn't even begun to do you justice."

Taylor looked away again, feeling her heart beating too fast.

"Toward the end of that summer, we were all at that party at the Robert Moses beach. Do you remember?" His voice softened and Taylor had trouble meeting his gaze. She knew where this memory was going. "I saw Ed off talking to some girl and you were sitting all alone by the fire. You looked so sad." Mike released Taylor's hand and took another drink of his beer. "I came over to sit by you and we talked for a long time."

She nodded. "You were very nice to me, Mike," she said, studying his face.

"The thing is, Taylor, you were nice to me."

Confusion covered her face. "I don't understand."

"Everyone knew I had a pretty wild past and not many people wanted me around. I had been arrested a couple of times, done time in juvie—hell, I was a mess. I used to hear people refer to me as 'the criminal.' You never did that." His eyes bored into hers. "That meant a lot to me."

"The way I saw it, there was no reason to bring it up. You were trying to get your life back on track and you weren't hurting anyone. And besides, everyone deserves a second chance." It was true. Taylor hated the way her friends had treated Mike back then. It had shamed her even to associate with some of them. They seemed to tolerate him for Eddie's sake, but the truth was that none of them wanted Mike around. She had argued with them over it more than once. Taylor had always tried to look for the best in people, and in her opinion, at the time Mike started coming around, he was a totally nice guy— he was funny and genuine, and he owned his mistakes. Unfortunately, she was in the minority with her feelings. The memory made her angry, but another came to mind that made her chuckle.

"What's so funny?" he asked, thoroughly confused considering the topic they had just been discussing.

Trying to maintain her composure, Taylor looked at him. "Do you know, to this day I still think about one of the most offensive lines you ever said to me?"

"Offensive? What did I say to offend you?" He was unaware of ever doing that and he racked his brain for what he could have said.

"When we were sitting by the fire, I noticed a tattoo of a cross on your arm and said it looked nice." She looked at him a little closer to see if he remembered, but clearly he didn't. "You looked me right in the eye and said, 'Got it in prison. Still think it's nice?'"

"I did not say that!"

She nodded. "Oh, yes you did," she said with a smile. "Believe me. There is no way I could possibly make up something like that."

And then he did remember and instantly sobered. "I was trying to scare you off."

"Why?"

"Ed was my best friend, and yet the more I got to know you, the more I wanted to get to know you. It wasn't right. I felt guilty."

"And right after you said that you leaned over and—"

"I kissed you." His voice was thick and deep and sexy.

"Yes, you did," she admitted shyly.

"I would have kissed you more, but there was a crowd."

For just a moment, Taylor allowed herself to get lost in his eyes and the memory of what the kiss had been like. "Well." She cleared her throat. "It was a long time ago."

Mike saw the hint of promise in her eyes, but it was gone in an instant. "What I was getting to was, well, I never did understand how Eddie was crazy enough to let you go. He had it all and he blew it for a quickie with someone he had no interest in. It just never made any sense to me."

A bit of the anger Taylor normally felt when she thought about that time in her life was right there. "I never understood it either," she said tersely. "I guess I just wasn't enough for him." She gave a mirthless laugh. "That's what I got for trying to be rebellious and dating the guy everyone warned me about. Guess I should have listened." She played around with her silverware, her drink, her plate…anything to keep from having to look at Mike and see the pity in his eyes. She had seen it enough in everyone else's over the years.

"I hated him for doing that to you," he said to break the silence.

"Me too." Her voice was small and she still couldn't look at him. It wasn't easy sitting here talking about the biggest failure in her life.

"That night at the beach, after he drove you home, he came to my house and we talked." Now she did look up. "We were shooting the breeze, nothing major, but he kept bringing you up in conversation. Things like, 'Did you know Taylor likes this?' or, 'Taylor and I are planning that.'" Mike took a deep breath. "I think he saw me kiss you and he was reminding me who you belonged to. Then he went on to talk about my screwed-up life." His gaze was fixed on hers. "It was his way of telling me to back off because I wasn't good enough for someone like you. I didn't get invited around much after that."

"I wondered what had happened to you."

"After the two of you broke up, he made sure I was with him at all times," he said with a hint of sadness. "I saw him more in those first few months after your breakup than I had in years. He practically lived with me. I think he felt that if I wasn't hanging out with him, I'd be out looking for you."

Taylor went still at his words, afraid to breathe, afraid to blink. What was he saying? That he had been interested in her back then and Eddie had prevented it from happening? Mike saw the questioning in her eyes and answered it. "I would have," he said softly.

"I never knew," she said, her voice barely audible.

"How could you? You were in love with Ed, and then when the two of you broke up," he said with a shrug, "I figured I was the last guy you wanted to see. Besides him."

"I...I don't know what to say, Mike."

He gave her a sad smile. "I didn't think you knew or anything, but...there it is." He finished his beer. "I found out about your writing purely by chance. I'm addicted to the news and current events. Weird, right?" Taylor smiled and nodded. "I saw one of your articles in *Newslink* on the closing of some of the area's libraries and—first, I was impressed with your writing, but then I realized how long it had been since I'd seen you."

"You obviously knew where I worked. Why didn't you reach out?" It wasn't an accusation; she just wanted to know why he waited so long to get in touch with her.

He shrugged again. "I had no idea what else was going on in your life. I didn't want to disrupt it and bring back memories I was sure you'd rather forget."

While she understood his reasoning, she wished he had opted to be less reasonable. "I would have loved to hear from you. All things considered, I still thought you and I were friends. I missed seeing you. Even after things happened the way they did with Ed, I still thought about you and missed talking to you."

"I never knew," he said, repeating her earlier words. There didn't seem much more to say.

"I'm sad to think he's gone, that he's got children who are never going to see their father again, but I can't say I'm surprised. He always seemed to live on the edge a little too much for my liking."

He chuckled. "I used to wonder how such a sweet girl like you ended up with someone like him."

"Unfortunately, I'm your typical cliché. There's something about bad boys that makes girls want to change them." She sighed. "I truly thought it was going to happen."

"If it counts for anything, I think Ed always regretted messing up with you."

"Thanks," she said, her voice distant and quiet. To distract herself, she stood up and began to clear the table.

"Didn't we already go over this?" he asked as he

stood to join her. "You're a guest here and you don't have to help with things like this."

She waved him off. "It makes me feel good to help. You've done nothing but listen to me talk all day and show me around and I get to stay in this beautiful house—it doesn't feel like work. Trust me when I tell you that I'm normally not a fan of housework of any kind, but helping around here makes me feel good. I feel…useful." She avoided his gaze as she gathered their dishes from the table and took them to the sink.

For a moment, Mike could only stare. Did she have any idea how incredible she was, how amazing? But he could still see the scars Ed had put on her and he hated it. Over the years, Mike had remembered Taylor as the girl with the big smile and bright eyes who was full of laughter and confidence. The woman in the kitchen now had a bit of an edge to her—and a defensive wall around her that hadn't been there before. It wasn't right to curse the dead, but in that moment, he did.

Glancing at the clock, Mike realized that he wasn't ready to part with Taylor for the evening. "I know we just finished eating, but I'm hoping you'll want to have dessert." He walked over to the refrigerator and pulled out a covered dish. "It's an Oreo pie."

Taylor's eyes went wide with delight. "Shut up!" she said even as she laughed. "Tell me you did not make that yourself!"

He had the good sense to look bashful. "Hey, when you're a bachelor, you learn to do these things for yourself, otherwise you'd go broke eating out and getting takeout all the time. It's not a big deal—it's a mix. Really, it's nothing."

Taylor thought he was possibly the most adorable man alive. No, that wasn't true — adorable was too mild a term. He was handsome and smart and sexy. And the fact that he could cook and make an Oreo pie tipped the scales.

"I know I shouldn't, but you've found my weak spot. I can't say no to an Oreo pie." She threw down the dish-towel she had been holding, suddenly feeling ashamed at her admission, when she remembered something. "Wait a minute. Did you…?" She shook her head in disbelief.

"Did I remember that Oreos were one of your favorite snacks?" he asked with a lopsided grin. "Absolutely."

A million questions ran through Taylor's mind. Too many coincidences, too many revelations. And if it weren't for the Oreo pie sitting there looking too delicious for words, she would excuse herself and go up to her room to think about everything she had learned that night. "Well, that was pretty darn sweet of you," she said instead. In one smooth move, Taylor turned and opened the cabinet to get two plates. It wasn't until she placed them on the table that she noticed the odd expression on Mike's face and realized what she'd done. She had never seen Mike set the table or where anything was in the kitchen, but it was like she somehow…*knew* where to find them.

What could she say? There was no explanation for how at home she felt — so she brought their attention back to the pie. "Can we eat it out on the porch?" she asked, her eyes bright, her expression hopeful.

"Uh…it's kind of chilly out, Taylor. It's a lot colder up here than it is in New York."

"Then I'll grab a sweater," she said. "Please? From the minute I drove through the trees today I've thought about sitting on that porch. Of course, I had pictured watching the sunset or sunrise, but being out there in the quiet would be a perfect way to end the day. Can we?"

He couldn't say no to her. Even though he had thought to take their dessert into the den and light a fire in the large hearth, he supposed there was something to be said for sitting outside in the cold.

At night.

While trying not to freeze.

—◦◦◦—

Within ten minutes, Taylor realized Mike was right. It was freezing. And pitch black. Oh, and freezing. Doing her best to keep her teeth from chattering, she had nearly inhaled her slice of pie and noticed Mike doing the same. When they both finished, Mike took their plates and set them down next to the porch swing. As much as she wanted to swing, the thought of propelling back and forth—even slowly—in the cool night air was too much for her.

"Okay," she said. "Lesson learned. You definitely know more about how cold it gets than I do and I'm ready to admit defeat."

Beside her, he chuckled. "It's not so bad," he said as he moved closer and put an arm around her, pulling her nearer. "I've almost forgotten what it's like to have feeling in my fingers." Together they laughed and Taylor playfully elbowed him in the ribs. "Ouch!"

"I should have listened, but all I could think about was getting to sit out here." She looked at him. "Any chance of the weather warming up this week?"

He shook his head. "Some, but not by much. But

there's a great fire pit out back. Maybe tomorrow night we'll sit by the fire."

"That would be nice," she said as she settled against him. And then she realized that this right here was also nice. Mike's body was shielding hers from some of the wind and he was very warm—despite what he had said. She rested her head on his shoulder, feeling at peace.

As if reading her mind, Mike said, "This is nice." Startled by how in sync they were becoming, Taylor lifted her head and looked at him. Though it was dark all around them, she could see his face across from hers. "What's the matter?" he asked.

Everything. Nothing. Past and present were swirling together in her brain and the only thing that stood out was how she wanted to experience that one moment in time with him again. That one moment when he had kissed her more thoroughly than any man ever had before—or since. She wanted to know what it would feel like to have him kiss her when nobody was watching.

Taylor wasn't sure she should initiate a kiss. What if everything he had said was how he felt years ago but not anymore? Would she be able to handle the rejection and continue to work with him all week? Indecision warred within her until she felt Mike's hand gently cup the back of her head.

"Let me help you make that decision," he said in a deep, husky voice.

And then he kissed her.

Chapter 5

Yes, she'd been in a dating dry spell.

And yes, she'd said it wasn't a big deal.

And yes, she was lying to herself.

This kiss, this searing-hot kiss was like nothing she had ever experienced. *Liar*. Once, with Mike, but it was clear he had learned some things since then.

Mike took Taylor's face in his hands. His skin was warm and rough, his touch gentle.

It didn't take long for Taylor's tongue to deliciously dance with his. She edged closer and the swing swayed a bit, causing Taylor to reach out and curl her fingers in his shirt. His kiss grew more and more urgent. It wasn't hard for her to keep up—she wanted this kiss more than her next breath. And it was exciting to feel this wanted—this needed—as if he couldn't breathe without her.

She wanted to ask him if they could go up to her bedroom—anywhere—so that they could be closer. Taylor hadn't realized how badly she missed the feeling of a man's body pressed against hers until now. She was about to say so when Mike abruptly pulled away. His breath was ragged as he rested his forehead against hers, his hands still cupping her face.

"Mike," she panted, but didn't get to finish.

"I'm not sorry for that, Taylor, but I also know this isn't the reason you're here." Without warning, he removed his hands and stood. Even in the darkness, she could see the conflict within him. His eyes were dark and stormy and his breathing still hadn't settled. "Good night," he said and walked off of the porch until he was swallowed by the darkness of the field.

For a minute she sat there, speechless. What had happened? One minute she was ready to ask him to make love to her and now she was sitting alone on a porch swing. Taylor got off the swing, though her legs weren't completely stable, and tried to see if she could spot him from where she stood. But she couldn't.

"So much for the audience being the reason he wouldn't kiss me for longer," she muttered and walked dejectedly into the house. Earlier in the day she had wanted to explore it—but right now she wanted to see her room. And close the door. And wallow.

Which was what she did as soon as her door was closed. The room she had marveled at earlier now seemed to mock her. She fell backward onto the bed and threw her arm over her face to block out some of the light, mocking herself. "What an eventful day you've had. Fly to Maine, drive a new car, tour a farm, start the article that is supposed to launch your career, and get kissed by a man you haven't seen since you were eighteen." *Yup. Eventful.* And what sucked the most was that Mike's kiss had excited her more than it had ten years ago. Tonight's kiss definitely had an edge—a promise—and yet here she was in bed alone.

"Oh, yeah," she said with self-loathing, "you've still got it."

She didn't have it in her to work, so instead she rose wearily from the bed and headed for the private en suite, drawing herself a bubble bath. Not that it was going to clear her mind, but at least she could unwind in luxury.

"No," she admonished herself, "it *is* going get your mind clearer." She was not here to play catchup with Mike Greene. No matter how great he looked. And kissed. And felt. "Dammit." No, she was here to do a no-holds-barred interview with Jonathan Wade. And she had to remember that at all costs.

Tomorrow she would need to keep things professional with Mike. No more talks about the past, no more cozy meals together, and certainly no more kissing. Maybe. She didn't want to jump to any rash decisions and then regret them, so she put kissing on the shelf for now.

She needed to start gathering some real information— the kind that was going to make this article a must-read for every fan of Wade's.

Why had she lost sight of her goal? Excitement from the day and lack of sleep all week were catching up with her—that's what it must be. Mike was here to help her get the information she needed for her job.

As she lowered her body into the steamy water, she allowed herself one more moment to think about Mike's kiss. She sighed. Who was she kidding? If he knocked on the door right now, she'd willingly tackle him onto her bed and forget about the damn interview, her job, everything.

But he wasn't going to knock. And tomorrow was another day.

—⁓—

Saturday morning was gray and bleak. Taylor kicked the warm blankets off and strode over to the large bay window to look out at the new day. Nature didn't look quite so friendly today. Even though her room was warm and toasty, she could tell the air outside was cold and brisk. She had a good view of the farm's property from this window and looked around for any signs of Mike. "Get a grip," she murmured as she snapped the curtains shut and forced herself away.

"Focus today," she chanted as she reached into one of her bags and pulled her iPod out to listen to one of Wade's books. The voice in the audiobooks always seemed to soothe her. She had already listened to this one, but as she relaxed on the bed and pressed play, it hit her—she was listening to Mike's voice! Groaning, she ripped the earbuds from her ears and threw the iPod across the room. *Great!*

Taylor padded across the room to retrieve it. "I'm pathetic," she said as she picked it up, put her earbuds back in, and went back to lie down. There wasn't time to listen to the entire book, but listening to the first chapter put things into perspective for her. *Work.* She was here to work. Not to play with Mike. And his sexy voice.

"Okay, no more!" she said as she threw the iPod again. "I'm done!" Jumping off the bed, she stormed into the bathroom to shower and get dressed. The entire time she was getting ready, she reprimanded herself for her lack of professionalism, thinking of what her editor would say if she found out that Taylor had spent the night making out with Jonathan Wade's assistant rather than getting information *about* Jonathan Wade.

"I'd be fired in an instant," she said to her reflection as she applied her makeup. When that thought got her heart rate going—and not in the sexy way it had last night—she reminded herself of why she was here.

"Jonathan Wade wanted you and only you for this interview. He obviously thinks your writing is good and he trusts you with this monumental task. You will be witty and charming as well as firm with your questioning. You're here for the next week to get a broad picture of the author so you will be well-prepared for when you face him."

A quick nod finalized the thought. Looking at the mirror, she was pleased with what she saw: her hair hung loose about her shoulders and she had popped her contacts back in today. With a touch of makeup, she felt she looked fresh and a lot less tired than she had the day before.

Not knowing what was in store for her today, she dressed casually in jeans and a sweater. For all she knew they were going to stay in the house and talk, but just in case Mike wanted to take her out and show her around the town or some of his boss's favorite places, she wanted to make sure she was dressed warmly enough.

The clock read nine, and on a working farm, she was rising pretty late. No doubt Mike had already put in several hours at the barn or on the property. She skipped down the stairs and headed straight to the kitchen to grab some breakfast.

Taylor didn't hesitate to put on a pot of coffee. She had no idea if Mike drank it, but she needed it to start her day. Once it was brewing, she looked through the window and saw Mike walking out of the barn. There was no way to avoid him—not that she wanted to—so she decided to act as if last night hadn't happened.

Stepping outside onto the side porch, she called out to him and waved. Mike strolled over and looked up at her from three steps below. "Good morning," he said with an easy smile. "Did you sleep okay?"

"Yes, thank you." She couldn't help the blush in her cheeks. Hearing his voice after discovering it was the same one that had been washing over her all week was enough to make her skin burn hot. "I'm making some coffee and wanted to know if you wanted any."

If anything, his smile grew. "Sure. Thanks," he said as he climbed the stairs. Opening the door, he let Taylor enter the warmth first. The coffee smelled good, and he watched as Taylor moved about the kitchen as if she'd lived there for years. "Have you been up long?"

She shook her head. "Maybe an hour. I realized with this being a working farm, you've probably been up since dawn."

He chuckled. "Close. Luckily, we have a great staff here, so it's not necessary for me to be out there with them every minute. I was going to ask you last night if you wanted to get up early and see what morning on the farm is like, but I figured you might enjoy sleeping in."

She nodded. "I did. I did so much this week to prepare that I haven't slept a lot. I pretty much crashed as soon as my head hit the pillow last night." *Liar, liar, liar!* Leaning against the counter, Taylor looked around for something to do while they waited for the coffee.

"If you're hungry, there's plenty of breakfast foods to choose from. Please, help yourself."

"I'm not much of a breakfast person," she confessed as she set out the mugs and reached into the refrigerator for milk. On a lower shelf, she spotted some yogurt and decided one little cup of yogurt couldn't hurt. Closing the door, she waved it at Mike. "Something like this is perfect."

Mike poured them each their coffee and then joined Taylor at the table. "Have you explored the house yet? It's quite impressive."

"I am curious to see the whole thing, but I wouldn't feel right doing that on my own. Exploring the property with you yesterday was fine, because it was all outdoors. I think going through someone's home is a little too personal when they're not actually at home."

"Well then, lucky for you that I'm done with what I needed to do out in the barn."

Taylor looked at him curiously. "What do you mean?"

"How about as soon as we're done with our coffee— and your yogurt—we take the grand tour?"

Her eyes went wide. "Seriously? He won't mind?"

Mike relaxed back in his seat and laughed. "Taylor, he invited you here. He didn't expect you to sit only in the kitchen or your bedroom. He's actually very proud of this place and likes to show it off from time to time."

That piqued her interest. "But from everything I've learned about him—which isn't much—Jonathan Wade is fairly reclusive. Who would he show the house off to?"

Mike shrugged. "He is reclusive to the public by Hollywood's standards. But believe it or not, he does have friends."

"They must be good friends if they haven't outed him to some magazine or tabloid by now."

"He's very selective." Mike left it at that and waited to see if Taylor would ask any more questions. When she didn't, he leaned on the table and got a little closer to her. "So, what do you say? You up for the tour?"

She was cursing the damn yogurt. "Five minutes and

then I promise I'll be done," she said and began to eat furiously.

"Taylor," he said softly with a chuckle, "the house isn't going anywhere and we've got all day together. Take your time and eat."

She was thankful he wasn't staring at her while she finished, and as soon as she'd taken her last spoonful, she stood and threw out the container as if she was making one of those winning basketball shots. With hands in the air, she said, "Done!"

Mike stood and clapped as she did a mini victory lap around the center island, and when she came to stand beside him, he couldn't help but smile. "That was awesome."

"I know, I know," she gushed. She bounced on her toes in excitement. "Can we start the tour?"

"Do you want your camera or recorder or anything?"

"Hmm." She considered the possibilities. "Are you suggesting there may be things in the house that will be newsworthy for the article?"

Sticking his hands in his pockets, he tilted his head toward hers. "Maybe."

"Dang it," she muttered before racing from the room to get her equipment. Mike met her at the foot of the stairs and waited as she took a minute to catch her breath. When she finished fidgeting with her hair, and then the camera, and then the recorder, she looked up at him expectantly.

"Are you sure you're ready?"

"As I'll ever be." For two solid hours, Mike took her through every inch of the farmhouse. There were antiques, beautiful pieces of artwork, and of course tons and tons of books. Jonathan Wade's library was to be envied and it rivaled the one from *Beauty and the Beast*. Wade seemed to have books on every subject and in every genre. When Taylor noticed that he had his own books on the shelves, she turned to Mike.

"Please tell me something about him," she pleaded. "I mean, I know you've been showing me around the house and telling me why he chose a certain piece of art or furniture, but I'd like to hear something personal. I need something to tie me to this man whose home I'm in. Does that make sense?" Her big blue eyes were filled with hope as she asked the question.

"He likes his privacy," he said simply.

"I knew that, Mike! Hell, everyone knows that," she said as she placed a book back on the shelf. "Is he young? Old? What does he look like?"

"Oh, now, that stuff I can't tell you. What I can say is that he loves to read all types of writing—whether it's books, magazines, cereal boxes…" They shared a laugh. "His real interest of late is in new writers. He feels privileged that he had been given a chance when he was a young, struggling writer and likes to see the potential in others."

"Is that why he chose me for this assignment?" she asked, mesmerized by the thought.

"Yes." Mike's gaze locked with Taylor's.

She could get lost in those deep blue depths. "I hope I don't disappoint him," she said, her voice husky to the point that she barely recognized it. With inches between them, Taylor began to sway, to get closer, when her cell phone rang. She had grabbed it along with her other devices in case Victoria or anyone from her office called. Stepping back, she murmured an apology before answering. "Hello?"

"Is this Ms. Scott?" a male voice asked.

"Yes," she said hesitantly. "Who is this?"

"Ms. Scott, this is Tom Levinson. Mr. Wade's attorney? I believe we spoke briefly earlier this week."

She nodded. "Yes, sir. We did. How can I help you?"

"It seems we missed a signature on one of the documents. My assistant is going to email it for you to sign. We'll need it back before your interview with Mr. Wade begins."

"Oh, okay. That shouldn't be a problem."

"Excellent. Thank you. Is Mr. Greene with you?" he asked.

"Yes," she said, "he's standing right here. Hold on." Mike stepped over and held out his hand for the phone, and Taylor watched as he took it and immediately walked several feet away from her. His tone was low, and she was too preoccupied watching him to decipher what he was saying. Wearing well-worn jeans, boots, and a gray thermal shirt under a navy flannel one, he looked like a true outdoorsman. Taylor felt her mouth go dry.

Leaving him to his conversation, she headed back to the kitchen to grab a glass of water. She tried not to think about having another five solid days here with only Mike for company. She was going to have to find some way to spend her time when they weren't talking about things for the interview, because she was picturing—all too vividly—the things she'd *like* to be doing with him, like taking off the flannel and thermal and getting down to skin.

She had to fan herself.

Bad Taylor!

There was no doubt he would have work to do that didn't involve her, and Taylor figured she'd drive into town to explore the area, do a little window-shopping and whatnot to pass the time. Unfortunately, her meager journalist salary didn't allow for the freedom to shop at will. No, she'd have to be happy browsing and exploring the town.

"Sorry that took so long," she heard Mike say as he entered the kitchen, handing her the phone back.

"That's okay. Was everything all right?"

He nodded. "He just wanted to let me know the paper was coming over and to make sure you sign and send it back to him as soon as possible. Unfortunately, it's something he'll need before you can talk to Wade."

Taylor frowned at the thought. "Why? What's the big deal about this particular document?"

He shrugged and poured himself something to drink. "Basically, it says Wade will get final approval of the article before it can go to print."

"What? Wait…that wasn't discussed before." She pulled up her contacts and then Victoria's number. "She is going to flip."

"Who?"

"My boss. She's going to freak out that this wasn't covered in negotiations."

"Taylor…" Mike began, but she was already talking on the phone. He stood back, wanting to bang his head against the wall. What freaking timing! If her phone hadn't rung, she would have kissed him. He knew it like he knew his own name. It had been painful to walk away from her last night—she was as sweet as he'd remembered and the thought of doing more than stealing a kiss… The more time he spent with her, the harder he was finding it to control himself.

Across the room, Taylor was pacing. "Are you sure, Vic?" he heard her ask. It ticked him off to no end that the document had been missed and he had no doubt it could potentially bring an end to all of this. He could only hope and pray Taylor would be able to smooth things over with her boss so they could move forward. He heard her saying goodbye and held his breath. "Everything all right?" he asked.

Sighing, she placed the phone down on the kitchen table and pulled out a chair to collapse into. "To say that she is pissed would be an understatement. I think she'll get over it, but right now she's having an absolute fit. I need to forward the document to *Newslink*'s office so legal can look over it before they allow me to sign—or not—and then I guess we'll move on from there." She looked up at him. "So, what does this mean? Am I supposed to stop talking with you about all things Wade until this is cleared up?"

Mike wasn't sure how to answer that. "I wouldn't imagine so…I think…"

"Because if this whole thing is going to crash and burn and be yanked away from me, I'd rather not have any information that someone might try to get out of me to sensationalize." She stood up and began to pace. "I know how important Wade's privacy is to him," she said quickly, "and if you and I talk and you start telling me more things about him and then the paperwork doesn't clear and I have to leave? I don't want anyone to go after my notes or recordings to try to make their own story out of it and destroy everything he's built here." Her eyes looked up at his pleadingly. "Does that make sense?"

"Taylor, you shouldn't worry. I'm sure everything is—"

"But *if* I can stay—if this document goes through—I want to know all of the details about this man, and I don't want him to be disappointed in me or in what I write." It was suddenly coming into view for Taylor—writer to writer, she wanted to do Wade justice. "I want to know what inspires him to write, where he does his writing—I didn't see any place like that when you showed me around the house." Taylor looked around thoughtfully. "When I write, I have a complete ritual—I bike for thirty minutes to clear my head before I begin. Then I pour myself a glass of wine and sit down at my desk. I have a picture of the lighthouse at Montauk Point sitting there that I can look at and...then I can begin."

"Why the lighthouse?"

She shrugged. "I only went there once. The last time I went was..." she looked away, suddenly shy.

Mike silently stepped up behind her. "When?" he asked, low.

Turning, she looked up at him. "That summer with you. Do you remember? It was just me, you, and Eddie, but we got up at the crack of dawn and drove out to spend the day on the beach, and we took a bunch of pictures at the lighthouse. I still have them, but there's one of the lighthouse that is just...perfect. I look at it and it soothes me."

He understood. More than she knew.

"I want to know if Wade has such a ritual. I wish I had more time to spend here."

"So, stay longer."

Taylor's eyes went wide. "What?"

"Stay. Longer."

He could tell she was tempted and hoped it wasn't just because of the assignment. That maybe, just maybe, she wanted to spend the time with him too. "I—I don't think my editor would like it or…"

"She's already been notified," he said softly.

"But…how? How did you know?"

"Taylor, the agreement was always an open-ended one. It was written up as a two-week deal to get things going but…let's just say Wade doesn't necessarily like to work under time constraints."

"But surely he understands deadlines. I mean, he does have a publisher he has to report to, doesn't he?"

He nodded. "Absolutely, but if there's one thing I've learned about him, it's that he also knows the importance of having the time to get the job done right. So I don't want you to feel rushed. You have all the time in the world to make this article everything you want it to be."

She looked at him warily. "How—how come I didn't know about this?"

"Probably because your editors are overzealous and want this piece as soon as possible. If they told you to take your time, they may have feared missing the next issue deadline."

He knew it all made sense and yet—he couldn't be sure she'd believe it. Her face was so expressive that he could see the conflict waging within her. He watched every play of emotion on her face and was even mildly amused by how transparent she was. He stepped in close—needing to feel the heat of her, to smell her perfume. "Will you stay?" he asked, noting her look of panic. "I mean…if you need to."

Taylor stepped toward him, leaving barely a breath between them. "Do you want me to?"

Mike closed the distance and claimed her lips with his. It was what he'd been wanting to do all morning. Who was he kidding, it was what he never wanted to stop doing last night. He sipped at her lips, giving her time to stop him if she wanted to, but her arms came up to twine around his shoulders and then her fingers threaded into his hair, and he took that as the green light. "Taylor," he murmured against her lips.

Honestly, he didn't want to talk. That was all they'd been doing since she'd arrived. Now that he'd had a taste of her, he wasn't willing to let it go at just the one kiss last night.

Or ten years ago.

His arms wrapped around her, and her breasts pressed against his chest as they embraced tighter than was possible on the swing last night. His tongue gently teased at her lower lip—he didn't want to rush her—but Taylor was having none of it. Her tongue, as delicate as her movements were, teased and tormented him.

Did she have any idea how much he wanted her? How long he had dreamed of being able to kiss and hold her like this? His mouth left hers so he could get some much-needed air and so he could kiss her cheek, her throat—which smelled so sweet he felt intoxicated. "I told myself I wouldn't do this again. Not yet," he said.

With her head arched back to give him more room to explore, Taylor sighed. "And I told myself I wouldn't either." She moaned when he bit down gently on her skin. "We're really bad at keeping promises to ourselves."

His tongue ran from her earlobe to her collarbone. "I'll feel bad. Later."

"I won't," she purred.

"Good. Because I won't either," he said in between kisses. His hands held her hips, his fingers gently kneading her curves.

"Mike?" she whispered.

"Hmm?"

"Stop talking." And she smiled when he did just that and came back to devour her lips. It was intense and yet so innocent at the same time. They were standing in the kitchen; his hands hadn't done more than stroke her back and hold her hips, yet Taylor felt ready to explode in his arms.

Taylor took her arms from his shoulders and her hands caressed the strong column of his throat. Then she massaged his shoulders before moving down his arms and squeezing his biceps. When he groaned with pleasure, she moved her hands to his chest and he wished she would push his shirt aside.

Something in her touch ignited a strong desire in Mike. Releasing his grip on her hips, his hands skimmed up to her waist and then slowly, ever so slowly, moved up her rib cage to just under the swell of her breasts. Taylor's breath caught in her throat at the contact and she let out a small growl of frustration. He was on the verge of losing control and had to mentally count to ten to calm down and rein himself in. He felt like a teenager with his first girl. The thought made him chuckle against her lips.

"Patience," he whispered as his hand crept even more slowly—if that were possible—to her breasts.

Taylor cried out as he cupped, then squeezed, then simply teased her nipples with his thumbs. Her response to him was more of a turn-on than he could ever have imagined. All he could think of was finding more ways to please her. She was beautiful and sexy, and to know that he had her panting in the middle of a kitchen had him ready to lay her down on the nearest surface and give them both what they wanted. An idea was starting to form when suddenly she stiffened in his arms.

And not in a good way.

"Mike?" she said softly, but his mouth was already working its way down to join his hands. Taylor was momentarily speechless as his mouth closed over one distended nipple and then she cried out at the pleasure of it. When she called out his name this time, it was more of a plea to keep going rather than to stop.

She said his name again—this time with a little more clarity, and he instantly raised his head. Her hair was disheveled, her lips were swollen, and her breath was ragged. "I'm sorry," she said, as he was trying desperately to catch his own breath. "But I can't do this. Not here. Not like this."

He came out of his own daze and looked around. "Oh…God, Taylor," he said with a hint of self-loathing and took a step back, lowering his head. "What the hell was I thinking?"

"Probably the same thing I was," she said, her tone light, as if she was trying to break the tension. "That we both wanted to do that. I'm just not the type of person who's willing to do…it…in a stranger's kitchen."

He stared back at her as if he didn't quite understand her. "What do you…?" And then it clicked. "Oh. Right." Walking over to the window, he took several deep breaths and pulled his fingers through his hair. It took several minutes for him to turn around again and when he did, he looked more relaxed. "Okay, let's admit that we obviously have an attraction to one another, right? I'm not going to pretend we don't, Taylor, so please don't ask me to."

She shook her head. "I—I wasn't. I couldn't."

"I guess, then, we just need to try our best to be a little more aware of where we are when we get…the urge…to do that again. Okay?" She nodded. "Good. Let's agree then that what just happened isn't a bad thing and we'll continue it later." Taylor blushed, and even that was sexy as hell on her. "In the meantime, let's get back to business." He took a moment to gather his thoughts and regain some sense of professionalism, for both their sakes. "We were talking about the possibility of you staying longer if you need to and your worries about the article."

He took another deep breath. "First things first— don't worry about what Wade is going to think about the article. Don't put that kind of pressure on yourself. We'll print the document out downstairs so you can look it over and have it ready to sign and get it over to *Newslink* and—"

"Downstairs?" she interrupted. "There's a downstairs?"

He had the decency to look mildly ashamed. "I wasn't going to show you just yet. But seeing that we've had a slight change of events here, I think it's safe to show it to you."

"Safe?" she repeated, feigning offense.

He leaned in close and gave her a wicked grin. "Sweetheart, we've only begun to scratch the surface on many things. I can't bring it all out at once." He winked and turned away, but not before catching Taylor's soft gasp and the widening of her eyes.

Chapter 6

IT WASN'T QUITE AS EXCITING AS SHE'D HOPED.

But then again, Mike hadn't let her see what she wanted to see. The entire lower level was finished and housed an impressive home gym, a theater room, and Wade's office. That's where the printer was, but Mike had essentially held Taylor off at the door while he made a copy of the document for her. Taylor had been dying to go inside the office—especially to find out if this was where Wade did his writing—to touch things and look at what was on the shelves, but Mike had explained it was something his boss wanted to show her in person, and that she needed to be patient.

Pfft. Patience. It was highly overrated.

To say that she was disappointed was a given. Her enthusiasm returned—somewhat—when she got to see what equipment the gym sported: aside from weight machines and treadmills, there were also stationary bikes. "Oh my gosh!" she exclaimed. "The man must enjoy keeping in shape," she observed, walking over to one of the bikes and staring at it in awe. "I've always wanted one of these. It would be great in the winter months. I have a regular outdoor bike, and I had to buy it at a garage sale." She ran her hands lovingly over the bike and then noticed Mike's amused expression. "I know it's weird to get so excited over a bike, but it's my favorite hobby."

"Wade says you are to have full access to the gym while you're here," he said with a smile. Next, he took her to see the media room, and soon they found themselves back up in the kitchen. "If you're interested, we can take a ride into town. I'll show you some of the highlights and maybe we could grab lunch. What do you think?"

She thought it sounded like a date but kept that observation to herself. "Sounds good to me. Let me get a jacket and my purse, and I'll meet you outside."

Rushing up the stairs, she ran into her room and was outside within a matter of minutes as Mike was pulling another SUV out of the garage. She wanted to ask him if this was his car or one of Wade's, but wasn't sure how to phrase it without possibly insulting him. Not that it mattered whose car it was—there would be time to find out about Wade's tastes later. "So where are we going?" she asked as she climbed in.

"Into town. There's not a whole lot there—lots of mom-and-pop stores—but there's a great diner where I figured we'd go for lunch. I eat there often."

"Really? But you're such a good cook."

He smiled at the compliment. "Sometimes it's nice to go out and let someone else cook. Plus, it's not as much fun cooking for one."

She was going to ask how often he cooked for two—or more—but thought better of it. They drove the rest of the way in silence as Taylor sat back and enjoyed the scenery. When they pulled up in front of the diner, Mike was at her door before she even had the chance to open it, and helped her out. Taking her hand in his, he led her into the restaurant and Taylor couldn't help but smile.

This was definitely a date.

For such a small town, they were certainly able to kill a lot of time. Lunch at the diner was way better than she had expected, and it seemed like everyone who came in knew Mike. She met what seemed like dozens of people, and for each one who stopped by the table, Mike made sure to introduce her, engaging in conversations that centered on the other person—not Mike. Taylor made a mental note of that—the man certainly was humble and didn't like any attention on himself. She admired that.

After their lengthy lunch, they walked hand in hand around town. Mike took her into just about every store, and he was able to give her the history of each of them along with the history of the town itself. It wouldn't make for anything interesting in her article, but it would make for good filler material if she needed it.

She took pictures of some of the older buildings, and at one point Mike stopped someone he knew and asked them to take his and Taylor's picture together. It meant more to her than it should have to finally have a picture of just the two of them, but she couldn't help it. In the back of her mind she had a feeling that once she printed the photo, it was going to become the new inspirational picture that could replace the Montauk lighthouse.

Not maybe. Definitely.

The weather wasn't as cool as she'd feared, but as they continued to walk and the sun began to set, the chill started to come back. She shivered and Mike pulled her close. "Tomorrow's supposed to be warmer. We'll be able to enjoy being outside a lot more."

She looked up at him and arched a brow. "We'll be outside again tomorrow?"

He nodded. "Actually, we're taking a bit of a road trip tomorrow. I'm going to take you to Wade's second home. It's on the coast and we'll probably end up staying there the night. I thought it would make a great addition to your article—you could tell a little more about him."

She gave him a warm smile. "Is it big like the farmhouse?"

Chuckling, he hugged her close for the briefest of moments before leading her back to the car. "You know, I don't remember you being this nosy or impatient when I knew you before."

Now it was her turn to laugh. "Well, you get enough unpleasant surprises and you learn to be cautious and know what you're getting into beforehand."

Mike stopped in his tracks and instantly sobered. "I just wanted to give you another view for your article, that's all."

If Taylor didn't know any better, she'd swear he was panicking. But why? "I wasn't accusing you of anything," she reassured him. "I was just answering your question—or, rather, defending your observation. I'm sorry. I didn't mean to upset you."

He shook his head, feeling slightly foolish. "You didn't and...I shouldn't have gotten defensive. It's just...after what you told me last night about you and Ed, I didn't want you painting me with the same brush, you know?"

She nodded. "I don't. I could never."

That pleased him. "C'mon. Let's get back to the farm. I've got some work to do and I'm sure you want to get some work done on the article and maybe put a call in to your editor about the document we sent over. And then I've got a couple of great steaks I want to grill for dinner."

While it all sounded good, she couldn't help but feel a little disappointed that he wasn't talking about picking up where they'd left off earlier. Mike was going to read her like a book. They got back to his vehicle and he unlocked the doors, opening hers. As he helped her inside, he captured her hips with his hands and leaned in to kiss her thoroughly. "What was that for?" Taylor asked, feeling slightly breathless when he released her lips.

"That was a preview of what's to come for dessert."

The alarm went off way too early for Taylor's liking. She had gone to bed early—not by choice—but hadn't slept well.

Last night held so many promises. She and Mike had shared a wonderful dinner out on the back porch with the help of a couple of heat lamps, and they talked until Taylor's voice was almost hoarse. As soon as they had cleaned up the dinner mess, Mike got a call about a problem with some of the cattle and he'd left. He had apologized profusely but told Taylor not to wait up for him. He wouldn't be back.

Staring up at the ceiling, she let out a long breath. It wasn't as if she'd expected much—not really—but she had been looking forward to the dessert he had alluded to earlier. The practical side of her reminded herself that she had only been there for a couple of days and it was too soon to be thinking about getting physical with him.

But the little devil sitting on her shoulder reminded her that she'd been fairly close to Mike years ago and it wasn't like he was a stranger.

And then it hinted at how long it had been since she'd had sex.

Stupid devil.

Rising from the bed, Taylor told herself that today was a new day. They were going out of town—and spending the night somewhere else—so maybe it was all for the better. Knowing this was Jonathan Wade's primary residence made her a little uneasy. She shouldn't even be considering getting physical with Mike here. She had hoped he would take her to his place. It was true there was the possibility he lived on the property, but Taylor knew she'd prefer going there and doing whatever they were going to do than doing it here.

Okay, stop thinking about doing it, she admonished herself as she gathered up her things and headed for the shower. It was bad enough that she had erotic dreams of him all night long. She had tossed and turned and was now feeling more than a little on edge. The hot spray did wonders for the tension in her tired muscles but little for her wayward thoughts.

By the time she was downstairs making coffee, Taylor had begun to wonder if they were still going out of town. She had no idea what a "cattle emergency" even was or if Mike had gotten any sleep last night. For the moment, she relished time alone in the kitchen to clear her mind.

Staring out the big window and looking toward the barn, she sighed. "Did you sleep okay?" the deep voice said behind her and she very nearly jumped out of her skin. Mike placed his hands on her shoulders to steady her when she turned around. "Sorry, didn't mean to scare you."

Taylor's hand went over her heart to try to calm it. "Well, you did," she said, forcing a smile. "Sorry." She shook her head to clear it. "I slept fine, what about you? How late were you out there?"

Stepping away, he poured himself some coffee. "It was after two when I finally crawled into bed," he said wearily.

"Does this sort of thing happen often?"

He shrugged and took a long drink from his steaming mug. "Not really, and when it does, it can't be helped. I'm used to it."

"If you want to postpone our trip, that's fine with me. I'm sure I can find something to do around here to keep me busy."

Mike placed his mug on the counter and considered her. "What would you do?"

"I'm not sure. I'm always thinking of new questions I want to ask in the interview, and I wouldn't mind going back into town and looking around a little more. I'll probably have to wait until tomorrow to hear back from Victoria and our legal department on the document we sent them—or," she said as the idea hit her, "I could go for a bike ride."

"All good possibilities," he said after a few awkward minutes of silence. Then he turned and picked up his mug and started to leave the kitchen. "But all unnecessary. Meet me outside in fifteen minutes."

And then he was gone.

Taylor stood there dumbfounded for a full minute before she actually moved. Then she quickly ate a cup of yogurt and took her coffee up to her bedroom to finish packing. Most of it was done, but now it was a matter of getting it all down the stairs and out to the car.

Once outside, she saw Mike pulling the SUV out of the garage. "You know, *Newslink* is paying for this rental. Why don't we use it?" she suggested.

"It's not a big deal," he said when he took her bags and put them in the trunk. When they were both seated and buckled in, he turned to her. "Ready?"

Nodding, she smiled. "You never told me where it is that we are going."

"Kennebunkport," he said as they drove down the long driveway.

Unfortunately, Taylor didn't know too much about the area, so she simply had to sit back and trust him in where they were going. They drove down many two-lane roads through small communities, and it gave her a sense of peace. "I would love to drive like this every day and not have to deal with the crazy pace of the city," she sighed.

"Why do you stay there?" he asked, glancing her way.

"I'm used to it now, I guess. Besides, I'm rooted there. My job's there. I have nothing to move to." It was a sad but true statement. Taylor had no real family left. Even though it meant there was no one to keep her where she was, it also meant there was no one to move for.

"You think you would enjoy country life after all this time?"

"Absolutely. In the last two days I've felt better than I have in a long time."

"In what way?"

"I'm relaxed, for starters. I find that I'm sleeping better, plus I haven't had to yell or curse at anybody in at least forty-eight hours. That's a record in my book!" They laughed and Taylor sat back and enjoyed the ride.

She must have nodded off because she felt herself gently nudged and heard Mike's soft voice telling her they had arrived. Opening her eyes, she noticed they were parked by a marina.

"What are we doing here?" she asked, blinking at the sights.

"I told you we were going to see Wade's second residence." He nodded his head toward the marina. "It's down there."

"He has a boat?" she croaked. Mike was already out of the vehicle and gathering their bags from the back. He opened the door for Taylor and held it for her as she climbed out. There were dozens of boats docked at the marina, and Taylor wished she had some knowledge about Jonathan Wade that she could guess which one was his. Judging from his need for privacy, she'd imagine it would be plain and unobtrusive.

Watching Mike walk ahead of her, she was shocked to see him stop in front of a rather large yacht. Surely, he was stopping there to wait up for her. She picked up the pace and when she was by his side asked, "Well, which one is it?"

"We're here," he said and handed the bags to the captain waiting at the side of the boat.

"This is the boat of a man who craves anonymity?" she cried as she climbed on board. "This thing is easily fifty feet long!" Noticing other uniformed people on board, she added, "With a crew!"

Mike walked behind her, laughing. "Fifty-five feet,

actually," he corrected, and when she turned to him with wide eyes, he reached out and took her hand. "Relax, Taylor. Just because the guy likes his privacy doesn't mean he doesn't enjoy the good life. You make it sound like he should be living in a cave or something."

He was right. Thus far, Jonathan Wade had been nothing that she'd expected—even though she'd yet to meet him. In a million years, she never would have pictured him living on a working farm, or having such a…normal home. He obviously trusted his employees with all he had since Mike seemed to have free rein of the place and all that went with it. And then there was the yacht. She didn't even know how to begin to process it all. Shaking her head in disbelief, she let Mike lead her on the tour.

The boat housed four bedrooms, three bathrooms, a large living and dining area, and a fully equipped kitchen. The captain, as well as two crew members, were there to assist them. The furniture was very modern and inviting—it was almost possible to forget she was on a boat and not in a luxury apartment. After the tour, Taylor sat down in the living room and thanked one crew member as he handed her a glass of iced water. She was still a little in awe of her surroundings and watched as he walked away. Mike sat down beside her.

"Well? What do you think?"

"I think I feel a little on display," she whispered, glancing at the crewmen. Before she could stop him, Mike walked over to them and told them their services were not needed at the moment. Her jaw dropped. She was frowning when he rejoined her on the sofa.

"Now what's wrong?" he asked with a dramatic sigh.

"This isn't right," she said as she faced him. "All

of it. The car, the boat, the crew…" She stood up and began to pace. "I mean, I feel like I had to jump through all kinds of hoops to get here. I know the agreement we had, but I'm not okay with it. I should be sitting down like a serious journalist interviewing her subject, not tooling around with one of his employees!"

The look on Mike's face told her that her ranting had hit a nerve. His jaw clenched and she saw a spark of anger in his eyes.

"I'm sorry, Mike. I didn't mean that the way it sounded. It's just…well, the man should be here doing all of this himself. If he was serious about this interview, he'd be the one here, not having you drive me all over the place and entertaining me. Maybe it's because of his reclusive lifestyle—he doesn't realize how all of this would be considered odd."

"I'll be sure to tell him," he answered in a tight tone. Standing, he walked to the kitchen to grab a beer. "You want one?" he asked coldly, seemingly unaware that it was barely eleven o'clock in the morning.

Taylor went to him. "I'm sorry. Please don't be angry with me," she pleaded. "I'm not used to being idle for this long. I work a lot. I don't take vacations. Maybe he thought this would be a treat, but it isn't for me. I was looking forward to working with a great author. Everyone back at the magazine is counting on me, but instead of working, I'm traipsing all around Maine!"

"There's nothing I can do about it, Taylor, so you might as well concede defeat and go with it." He took a sip of beer so he could gain a moment to get his emotions under control. "The plan was to take you out for a sail today and on a bicycle tour tomorrow. The weather is going to be unseasonably warm so I thought you'd enjoy it. We can head home after lunch if you'd prefer." He turned to walk out before she could respond, but she stopped him.

"Wait a minute," she called after him in an angry tone. When he turned around and faced her, she stormed over to him. "I said I was sorry, dammit. What more do you want from me?" He didn't say a word, but a blaze of emotion flashed in his eyes. "Why is it that we've been able to talk about nearly anything and everything, and yet when I happen to express my feelings—my frustrations—you get ticked off? This is who I am, Mike. I'm not the quiet girl you used to know. I have emotions and there are times when I'm out-and-out bitchy. If you can't deal with that, then okay, we'll head back to the farm. We don't even have to wait until after lunch. Let's just go now." She turned to head down the hall, where she had seen one of the crewmen place her luggage, but Mike reached out and grabbed her gently around her upper arm to stop her.

"Hey," he said softly. "You're right. I overreacted and I'm sorry. I guess it didn't occur to me that you wouldn't be pleased with all of this. Most people would kill to play 'lifestyles of the rich and famous' for a few days. I'm used to people being okay with taking advantage of what Wade's money has to offer."

"Well, I'm not," she replied in the same quiet tone. "I don't expect to be treated like this, like I'm somebody who needs to be pampered and spoiled. To be honest, it makes me a little uncomfortable."

He tugged her closer. "I was hoping you'd be pleasantly surprised by the bike tour, though. I thought it was perfect for you, and technically not a very pampering experience." A lopsided grin crossed his face and Taylor couldn't help but grin with him. "I would really like to take you on the tour."

"I'd really like to go on the tour. Thank you."

He slowly released her arm and took a drink from the frosted bottle in his other hand, his eyes on Taylor the entire time. Carefully, he placed it down on the butcher-block counter and visibly seemed to relax. "If it's okay with you, I'll tell the captain we're ready to go, and we can get some good time out on the water today. Would you like that?" She nodded and all the remaining tension left his body. "Good. I'll be right back."

"Mike?" she called out when he was halfway out the door. "I'm sorry about what I said before. I didn't mean it."

"I know," he said and walked out the door.

Two hours later, Taylor felt like she had stepped into the pages of some amazing travel magazine. The view of the water was breathtaking—the weather was perfect and there wasn't a cloud in the sky. They enjoyed their lunch out on the deck and for the most part, they kept their conversation to a minimum.

Taylor didn't mind. She had said enough earlier and didn't want to risk saying anything else that would upset Mike. Once she was done with her lunch, she took out her camera and got some shots of the ocean. Not that there was much to see, but she had never gone sailing in any way, shape, or form in her life, so the experience was new and she wanted to capture it on film.

"We'll continue on this course for another hour or

so," Mike said as he came to stand beside her. "Then we'll stop for a while. I wish it was warmer so we could have gone for a swim."

"Oh, I don't know if I would have been ready for something like that. I'm a big baby when water is involved. And I'm pretty sure it's super deep out here with lots of slithering creatures swimming about. No thank you." He chuckled at her words and they shifted positions so Taylor was leaning against the rails as Mike wrapped his arms around her from behind.

It was a good feeling. Very good. Taylor couldn't help but lean back into him so she could feel him firmly pressed against her, practically from head to toe. Without thought, she tilted her head to the side and was thrilled when he took that as a sign to begin nuzzling at her neck. She hummed her approval and soon found herself turning in his arms.

"Hi," he said softly as she faced him.

"Hi, yourself." Her arms came up and twined their way around his shoulders as she pressed closer to him.

"You're missing a pretty spectacular view," he said, leaning his forehead against hers.

"I think this particular view is pretty spectacular, too." Then she leaned up and kissed him gently on the lips, and was rewarded when he groaned right before his arms banded around her.

"If we start this, you're going to miss the rest of the sights," Mike said, his voice a little gruff.

"I think I'd be more than happy with the sights below deck," she said with a wicked grin so that Mike couldn't miss the double entendre.

Wordlessly, Mike took Taylor's hand and led her

back into the main cabin, and then down the stairs to the master stateroom. He closed the door, watching as she slowly wandered the room, touching the furniture and the bed. She was slightly nervous. "We don't have to do this, Taylor. Not if you're uncomfortable."

Looking over her shoulder at him, she smiled and chuckled. "You may not believe this, but the only thing making me uncomfortable is how much I want this and the fact that I want to…push you up against that door and have you kiss me like you did in the kitchen yesterday. Until neither of us can catch our breath."

A lazy grin crossed his face. "And yet you're standing all the way over there."

Slowly, so slowly, she walked toward him until he had no choice but to back up against the door. Her breathing was ragged, and the intense look on Mike's face was the sexiest thing she had ever seen. "Are we crazy?" she asked softly. "We barely know each other anymore."

Mike shook his head. "We're not crazy, Taylor. I never forgot you. Couldn't forget you." He reached out to stroke a hand across her cheek and she was surprised to see it was shaking. She was relieved to know she wasn't the only one feeling that way.

"Me too, you know. I never forgot you, either. I felt guilty—"

"Shh…" He placed a finger over her lips. "I don't want to talk about the past. Not anymore." She nodded in agreement and stepped closer to him until her breasts were pressed against his chest. He removed his finger from her lips and caressed her cheek with it. "You're so soft, Taylor. So beautiful."

She blushed at his words. No one had ever said

anything like that to her before. Not ever. Only him. "I need you to touch me," she said boldly.

It was all the encouragement he needed. As she rose on tiptoes to press her lips to his, Mike's hands immediately went to her waist before he let his hands roam up her back and then down to her bottom, where he gently squeezed, and then back up and around until her breasts filled his hands and his thumbs were teasing her nipples.

Taylor kissed him all the while, not wanting to stop, needing him desperately. Without even realizing it, he began to walk her backward toward the bed. When the back of her legs touched the mattress, she jumped, breaking the kiss. There were a million questions in Mike's eyes as she looked at him. And her answer to every one of them was *yes*.

She reached down for the hem of her sweater and lifted it over her head. Looking up at Mike, she was surprised to see he was still looking at her face, her eyes. He was wearing his standard attire of thermal layered with flannel. Taylor's hands went to work on the buttons of the flannel shirt and she smiled up at him. "I've been wanting to do this for days."

"Days, huh?" She nodded. When the last button was undone and she pushed the shirt from his shoulders and down his arms, he let it fall to the ground before he took care of the thermal shirt himself. It joined the pile on the floor as well.

Unable to help herself, Taylor leaned in and let her hands finally feel the strong expanse of his chest. It was even more impressive than what she'd imagined. His skin was warm and smooth, with a smattering of hair that was perfect to her. Her mouth actually watered and she closed the distance to rain tiny kisses across his chest until she heard him hiss.

Lifting her head, she looked up at him. Their gazes never wavered as she reached behind her and unhooked her bra and let it drop to the floor. Next, she kicked her shoes off and then shimmied out of her jeans and panties. When she straightened and looked at him, she saw a fire in his eyes that excited her more than any caress ever had.

"I seem to be a little overdressed," he said thickly, his eyes still on hers.

"I doubt you'll stay that way for long," she said wickedly as she wrapped an arm around his shoulders and carefully pulled him down onto the bed with her.

And she was right.

———

Later, as Taylor lay in his arms, she couldn't help but marvel at how right everything felt, as if her entire life had been leading up to this specific point in time. She sighed and snuggled closer to him. "That was pretty amazing," she finally said.

He kissed the top of her head. "I have to agree. But then again, I knew it would be."

Slowly, Taylor lifted her head. "You did, huh?" He nodded. "How could you be so sure?"

"Because it's you," he said simply. "I knew ten years ago when I kissed you that if we ever had the chance at more, it would be incredible." His hand reached out and softly skimmed her cheek. "You were worth the wait."

Everything inside of her melted and she had no idea what to say. She felt the same way about him. It was hard to be with him—and not just like this—but in any capacity and not regret the past. If she had been stronger, more confident back then, maybe she would have sought him out after she and Eddie had broken up. To think of all the years they wasted just wondering what could have been.

Leaning down, Mike kissed her thoroughly. "As much as I'd like to keep you down here all day and night, I need to go back on deck and make sure things are running smoothly and see about dinner."

"Is it dinnertime already?" she asked, looking at the clock in surprise. They had been locked away for hours. A blush crept across her cheeks. She was going to say something flippant about time flying and all that, but it would have been ridiculous.

Mike rose from the bed and went in search of his pants. "I made sure everything was stocked for us for dinner so all I have to do is cook it up." He glanced at the clock. "Why don't you stay down here and relax or write or whatever you want to do. I'll call for you when dinner's ready. How does that sound?"

"Like you're spoiling me," she said as she sat up and stretched. The sheet she had been carefully clinging to slipped down around her waist, baring her to him. At first Taylor was oblivious to what she'd done, but one look at the heated expression on Mike's face and she knew. Her hands immediately went to pick up the sheet and cover herself, but Mike placed one knee on the bed and his hand reached out to stop her.

"Don't," he said, his voice low. "You're so beautiful, Taylor. I look at you and I ache." His head lowered to her breast and Taylor felt herself slowly falling back onto the pillows, Mike's body carefully covering hers.

His lips gently suckled and a moan escaped Taylor's lips before she could stop it.

"What about dinner?" she whispered breathlessly.

"It can wait," he growled as he kicked off his jeans and dove under the sheets with her.

—∽∿∽—

Taylor was positively boneless by the time Mike left to go up on deck, yet she felt energized. Her life was spinning out of control in the most amazing way and oddly enough, she felt motivated to get some writing done for the article. She climbed from the bed and walked to the room she originally thought she'd be staying in and grabbed her laptop. Did she go back to the room she and Mike had shared or stay here in the one with her stuff?

Thinking of how she'd spent the last several hours, she opted to go back to Mike's room.

Sitting down on the bed, she began typing notes on the weekend thus far: her anticipation about meeting Jonathan Wade, his farm, the house, and now the boat. Could she even call it a boat? She wrote about the two different towns he resided in—one was coastal and touristy while the other was small, quiet, and isolated. Even with all of this information, it wasn't possible to form an opinion or a vision of the man himself.

The wait was killing her, even though being with Mike was an extremely pleasant distraction. The thought of the way they had spent the last several hours made her sigh. How could she have been so blindly in love with Eddie when Mike had been right there?

It was too late to think about all that could have been. She needed to focus on the here and now. Looking at her watch, she realized a little more than an hour had passed since Mike had gone up on deck. While he had said he'd come back and get her, Taylor missed being in his company. Putting her laptop and notes away, she freshened her hair and makeup and ran up on deck to look for him. She spotted him at the bow, talking to the captain. The two men appeared familiar with one another and seemed to be sharing a joke.

Mike looked extremely handsome, especially when he smiled. He always seemed to be relaxed, but his smile could thaw an iceberg, Taylor thought. He was dressed in black jeans, as she was, but had changed out of the thermal and flannel from earlier into a deep maroon sweater and his standard work boots. Very rugged. Very masculine. As she was standing there admiring his form, he looked down and saw her. Taylor gave a slight wave and he immediately started for her.

"I didn't want to disturb you," he said as he climbed down the small flight of stairs. "Did you get some rest?"

"No. I did some work." At his frustrated expression, she began to laugh. "I told you! I need to work. I don't do vacations. Like, ever." She could tell he wasn't amused. "I'm a single woman who lives in one of the most expensive cities in the world with no means of income other than my writing. If I don't work, I don't eat." She shrugged and tried to make light of it, but his frown didn't ease. "So…what's for dinner?" Maybe a change of subject would work.

As if on cue, one of the crewmen came out to announce that everything was set up for dinner. Mike thanked him and then without a word took Taylor by the hand and led her inside to a table with an open view of the entire back of the boat, where he held out a seat for her before taking his own. There was a traditional clambake waiting for them, complete with lobster, mussels, crabs, steamers, corn on the cob, and potatoes. Taylor was overwhelmed. On her salary, she didn't eat this much seafood in a year, let alone in one sitting!

"I could get used to this," she joked midway through the meal. "So, did your boss ask you to dazzle me with all of my favorite foods so I wouldn't whine so much about having to wait to meet him?"

Mike chuckled. "No. He's not that devious. The food was my idea. I thought it would be nice to have a traditional coastal dinner while out on the boat."

"Well, you thought correctly," she said with a smile, happy to see him relaxing again.

"And for the record," he said with a grin, "I don't think I should have to dazzle you with food to keep you from whining."

She blushed. "Do you have any idea how frustrating this assignment is?" She was hoping that yet another change of topic would distract him. The last thing she wanted was to crawl across the table and throw herself at him, which was a very real possibility if he kept looking at her like he was now.

"You're not very patient, are you?"

"Nope," she replied with an impish grin. "I'm used to knowing what I have to do and getting it done." They continued to eat for several minutes and as dinner wound down, she began to ask him questions that she actually could use for the interview—what it was like working on the farm and his apparent managing of all things Wade. His answers were always short and to the point and he didn't elaborate much on anything.

Time for a different approach.

"What initially brought you up here, Mike?" Taylor realized he had never told her how his life up here had begun and what it was that made him leave New York.

"It's a long story, Taylor, and not one I'm prepared to talk about with you." He wasn't being nasty, but his tone left no room for argument. Taylor clammed up immediately and ate the remainder of her meal in silence. It wasn't that hard to do, because the view off the back of the boat was enough to keep her captivated. Other boats out on the water were getting closer to land, so there was enough to keep her attention diverted from Mike.

When the crewmen appeared to clear the table and offer dessert, she declined. Mike waved them off, but made no attempt at conversation after shutting her out of her last question. With nothing left to do, Taylor rose and walked toward the back deck. The breeze off the water was cold now that the sun was down and she shivered.

Silently, Mike came up beside her and looked out at the water with her. "I'm sorry," he said as he continued to stare forward and not at her. "I didn't mean to sound so rude earlier. I'm just not comfortable talking about my past with anyone. Can you understand that?"

"I suppose," she sighed. "It's just…I'm here waiting to interview someone who doesn't seem overly anxious to talk with me, and then I'm sitting here having dinner with someone who doesn't want to talk either. In my position, where talking and interviewing are my life, it's extremely frustrating."

He couldn't help but laugh. "I guess I didn't look at it like that." He moved closer and put his arm around her to keep her warm, and then took her by the hand and led her around to the front of the boat.

"What are we doing?"

"There's a blanket on the bench up here, and I think you'll enjoy the view as we pull into the marina." They reached the bench, tucked away under the upper deck where the captain and the crew members now were. They were out of sight and, as they settled in with the blanket wrapped around them, Taylor felt like they had gotten something back that they almost lost earlier.

"This is nice," she said quietly, resting her head on his shoulder. The truth was that it was beyond nice. Even if she didn't factor in how romantic it was to be here like this with Mike, the entire experience was something she'd never forget. Her legs were curled up at her side and she slipped her shoes off for more comfort. Mike's arms were around her and the movement of the boat on the water was almost lulling. She shifted slightly to get more comfortable and was content to watch the shoreline coming into view.

"When I turned nineteen," Mike began slowly, seemingly out of nowhere, "I saw how my life was going nowhere." Taylor desperately wanted to raise her head and look at him, but she knew he was answering the question he had refused earlier. "I had been in trouble for so many years, and I knew I had to change or my life would be ruined forever."

She hadn't known him at nineteen. It wasn't until several years later that they had met.

"Because of my own rebellious attitude, I'd done a

lot of stupid things. I was several years older than most of the people I hung out with, mainly because I had been left back in school so many times." He paused for a moment. "Did you realize that I'm four years older than you?" Taylor shook her head. She had known he was a little older, but she never would have guessed how much.

"Anyway, it took a while for me to actually get my shit together and to realize I was going to have to break some patterns of behavior and step away from the people I had been associating with." He didn't have to name names; Taylor knew who he was referring to. "I took a job in the mailroom of a publishing house in Manhattan about five years ago, and that's where I came to know Wade." When he didn't continue, Taylor began to put it all together. He and Wade had somehow become friends and when Wade moved to Maine, he offered Mike a job with him, managing his properties because he saw potential in Mike that no one else had bothered to see.

She wrapped her arm across his chest and hugged him tightly before placing a soft kiss on his chest. He stiffened for a moment before relaxing again. "Was it Jonathan Wade who brought you up here to Maine?" she asked softly.

"Yes." No more was said on the subject and they leaned into one another for several minutes. Taylor loved the feel of being wrapped in Mike's arms, and between his warmth and the sounds of the water, she felt more at ease than she ever had before in her life.

Wordlessly, she turned and straddled his lap before taking his face in her hands and kissing him. It was an impulsive move, yet she couldn't have waited another moment to kiss him if her life depended on it. His hands grabbed her hips and pulled her snugly against his already-growing hardness, and Taylor couldn't help but sigh at the feel of it.

With the blanket and overhang for cover, she felt bold. She felt naughty. No one could see them. As if sensing her thoughts, one of Mike's hands came up and cupped the back of her head as he deepened the kiss. His tongue stroked hers and he moaned with pleasure as she began to rock against him. Taylor had never been sexually aggressive, and yet something about Mike brought out that side of her.

Slowly, rhythmically, Mike rocked up into her. Tearing his mouth from hers, he whispered her name and nipped at the column of her throat. "In a perfect world, I'd be inside of you right now, under the stars, in the moonlight." He licked a trail up to her earlobe. "I want to strip you bare and make love to you."

Now it was her turn to moan. The thought of doing exactly what he said was more tempting than she'd ever thought possible, and when she reached between them and grasped at the button-fly of his jeans, one strong hand clamped over hers to stop her. She raised her head, her breathing ragged, and looked at him with confusion.

"We're not alone," he said, his voice gruff, his frustration evident. "There's no way I'm going to compromise you and risk having anyone see what we're doing." He rested his forehead against hers for a moment. "Wrap your legs around me, sweetheart." She obeyed and as soon as her ankles locked behind his back, he stood. One hand cupped her bottom and secured her to him while the other held the blanket in place.

"What are we doing?" she asked, dazed and more than a little turned on.

"We're spending the night on the boat and I plan for our night to begin right now."

As he carried her, Taylor looked up to where the crew was standing on the top deck. "What about them? Won't they need to talk to you once we dock?"

He shook his head. "Once we dock and the boat is secured, they are off the clock. They'll leave, and then we'll have the whole place to ourselves." Images of the two of them naked up on deck ran through Taylor's mind and some of those thoughts must have been transparent enough for Mike to know what she was thinking. "Still too risky," he said as he maneuvered them through the open doors at the back of the boat, through the dining area, and down the stairs to the stateroom.

Inside, he set her down on the bed before pulling the blanket away. With her hair fanned out around her and her arms thrown back in surrender, she watched him and waited. His expression was dark, possessive, and it thrilled her. She wished he would move—join her on the bed and finish what they started.

"Mike?" she whispered hesitantly.

"Someday, Taylor..." he began in a low voice. "Someday we will do that. We'll go out on the water alone, the two of us, and then I'll spend hours loving you under the sun, the moon, and the stars. I promise."

She wasn't going to question how he was going to get the boat out again. It wasn't important. The imagery, the intent, and the emotion in his voice was quickly sending her up in flames. "I don't need the sun or the moon or the stars right now," she said, her eyes never leaving his.

"What do you need?"

"You," she whispered. "Just you."

Control be damned.

Chapter 7

MORNING CAME WAY TOO SOON AS FAR AS TAYLOR WAS concerned. She had spent the night in Mike's arms and it was a glorious feeling. They had made love more times than she could have imagined. And now that it was Monday, she felt a sense of disappointment she hadn't felt in a long time. She wasn't ready for the weekend to be over—or for reality to set in. For almost twenty-four hours she and Mike had existed in a world of their own, and no matter how much she wanted to do this interview with his boss, she was slowly coming to realize that she wanted the time with Mike more.

Turning her head slightly, she looked at him as he slept. Who would have thought that the boy she once knew would turn into this incredibly sexy man who seemed to find great joy in entertaining and pleasing her? He seemed to know more about her than he had ever let on. Was she that transparent? Taylor hadn't spent a whole lot of time alone with him all those years ago, and even Eddie wasn't aware of who she was back then.

No, back then she was a girl of eighteen. Her head was full of dreams that she didn't share with anyone because she didn't have the confidence to do so. Eddie only knew the side of her that had wanted to be a wife and mother. He never knew her dreams of being a journalist, or of leaving New York altogether. All of their plans back then had been focused on *his* future. Looking back, she realized how sad it would have made her. Maybe now she could finally let go of the feeling of betrayal and focus on the man lying beside her who seemed genuinely interested in knowing who she was and giving her what she wanted.

She jumped when the alarm went off at eight o'clock. Mike stirred beside her and reached out to shut it off. Without missing a beat, he rolled over and tucked Taylor beneath him, kissing her until they both were breathless. "Good morning."

Unable to help herself, she smiled against his lips. "Good morning. I didn't realize you had set the alarm."

"I wanted us to have time to get up and have some breakfast before heading over to pick up the bikes. We can do the tour at our own pace, but I reserved the bikes for eleven o'clock. Will that be enough time, do you think?" Taylor thought about it for a moment and then her expression changed, fell. "What?" he asked as he sat up, alarmed by the look on her face. "What's the matter?"

"I had no idea you had planned something like this, and I didn't pack for a bike ride." She was sure her disappointment was palpable, and she hated that she was going to miss out on something as wonderful as this over a change of clothes.

"Is that all?" he asked.

"I don't think you understand. I can't go for a bike ride in boots with heels, trust me."

Mike rolled his eyes. "Seems to me if your love of biking is all you say it is, something like boots wouldn't stop you." He was challenging her and he loved the immediate spark his words put in her eyes.

"It's not that," she said and swatted playfully at him. "I prefer to be comfortable when I'm biking."

"So, we'll go shopping. There. Problem solved."

How could she possibly even begin to tell him that her life wasn't as simple as that? How she couldn't go into a store and buy herself new pants, shirt, and sneakers on her small salary? She budgeted every penny and while there were some things she could do, an entire outfit wasn't one of them right now. "Mike," she began and was surprised when he placed a finger over her lips.

"Shh... We'll eat some breakfast and then drive into town to shop." When she began to protest again, he pressed his finger a little more firmly against her lips. "Consider it a gift. I should have told you what I had planned so you could be better prepared."

"I can't—"

"A gift. You're supposed to say thank you," he teased and placed a gentle kiss on the tip of her nose.

It was pointless to keep arguing with him, she realized, and instead raked her fingers into his hair and pulled his lips down to hers for a more thorough kiss. When they finally resurfaced, they were both breathing hard. "Thank you," she whispered and gave him a sexy smile, hoping to entice him into staying in bed a little longer. For a minute, she thought she had as his body seemed to relax against hers, but at the last moment, he pulled back.

"As much as I want to spend the day in here with you like this, I think it would be wiser to get up and go on that bike tour." His tone lacked any real enthusiasm. "I do have some things that need to be handled back at the farm early tomorrow morning, so we'll have to head back tonight."

Taylor wanted to be disappointed, but Mike had already given her so much that she couldn't. The reality of it all was that she was here to do a job, an interview. This new development should be a perk, but the more time she and Mike spent together, the less interested she became in the interview with Jonathan Wade. Knowing her boss would kill her if she didn't follow through and finish what she came her for, Taylor would do the interview—it was just that her enthusiasm was no longer directed at Wade and was instead fully directed at the sexy man getting up from the bed.

She sighed with appreciation at the sight of him. He was a man who did physical labor and it showed. Every inch of him was muscle, and it took every ounce of self-control she had to keep her hands to herself while he went in search of clean clothes to wear.

With clothes in hand, Mike turned and walked into the en suite. He couldn't miss the way Taylor was watching him. Even though they were on a schedule, he couldn't help himself. Without a word, he walked back to the bed and pulled the blankets back. A small scream escaped Taylor's mouth at the surprise attack.

"Mike! What are you doing?"

Still silent, he scooped her up in his arms and headed toward the bathroom. Placing her on her feet, enjoying the delicious slide of her naked body against his, he smiled wickedly. "Trust me. We'll save time showering together."

Taylor's smile lit up the room, and as he reached behind her to turn on the water, he realized he didn't care if it saved time or not.

They stepped off the boat a little later with their coffees in travel mugs. Mike was determined to get Taylor outfitted early so they could pick up their bikes and begin the tour. By ten o'clock, Taylor had new sneakers, thick socks, sweatpants, and a sweatshirt that said *Kennebunkport* on it. She had rolled her eyes when he picked it up, claiming she had a sweatshirt she could wear, but Mike had insisted she needed it so she would remember her time there.

As if she could forget it.

They made a quick stop back at the yacht for Taylor to change and grab her camera equipment. In the back of her mind, Taylor had decided that even if she didn't use the pictures for her piece, she'd love to have them for her personal album. Once she had everything loaded up and ready to go, Mike led them back to the car and drove across town to where they would pick up their bikes.

The tour he had chosen would take them to Cape Porpoise on a route parallel to the Kennebunk River, a view of where it emptied into the Atlantic in sight. Taylor stopped many times to take pictures, but rather than get annoyed, Mike stood back and watched her work, marveling at the way she found joy and wonder in the smallest of things. It didn't matter if it was a flower, a tree, or people, Taylor found a way to photograph them to tell a story. Along the way, they had seen an old fire station, and she had stopped the bike to photograph it as well. As they rode away, she spoke of what she imagined its history to be. Between the pictures, the conversation, and the ride itself, Mike thoroughly enjoyed himself.

The route ended at Cape Porpoise, which was a

working fishing village with great vistas and tons of traditional Maine fare. Feeling invigorated from the ride, they locked up the bikes and walked through the town to window-shop. They had been walking for several minutes when Taylor realized they were holding hands. It was such a natural thing for them to do, and she wondered when it had happened. When had they gone from two people who hadn't seen each other in years to comfortable lovers?

Noticing the direction of her gaze, Mike gently squeezed her hand and led her to a shack out on the pier. "Have you ever had a lobster club?" he asked, walking up to the window of the shack.

"I don't think I've ever even heard of a lobster club," she said with a chuckle.

Not waiting for further input, Mike ordered them two sandwiches and drinks. After paying and taking the tray, he led her to a spot further out on the pier. Sitting down and hanging his legs from the side, he patted the spot next to him.

Taylor obliged and readily sat down, accepting the sandwich. Biking always gave her an appetite and the sight of the sandwich was enough to make her almost forget her manners. "Thank you," she said as she accepted the plate he handed to her. She purred with contentment after the first bite.

"There's nothing quite like it," Mike commented as he watched her eat. "I know New York is famous for its food, but they can't do something like this. This is fresh out of the ocean."

Delicately wiping her mouth, Taylor nodded. "Like I said last night, I could definitely get used to this."

She finished eating in silence and then leaned back and closed her eyes, letting the sun touch her face.

Silent beside her, Mike watched. He'd seen her relax more and more over the last several days, but this was, by far, the most serene he had ever seen her. She looked even younger than her years—almost as young as when he'd first met her, if that were even possible.

Actually, something about her today reminded him of the girl he had known back then. Her hair was pulled back in a ponytail, her cheeks were flushed from the bike ride, and she had a smile that seemed to say that she didn't have a care in the world. It was a good look.

Finishing his sandwich, he looked out at the water. The air was cool, typical for a fall day. He watched many boats off in the distance and wished they could spend more time here without the crew and go off sailing on their own. No interruptions. No watchful eyes.

No schedule to keep.

The thought made him look at his watch. It was already after two in the afternoon, and he knew the ride back would be shorter since Taylor wouldn't need to stop for as many pictures, but it was still going to take them at least two hours to get back. Turning, he looked at Taylor, hating to disturb her, to break the peace she was clearly experiencing.

It was an unfortunate necessity.

"I think we need to start heading back," he said quietly and nearly groaned with desire as Taylor turned to him with slumberous eyes and a serene smile on her face. She looked like an angel to him—unfortunately, the thoughts going through his mind were far from angelic.

"So soon?"

He nodded. "It's still a couple of hours of riding, and then we have to return the bikes and get back to the boat to pack and then drive home." Her expression didn't change as he spoke, and he wondered if she was even listening. "Taylor?"

"Hmm?"

"I hate to cut our day short…"

"It's so peaceful out here. We're surrounded by people and the water, and there are boats and birds and conversations going on all around us, yet it's so peaceful." She took a deep lungful of fresh air and let it out slowly. "I know we can't stay here, but I'm enjoying our last minutes."

He felt guilty. There were probably a dozen different ways for him to get out of his responsibilities for at least another day, but that wasn't who he was. He took his job seriously, which was why people respected him. It had taken a long time before anyone showed him any kind of respect, and it had taken moving hundreds of miles away from everything he had ever known to make it happen. He wasn't about to shirk it all now.

Standing, Mike collected their trash and gave Taylor another minute to enjoy the view. By the time he had turned around, she was walking toward him with a lazy gait. "Any chance of someone picking us up and taking the bikes back?"

He laughed. "Come on, now. That doesn't sound like the bike enthusiast you bragged about being."

"Yeah, well…that bike enthusiast never rode for hours followed by a lazy and filling lunch on the water. I could very easily take a nap right now."

He made a *tsking* sound and took her by the hand.

"I'm not saying it's going to be easy, but we can do it, right?"

Protest was on the tip of her tongue, but she let it go. They walked along quietly to where they had locked up the bikes and soon were on their way. The sights were no less spectacular, but this time Taylor was satisfied watching them go by rather than stopping to photograph them. She sighed with contentment, happy to be riding behind Mike and watching his adorable rear snugly covered in denim. Now, that was something she could watch all day long.

At the midway point, Mike surprised her by pulling his bike over to a shady spot beside the river. "What are you doing?" Taylor asked as she pulled up beside him.

"I'm not as in shape as I thought I was." He laughed through a ragged breath. "I need a break!" Parking his bike against a tree, he walked slowly toward the water, holding his side for dramatic effect.

Taylor had to admit she felt a little winded herself, and the thought of taking a short break by the river sounded very appealing. After parking her bike next to Mike's, she followed his path through the trees and found him lying on his back on a patch of thick grass, eyes closed, hands behind his head. She sat down beside him and looked out at the water. His hand on her shoulder made her jump, but soon she found herself lying down beside him.

"Relax," he whispered, his eyes still closed.

Obeying, Taylor lay there on her back, hands above her head in surrender. It felt wonderful to lie there with the sun shining down on her face. She closed her eyes and let her body go boneless. "I may never get back on that bike after this," she murmured and heard his soft chuckle next to her.

Moments later, she noticed a shadow over her face. Opening her eyes, she found Mike leaning up on one elbow, looking down at her. No words were exchanged; it was all in their eyes. His asked. Hers answered. Slowly, Mike lowered his head as Taylor reached up to wrap an arm around his shoulder to bring him closer. When his lips met hers, Taylor melted. It was so good, so sweet. His lips were so soft, so gentle, coaxing hers to open under his. It didn't take long for her to give in, and for as much emotion as they each poured into the kiss, it didn't feel hurried or frantic.

It felt…right.

Mike sighed deeply into her mouth and Taylor felt all of his longing in this one exquisite kiss. She rolled onto her side so she could press herself against him. He ran a hand down her back and let it rest at the base of her spine and held her to him. Their tongues teased shyly at first— aware of kissing in the middle of a fairly public area— but when Taylor wriggled against him to fit more snugly against his growing arousal, Mike's control broke.

All thoughts of being out in public were forgotten. Turning Taylor onto her back, Mike stretched out on top of her and his kiss became more urgent, demanding. Taylor clung to him, wanting all of his strength and heat. Tongues mated, hands roamed as she raked her fingers up through his hair. His mouth left hers briefly to kiss her throat, focusing all of his attention there as she let out a moan of approval. She arched her head back to give him better access and he sucked where her pulse was racing. Unable to help himself, Mike ground his hips against hers and Taylor had an overwhelming need to wrap her legs around him to keep him secured against her.

Sounds of approaching voices broke them apart. Mike jerked his head up and looked around, seeing a group of people off in the distance. He quickly rolled off of her before looking back at her face. When he did, it took all of the self-control he had ever had to not take her right then and there. Her eyes were dark with desire, her cheeks flushed and her lips full and red from their kissing. When her tongue darted out to moisten them, he groaned and buried his face in the crook of her neck and shoulder, inhaling her sweet scent. He hugged her close one last time before rising and extending a hand to help her up.

It was odd, but for all that had happened, not a word had been spoken. It was as if they were of one mind. Walking slowly back to their bikes, Taylor smiled shyly at him as she got ready to climb back on. As before, he led the way back to town. The rest of the scenery was lost on her, anyway. All Taylor could think about was how she didn't want to drive back to the farm; hell, she didn't want to drive anywhere. She wanted to get back, return the bikes, and go back to the yacht where they could spend another night in each other's arms.

They hadn't discussed it, but the reality was that Taylor would not be comfortable spending the night with Mike back at Wade's farmhouse. She'd have to address that with him. Although, was there a difference between sleeping with him on the yacht and doing the same back at the farm? For some reason, it seemed like there was. Even without Jonathan there, the farm seemed like it was a personal residence.

She sighed. It sucked not being more in control of their surroundings and where they were staying. She'd love to find a little bed and breakfast or hotel and hole up there for a few days with him. The thought of taking any more advantage of Wade's hospitality didn't sit well with her—all she wanted was to find a place that was only for them.

When they returned to the bike rental shop, Mike took care of everything but then excused himself to make a call. Taylor made small talk with the sales clerk regarding their tour, and she told him about all the pictures she had taken. It was so nice to be able to sit and talk to the shop owner. Mike reappeared moments later and she followed him to the car and climbed in. Her body was still humming with anticipation and she could sense Mike's urgency to get back to the marina. She only hoped his urgency had to do with them and what they had shared in the park rather than getting back to the farm.

He parked the car a little haphazardly in the marina parking lot and quickly climbed out. Taylor joined him and Mike took one of her hands, kissed her palm, and led the way back to the boat. She thought she knew what was going to happen—they were going to pack and get their things and head back to the car.

"I'll just be a minute," she said and started toward her stateroom, but Mike didn't release her hand. She turned to him questioningly. "I need to pack up my stuff so we can get on the road."

He pulled her toward him and then into the main living area, shutting the door. "We're not getting on the road."

She arched a brow at him. "We're not? But you said—"

"I've made other arrangements." His voice was deep and a little gruff. "Do you want to leave?" Taylor shook her head. "Good."

Without another word, he led her back to their stateroom and finished what they had started in the park.

Repeatedly.

Chapter 8

TAYLOR NEVER ASKED HOW IT WAS THAT MIKE HAD GOTTEN them an extra night on the yacht, and to be honest, she didn't care. After they had closed the door to the stateroom the night before, it was as if they were alone in the world. They had made love fast and furiously, letting their pent-up passion carry them away. And much later, Mike had taken her up to the control room, where he steered the boat out of the marina and far enough out into the water so they could drop anchor.

And then he made love to her under the stars as he'd promised the day before.

As they drove in companionable silence back to the farm, Taylor could only marvel at the man. He worked hard at everything he did, and he seemed to know how to do everything. She could only hope that Jonathan Wade appreciated all Mike did for him—she had a feeling she was going to mention that to the man when they were "off the record."

"Do you want to stop for lunch, or wait until we get home?" he asked, his eyes never leaving the road.

The question struck her as a bit odd. Home? It could have been a slip of the tongue, but then it hit her how much she wished it were true. "I can wait until we get back to the farm," she said with a lazy smile. Truth be known, she was exhausted. They hadn't slept much the night before and she had a feeling that a nap was definitely in her future. At that thought, she yawned.

"We've only got another thirty miles to go," Mike said softly. "Why don't you rest your eyes and I'll wake you when we get there."

Her eyes were closed before he even finished speaking.

Mike's voice brought her to wakefulness. He was standing next to her on the passenger side of the car with the door open. Taylor gave a catlike stretch and yawned. Her eyes felt too heavy to open and it was tempting to turn her head and continue sleeping. Without warning, Mike gently lifted her into his arms and carried her into the house. Snuggling into his warmth, she curled her arms around his neck as he closed the front door and continued up the stairs to the bedroom she had been using.

Carefully, he placed her on the bed before closing the blinds and the curtains. Next, he came back to remove her shoes. Taylor made an attempt to sit up, but between the comfort of the bed and the dimness of the room, she decided to stay where she was. As her shoes hit the floor with a soft thud, Mike straightened to look at her, indecision written all over his face.

"Thank you for a wonderful weekend," she whispered, slowly propping herself up on her elbows.

"You're quite welcome." Mike stood completely still, unsure of what to do or say next. There were chores to be done; he had a job. Responsibilities. Yet being here like this with Taylor made him want to forget everything else. He hadn't thought that by now he would feel this strongly toward her—that he'd be a little more in control of his need for her. But as she looked up at him through sleepy eyes, all thoughts of what had to be done outside of this room vanished.

She sat up fully now. "I really enjoyed the bike tour."

Memories of their time together on the boat came rushing back to him and without conscious thought, he placed one knee on the bed before allowing himself to cover Taylor's body with his as he claimed her mouth. She went with him willingly, struggling to get as close to him as possible. "I know I should be letting you work," she said breathlessly as his hands began to roam her body, "but I can't."

"I'm not complaining," he replied before cutting off any further conversation.

Neither spoke beyond heated gasps and sighs of pleasure. Taylor greedily ran her hands over him. She leaned forward and rained tiny kisses along his chest and collarbone. Mike sucked in a breath as her tongue darted out to taste him.

Stretching out beside her, he kissed her ravenously along her neck and jawline, but Taylor grew impatient. She gave a slight shove against his shoulders and sent him rolling onto his back, right before she threw her leg over and straddled him. She pulled her sweater over her head and off, keeping her eyes fully focused on Mike's face the entire time.

He reached his hands up and skimmed over the lace of her bra, and Taylor's head fell back in sheer delight. He massaged, caressed, and with a growl of need, unclasped the front hook and freed her from the wispy garment. Leaning forward, she gave a wicked smile. "I think I'm a bad influence on you."

Mike couldn't help but give her the same smile. "Sweetheart, you couldn't be a bad influence on anybody. You're too good. Too sweet." His hands came back and cupped her breasts. "Too everything."

For the second time in twenty-four hours, he was done talking and set out to prove his words.

It was after dark when Taylor found herself alone in the kitchen. She had fallen asleep after she and Mike had made love and when she woke up alone, she assumed he'd had to get back to work.

Unsure of what to do with herself, she wandered around and tried to figure out what to make them for dinner. It felt weird to be planning on cooking a meal in someone else's house, and the more she opened cabinets, the guiltier she felt.

What had she done? She had promised herself she wouldn't sleep with Mike in Wade's house! She had planned on asking him to take her to his place, or a hotel, or...anywhere! But in her haze when they had returned, it had only taken one heated look from Mike to make her forget herself. To forget everything.

Her appetite was gone. What she did was completely wrong. It was unethical and Taylor knew she had to do something to make it right. While there was no way to undo what they'd done, she couldn't allow it to happen again. She wasn't sure if Mike would agree with her reasoning or if he'd be angry with her, but for the most part Taylor was a very honorable person. There was no way she was going to jeopardize her interview with Wade—or her job—over sex.

No matter how good it was.

Slamming a cabinet door closed, Taylor placed her hands on the granite countertop and bowed her head. She didn't want to end things with Mike, not now, possibly not ever—but while she was on this assignment, she had to get back into professional mode. It was imperative she not do anything else that would make her look untrustworthy to the man she was here to interview.

And that meant no more wild monkey sex with his assistant.

Again, no matter how good it was.

That's the way Mike found her, head bowed and bracing herself against the counter. He wondered what had her looking so tense. Tiptoeing up behind her, he carefully wrapped his arms around her waist and pulled her in close before kissing her gently on the neck. She nearly jumped three feet to get out of his grasp. "Taylor? What's the matter?"

She blushed and couldn't quite meet his eyes. "I didn't hear you come in."

"I got that," he said with a slight laugh, knowing immediately that something was wrong. "What's going on? Are you okay?"

Taylor walked around the center island to put some distance between them. How was she supposed to explain to him what was going through her mind? Unable to help herself, she looked at him. Her heart ached at the concerned expression on his face. Her shoulders sagged with defeat. "I can't do this."

Mike took a step forward, but stopped when Taylor took a step back. "Do what?"

She gestured between the two of them. "This. Us. Not here. Not in this house. I'm here on a job, Mike, and I can't believe what I've done." Tears welled in her eyes and her voice shook as she spoke, but Taylor did her best to keep herself together. "I came here to do an interview. I was supposed to talk with you, spend time with you"—she swallowed hard—"not sleep with you."

Panic grabbed Mike by the throat. "Taylor, I know you didn't come here for that," he said, trying to reassure her. "I'm not going to lie to you. When I...recommended you...for this job," he began carefully, "I had hoped there would still be something there between us, that I hadn't imagined it all those years ago. But I don't think what's happened between us has anything to do with your job."

"But it does!" she cried. "Don't you see? Jonathan Wade took your advice and chose me for this interview. I'm supposed to be getting ready to talk to him! And instead, I'm...I'm sleeping with the hired help!"

As soon as the words were out, she regretted them. Again. She remembered saying them not so long ago and one look at Mike showed that it enraged him as much now as it did then. Unfortunately, she couldn't take it back. He had to understand how dire the situation was.

"He could have given this assignment to any veteran reporter. God knows there are dozens of them who would have gladly taken him up on his offer and done a hell of a lot better with it than I'll probably do—"

"Taylor..."

She shook her head. "What if he had come home

early?" Hysteria was slowly starting to set in as that thought came out of nowhere. "What if he had found me in bed with—"

This time he succeeded in cutting her off. "With his farmhand?" he said sarcastically.

"That was not what I was going to say, dammit! Don't put words in my mouth." Taylor began to pace the kitchen. "It doesn't look very professional of me to be sleeping with someone in this man's house while he's away. To the average person, they'd take one look at this situation and think I'm sleeping with you to get more information on your boss!"

"Are you?" he asked with a deadly calm he didn't feel.

Taylor looked as if he'd slapped her. "Is that what you think?" she whispered. "Do you honestly think that's the kind of person I am?"

"To tell you the truth, Taylor, I'm beginning to think I don't know the first thing about the kind of person you are. I still can't believe we're having this conversation!"

Taking a deep breath, Taylor mentally counted to ten before responding. "I take my job very seriously, Mike. I have to. There is a lot of competition out there and it's hard enough to make a living at it, let alone make a name for myself. I would prefer not to have my name be followed by 'You know, the reporter who got caught in bed with Wade's assistant and blew the interview.' I've worked too hard for this. I have to be professional. I have to—"

"To hell with being professional!" he yelled, his control finally snapping. "You're afraid of what it'll look like if you're sleeping with one of his employees, isn't that it? I wasn't good enough for you ten years ago, and I think you still feel that way! It was all right to get a little down and dirty with me on the coast because no one was looking, but here at the farm, there's a chance someone will see. Someone will notice." He took a steadying breath. "I thought you were different, Taylor. Back then and now." He looked at her with disappointment. "I guess I was wrong."

Her silence spoke volumes.

Taylor stood rooted to the spot. Maybe that was it. She had been so lost in the intense emotions Mike brought out in her that she had temporarily forgotten her purpose in being here. Being thrown back into the reality of it all, she feared what it would look like to others for her to be found in bed with Mike.

Hanging her head in shame after seeing the hurt in his eyes, Taylor realized he was right—she was no better than all the friends who had simply tolerated Mike's presence but secretly thought him beneath them. Though it hadn't been her intention, that's exactly what her reaction had screamed.

Walking over to the refrigerator, Mike pulled it open and grabbed a bottle of water, showing no outward sign of emotion. He closed the door and turned to Taylor, his expression carefully blank. "I won't embarrass you by having you be found sharing a bed with me. And you don't have to worry about me telling Wade about this either."

His words were ice cold and cut Taylor like a sword.

"Help yourself to whatever you want in the kitchen. It's been stocked." He turned and walked toward the door. Because he was clearly a glutton for punishment, he looked back at her one more time. "For what it's worth…thanks."

Taylor was practically choking on the sobs that wanted to come out. "For what?" she whispered.

"For being willing to slum it for a weekend." And then he was gone.

Taylor stood stock-still for long minutes before her brain began to function again. Her appetite was long gone, so she very calmly left the kitchen, shutting off the light as she left, and walked as if in a daze back to her room. Once inside, she stripped, found a pair of pajamas, and then crawled under the blankets. She could still smell him from earlier.

How could she have been so…what was she? Was it so wrong to want to make a good impression on Jonathan Wade? Was it wrong to not want to be labeled a slut who was sleeping with an employee to get information? Even though Taylor knew that had nothing to do with why she'd slept with Mike, others might not view it the same way.

While it was true she had temporarily lost her focus, she could see now how much spending time with Mike had meant to her. But even so, it couldn't be—at the end of the day he lived in Maine and she lived in New York. Any kind of future relationship between them wouldn't be practical.

And if Taylor was one thing, it was practical.

She had been living a lonely, solitary life for so long that this weekend had given her a glimpse of what a shared life could be like. It made her long for what she had never known. Mike's lovemaking had brought her body back to life and she knew it would be a very long time, if ever, until she got over it. She couldn't imagine any other man touching her soul the way Mike had touched hers with just a look.

Wiping away a lone tear, Taylor finally let exhaustion claim her and she slept.

~~~

It was after nine on Friday morning when she woke up. Gasping when she saw the time, Taylor jumped from the bed and grabbed her robe. Today was the day: her first meeting with Jonathan Wade.

Mike had been painfully absent for the past few days. Taylor had been completely alone, and the only reason she was aware of Wade's return to the farm was because his attorney had called her the day before to let her know. She had eaten and slept alone and was miserable. She missed Mike with an intensity she couldn't believe. Perhaps having Wade here and getting to the heart of her assignment would help her get over the feeling of loss.

She doubted it, but tried to be hopeful.

With her clothes for the day laid out on the bed, Taylor was heading into the en suite to take a shower when her cell phone rang. It was Victoria. "Hey, Vic," she said, forcing enthusiasm into her voice. Taylor had a feeling she was in a bit of trouble for not calling the office more, but she didn't even have the energy to care.

"I thought we understood one another, Taylor," she said by way of greeting. "You were supposed to keep in touch with us."

"There wasn't anything to report," Taylor said with a hint of irritation.

"Be that as it may, we expected you to be a bit more professional." She waited to see if Taylor would say anything and when she didn't, Victoria went on. "Anyway, legal looked over the document you sent over and we emailed it back with our approval. Did you get it?"

Taylor had completely forgotten about it. "Actually… no."

Victoria sighed loudly. "This is why you should have checked in!" She quickly regained her composure. "I'm sure it's there in your inbox. We also copied his lawyer on the email, so be sure to sign it today before you go into your first meeting. Understand?"

"Yup."

"What's going on with you?" Victoria asked, and Taylor got the feeling that Victoria knew she was hiding something. "Did something happen up there that you're not telling me?"

There was no way she was going to share anything about what had happened with Mike with Victoria. Ever. "No. I'm just…it's been a lot of sitting around and waiting. I'm not used to this slow of a pace. I'm ready to get moving on this and get home."

"Ah," Victoria said, seemingly pleased. "Well, don't you worry. Once this piece goes to press and is out there, you will be in big demand. You won't have to worry about boredom ever again!"

Somehow Taylor doubted that, but she kept that observation to herself. "I hope so."

"Okay then. I want you to do a better job of keeping in touch from this point on, Taylor. Remember to sign the document, and I want daily updates from you."

"Not a problem." What else was she going to do in

her spare time? Somehow, she doubted Wade was going to entertain her from sunup to sundown. There was only so much writing she could do to pass the time. There was a very real possibility that talking to Victoria was the only thing that would keep her sane.

Taylor glanced at the bedside clock and saw it was getting late. "Listen, Vic, I was about to get in the shower when you called. I'm supposed to meet him for lunch and then start the interview."

"You sound so calm, Taylor. I'm very proud of you. I know you're going to do a great job on this piece."

"Thanks, Vic." Hanging up, Taylor felt a sense of calmness come over her. She took her shower and got dressed, doing her hair and makeup all without worrying about meeting a man considered to be a living legend.

The plan was to join Wade for lunch downstairs at noon, but by eleven thirty, Taylor had nothing left to do with herself in her room. Gathering everything she was going to need for their first interview session, she left the security of her room and went downstairs. She put her satchel down in the kitchen next to the table. For all she knew they were going to use part of their lunch conversation for the article.

The table was set, but there was no one in sight. She wondered if Mike had done this or if someone else had been brought in to handle it. The house had been silent for days, and if Wade was in residence, she never heard him. True, the house was large enough that she might not hear another person walking around, but she couldn't imagine anyone being that quiet.

As if on cue, the front door opened. Taylor's heart skipped a beat. Was it Mike? Was it Wade? Straightening her slacks and sweater, she ran a hand over the sleek ponytail she was sporting and took a deep breath. "This is it," she whispered as she walked toward the entryway.

A well-dressed man stopped when he saw her. "Ms. Scott?" he asked as he straightened the wire-rimmed glasses on his nose.

Taylor smiled brightly as she approached and held out her hand. "It's a pleasure to finally meet you, Mr. Wade."

The man gave a chuckle. "I guess I should have introduced myself first," he said. "I'm Tom Levinson, Mr. Wade's attorney. We've talked on the phone."

Taylor deflated. "Of course. It's nice to meet you. I didn't expect to see you here today."

Without waiting for an invitation, he walked into the kitchen and placed his briefcase on the countertop. "Your office approved the last of the paperwork that requires your signature. I wanted to get that taken care of." In a no-nonsense manner, he pulled a file out of his briefcase along with a pen and laid them out for Taylor. "If you'll sign here…here…here…and here," he said as he indicated all of the required places, "I'll get this filed with the rest of the contract and then I'll take you down to meet Mr. Wade."

Taylor's eyes went wide. "He's here?"

Tom chuckled again. "Of course he's here. He knows the two of you have an appointment at noon for lunch. He's very much looking forward to getting the process started."

That greatly relieved her. Quickly, she signed the document and handed the pen back to him. "That should be everything, right?" Oh gosh…could she sound any more anxious?

He smiled at her before placing the document and pen back in his case. "If you'll follow me." Not waiting to see if she was following, Tom walked out of the kitchen and through one of the living areas toward a door in the far corner of the house. Taylor remembered that it led to the downstairs, to Wade's office. She had hoped to save that for later and have him greet her over lunch. With a mental shrug, she continued to follow Tom down the stairs.

Walking through the gym area behind him, she began to feel a bit nervous. This all suddenly felt too formal, too…orchestrated and calculated. Why did this have to be so dang complicated? Was Tom going to stay with her through the introductions? Through lunch?

The door to the office was ajar and Tom gave a light knock before entering. Taylor needed a minute. This was it. Once she walked through that door her life was never going to be the same. She had been given the assignment of a lifetime on a silver platter; all she had to do was take those last five steps.

Tom turned and looked at her expectantly. Snapping out of her haze, she walked toward him until she was in the office standing beside him. Looking around the office, Taylor didn't see anyone other than the two of them. She stared at Tom in confusion and was about to ask what was going on when she heard someone coming down the stairs behind them. Her breath caught in her throat when Mike walked through the door. He wasn't dressed in his customary jeans and flannel. Today he had on khakis and a thick cable-knit sweater. Taylor looked from him to Tom and back again.

"Taylor," Tom said, "allow me to introduce you to Jonathan Wade."

Chapter 9

EVERYTHING IN TAYLOR WENT NUMB AND HER KNEES almost gave out. Mike's eyes never left her face, as if he was daring her to say something. So she did.

"You son of a bitch," she snapped, tossing a glance at Tom Levinson before storming from the room. "Excuse me." She ran up the stairs and made her way to the kitchen to grab her satchel and was about to exit the room when she heard both men coming up behind her. Turning, she gave them an icy stare. "Is this some sort of joke?"

Tom stepped forward first. "Ms. Scott, there is no joke here. Mike Greene *is* actually Jonathan Wade. It's his pen name. Surely you're aware that authors use those."

She gave him a disgusted look. "Of course I'm aware of that. But if that was the case, then why go through all the nonsense? Why not say who he is, let me come in here and get the interview, and go? Why did I have to be here for two weeks? Why did you have me believe I was going to be meeting *two* different people?" She wouldn't even look at Mike at this point. She couldn't. Betrayal made her feel sick.

Tom looked nervously from Taylor to Mike, unsure of how to answer her question. "Maybe I didn't know if you could be trusted," Mike said, his voice cold and unlike anything Taylor had heard from him all week.

"Oh, that's rich coming from you," she snapped. "*I'm* the one who can't be trusted? I'm not the one who lied!"

"I don't see it that way," he said with a shrug.

"Really? You don't see how you utterly misrepresented everything that's happened since I arrived here?"

Tom stepped between them. "Why don't we all sit down and have some lunch and discuss this calmly? I think you've both come a long way into this process, and it would benefit everyone to see it through to the end."

She wanted to argue, or at least tell the lawyer to mind his own damn business. She wanted to yell and scream—not just at Mike, but at herself. How could she have been so blind? So naive? She was a journalist, for crying out loud! What did that say for her as a reporter? How could she move forward without second-guessing herself time and time again?

As much as Taylor wanted to flee, her curiosity got the better of her. She'd invested too much time and had to see this through. And as much as she'd resented Tom a moment ago, Taylor realized she was secretly glad for his presence. No doubt if it had been solely her and Mike, she'd be hurling insults and accusations, professionalism thrown out the window. The three of them sat down at the large kitchen table that was now laden with food, and it didn't take a genius to know that Mike had done all of it—as he had since her arrival.

Silence stretched uncomfortably and her head began to spin as she tried to come to grips with what was going on. Glancing at Mike, she noted that his expression held a touch of contempt and she wanted to smack that look right off his face. How dare he play the injured party! For a full week, he'd led her to believe he was someone he wasn't, and in the process, made her look like a fool. And worse, now she was forced to stay here and carry out this farce of an interview. If she didn't, she'd be the laughingstock of the journalism world and probably be out of a job, too!

Deciding to be the more mature party at the table, she took her napkin and placed it in her lap. She looked at Mike, her gaze narrowing. "Are we officially going on the record as of now? Do I need to get my recorder?"

"Why don't we try to get through lunch before the interview starts," Tom answered for him.

It miffed her a bit, but she shrugged and helped herself to a fresh-baked roll and some salad. The two men waited for her to serve herself before doing the same, and she feared that lunch might go on in this state of hostile silence, when someone's phone rang. "I'm afraid that's mine," Tom said as he stood. Taking his phone from his briefcase, he strode from the room.

"Was lunch necessary? Couldn't we start the damn interview?"

Without missing a beat, Mike shrugged and took a forkful of pasta salad. "Everyone needs to eat, Taylor. I figured we might as well start with this so we could have the entire afternoon to work."

"Oh, so we're going to work? You're going to do an interview?"

He looked at her as if he didn't understand the question. "Of course I'm going to do the interview. Why would you think I wouldn't?"

Now it was her turn to look at him as if she didn't understand. "Seriously? You lied to me about who you are. That contract is kind of a joke now. For all I know, this was all some sort of game for you to get me up here and then take the interview away."

"I wouldn't do that, Taylor," he said, his voice deadly serious. "I'm a man of my word."

She rolled her eyes and was about to respond when Tom walked back into the room. "I'm so sorry, but I have a difficult client I need to deal with." He quickly gathered his briefcase and belongings and looked at Taylor apologetically. "Thank you for signing the paperwork, and if you or your office have any questions, please feel free to call me." He left and the front door closed with a final *thud*, leaving Taylor and Mike sitting alone in the kitchen.

Calculated.

Orchestrated.

Those two words played over and over in her head as she focused on her lunch and refused to say another word to Mike. If he thought she was going to be impressed with his secret identity, then he was wrong. If anything, it made her like him even less. When she'd had no idea who Jonathan Wade was, it was safe to consider him to be a man without faults, someone she could almost put on a pedestal. The reality was that Jonathan Wade was someone who'd lied to her, slept with her, and now was going to force her to stay in his presence when he knew she wanted nothing more than to leave.

She wanted to forget about the article.

They ate in silence and when they were done, worked together to clean up. Taylor cursed her stupidity—she wanted to make him do it himself but wasn't that petty. Once everything was put away, Mike faced her. "Would you rather work in the office, or maybe in the living room?"

She didn't want to be comfortable—and she certainly

didn't want him to be comfortable either. "The office," she said simply and walked over to get her recorder and laptop before leaving the room.

Once they were downstairs, Mike took the seat behind his desk and watched as Taylor got herself situated in a chair facing him.

"Do you mind if I record this?" she asked, her tone cool, professional.

"Not at all," he replied as he sat back in his seat.

Clearing her throat and opening her notepad, she tapped a pencil against it several times before speaking. "For the record, would you mind telling me your name?" She was grateful this wasn't a video interview. "Your real name," she prompted.

Meeting her stare, Mike reached across the desk and clicked the off button on her recorder. "Let's clear the air before we begin, shall we?" he said, his voice strained.

"Please do." Her voice dripped with sarcasm. "Since we both know exactly who *I* am and why *I'm* here, why don't you go ahead?" She continued to tap her pencil lightly on her pad as she watched him, daring him to give her an argument.

Taylor noted the look of irritation on Mike's face but wasn't prepared for his quick action of stepping around the desk and taking the pencil out of her hand before snapping it in half, throwing the pieces across the room. The gloves were off; it was just a matter of who was going to throw the first punch.

Her first instinct was to yell and scream and tell him how rude she found him and how offensive his behavior had been. Instead, she reached down into her case and retrieved another pencil.

"If you tap that thing, Taylor, so help me…" he said, exasperated.

Hoping her heart—which was threatening to beat itself out of her chest—didn't show, she feigned indifference and shrugged at him with a bored expression.

"I didn't mean for things to go the way they did," he said, taking a deep breath to get his temper under control. "I had planned on telling you when you arrived, but then you recognized me almost immediately and… hell, all that went out the window. I wanted time with you as me, Mike, not as Jonathan Wade."

Taylor stared at him as he made his way back around the desk to sit down, not trusting her own voice to respond in any way.

"So many times over the years I thought about sitting and talking with you, getting reacquainted with you, but I never did. At first it was because of Eddie, but then afterward, when he married and moved away, I wanted to get my life together before I looked you up." He ran a hand over his face and watched her for any sign of a response.

He received none.

"Anyway, as the week went on, I found I didn't want to be Jonathan Wade with you. I didn't want to share you with anyone. Even if the 'anyone' in question was my alter ego. It had been such a long time since I'd been out and relaxed with anyone like I was with you and I was enjoying myself too much to give it up."

Still she said nothing.

"Then Tom reminded me I was playing a dangerous game. If the author part of me didn't reveal himself and make an appearance, your magazine would have a field day with me for breach of contract."

Now she'd had enough. "So, you're telling me the only reason you decided to be honest here is because of the threat of a lawsuit?" Her voice was much louder than she'd intended. "Do I have that right?"

He nodded his head solemnly. "I'm so sorry, Taylor," he said in a pleading tone. "I can't believe how out of hand I let this get."

Rising from her seat, Taylor began to pace his office, unsure of what she was supposed to be doing at this point. How could she possibly spend another week here and interview this man, knowing exactly who he was and what he'd done? Then again, how could she be the one to back out of such an important assignment? Wasn't sometimes doing something you found distasteful part of being a professional?

She glared at Mike. How many times had she interviewed people she had no respect for just because it was newsworthy? Too many to count—but she hadn't slept with any of them! It was a no-win situation and Taylor knew it. She was trapped. She had no choice but to figure out how to write this piece and live with this man for the next five days.

Thinking it through a little further, Taylor realized she'd have to pretend the last week had never happened and she was meeting Jonathan Wade—oh, how she was beginning to hate that name!—for the first time today. It wouldn't be easy, but there was no other option for her.

Sitting back down and gathering her pad and pencil, she forced herself to look at him. "Fine," she said coolly. "You've said your piece. I'd like us to start this process as if we'd never met before." She saw the same hurt expression she'd seen in his eyes several days ago before he left her room. "It's easier that way." She saw his curt nod. "May I begin taping?" He nodded again.

Taylor began her interview as she had planned it. She couldn't quite bring herself to meet his eyes but kept her professionalism in check, and for the next several hours, they spoke about his childhood up to when he went to work in the mailroom for a publishing house.

It was impressive the way he openly discussed his past, legal troubles and all. In her experience, most people chose to omit them, but she figured Mike had no choice but to discuss something she already knew. Whatever the reason, she was glad he was being honest.

When she decided they'd done enough for one day, she reached to turn off the recorder. "We'll start up again tomorrow, if you don't mind," she said as she placed her belongings back into her case. "Would after lunch work for you?" There was no way she was going to try to sit through another meal with him, but she kept her tone neutral.

"That would be fine," he said, his voice void of emotion.

"I'll see you tomorrow afternoon, then." With her belongings in hand, she walked to the office door and stopped for a moment, wanting to ask him something, but then thought better of it and left. She climbed the two flights of stairs up to her room with as much dignity as she could find. Chin up, spine straight, she walked. Once inside her room, however, she crumbled.

She turned on the shower, shedding her clothes and stepping in. The hot water scalded her skin, but the sound of it beating against the glass walls muffled her sobs. *Betrayed again*. Her mother had been right. Once you give your heart to someone—and she realized right then and there that she had given hers to Mike this last week, if not before — it was easily hurt.

Dragging in deep breaths, she sat on the tiled floor. Work would keep her busy and she would truly only have to spend a couple of hours a day with him before she could retreat to her room, but there was only so much time she could spend working. Hopefully, the piece could be completed and emailed to Victoria before she even left the farm.

Taylor's pessimism taunted her to remember the last time that something had actually gone as she'd planned. Never, it seemed. With any luck, she might get out of this situation and actually survive it.

Right now, it didn't feel like it.

Emerging from the shower some time later, her skin was red and her entire body hurt from the emotional cry she'd given in to. Rummaging through her clothes, she found a clean pair of jeans and a sweatshirt to throw on. It surprised Taylor to find that she was hungry.

After drying her hair, she decided to go into town for something to eat. Sure, it would damage her dwindling savings account, but it would be worth it not to chance sitting through an awkward meal with Mike.

After grabbing her purse, she headed down the stairs and out the door to her rental car. As she crossed the yard, she spotted Mike over by the barn and hoped he didn't hear her leaving. No such luck. As Taylor unlocked the car door, Mike started to jog toward her. Gone was the professional-looking man from the interview — the farm-hand was the man who came over.

"Where are you going?" he asked, concern creasing his brow.

"To town to grab something to eat," she said casually as she climbed into the SUV, avoiding his gaze.

"Taylor, you don't have to do that. I told you, the kitchen is fully—".

She held up a hand to stop him and then started the car. "I think I've taken advantage of Jonathan Wade's hospitality enough, thank you." She couldn't help how she responded to him.

Mike took a step back and conceded defeat. He knew he had her anger coming and he deserved it. With nothing left he could do or say, he could only watch as she pulled away and drove through the trees and down the long driveway. Away from him.

There wasn't a whole lot more to see or do in town that Taylor hadn't already done, but it was still somewhat relaxing to wander around and window-shop. Stopping at a small café, she had a simple dinner that consisted of little more than a cup of soup and a salad. Sitting by the window, she watched people walk by and it reminded her of their weekend in Kennebunkport. Feeling disheartened, she forced down the last spoonful of soup, paid her tab, and left.

As Taylor exited the café, she spotted a small bookstore several doors down that they hadn't stopped in before. It was nice to be inside the cozy yet cluttered space. There were floor-to-ceiling bookshelves, as well as many tables and tall racks of books from every genre. Most of the tables in the center dealt with local topics and she stopped to look through a few of them. A store like this was a treat to her and oddly refreshing.

Walking up and down the aisles, she spotted the section that was dedicated to Jonathan Wade. Without conscious thought, she picked up the latest one. It was the only title she hadn't been able to get a copy of before leaving New York, and before she knew it, she had it tucked under her arm and was walking toward the front of the store. Along the way she picked up a couple of books on the area to help add a little more local flavor to her article. More receipts to add to her growing reimbursement pile.

Stepping outside with her purchases, she noticed the setting sun and the cooling temperature, and realized there was nothing else she wanted to do. With a sigh, she headed back to her car and resigned herself to going back to the farm, hoping to avoid seeing Mike.

The drive back was short and did nothing to ease her mind. Mentally, she began writing her story. It would be hard for her to write without being able to partake of her usual writing routine. She had become an unfortunate creature of habit and realized that maybe she was too rigid in the way she was living.

Stopping the car in the middle of the road less than a mile from the farm, Taylor had a thought. Did she have to do without her routine? If she had to, sure, but maybe she could improvise. Turning the car around, she made the quick drive back into town and picked up a bottle of wine. With a sense of purpose and a little less dread than she'd had thirty minutes ago, she began her journey back to the farm.

Back at the house, Taylor grabbed her books and her wine and went inside. Running up to her room, she changed into comfortable clothes, grabbed her iPod, and went down to the basement where Mike had a few stationary bikes. She could easily get a ride in and then come upstairs, have her glass of wine, and maybe find another picture to meditate on before sitting down with her laptop to write.

Her steps were light and bouncy as she went down the stairs. She noticed the door to Jonathan—no, Mike's office was closed and Taylor hoped she wouldn't be distracting him if he was working. Picking a bike, she set the timer for thirty minutes, placed her earbuds in her ears, and began listening to the day's interview while she rode.

When the timer went off, she felt energized and invigorated. The story was already beginning to form in her mind and, although she didn't get through much of the interview in the short amount of time, it was enough for her to figure out where she wanted to begin. Taking her towel off the handlebar, she wiped the sweat from her brow and turned to see Mike standing in his office doorway.

"Sorry if I disturbed you," she said as she dismounted. "You said I could use the gym." Her tone was defensive.

"You didn't disturb me," he said, his voice hoarse. He was watching her intensely, struck nearly speechless by the way her body shone with sweat and how her tank top clung to her breasts. He swallowed hard.

Seeing the direction of his gaze, Taylor picked up the sweatshirt she had discarded five minutes into her ride. "Excuse me," she said as she gathered the rest of her things. "I have work to do."

"Taylor, wait." Walking across the room, he came to stand in front of her. "Are you going to keep ignoring me for the remainder of your time here?"

Honestly? She didn't know. It was the easiest way to keep her heart intact, but she knew it wasn't very professional of her. She wasn't sure which one was more important. Her eyes searched his face, wanting desperately to reach out and touch it, kiss it, but she didn't have the nerve. There was no way she could possibly open herself up to him again and risk him betraying her again. She could tell Mike was straining his own self-control not to touch her either.

Forcing herself to look away, Taylor whispered, "I have work to do."

He didn't stop her this time.

Taylor stopped in the kitchen on her way up to her room to grab a wineglass and a bottle of water. Once in her room she decided to change her routine and shower again. If nothing else, she would leave this trip being, perhaps, the cleanest person on the planet! Although this time, it wasn't because she needed to cry or escape her feelings for Mike, but simply to wash the workout off of her.

Wrapped in her robe, she pulled out her laptop, set herself up at the desk Mike had supplied for her room, and poured her glass of wine. Once she got comfortable, the words seemed to write themselves. She was like a woman possessed. Jonathan Wade came to life on the pages, at least the first twenty-two years of his life did.

When she reached the end of the tape and finished interspersing tidbits of quotes and phrases from his library of work, Taylor stood and stretched. Drinking the last of her wine—well, the last of what she'd allowed herself to drink—she looked over at the bedside clock. It was after two in the morning! Padding across the room, she pulled on a pair of silk pajama pants and a tank top to sleep in.

As she pulled the comforter back and got ready to crawl between the sheets, she paused. Though she had just finished the wine, she had finished the bottle of water hours ago and was still thirsty. Taylor tiptoed down to the kitchen to get a glass of something cold to drink, pouring herself a glass of juice before quietly heading back toward the stairs.

"Done working?" came the familiar male voice out of the darkness.

Looking around, Taylor spotted Mike sitting in the darkness of the living room. The moonlight reflected off of the tumbler he held in his hand. She stood frozen at the bottom of the stairs. When she didn't answer, he rose and lazily walked toward her.

"So? Are you finishing work or were you having trouble sleeping?" His voice was silky and seductive and Taylor wanted nothing more than to lean into him and feel his breath on her face, her throat, anywhere and everywhere on her body. Shaking her head to clear it, she cleared her throat.

"I just finished typing from today's interview and needed something to drink before I went to sleep."

He nodded. "I see." His hand slowly came up to caress her face. Taylor gave in to the need to lean into it and inhaled deeply. She craved contact with this man like she did air. They stood like that for what seemed like an eternity. Taylor felt too tired to stand and had to move away, placing a hand on the railing.

"I...I, um, I need to go to sleep, Mike. I'll see you after lunch." She turned and walked up the stairs; he watched her go.

Crawling into the bed, she took one sip of her juice before placing it on the nightstand and turning out the light. Extreme fatigue—mental and physical—claimed her almost instantly.

Chapter 10

THE FOLLOWING AFTERNOON, TAYLOR MET MIKE IN HIS office for their next session. She found him sitting behind his desk, deep in thought.

"Would you mind if we sat someplace else today?" he asked, appearing distracted.

"Sure. Is there a problem?"

"It's just that I'm in work mode down here, and I think I would be able to focus on our interview more if we weren't in here." He ran a tired hand over his face. Being a writer herself, Taylor knew the mode he was in, and as anxious as she was to get this interview over with, she respected him as a writer.

"Why don't we put off the session until you're ready?" she suggested and watched as he sagged with relief.

"I have no idea how long I'll be, Taylor. I could be ready in fifteen minutes or four hours. Are you willing to hang around the house and wait?"

She shrugged. "Sure. I can bike or read or something. It's not a big deal." He gave her a look of gratitude as she excused herself and closed the door behind her.

He must have been on a roll because Taylor did not see or hear from him for several hours. As with the day before, he found her on the bike, earbuds in as she listened to an audiobook. She was cycling with her eyes closed and she screamed when Mike's hand touched her shoulder.

"Oh!" she cried as she pulled one bud from her ear. "You scared the life out of me!"

"I'm sorry," he said with a grin. "You were so lost in thought you didn't hear me call your name."

"You could have called more than once," she said with a hint of irritation.

"I called you five times," he said as he continued to grin at her. "Louder each time."

"Oh. Sorry," she said as she climbed off the bike. She hadn't shut off her iPod, and then it hit her that she had made the discovery days ago but never mentioned it to him. "It's you on these audiobooks, isn't it?"

"Yes."

Taylor's heart raced at the confirmation. No wonder she had found such comfort in listening to them. Secretly, she liked knowing that even when she left this place, this haven she was coming to love, she'd still have a piece of Mike with her. Not wanting to give her thoughts away, she gave a curt nod. "I had been wondering who did the readings. Most authors hire voice actors to do them." She reached for her towel and moved to put some distance between them, looking around for a clock. "What time is it?"

"It's a little after four. Are you still up for doing our session?"

"Absolutely. Would you mind if I freshened up first?"

"Take your time. I'll meet you in the kitchen in an hour."

Taylor nodded in agreement and grabbed her things before leaving the basement.

⁓

An hour later she found Mike in the kitchen grilling steaks on his indoor grill. "I hope you don't mind," he said when he saw her standing in the doorway. "I thought we'd eat an early dinner tonight." Taylor knew it sounded innocent, but she had a sneaking suspicion it was also his way of keeping her in the house.

"That's fine," she said as she sat at the table and put her bag of interview supplies down on the chair beside her.

"We could even start the session while we eat," he suggested over his shoulder as he continued to prepare their meal. "Would you like some wine?" He motioned to an open bottle on the center island.

"What are we having?" she asked as she got up to pour a glass of wine.

"I'm grilling some steaks and I've made a Caesar salad. I've got some potatoes baking in the oven." Taylor was impressed. The man could write, he ran a successful farm, and he could cook. He was the complete package that most women dreamed of.

Including her.

Dammit.

Frowning at her thoughts, she turned back to the table to set her things up.

Mike turned to look at her and saw the expression on her face. "Everything okay?" he asked, concerned.

She shook her head to clear it. "Everything's fine," she lied. "Just collecting my thoughts on where I want our interview to go tonight." Trying to look professional, she took out the tape recorder, pad, and pencil and put them next to her place setting, then sat and took out her notes, sipping her wine as she read.

Soon, dinner was placed before them and once Mike

took his seat across from her, he looked at her expectantly. "Well?"

"Well what?"

"Are we going to start the interview over dinner or are we waiting until we're done?"

"Now, if you're sure you don't mind," she said. Mike nodded and cut into his steak. Taylor took a few bites of her own before launching into her questions.

Conversation flowed and Taylor learned that Mike had led a fairly fascinating life—they were now up to the years after she had stopped seeing him, so a lot of it was new information.

"So, how did it all begin? How did you come to be a writer? Was it something you set out to do?"

He shook his head. "Far from it. I was working in the mailroom, and one afternoon during my rounds, I heard one of the executives yelling from his office. So, I go in with his mail and see that he's not yelling at anyone in particular. He was alone in the room and simply having a temper tantrum." Taylor laughed.

"Anyway, he takes one look at me and tosses a bundled manuscript at me and says, 'I'll give you a hundred bucks if you read this piece of crap and give me an honest opinion on it.' So, I figure, sure, what do I have to lose? I took it home that night and read through the entire thing, which was amazing in itself because at that point, I hated to read. But I did it and brought it back to him the next day. 'What'd you think?' the old guy asks, and I told him. It sucked." Taylor looked at him, wide-eyed with shock, and he chuckled at her expression.

"It couldn't have been that bad," she said.

"It was horrible. No redeeming qualities at all. We

talked for a while and he asked what I would change or what would make it readable and appealing to the general public."

"Why was he working so hard with it? Why not put it in the slush heap and be done with it?"

Mike laughed. "You'd think, right? But apparently it was one of their top authors and they had a contract with him and no matter what, he owed them a book. They had to do something with it to make it publishable and make the readers like it."

"Seems like an awful lot of trouble."

He nodded in agreement. "He took me to lunch and we brainstormed. Why he chose me, I'll never know. Or why I suddenly had the ability to visualize and come up with the ideas I did. But basically, he loved my ideas. He asked what I liked to read and I told him that I didn't. He thought that was hysterical, because I had a great imagination."

Stopping, he rose and poured them each another glass of wine before continuing. "Anyway, lunch ran into dinner and I was fearing for my job. He pulled some strings and quickly got me out of the mailroom and hooked me up with some of his staff. He promised me payment if I could flesh out one of my ideas into a rough draft in a week!"

Taylor choked on her wine. "Are you kidding me?"

"Serious," he said as he placed his glass back on the table. "So I stopped at the local thrift store and bought a typewriter and went home. I was too poor to buy a computer and figured I had to start somewhere. In four days, I had a rough draft done. I couldn't believe I was able to do it, but once I started, it was like I couldn't stop. The old guy went crazy for it!" Mike laughed at the memory. "Who knew someone like me could actually have any talent?" His expression sobered. "This man was willing to take a chance on me and get my story published. We decided to do it as a series, so there was a commitment he was making to me. No one had ever put that kind of faith in me, Taylor. My own parents had washed their hands of me after I was put in that juvie center for breaking and entering."

"Did this man know of your past?" she asked.

He nodded. "I laid it all out for him that first day over lunch. I mean, if he was willing to work with me, he deserved my honesty."

"Very commendable of you," she said evenly, even though in the back of her mind she was screaming with frustration as to why he couldn't have been that straight-forward with her. If he had, they'd still be doing the interview right now, but they'd also get the pleasure of sleeping together tonight. Sighing at her thoughts, she brought her attention back to Mike. "So how long does it take for you to get a story down on paper?"

For the next hour, he went through his writing process with her. They moved the conversation to the living room, where they sat on opposing couches. Taylor had kicked off her shoes, reclining, and Mike had done the same.

"I know for me," she said as they got comfortable, "I have the picture of the Montauk Point lighthouse on my desk that gives me peace to look at. It puts me in the right frame of mind to write. Do you have anything like that?"

He considered her for a long moment. Taylor started to squirm under his watchful eyes. When he finally answered, it wasn't with words. He stood and walked over to her and held out his hand. Taylor hesitantly took it and felt a charge of energy surge through her. Did he feel it too? He led her in silence down to his office and motioned for her to sit in his chair.

"Now," he said softly, "look around and see what I see."

Taylor positioned herself comfortably in his chair and looked at her surroundings. There was his computer, but no screen saver was showing. There were odds and ends on his desk, but nothing that grabbed her attention. Swiveling the chair around, she faced the bookshelves but couldn't read any of the titles from where she sat. She looked at him with raised eyebrows. "Keep looking," he prompted.

Feeling slightly annoyed that he wasn't helping her, she continued to peruse the room. Off in the corner, she saw it. There was a small table and the only thing on it was a framed photograph. She looked to Mike for confirmation, but his expression was closed. Rising from the chair, she walked over and lifted it off of the table, gasping with surprise.

It was taken the summer they had spent together: Taylor sitting between Eddie and Mike on a log by a fire at the beach. She ran a finger over it as tears welled in her eyes. Her first thought was of Eddie and how his life was over; the next was of how Mike had kept this picture for all these years.

Taking her eyes from the picture, she looked at him as the first tear fell. "Why?" It was barely audible.

"It was the only picture I ever had of you, and I took it from Ed," he said quietly. "When I look at it, it reminds me that there was a time when someone was nice to me." His words were raw with emotion. He didn't move from where he stood. "I remember the girl who, for one short span of time, saw something good in me."

Taylor placed the photo back on the table but continued to look down at it. She willed the tears to stop falling, but to no avail. He was behind her in a heartbeat.

"You are what inspires me to keep writing, Taylor." His words were the caress on her face she had craved last night. He turned her to face him as his hand came up and cupped her chin, forcing her to look at him. "You have no idea the impact you've made on my life. You make me want to be a better person."

Taylor was afraid to open her heart to his words. "I don't know what to say," she admitted in a soft voice.

Mike tucked a stray strand of hair behind her ear. "I don't want you to say anything unless you want to," he assured her. "Come on. Let's go back upstairs. Do you have more questions for tonight?" They walked up to the living room as he waited for her reply.

Taylor glanced at her watch and saw it was near midnight. "I think I'm done for now," she said, yawning. She began to collect her things and wiped away a few lingering tears. "Would you mind if I took some pictures of you tomorrow for the piece?"

She turned and saw the hesitation in his eyes. "I wasn't sure if you wanted to be seen as well as known from this story," she said. "You don't have to do it if you don't want to."

Mike seemed to be mulling over the idea, but before he could answer, Taylor had one last question. "Why did you want me to write this article?" Her words were barely above a whisper but were filled with such desperation, she ached for an answer.

"I wanted to let you—as well as anyone who reads this—know me. I felt like I'd be introducing the real me to you first. I trust you implicitly, Taylor, to portray me as you see me."

The man was killing her. How could she keep her heart closed to him when he was baring his soul to her with every word that escaped his lips? "I hope I don't disappoint you," she said quietly as she began to walk toward him.

"You never could."

When they were close enough to share a breath, Taylor reached for him and touched the strong line of his jaw with the gentlest of touches. His eyes closed as he let out a ragged sigh.

"How do you see me, Taylor?" he asked as she continued to study his face with her hands.

"I see you as you are right now. A man who has captured my heart and my soul. A man who I want desperately to touch me." The words came out as a near sob, but before any tears could fall, Mike scooped her up into his arms and took her to his bedroom.

Taylor had not seen this room before—the door had been closed and Mike had assured her it was merely a storage room. But as he opened the door and Taylor looked around, all she could see was the enormous bed and the stone fireplace that took up one whole wall. It was strong and masculine—just like the man who was carrying her.

Mike kicked the door shut carefully before stepping further into the room. "I don't want to rush you," he said quietly as he came to a stop. "I want you, I've always wanted you, but I need to know you want this. That you want me."

Taylor looked up at him. Rather than answering him with words, she wound her arms around him, raking a hand into his hair and guiding his lips down to meet hers. The kiss was a gentle reacquaintance at first, but then heat and need took over. She was hungry for him, and although she knew they should go slowly, her body screamed otherwise.

After gently laying her down on the bed, his hands roamed everywhere they could reach. Mike's need for Taylor seemed just as frantic as hers was for him. "You are so beautiful," he groaned as he began to kiss her again. He trailed kisses down her neck and back again as his hands reached up to cup her breasts.

The last several days had been sheer torture, having Taylor in the house, so close, yet not being able to touch her. But she was here now—here in his bed—and Mike vowed he would prove to her he was worthy of her. He didn't care how long it took, in the bedroom or out, but he was determined to win Taylor back.

She cried out his name as he nipped at the pulse in her neck, and he smiled against her throat. "I like it when you say my name like that," he growled.

A slow smile crept across Taylor's face as well. "Hmm..." she purred. "I bet you can't make me do it again."

Pushing up on his arms, Mike looked down into her beautiful face, his expression heated. "Sweetheart, I guarantee you I'll not only make you say it, I'll make you scream it."

Taylor hooked one leg around Mike's waist and pulled him down on top of her. "You're on."

Within minutes, he proved his point.

—∿∿—

Taylor opened her eyes to the brightness of the sun shining through Mike's bedroom windows. Her back was pressed against his chest and his arm was curved possessively over her hips. She was exhausted. Neither of them had slept for more than an hour at a time before one would wake the other with gentle caresses or bold invitations. Taylor smiled at the mere thought of it.

Never in her life could she have imagined the feelings such intimacy could bring to life. Thinking over her time here with Mike, she realized what he was willing to sacrifice to be with her. He had obviously led a reclusive existence for a reason and yet here he was, willing to give it all up for her.

She snuggled closer to him and felt a sudden surge of protectiveness toward him. There was no guarantee what the future held once his identity was known to all. Would he, in time, come to regret his decision? Would he hold it against her? The thought made her frown.

The feeling of his warm hand cupping her breast, however, eased her mind for the moment. "Good morning," he murmured against her ear.

The sensation sent chills up her spine and she shifted her rear to cradle his growing erection. "Mmm," she moaned as she wiggled against him. "Good morning to you, too."

Mike kissed her temple, her throat, and her shoulder before taking a light bite there. "Dammit, woman," he snarled playfully, "you're killing me." Taylor giggled as Mike traced a light path down her body with his fingertips. "It's like I can't stop touching you."

Another moan escaped as his hands continued to tease and explore her. "Don't we need to get up?" she managed to ask, even though it was the last thing she wanted to do.

Mike rolled her beneath him and silenced any further questions.

—◇◇◇—

The rest of the day was a blur. Day turned into night and even then, Taylor couldn't be sure of what time it was at any given point; talking and making love consumed her attention. Even though she was still gathering information for her article, she took her time now.

The next day, Taylor did manage to get all of her recordings transferred onto her laptop and had a rough draft of the article completed. Then she headed outside to get some pictures of Mike working at various places around the farm. She could tell he wasn't comfortable with any of it, but he never uttered a word of complaint.

Lying in front of the fire after dinner, she asked him about it. "I know you let me take those pictures today, but if you'd prefer I not use them, then I won't." They were reclining on plush, oversized pillows, cradled in one another's arms as they watched the flames.

He sighed and hugged her close. "I'm feeling a little apprehensive about the whole thing, Taylor," he admitted.

"Anything in particular bothering you?"

"I knew what I wanted when all of this began, interview-wise, I mean. But now that it's happening, I'm not sure I can go through with it all."

Taylor couldn't help but stiffen a little. The journalist

side of her wanted to remind him of their contract and
how he needed to follow through. This was her career he
was messing with, after all. But there was also the side
of her that wanted to soothe all of his fears and reassure
him that everything was going to be fine.

"What part do you not want to go through with?" she
asked cautiously.

"I'm not ready to put my face out there." He paused
as if to collect his thoughts. "I don't like the idea of
having my picture taken and seeing it plastered around
with some idiotic caption under it," he explained as he
sat up.

Rolling over, Taylor looked at him. "Okay, so we
won't put any pictures in the piece. I mean, sure, it's a
little odd, but I can make it work. I can use pictures of
the farm and pictures from the coast." She felt relieved
that she had found a solution.

"What if I asked you not to print this interview at
all?" It was a challenge. Taylor sat up straight and
faced him.

"Is that what you're asking?" She needed the guide-
lines to be clear—even though her heart was hammering in her chest. She felt like she was going to be sick.
She needed to make sure she understood exactly what
he was saying.

"If I were, what would you do?"

"Stop answering my questions with questions!" she
shouted as she stood. Looking down to where he sat on
the floor, she repeated her initial question. "Are you
asking me to not print this story?"

He stood and glared at her. "Yes. That's what I'm
asking you. I've changed my mind. I don't want to be in

the public eye." He walked over and poked at the fire. "I'm asking you to forget about the whole damn assignment. Will you do that?" Again it was a dare.

Taylor was torn in two. It was as she'd feared — she had come up here in hopes of moving ahead in her career, but instead she'd be stuck in the same tiny cubicle, if she was even allowed to keep her job. He'd duped her to get her here, and now...well, now she had no idea what was going on!

"You know, Mike, since you initiated this whole interview, you've been calling the shots and pulling the strings. I've had to sign all kinds of confidentiality agreements, fly up here into the unknown, been lied to repeatedly, and *now* you want to pull it all out from under me? What kind of game are you playing?" Taylor was furious now.

"Taylor—"

"Hell, if you just wanted to meet up with me again after all these years, you could've called me! You didn't have to set up this elaborate ruse and jerk my career around in the meantime!"

"I'm not jerking your career around, Taylor! Don't be so dramatic." He turned from the fire to face her. "I am entitled to have a change of heart. In fact, it's in the contract! No one will look poorly upon you and your precious career, so you don't have to worry. I'll come out looking like the bad guy here, not you."

"The only difference, Mike, is there'll be no face for the bad guy. I'll be the only one identified in this scenario." Stalking from the room, she went upstairs to her room. Mike was quick and caught up with her at the doorway. Reaching out, he spun her around.

"What are you going to do?" he demanded.

"I think we're done here. I'm getting my things together and going home." Angrily, she pulled out of his grasp and went about retrieving her luggage from the closet. Throwing the cases on the bed, she began stuffing her belongings into them. When her clothes were packed, she went to work on her supplies. As Mike watched, Taylor took the flash drive out of the laptop and threw it on the bed.

"So, was sleeping with me again part of the assignment?" he asked, stalking into the room. At her shocked expression, he continued to taunt. "Did you think I would give you even more information because we had sex? And now that the assignment is over, you're able to just walk away, is that it?" Taylor glared daggers at him, but refused to take the bait.

"Well, I'll give you one thing, Ms. Scott," he spat, "you certainly give it all you've got for a story. Well done." He strode from the room as Taylor picked up her alarm clock and hurled it at him. It barely missed his head as it shattered against the door.

When the last of her things were packed, she started hauling it all down the stairs and out to her SUV, muttering under her breath all of her pent-up rage toward Mike as she went. "*Interview me, don't interview me! I'm Mike Greene, no, wait…I'm Jonathan Wade*," she mocked. When at last all of her things were cleared out of the room, she stormed from the house.

Pulling away from his property, hot tears finally came and streamed down her face. Looking in her rear-view mirror, she saw the road was clear behind her. "Of course he's not going to follow you," she scolded herself. "It would mean leaving the security of his little world and actually showing his face someplace."

The clock on the dashboard read six thirty p.m. Reaching for her cell phone, she called the airlines to see about getting a flight back to New York that night. If she couldn't, she'd sleep at the airport. Luckily that wasn't necessary, because there was one last flight, but it was going to be tight for her to get there and return the rental car in time.

As it turned out, traffic was on her side and by nine o'clock she was sitting in the terminal, waiting to board her flight. Waiting for her row to be called, she found herself looking around, secretly hoping *someone* would come looking for her.

No one did.

There wasn't time for self-pity. There were too many other things to consider at this point. First was how she was going to tell Victoria that Mike, a.k.a. Jonathan Wade, had backed out of the interview without incriminating herself in the process. Next came the possibility that she may very well have to start looking for another job by tomorrow afternoon. With her mind reeling from those two thoughts, she barely acknowledged her broken heart.

That would come later.

"This is the last call for Flight 752 to New York's LaGuardia Airport..." came the voice over the loud-speaker. Taylor stood with great effort and boarded the flight.

It was uneventful, and Taylor was relieved to find her ratty old Jeep waiting for her in long-term parking. It started on the third try—a new record—and she headed for home.

Back in her tiny, solitary apartment, she walked listlessly about, checking phone messages and sorting through her mail. No one missed her; no one cared that she'd been gone. Without paying any mind to her luggage, Taylor merely stripped and climbed into her bed.

There would be no clear decisions made tonight, and she had a feeling tomorrow was going to be more than she could handle.

Chapter 11

TAYLOR ARRIVED AT *NEWSLINK* AFTER TEN THE NEXT morning. She hadn't called Victoria to let her know she was back; she was hoping the element of surprise would work in her favor. Not bothering to stop at her desk, she went directly to her boss's office.

"Knock, knock," she said as she entered, forcing a cheery smile on her face.

"Taylor! You're back!" Victoria rose and walked around her desk to greet her. "Why didn't you call me and let me know you were back?"

"I got in late last night," Taylor supplied as Victoria led her to a chair.

"So…?" she asked giddily. "How was it?"

Taylor had thought of this moment so many times since the assignment was first given to her. She'd dreamed of arriving back here to a hero's welcome, all praise and glory. She drew in a deep breath and prepared for the inevitable. "Mr. Wade backed out of our agreement last night."

Victoria sat in silence for a moment and stared blankly at Taylor. When she finally found her voice, she said, "Excuse me?"

"We were discussing the use of photographs in the piece and he was opposed to it. After I said I wouldn't use them, he pulled out of the deal."

Victoria stood and paced behind her desk. "Tell me

that you still have your recordings…your notes…the files!"

"Yes. He has a copy of my draft on a flash drive. I thought it best." Taylor's head was hung low, as was her voice. She couldn't bear to witness the look of disappointment she was sure to see on Victoria's face.

"Well, we'll have to see about all of this," Victoria murmured as she picked up her phone and punched a few numbers. "Get me legal!" she snapped.

Taylor could do nothing but sit back quietly as Victoria ranted and raved into the phone at the magazine's legal department about Jonathan Wade's behavior and what they should be doing about it. There was still a soft side of Taylor that wanted to jump up and shout at Victoria to leave him be, that the man deserved his privacy, but she couldn't find the courage to do it.

Sometime later, Victoria slammed the phone down and faced Taylor.

"I want you to rewrite the article—or do edits if you have a final copy on your computer."

"What?" she asked, confused.

"We have his signature giving us permission to write this piece. As long as you're willing, we have a right to get this story out."

"But…he said he had the right of refusal," Taylor said, matter-of-factly. "He said it's in the contract."

Victoria waved her off. "There are ways around that, Taylor. Trust me."

Taylor stood, slack-jawed, staring at her editor. She wasn't fired! She still had a job! Her career wasn't over! She should be thrilled. She should be whooping it up with relief. Instead…

"I can't do that, Vic," she stated.

"*What?*" Now it was Victoria's turn to be stunned.

"I can't write this article."

"May I ask why?"

"I told him I wouldn't. If I go ahead and do it, my credibility is shot." There. She'd said it and the sky didn't fall.

"Taylor," Victoria said with a deadly calm voice, "the man doesn't speak to anyone. No one will ever know you *mistakenly* said you'd abandon the project. Trust me, he's not going to tell anyone. He'd have to go out in public, and I think we've all seen to what degree he'll go to keep his privacy intact."

It was a side of Victoria that Taylor had never seen before, and she really didn't like it. What she was being asked to do was unethical and she wasn't comfortable with it. "It's in the contract, Vic. He has the right to back out."

"We'll get to press before he can stop us," she countered. "Taylor, I want this story. *You* should want this story! More than any of us, you should be fighting for it!"

But Taylor shook her head sadly. "I can't do it, Vic. I just can't."

"Then you leave me no choice, Taylor." Her words were cold, but Taylor was prepared for them. "I'm sorry."

"Me too," she whispered as she walked out of the room.

After stopping at her desk for a few minutes to collect her things, Taylor found herself back home before noon. Dropping the box of her belongings on the floor of her living room, she collapsed on the couch.

Deep down, she knew she had done the right thing. Boosting her career by betraying someone's trust wasn't worth it. But what on earth was she supposed to do with herself now? Kicking off her shoes, she reclined on the sofa and rubbed her temples.

If it were any other time in her life, Taylor would be freaking out right about now, but for some reason, she felt a sense of peace with the situation. Was she sorry to see the job at *Newslink* go? No. It didn't fulfill her the way she had hoped it would, but what was she going to do now to earn a living?

A glass-is-half-full person would be excited about all of the possibilities that lay ahead, but the glass-is-half-empty side of Taylor looked around her tiny apartment and wondered if she was going to have to move or get a roommate or start selling her belongings before she found another job.

Rising from the sofa, she refused to give in to the negative thoughts. "Power of positive thinking," she chanted as she walked into her bedroom and changed into casual clothes. Stepping back into the living room, she grabbed the box and put it in a closet so she didn't have to look at it—or have it sit there mocking her. Out of sight, out of mind. Grabbing her coat and keys, she left the apartment—determined to find something to fill her days and hopefully give her a sense of purpose.

The air in the city was cold and she felt like she'd walked about a hundred blocks, but it paid off. On a tiny street, not too far from her apartment, she had wandered into a mom-and-pop bookstore not unlike the one she had shopped in up in Maine. After striking up a conversation with the owners, she found out they were looking for some part-time help. It wasn't ideal, but it was something Taylor knew she'd enjoy and if she had to take on a second job for a little while, so be it.

She left the store with a renewed sense of purpose, and as she walked home, she began to think about Mike. Would he realize what she had given up for him? Should she call him now that this interview was no longer between them? No. He had once decided to wait until he had gotten his life together before contacting her; she could understand that now. She didn't feel comfortable calling him fresh off of losing her job; it might look like she was blaming him for her misfortune.

No, waiting was definitely the way to go.

No matter how much her heart ached to go home and call him right now.

A month after her return from Maine, Taylor came home after a full day at the bookstore. Her arms were full of groceries and mail and her phone was ringing. She dropped everything and fished her phone out of her purse.

"Hello?" she answered, breathless.

"Taylor? It's Victoria! How are you?"

Taylor pulled the phone away from her ear for a moment and looked at it in disbelief—and disappointment. "Oh…hi, Victoria. I'm fine. How are you?" She had no idea what her former boss could want. Ever since she had refused to write the Jonathan Wade story, no one from *Newslink* had contacted her. She never even got reimbursed for her expenses from the trip.

"I'm fine, sweetie. Just fine. But the big question is—how did you do it?"

It had been a long day and there was ice cream that was going to start melting on her living room floor. She was in no mood for confusing conversations. "What exactly did I do, Vic?" She took off her coat and wearily sat down on the sofa.

As if not even hearing Taylor's question, Victoria went on. "I want to meet with you tomorrow as early as possible. Can you come to the office around eight?"

"Look," Taylor began diplomatically, "I do have another job to get to and—"

"Forget that!" Victoria interrupted. "You'll have to quit it. Trust me, Taylor, you're going to be thrilled at what we're offering."

She'd had enough. Sighing heavily with aggravation, she snapped. "Victoria! What the hell is this all about?"

"Jonathan Wade agreed to have the interview printed! It's hitting the newsstands tomorrow! *Newslink* gave it the cover! You've got a cover story, Taylor! Can you believe it?"

Taylor dropped the phone and fell to the floor as nausea overwhelmed her.

"Taylor? *Taylor!*"

She picked the phone back up. "Why am I just hearing of this now? How did you get a copy of my story?" she demanded.

"I was all Mr. Wade's idea. When we notified his people of our displeasure at his refusal to do the story and your subsequent dismissal, he reached out to us, and he was furious. These were the terms he demanded in order to print the story—you weren't to be told until it was a done deal and on the stands. You obviously made quite an impression on him, Taylor. Bravo!"

Her eyes filled with tears. He'd given it all up for her. Wiping furiously at her eyes, she cleared her throat to finish the conversation. "Um, what does this mean to me in regards to *Newslink*, Vic?"

"We want you back, Taylor. I am so sorry for how I behaved when you got back from Maine. I cannot even begin to explain myself." She paused. "The important thing here is that we all got what we wanted, didn't we? You've got your job back with a cover story, we got the exclusive of the year, and Wade's got publicity for his new book!"

"Oh…right."

"It's coming out tomorrow too, funny, huh?" Victoria let out a laugh. "What timing! So, when will you be in? I'll pick up a couple of lattes and those muffins you like so much."

"I won't be," Taylor replied flatly.

"Excuse me?" Disbelief oozed out of the phone.

"I do, however, expect to be paid for my article and to get reimbursed for the receipts I submitted after I was fired. But honestly? I have no desire to return to *Newslink*. You have my address. Just mail me my check." With that, she hung up her phone and then shut it off.

Sitting in silence, she looked around her. In the last month, she'd had to sell her beloved bike, some jewelry, and had eaten more ramen noodles than she'd thought possible, but it had been worth it to have her peace of mind. Now, however…now people would see her article and doors could possibly open for her again. Reality hit her and she jumped around her apartment with glee. She had stood up for what she believed in again and it felt great!

Taylor thought about her job at the bookstore. As much as she loved it, it wasn't what she wanted to do with the rest of her life. Perhaps if she went into freelancing, she'd have some freedom to write what she wanted to and actually accomplish getting her life back from this setback.

She'd get herself a new bike.

The thought made her smile.

At work the following day, Taylor stocked the shelves with the latest copy of *Newslink*. Her bosses took great pride in pointing out to all of their customers how it was their employee who'd written the cover story! Next came the task of stocking the shelves with *Misty's Return*, the new Jonathan Wade book.

She couldn't help the sense of pride for Mike as she placed the numerous copies on the shelf. Taylor took one for herself and held it behind the counter. She'd curl up with it tonight, maybe even splurge and download the audiobook, too. Not a night had gone by that she hadn't listened to Mike's voice on her iPod, listening to one book or another each night on her walk home and then again as she lay in bed trying to fall asleep.

Eager with anticipation for the workday to end, she bolted out the door at 5:01 p.m., waving to her bosses as she left. Deciding she deserved one more splurge, she stopped at a local Chinese restaurant and grabbed some celebratory takeout. Once her check from *Newslink* came in, she'd be okay, and the thought of one more night of ramen noodles almost made her stomach turn.

In the comfort of her apartment, she quickly changed into a pair of yoga pants and an oversized T-shirt, curling up on the couch with the Chinese food and her book.

Four hours later, she found herself crying. The hero of the story had finally found the woman he had been longing for, Misty. And she didn't leave him or escape in the night. The ending had made it abundantly clear that the series was over. Misty had returned and our hero could finally live happily ever after in peace with the woman he adored.

Placing the book down on her coffee table, she went in search of tissues. "Dammit," she cursed as she saw her reflection in the bedroom mirror. She looked frightful—red puffy eyes, a red nose, and mascara running down her cheeks.

"Why me?" she asked her reflection. "Why didn't I put up more of a fight? Why didn't I go back to him?" She had no answers. Walking into the bathroom, she quickly washed her face, but even that didn't make her look—or feel—any better. Then she shifted the blame onto Mike. Why hadn't he called her? Why didn't he come after her? What was the message at the end of the book supposed to mean? Was she Misty? Was Mike supposed to be the hero?

The damn questions were giving her a headache. Clearing up her dinner mess, Taylor headed to bed, setting the book on the nightstand next to her. She realized she'd never downloaded the audio version—but tomorrow was another day.

Wednesday was her day off, so Taylor took advantage of the opportunity and slept in. Or at least she tried to. Rising from the bed earlier than she wanted to, she was surprised to hear a knock at her door. Padding into the living room, she peered through her peephole to see who it was. Her neighbor, Mrs. Martinez, was standing there.

"Good morning, Mrs. Martinez," she greeted sleepily as she opened the door.

"Good morning, Taylor. How are you this morning?" The plump and petite gray-haired woman entered her apartment without waiting for an invitation.

"I'm fine," Taylor managed to say with a smile. "What can I do for you today?"

"I'm sorry to come by so early, but the mailman delivered this to me by mistake yesterday," she said as she handed Taylor a small package. "I got home late last night and forgot to bring it over, dear. I'm so sorry."

Assuring the woman it was all right, they chatted about the weather and other niceties before her neighbor was on her way. Closing the door behind her, Taylor glanced at the package. There was no return address on it. Tearing into it, she found an iPod wrapped in a sheet of paper.

"I know you enjoy listening to these" was all that was written on the paper, but Taylor was certain it was Mike's writing. She searched the room for her earbuds and then plugged them into the iPod, sitting down on the couch. It didn't take long for Mike's voice to start speaking—it was the audio version of *Misty's Return*, read by him.

Smiling, Taylor curled up on the couch and let the sound of his voice wash over her. Hours later, when the story was coming to an end, Taylor sighed. It was an even more emotional experience than reading the physical book, because she heard the emotion in his voice as he read it. Not only that, the happily ever after would be so hard to hear coming from his voice—especially because they never got to have one.

When at last it ended, there was a short silence and she was about to shut the iPod off when his voice came back on. "Baby, I love you. Please come home. I miss you." Taylor stopped the recording and rewound it, playing the message over and over again.

Running to her bedroom, she jumped across her bed and grabbed the book. Nowhere in the end did it say those words. He was saying them to her—it wasn't part of the book at all! It was his message to her, Taylor!

Dare she hop in her Jeep and drive up to Maine? Of course, she'd have to take the train out to the Island to pick the car up first before she could leave, but…if it meant going back to him? It would be worth it. Walking quickly across the room, she picked up her phone and called the bookstore to let them know she needed a couple of days off. Her boss gave her more grief than she'd anticipated, but he finally gave in. Next, she showered and packed. Anticipation bubbled up inside of her and her hands were shaking when she finally picked up her bags and locked up her tiny apartment— feeling as if the weight of the world had been lifted off of her.

She had packed lightly, but it was still going to be a little awkward to carry it all the way to the subway and then around Penn Station to catch the train out to Suffolk County. "It will be worth it…it will be worth it…" That's what she kept telling herself as she made her way up the block.

Taylor was minding her own business when she felt someone tap her on the shoulder.

"Can I give you a lift somewhere?" came a voice from behind her.

Everything in Taylor stilled for a second before she turned around. "Mike?" She was stunned by the sight of him. "What…? How…? What are you doing here?"

"I sent you a package yesterday," he said instead of answering her question. "Did you get it?"

She nodded. "This morning. It went to one of my neighbors by mistake." Her eyes wouldn't leave his face. She couldn't believe he was standing here in front of her, in the middle of the city. "That still doesn't explain why you're here. Or how you found me."

"I was making sure you came home," he said confidently as he moved closer, until he was toe to toe with her.

"I wasn't sure you'd want me," she said huskily, wanting so badly to lean in and kiss him.

"Oh, I want you, Taylor. I've always wanted you." Pausing, his loving eyes scanned her face. "I was pulling up to your place and saw you walking away. I double-parked so I could get out and catch up to you."

"Wow," she said with a happy sigh. "Talk about perfect timing."

She got up on tiptoes as she tried to kiss him, but he dodged her advance. At the look of confusion on her face, he chuckled. "If I kiss you here, I'm not going to stop." He rested his forehead against hers. "And if I don't stop, I'm going to end up making love to you right here in the middle of this city street. People will recognize me now and it will be all over the tabloids." He pulled back with a knowing smirk. "There's a big story on me in *Newslink*. Maybe you've seen it?"

She swatted playfully at him. "Oh, I've seen it and I'm going to want to hear all about how you came to change your mind."

"Well," he began, "I realized—"

She cut him off by putting a finger to his lips. "Later. We'll talk about it later. Right now I want to get out of the street and go someplace where we can be alone."

His gaze heated. "I like the way you think." He took her bags from her hands. "Let's get back to my car so I can park it properly. Hopefully before I get a ticket." She nodded and they began walking back toward her place.

At his car, he kissed her quickly and promised to be right back. "I'll meet you inside as soon as I find a spot." She almost argued that she'd just go with him, but it seemed silly.

"Okay," she said with a small pout. Now that he was here, she didn't want to let him out of her sight.

Within minutes, he was back. And when she opened the door to him, she felt embarrassed for him to be there, knowing how Mike lived. Sensing her uneasiness, he pulled her into his embrace. "I don't care where you live, Taylor." It was a hushed whisper against her throat as he began to trail kisses upon her. Her head fell back in abandon. "Besides, after today, hopefully you won't be living here anymore."

That got her attention. Snapping her head up, she met his eyes.

"I meant what I said on the recording, Taylor. I want you to come home with me and stay there."

"You want me to move in with you on the farm?"

He shook his head. "Baby, I want you to marry me

and live with me on the farm. Will you?" His plea was so full of emotion and Taylor could read it all in his magnificent eyes.

"Yes," she whispered. "Yes, I will marry you and go home with you and stay there with you forever."

He lifted her into his arms and wrapped her in his embrace. He kissed her thoroughly before setting her back on her feet.

"Thank you for coming back for me," she said, looking up at him, smiling with pure joy.

"I should have done it years ago," he said solemnly and then took her hands in his to lead her toward the bedroom. "But I believe you were worth the wait."

Kicking the bedroom door closed behind her, Taylor intended to prove to him how much she appreciated his patience.

Epilogue

"Okay, camera two will be on you in one minute, Taylor. The red light will go on and Julie will begin her introductions." Taylor nodded in understanding as the microphone attached to her blouse was adjusted.

"Mike? Are you all set?" the director asked. Mike gave a curt nod and turned his attention to Taylor.

"I can't believe I let you talk me into this," he whispered in her ear.

"I can be very persuasive when I need to be," she said with an angelic smile.

They were sitting on the New York set of a popular morning show. It was the second such appearance in a week. Since her story in *Newslink* had come out, Jonathan Wade was more popular than ever. The offers had started pouring in to his agent by noon that first day. Taylor saw the tension in his body but knew that as soon as they started taping, he would be a natural.

"Okay, people! Bring it in five, four…" came the prompt from behind the camera.

In fifteen minutes, it was all over and they were being thanked and sent on their way. Climbing into the waiting limousine, Mike reached for Taylor's hand and pulled her to him. "Thank you," he whispered right before kissing her.

"For what?" she asked, kissing him in return.

"For everything you've done for me. This isn't as

awful as I'd thought it would be—the media frenzy and all." She gave him a look that screamed "I told you so."

It had been barely a month since the story had been released and in that time, Taylor had indeed moved up to Maine with Mike; they had gotten married on his boat that weekend by a justice of the peace and honeymooned on it as well. They'd done nearly a half dozen talk shows and Taylor had been offered several jobs with different publications, but she turned them all down.

"Do you miss writing?" he asked as the private car drove them toward their hotel.

"I haven't had time to miss it yet. Touring with Jonathan Wade has kept me very busy," she teased.

"Well, I have a plan that I think could keep you very busy for a while if you were to agree to it." His tone was very businesslike, but his eyes were dark with desire.

"Really?" she inquired. "And what exactly were you thinking of?" She reached over and ran her hand over his chest, purring like a kitten as she did.

"I was thinking that having a baby would keep us busy for a while," he said softly, leaning forward to taste her lips as his hand skimmed her body and came to rest on her abdomen. "We've done quite well with this first collaboration. I figured we could branch out."

She smiled against his lips. "Hmm. I like the sound of that."

The car came to a halt in front of the Plaza and Mike helped Taylor out, thanking their driver before they headed up the stairs to the hotel entrance. Then all bets were off. Taking Taylor's hand, he pulled her toward the elevator, thankful no one else was standing there waiting to get in with them. Once on their floor, they nearly ran to their suite, anxious to get started on this new assignment.

A TOUCH of HEAVEN

Chapter 1

"OH, THEY'RE PERFECT! EXACTLY WHAT I WAS LOOKING for."

Regan Amerson looked at her mother as if she had lost her mind. "Um, they're not exactly what we had discussed."

"Of course they're not—they're better."

"They're bedazzled."

"Exactly. I think they really grab your attention."

Regan pinched the bridge of her nose, mentally counted to ten, and sighed. "Mom, we agreed the shirts would be basic black or white with our logo *tastefully* placed in the corner." She pointed to the shirt her mother was holding up. "That's not what I see."

Caroline rolled her eyes. "I know what we discussed, but those were boring. These are much better."

"No, Mom, they're not. They're the opposite of better!" Regan rarely raised her voice, particularly at her mother, but this time she had been pushed to her limit. "First, they are tacky. Second, we have *male* employees. Do you honestly think they are going to wear a bedazzled T-shirt?"

"Don't be ridiculous, Regan," her mother scolded. "I kept your *boring* design for the guys. I just thought the ladies would appreciate something with a little more…bling."

"I hate bling! You know it's one of my pet peeves,

and yet you did it anyway! We're partners, Mom, and we're supposed to discuss things like this before making a decision. What were you thinking?"

"I was thinking it wouldn't kill you to open your mind a little bit." Reaching into the box in front of her, Caroline pulled out a shirt in Regan's size. "Just try it on." She held it up in front of her daughter and measured it against her just like she had when Regan was a child.

Regan shooed her away. "Stop that!" she snapped. "I'm not wearing that shirt and I won't allow my girls to wear that shirt. You'll just have to send them back."

"Excuse me, but your girls? *Your* girls? I'm a partner in this business. I think it's fair to say that they're *our* girls, and I say they can wear them."

"Don't you see what you've done?" Regan asked, bewildered. "Don't you see what makes them so offensive?"

Caroline looked at the shirt and could only smile. "Regan, they're perfectly acceptable. It's a basic T-shirt, no plunging necklines, not too tight…I don't see the problem. Here." She shoved the shirt into Regan's hand. "Go ahead. Try it on and show me what is so offensive about it."

"I really don't think—"

"No, go ahead," Caroline urged. "Clearly you see something that I don't. So please, enlighten me."

All Regan wanted to do was stomp her foot, but she knew her mother would eat that up. It wasn't easy being in business together—their mother-daughter dynamic followed them to work. Ignoring her mother's arched brow, Regan headed to the bathroom to change.

"For crying out loud, Regan, I'm your mother. You don't have anything I haven't seen before."

Regan knew the words were a dare but she took the bait anyway. "Fine." She stopped where she stood, whipped her own conservative shirt over her head, and reached for the bedazzled spectacle that her mother was so thrilled about.

"It wouldn't kill you to invest in some good underwear, you know," her mother taunted while Regan changed.

Deciding not to take *that* bait either, Regan pulled on the T-shirt and straightened it. Hands on hips, she faced her mother.

"I still don't see it."

"Really? You don't see any problems with this shirt?"

"It's the spa logo. What is offensive about it?"

Regan was done playing. This had gone on long enough. "It says *A Touch of Heaven* in bejeweled letters right across my breasts, Mom! For crying out loud, you don't think that's offensive?"

She saw the exact moment her mother caught on.

"Oh my goodness," Caroline gasped. "I hadn't thought of it like that! I just thought it would be better to have our logo stand out more—I didn't even think about the placement." Caroline turned a lovely shade of crimson as she placed a hand over her mouth to stifle a giggle.

"Don't you dare," Regan warned. "You can play innocent all you want, but I will not cave in and wear this shirt."

"Well, the logo certainly pops," Caroline said and then burst out laughing.

"Yes, yes," Regan said tiredly. "Yes, it's very clever,

Mom. My enormous chest really makes the words stand out. What's more flattering than someone asking what I do for a living and reading it across my breasts? Brilliant marketing strategy."

"Don't be so snarky. I honestly didn't think along those lines when I ordered them. You have to admit, though, the male clientele will increase."

"Mom!" Regan cried with exasperation. "We are a respectable day spa. We've worked so hard to get where we are, and I'm not turning to cheap thrills to boost business. You can't be serious."

Caroline waved her daughter off. "I was joking about the male clientele, Regan. Relax. I was only trying to go for something different, a little less practical and stuffy."

"There's nothing wrong with practical."

"What about stuffy?"

This was not a new argument. Lately there seemed to be a lot more of them. Originally they had agreed upon a standard uniform of black pants and white shirts. Then they added the option of black on black. The idea of a shirt with the spa's logo seemed to be a good one, and as far as Regan was concerned, the design she'd suggested made sense. Caroline hadn't argued about it, so Regan thought it was a done deal.

Clearly she was wrong.

"People come here to be pampered and to relax. They don't need flashy lettering on the employees' chests distracting them."

Caroline nodded. "You're right. I'm sorry that I tried to get too creative. I'll keep my opinions to myself from now on."

Great, the martyr act.

"I'm not saying you can't get creative. All I'm saying is that we're supposed to talk to one another before making decisions. Those are two completely different things."

Mumbling about minding her own business and maybe it was time to move her into a home, Caroline walked away, leaving Regan in the office wondering what she was supposed to do now.

Forgetting about the ridiculous shirt for a moment, Regan welcomed an incoming phone call, and for the next hour found herself placing orders for towels and candles while scheduling appointments for two upcoming bridal parties coming in for a day of pampering. When she looked at the clock, it was lunchtime, her stomach reminding her that she had skipped breakfast. Stretching, she stood up from her chair and headed into the spa to find Caroline.

"What are we doing for lunch today?" she asked as Caroline was coming out of the storeroom.

"How about sushi?" Caroline suggested.

"How about burgers?" Regan countered. It was a daily argument about what to eat—Caroline always ready to try new things, and Regan content with sticking to what she knew.

Sighing with defeat, Caroline spoke first. "I'm probably going to grab something while I'm out. I want to go to the home improvement store and get the paint for the kitchen and bathroom. The sooner we get them painted, the sooner I can get the Realtor over and the house listed."

It was a topic that made Regan's heart ache: her mother was going to sell the home Regan had grown up in. It was the smart thing to do; after Regan's father died ten years ago and with Regan living on her own, the house was too big for Caroline to take care of by herself. But it still made Regan sad. In a perfect world, she'd buy the house, but it was too much house for Regan as well. The practical thing was for them to sell the house and for Caroline to find someplace better suited for her. Regan just wished the thought of strangers living in her home didn't bother her so much.

"I still think we should hire a painter to come in," Regan reminded her mother. They'd had an earlier discussion on the topic.

"Nonsense. It will be fun for the two of us to do it together."

Fun wasn't quite the word Regan would have chosen. "But it would go so much faster if we had a professional." Plus, it would help Regan distance herself from the process. The thought of spending extra time in the house and painting over walls that held a lifetime of memories seemed too much to ask.

Caroline knew her daughter well and knew why she was so apprehensive. She stepped up and placed her arms around her. "Regan, it's just a house. Your memories are here"—she pointed to Regan's head and then to her heart—"and here. Just because the house won't be ours anymore doesn't mean you lose all those memories."

Tears threatened, but Regan willed them away. "I know, Mom, I really do. I can't help the way I feel, though."

Caroline stroked her daughter's cheek. "You just say the word and I won't sell. I'll find a way to make it work."

And we're back to guilt.

"I'm sorry. I know I'm being selfish. Selling the

house is the right thing to do. You deserve to retire and live someplace that doesn't require so much work." She hugged her mother and stepped back. "Go find your paint colors. Remember, the Realtor said neutrals. Don't go getting all flashy with the paint."

"I believe I've learned my lesson, dear," Caroline said as she grabbed her purse and headed out the door.

Regan watched her go and took a moment to enjoy the silence. There wasn't a doubt in her mind that the T-shirt debacle was an indication of bigger things to come.

"Regan? Are you there? Did you hear me? I've won a home makeover!" her mother trilled into the phone a few hours later.

Clearly, I've died in some sort of fiery crash and this is hell, Regan thought as her mother rambled on about her good fortune. "Mom, I'm sure you're mistaken. You did not win a home makeover."

"Don't talk to me like I'm senile, young lady! I'm telling you, I was walking around the home improvement store with a shopping cart full of paint supplies when a man with a camera crew approached me and asked what I was doing."

"They couldn't tell by the shopping cart full of paint?" Regan deadpanned.

Caroline ignored the comment. "So I looked around and asked for the store manager. He told me the man was legit and that I had, indeed, won a home makeover."

A migraine was building behind Regan's right eye. "We don't need a home makeover, Mom, we need to paint the kitchen and the bathroom. That's it."

"Well, I know that's all we had planned to do, but imagine how much more we can get for the house if it's been professionally made over! It will surely draw a lot of attention to the listing if we say a famous TV show did our whole house over."

A famous TV show? "Wait, wait, wait," Regan said, thoroughly confused. "What are you talking about?"

"Honestly, you never listen to me," Caroline said with a huff. "You know that show *The Bennett Project* on the Home Improvement Network?"

"What about it?"

"That's who stopped me today! Max Bennett! Oh, Regan, he's even more handsome in person!"

"Isn't he a little young for you, Mom?"

"Sheesh, Regan," Caroline said with exasperation. "Max is the father. You're thinking of Sawyer. He's the son."

"Not that any of this matters, Mom. We don't need the home done over. All we need is a coat of paint in two rooms. That's it. Tell them thanks, but no thanks."

"Oh, sweetheart, I can't do that. I already told them we'd do it."

"What?" Regan collapsed into her desk chair and nearly slid to the floor. "Didn't we just talk about not making any decisions without checking with one another?"

"That was about business, dear, not the house."

Seriously, I'm in hell. "Mom…"

"Anyway, they're going to meet me at the house in an hour, so I won't be back to the spa today. Kaitlyn can handle my appointments."

"Please don't sign anything before I get there!" Regan cautioned.

"You don't have to be there, Regan. I can handle this."

"Just…promise me you won't sign anything," Regan repeated for good measure.

"Fine, fine, fine. I won't do anything until you get there. But I'm telling you right now, Regan, I want to do this. You're not going to talk me out it."

We'll see about that, Regan thought before she hung up the phone.

"I thought you were going to wait for me before choosing someone," Sawyer Bennett said to his father as they drove down the highway in search of their latest project's address.

"I know, I know," Max said patiently. "But I saw her wandering the aisles with way too many paint supplies, and I knew she would be the perfect client."

"Dad, just because she was painting a room doesn't mean she's going to be a good fit for the show. You know there are certain criteria that have to be met. The producers—"

"I already talked to Devin and he is one hundred percent on board with this project."

Sawyer looked doubtful. "Devin is never one hundred percent on board with any project—he finds problems with everything. What makes this one so different?"

"Well, for starters, she's a widow."

"Oh no—"

Max held up a hand to stop him. "She's been a widow for ten years. She is getting ready to put her house on the market because it's too much for her to take care of."

"I'm still not seeing the draw."

"Her daughter isn't on board with her selling the family home, so it adds a bit of drama to the whole thing."

Luckily, they were stopping for a traffic light, otherwise Sawyer would have slammed on the brakes in disbelief. "So we are going to glamorize an emotional decision between a mother and daughter for the sake of ratings? When did we stoop to this level?"

"It's not stooping to anything, Sawyer," Max said in an even voice. "Devin and I both think that the show has been a little too predictable lately: Family needs a makeover, we give them a makeover, everyone's happy. There's almost no need to tune in because one show bleeds into the next. This time we're going to throw a little emotion into the mix, show another side to that scenario."

"I don't like it."

"Well, the network does. They're getting a little tired of the same old, same old, and if we don't do something different soon, we may not have a show to keep doing."

"It wouldn't be a catastrophe, Dad," Sawyer said, his voice weary. Truth be known, he was ready to be done with *The Bennett Project*. It had been a lot of fun at first, but now it was exactly as his father said: predictable. Sawyer missed being able to pick and choose the projects he wanted to do. He missed sleeping in his own bed more than a handful of nights per month. If the network decided to pull the plug on the show, Sawyer was confident that he would be okay. He had saved a lot of money and could readily go back to being a full-time contractor again.

He longed to do it.

"Don't talk nonsense," Max said. "This show has been a godsend for both of us. Why wouldn't you want to continue with it?"

"I'm just ready for a change, that's all."

"Well, get unready. I think this project is going to open a lot of doors for us and I want you to keep an open mind about it."

"When have I ever not had an open mind?" Sawyer asked with a scowl.

"Seems like it's happening more and more lately. It's not Devin who has problems, son, it's you."

"That's ridiculous," Sawyer snapped. "I'm just getting a little tired of not having a say in which projects we pick. In the beginning, they listened to my input, but now I'm supposed to go wherever they tell me—and personally, it's insulting. I have proven myself to them. I'm competent at what I do, and yet I'm being babysat like I'm a rookie!"

Max glanced at his son and sighed. "You're looking at this the wrong way. They want you to focus on the designing and the job so you don't have to worry about weeding through applicants and the paperwork end of it. They thought they were doing you a favor."

"Well, they aren't. I want to decide what jobs we take. I have to be honest with you. From what you've told me about this one? I am not interested."

"Look, let's just meet with Caroline Amerson and her daughter and take a look at the house. If you're still set against it after we meet with them, then I'll talk to Devin and the network and tell them we want to pass on it."

Sawyer looked at his father hesitantly. "You'd do that? You'd go against the network over this?"

Max nodded. "I want you to be happy, Sawyer. It's been a blessing to work with you like this for the last five years. I never dreamed after raising you on my own that you'd want to work with me. I don't want this to be a chore for you. I want you to enjoy what you do."

How could he argue with that? "Thanks, Dad."

Max reached over and squeezed Sawyer's shoulder. "You make me proud every day, Sawyer. I'm not going to let Devin or the network tell you what you have to do. I wish you had told me sooner that you were so unhappy."

"I guess it really didn't hit me until today, when I heard about adding this emotional angle."

"What did?"

"It just seems wrong to be using someone's emotional distress to sensationalize our show."

"Well, that's the way most reality TV is these days."

"That's not the kind of TV I want to be a part of, Dad." The conversation died off and they continued the rest of the drive in silence, listening to the GPS directing them to their location. Once off the main highway, they took the secondary roads until they came to a turnoff that could have been a road but seemed more like a driveway. "This can't be it," Sawyer mumbled, turning at the insistence of the GPS.

"We're definitely not in Kansas anymore," Max said.

"Not funny," Sawyer said, trying to get a grip on where exactly they were. There were houses lining the road on large, heavily wooded lots. "What number are we looking for?"

Max looked at his paperwork. "Number eighty-seven." He craned his neck and looked around. "Looks like it's coming up on the right."

Sawyer turned into the long driveway and parked behind a white SUV. Putting the truck in park, he took in the house. Maybe it wouldn't be so bad. It was a ranch with a detached two-car, two-story garage that could work as an income property, he thought. The outside needed some TLC and the landscaping was a little overgrown, but overall it wasn't as bad as some of the properties he'd worked on.

They climbed from the truck and Sawyer came around to stand next to his father. "First impression?" he asked.

Max walked a few feet away, taking a good look at the property, and made some notes in the notebook he insisted on carrying, still refusing to join the digital age and use a tablet. "First glance tells me there are some boards that need to be replaced on the siding, and we'll only need a cleanup crew for the yard. I like the detached garage, but the doors are in need of some paint." Sawyer nodded. "I think overall the paint looks good but could use a bit of sprucing up on the trim." He took a step back so he could get a better view of the roof. "I'll want someone to check the gutters and look for any roofing issues."

"Isn't this supposed to be an interior thing?" Sawyer asked, clearly confused.

"Normally, but I'm thinking if we're going to go a different route with this one, we might as well break from routine and throw in something new." Again, all Sawyer could do was nod. "What about you? What are you thinking?"

Sawyer shrugged. "I'm not thinking anything. I'm trying to keep an open mind as you suggested, and I'm trying to forget there is family drama here." He looked around and noticed only the one car. "Does the daughter live here, too?"

Max shook his head. "Caroline said her daughter lives in Raleigh, but the house is technically half hers. That's why it's so important we get the daughter on board with the project."

"What does that even mean? Technically?"

"The daughter's name isn't on the home—the title, the deed, none of it—but Caroline explained to me that when the house sells, half of the money will go to her daughter." Max paused. "If we wanted to push, we could point out that the daughter legally doesn't have a say in what we're going to do."

"I'm not going to bully anyone into this, Dad."

"I'm not asking you to. And I'm just speaking hypothetically. All I'm asking is for you to meet with them, look at the house, and see if it's something you can picture doing on the show. We'll be here an hour, tops."

Sawyer sighed with defeat. Hell, he had nothing else to do. The network wanted to do a couple of episodes in the area and he was stuck here until they lined up projects elsewhere.

They started walking toward the front door when Max stopped him. "Hey," he said quietly, "we're not heading off to our execution. Caroline's a very nice woman, and it would be helpful if you didn't look like you were here with a gun to your head."

"You're right. Sorry."

"I'll spring for dinner tonight," Max said to lighten the mood. "I'll even go for Mexican."

Sawyer chuckled. "Just as long as we're not sharing a room, you're on!"

"That's my boy." Max chuckled and led Sawyer to the front door, where Caroline Amerson was waiting.

The first thing Sawyer noticed was her wide and welcoming smile. He had no doubt she was going to hug them both as soon as they got close enough. If he had to guess, he'd say she was in her fifties, her blond hair highlighted with gray. She stood about five feet seven and still had a good figure. Out of the corner of his eye, he noticed his father was smiling just as broadly as she was.

Interesting.

"I see you found the place," Caroline said as she stepped out onto the porch, and as expected, she hugged them both. "I'm thrilled you're here. It's like an answer to a prayer!"

Sawyer hugged her awkwardly and was about to speak when his father suddenly took over. "I don't think anyone's ever told us that before, Caroline," he said as he inclined his head toward hers. Sawyer took a step back, a little in shock. Was his father flirting? *What in the world?* It's not that Max didn't date; hell, he had been single ever since Sawyer's mom had left when he was just a toddler. This was the first time, though, that Sawyer had ever seen his father in action.

"Why don't you show us around, Caroline, and tell us what you envision for your home?" Caroline hooked her arm through Max's and led him into the house, leaving Sawyer no choice but to follow.

Chapter 2

HER DAY HAD BEEN HECTIC AND ALL REGAN WANTED WAS to go home, have a glass of wine, and relax. But no, she had to make sure her mother wasn't getting conned into some crazy scheme by some shifty contractor. Regan sighed. Lately, it seemed like everything was a challenge with her mother. Regan wasn't sure which of them was being unreasonable, but they were butting heads with more frequency now than they had when Regan was a teen.

Deep down, Regan knew her mother was ready to retire and move on to something new, and that she was the one holding her mom back. Caroline never said it outright, but Regan had a sneaking suspicion something was definitely up.

It wouldn't be hard to run A Touch of Heaven on her own; Caroline made her own hours and mainly worked so she could keep herself busy. But it would be hard not to have her mom around every day. It wasn't that Regan was afraid to be on her own—quite the contrary. Regan loved her independence. She considered Caroline a friend as much as a parent and genuinely enjoyed the time they spent together.

Even when Caroline was making her crazy.

She pulled into her mother's driveway and parked behind a massive Ford pickup truck. *Oh, joy,* she thought, *they're already here.* With a fortifying breath, she climbed from the car. It was only four o'clock and Regan felt as though she had worked more than a full day. "Home makeover," she mumbled aloud. "There's probably a boatload of fine print saying how this is going to cost us a fortune."

A feeling of disgust stayed with her as she entered the house and called out for her mother. "In the kitchen!" Caroline shouted and Regan headed that way. She found her mother and an older gentleman sitting at the table drinking coffee and laughing like old friends. Max Bennett was a big, burly man who made Caroline look petite, and he had her laughing like a schoolgirl.

Interesting.

"Regan, this is Max Bennett. Max, this is my daughter, Regan." Max rose and walked across the room to shake Regan's hand. "As you know, Regan's not the most excited for the home makeover—but I hope you'll be able to change her mind."

"It's a pleasure to meet you, Regan," Max said, towering over her. Regan stood five feet four and always wore heels to keep from feeling her actual height. He had a great big smile, dimples, and twinkling green eyes. Regan had a feeling he was going to charm the two of them no matter how hard she tried to fight it.

"Same here," she said, forcing a smile. "My mother tells me she *won* this home makeover. I don't mean to sound critical, Mr. Bennett—"

"Please, call me Max," he interrupted.

Regan cleared her throat. "As I was saying, I don't mean to sound critical, but I find it hard to believe you're going to come in here and do a home makeover that won't cost us a dime."

"Regan Elisabeth!" Caroline hissed.

Regan turned toward her mother. "Look, I don't believe in wasting anyone's time. Let's just cut to the chase, shall we?"

Max held out a chair for Regan, but she shook her head, choosing to lean against the counter while he sat back down next to Caroline. "There is no chase, Regan," Max said. "Our show, *The Bennett Project,* chooses homes that need our help. The only cost to you is what you were going to spend to spruce up the place yourself."

The snort of disbelief escaped before she could stop it. "So what you're saying is that we're going to get a home makeover for the cost of a couple gallons of paint, do I have that right?"

Max nodded.

"And how does the show make money on that?"

"Product placement, advertising, media coverage of how we help in the community, that sort of thing."

"Look, Mr. Bennett—"

"Max."

Regan sighed irritably. "Max. We appreciate the offer, but I'm not interested in having the house torn up. As I'm sure my mother has shared with you, I already have some issues with selling this house. This is my home, where I grew up. The thought of another family living here is…" She had to take a moment to compose herself. "Let's just say it's hard to imagine another family here. Adding demolition to the equation and watching you and your crew tear down parts of the house… It's just too much. I'm sorry to have wasted your time."

Max simply nodded and looked at Caroline before addressing Regan. "Are you familiar with our show,

Regan?" She nodded. "Okay, then you know our motto is 'minimal demolition/maximum results,' right?" Again, she nodded. "So we're not going to be tearing down walls or ripping out things you don't want ripped out. What we do is enhance what's already there. If something needs to be repaired, we repair it. If it needs to be replaced, we replace it. Nothing gets demo'd unless you want it that way."

To say she was skeptical would be an understatement. One look at her mother told her she was alone in her feelings—if anything, Caroline was absolutely beaming. With a sinking sensation, Regan knew she was fighting a losing battle. "I'll want all of that in writing."

"Absolutely."

"And I'll want our attorney to look it over."

"Of course," Max said, beaming just as much as her mother was.

"What kind of timeline are we looking at?" Regan asked with resignation.

"That will depend on Sawyer," Max replied. When Regan looked confused, he clarified. "He's the host of the show and he does all the designing and planning. Once he gets an idea of what he wants to do, we can give you a better estimate."

Regan looked around. "Is he here?" she asked as an idea began to form in her mind. Maybe she could convince Sawyer that this was not a project for his show. She could be rude and difficult and make demands that would ensure he wouldn't want to take this on. "I'd like to meet him," she said, her tone suddenly sweet, hoping she'd be able to pull this off and get this father-and-son team out of here.

"He's walking around taking measurements and making notes," Max told her, seeming pleased that she appeared to be on board.

"Great," she said with a smile. "I'll go find him and introduce myself."

―――∿∿∿―――

As much as Sawyer hated to admit it, the house had potential. He knew he should pass on the job; there wasn't a challenge here construction-wise. It was structurally sound, and other than being outdated, the project would be a no-brainer.

It was a shame, because now, standing in the master bedroom, Sawyer had all kinds of ideas how he could renovate the space and turn the room into the sort of retreat a couple would love. Taking out his tape measure, he let himself get caught up in the design in his head. "Change the lighting," he muttered as he typed notes into his tablet, "add a ceiling fan and crown molding"—more typing—"rip up the carpet and replace with hardwood"—type, type, type—"put a king-size bed in here because what couple wouldn't enjoy a king-size bed?"

"My parents didn't, actually," a voice said from behind him. Sawyer turned and nearly forgot how to breathe. She was stunning and sexy and clearly mad as hell at him for being there, judging by her defiant stance in the doorway.

"You must be Regan," he said when he was able to find his voice. Walking toward her, Sawyer extended his hand in greeting. When she met him halfway and placed her hand in his, he felt as if he'd gotten an electric shock.

Meeting Regan's eyes, he was pleased to see he wasn't the only one affected.

"So," she began and Sawyer heard her voice tremble, "you seem to have a lot of ideas for this room."

Sawyer still hadn't let go of her hand. He nodded.

And that's when he saw it.

The T-shirt.

The bedazzled words emblazoned across Regan's ample breasts mesmerized him. *A Touch of Heaven*, he read and actually felt the sweat breaking out on his temple. His gaze lingered more than was appropriate and when he finally forced his eyes away, they met a very angry pair of brown ones.

"The room, right," he stammered and released Regan's hand. "I was thinking with the high ceilings, it's a shame crown molding was never installed. The lighting fixtures are outdated and a ceiling fan would work wonders. The French doors leading out to the yard could use a good rehab, as well as adding blinds for privacy."

It hit him in that moment that he was nervous—and not just because she had caught him blatantly staring at her breasts. For some reason Sawyer felt that it was vitally important for Regan to see his vision and to win her over. Never before had the urge to get a client's approval hit him so hard. It was quite disconcerting.

"That's all fine and well," she said, interrupting his thoughts, "but I don't want this room touched."

He turned and looked at her with disbelief. "Excuse me?"

"I'm sure my mother has already shared with you that I am against this project. If there was any way not to sell this house, I would do it. This is where I grew up. I have a lifetime of memories here, and changing all this around before we go is not something I'm happy about."

Sawyer crossed his arms over his chest and studied her until Regan started to squirm. Finally, he said, "If we take on this project, I won't be doing a lot of structural changes—if any. But you have to admit there is plenty here that's outdated and in need of renovation."

"Oh, I'm not denying it, Sawyer," she said, her voice sounding a little breathless and a whole lot sexy. "But the fact remains that I don't see why I have to make this house over for someone else to enjoy. I agree some paint is needed in the kitchen and the hall bathroom, but that was all I was willing to commit to. So, I think you can see this project is really a waste of your time."

It was exactly what he'd wanted to hear—all the excuse he needed to get him the hell out of here. Yet now that Regan had said it, it was the last thing Sawyer wanted. Leaving here would mean not getting to know her, and he knew right then, without a doubt, that Regan Amerson was someone he definitely wanted to get to know. It had been a long time since he'd wanted to get to know a woman, but something about this pint-sized beauty with wavy brown hair and angry brown eyes made everything in him want to know her. From the tips of her pink painted toes on up, she was like a present he wanted to unwrap.

In that king-size bed he imagined in here earlier.

Damn.

The smart thing to do would be to thank her for her time, collect his father, and leave—cut their losses and run. But suddenly that was the furthest thing from his mind. Honestly, now that he'd gotten a glimpse of

Regan, Sawyer knew he'd need to find a way to drag out the three weeks he'd anticipated the job taking so he'd have more time to win her over.

And there was no doubt he'd have to win Regan over. Between the issues she was having with her mother over selling the house and the fact that he was going to be the guy doing the work on the house, he was going to be persona non grata with her. Well, Sawyer could certainly be charming when he needed to be—and he needed to be right now.

"Why don't you let me present to you and your mother what I have planned for the house before you make a decision?" he suggested.

"I really don't think—" she began, but Sawyer brazenly placed a finger over her lips to silence her. They both stared wide-eyed at one another at the charged contact.

"Promise me," he said softly, "that you'll at least let me make my presentation to you before you say no. Your mother is very excited about this project and I know we can do everything that needs to be done here and please you at the same time."

If that wasn't a loaded statement, he didn't know what was.

~~~

Regan didn't know what to say or if she would be able to form the words at all. Goodness, but Sawyer Bennett was even better-looking in person than he was on TV. He towered over her much as his father did, but where Max Bennett was big and burly, his son was big and muscular. Her hands itched to reach out and touch one of his biceps to see if it was actually as hard as it looked.

Bad Regan! Knock that off! Clearing her throat, Regan tried to think of something witty to say but got lost in Sawyer's sea-green eyes. The whole making-him-go-away thing was suddenly not appealing at all.

Regan wanted to speak, but his finger was gently caressing her bottom lip. She wanted to be outraged that he was being so forward with her, but she honestly couldn't find the will to fight it. When Sawyer finally pulled his finger away, Regan delicately licked her lips and saw the heat in Sawyer's eyes. He looked at her expectantly, and then she remembered he had asked her a question.

"Okay," she said finally. "I will wait to see what you come up with, but I have to be honest with you, there's nothing that's going to make me get on board with this. I don't want to see anything changed in this house—I love it the way it is."

"Then why sell it? Why don't you buy it?" he asked, genuinely curious.

"For the same reason my mother is selling it: it's too big for one person to live in and take care of. There are four bedrooms, three bathrooms, and we're on almost an acre of property, as I'm sure you've already seen. It's not practical for a single woman to have this much space."

"But someday you'll be married and have children," he countered. "Wouldn't it be nice to raise your children in your childhood home?"

It bothered her that Sawyer seemed to know all the buttons to push. Of course she had thought of that; as a matter of fact, it had been all she had thought of. As much as she hated to admit it, the house did need some work and it wasn't a project she wanted to take on. Plus, she had her townhouse in downtown Raleigh. It was new and sleek and modern, and she didn't have to do a thing to maintain the grounds. That would not be the case here.

No, as much as she hated it, there was no husband, no children in her near future to make the idea of keeping the house feasible. Now she was angry at him all over again for reminding her of *that* depressing aspect of the whole damn thing. Taking a step back, she laid down the rules.

"Look, what I want and what is practical are two different things, and they don't concern you." There was an edge to her voice now, and she noticed Sawyer arched a brow at her tone. "For whatever reason, you and your crew latched on to my mother. Maybe you saw her as some weak older woman and thought she'd be a pushover, or maybe you figured she'd be so thankful to be chosen that she'd allow you to do whatever you want, but I'm here to tell you that is simply not the case. I don't want you here, I don't want your crew here. I've agreed that my mother needs to sell this house because the situation is hopeless. You can renovate the hell out of the house and it won't change the simple fact that it has to be sold. Maybe you should wait for the next homeowners so you can customize the house to what they want, but no amount of renovation is going to give me what I want."

She let out a breath, proud of herself for her little speech—at least until Sawyer stepped so close that they were practically touching. "How do you know I can't give you what you want?" he said in a quiet, husky tone.

Regan had to fight the urge to lean into him and

feel all the hard muscles her eyes had been feasting on. Taking a deep breath, she met his gaze. "Because you want to destroy everything I hold dear. Because of that, we'll never be in agreement." And before she did anything stupid, Regan fled the room.

———~~———

"Weren't they just delightful?" Caroline asked an hour later as she poured herself a glass of wine. She held up a glass to ask Regan if she wanted one, but Regan declined. "I think they're going to come back with some wonderful ideas. Max told me a little about what he was thinking, and if they can pull off even one-tenth of that, I'd be thrilled. What do you think?"

I think I'm ready to poke my own eye out because it would be less painful than this conversation. Taking a seat next to her mother at the kitchen table, Regan reached out and placed a hand on top of Caroline's. "Look, I know you are very excited about this whole thing, but I don't think it's a good idea."

Caroline looked devastated and pulled her hand from Regan's. "Why? How could you even think that? They were both professional and polite, and you've seen the show, so you know what kind of work they do!" she cried.

Regan wanted to point out that Sawyer's stroking of her bottom lip was far from professional but didn't want to open *that* can of worms right now. "It seems pretty pointless to do all this work when we have no idea who the new owners are going to be or what it is they might want to do. Which is why I suggested to Sawyer that maybe they should wait until the house sells to do the renovation."

"You did what?" Caroline shouted, jumping to her

feet. "Why would you do that? You know how excited I am about this, and you sabotaged it? I don't know what's gotten into you, Regan, but I am very disappointed!" With that, Caroline did exactly what Regan had done earlier and fled the room.

Regan thought about following her, but decided the best thing she could do right now was head to her own place, and they could talk about it tomorrow when they'd had some time to think about the situation.

Regan just hoped she'd be able to think about the renovations and not the man who wanted to do them.

Chapter 3

To say that things were tense the next morning would be the understatement of the year. Every time Regan asked her mother's opinion on something, Caroline merely shrugged and said, "Whatever you think is best, dear." Regan *hated* when she did that. By lunchtime, she'd had enough.

"Okay, look," she began as she dragged Caroline into their office. "I know you're disappointed in the way I handled things yesterday, but let me remind you that it was *your* idea to sell the house and you were the one who wanted to sell it 'as is' because you didn't want to do anything to it. I was the one who suggested slapping on a coat of paint to freshen up the place, and I had to twist your arm on that one! Now all of a sudden, you're all psyched to have some silly television show come in and fix the place up!"

Caroline sat quietly and examined her nails while Regan spoke. She waited another solid two minutes before speaking because she knew it would irk her even more. "Yes, I know how I felt when we first talked about selling the house and I know what I said. I'm entitled to change my mind, aren't I? I mean, I didn't carve my opinion in stone anywhere, so what's the big deal?"

"Don't be so dramatic, Mom. Sheesh."

"And just for the record, has it occurred to you how much more the house will be worth once the renovations are done? From the little bit of info Max shared with me yesterday, it sounds pretty darn impressive. I think we are going to benefit from this a lot. Think about it—you technically own half the house. You're going to get half of the profits. Wouldn't you love to have a little extra money in savings? Or for improvements here at the spa?"

"What's wrong with the spa?" Regan demanded.

"There's nothing wrong with the spa." Caroline sighed. "I'm just saying there may come a time when you want to do work here, and it would be nice for you to have a little nest egg. Or maybe you'll want to move out of that sterile townhouse you call a home."

"Now there's a problem with my townhouse?"

Caroline shrugged. "All I'm saying is we have nothing to lose and everything to gain here. Why are you fighting it?"

"Because then it means Dad's really gone!" Regan cried and quickly turned her back so Caroline couldn't see her tears, but she wasn't fast enough.

"Oh, sweetheart," Caroline cooed, wrapping her arms around her. "Is that what this is all about?" Regan nodded. "Your father has been gone a long time, Regan. The house isn't going to change that."

She wiped away the tears that were clouding her vision. "I know that here, in my head, but in my heart… well, it just hurts. Whenever I come home, I walk around the house and I can still picture him there."

Caroline helped wipe the stray tears away. "Your father loved that house, but he wouldn't want it to be a burden to either of us. We had always planned to retire to Florida or someplace warm. It was never going to be a forever kind of house for us."

"Sometimes when I'm there," Regan began, "I'll sit in his recliner and I swear I can still smell his cigars."

Caroline smiled sadly. "Those darn things stunk up the whole house, but he enjoyed them." Taking Regan by the hand, she gently tugged so they were sitting on the leather sofa they kept in the office. "The house is just a place. We'll take the memories with us. You can have the recliner or whatever else you want from the house, but it's time, Regan," she said softly but firmly. "It's time for us both to move on."

"I don't know if I can."

"You're stronger than you think. You're an intelligent woman with a successful business and I know you're going to be okay no matter where this whole house thing takes us or no matter where I end up."

Regan was almost in agreement until that last part registered. "Where you end up? Are you planning on going somewhere?"

"That's just it—I don't know. Once the house sells, I don't have to stay in Raleigh. I can retire like I had planned or move and do something new."

"But what about the spa?"

"Sweetheart, you and I both know I'm not really needed here. I am happy being a silent partner. This will give me an income to keep going, and I'll have the money from the house to get settled someplace new."

This was so not the conversation Regan thought they were going to have. It was like her entire world was spinning out of control, and she had no idea how to stop it. "But what about me? What am I supposed to do?"

"Regan, you're twenty-seven years old, you don't need your mother hanging around you all the time. I think you spend too much time worrying about me and not enough time taking care of you."

"What's that supposed to mean?"

"It means when was the last time you went out on a date?"

Regan racked her brain and she must have zoned out because Caroline jumped in. "Exactly! It's been so long that you can't even remember! It's not healthy. You're a young, beautiful woman. Why aren't you out there dating?"

"This successful spa keeps me quite busy," Regan said defensively. "You know the first couple of years are the hardest, and we're finally at a point where we're making a decent profit. Maybe in another year or so I can take some time off, but for right now, this is the way it has to be."

"Nonsense. I think if the right man came along, you'd find the time."

Regan's mind immediately went to Sawyer of the sexy muscles and rough and callused fingers, and wondered if her mother had a point. Regan had a feeling if Sawyer Bennett penciled her in for a little one-on-one time, she'd readily take the time off.

~~~

Two days later, Regan found herself cooking dinner with her mother. "So, what's the occasion?" she asked as she chopped vegetables for what seemed like an awful lot of steak kabobs.

"Does a mother need an occasion to have her daughter over?" Regan shot her mother a glance that clearly conveyed her disbelief. "Okay, fine. I just thought things have been a little tense with us lately and that it would be nice to have a peaceful dinner together."

How could she argue with that? "Well, it does sound much better than what I was thinking."

"What were you thinking?"

"That you invited me over for the presentation the Bennetts want to do."

Caroline didn't answer right away.

"Mom?"

"You're going to have to hear it eventually, Regan," Caroline said as she busied herself in the kitchen. "You need to accept it."

"I know, but not right now. I'm not ready." She looked around and saw the wine was already open. "Can you pour me a glass?" Caroline nodded, but Regan noticed that something was off. She couldn't put her finger on it, but there was something wrong. "Mom? Are you okay?"

"Hmm? What? Oh, yes, everything's fine, sweetheart. Did you see I booked the Miller bridal party for the full day of pampering? There's twelve in the party. It's going to be wild on that day, that's for sure."

"Did you offer them the brunch package?"

"Of course. I've already made arrangements with Posh Delights to do the food."

"That's awesome. That makes three bridal parties this month." Regan did some quick math in her head. "If we can get the word out on these packages, we'll have a leg up over the competition. Remind me to look into when the next bridal expo is coming to town. We'll see about getting a booth with them to advertise and maybe offer a package to one of the brides to drum up excitement."

"That's my girl, always thinking. You're a natural with the business."

Regan blushed at the praise and was getting ready to pull the marinated steak from the refrigerator when the doorbell rang. "Mom? Are you expecting anyone to join us for dinner?"

"What? Oh, don't worry, I'll get that."

Worry wasn't exactly what she was feeling, but it seemed odd for anyone to be showing up at their door at dinnertime. She was reaching for the platter of meat when she heard male voices coming from the foyer. *Oh no…*

"Regan, you remember Max and Sawyer Bennett, don't you?" Caroline said in a cheery voice, and Regan had the urge to smack her.

"Yes, of course," she said, recovering quickly. "This is a surprise. My mother didn't mention you'd be coming by tonight."

Both men looked at one another and then at Caroline. "Did we get the date wrong?" Max asked.

"No, no, you're right on time. It just slipped my mind to mention it to Regan." Caroline fluttered around the kitchen pouring wine and making small talk, and when she finally made eye contact with Regan, she was sure she got the point across.

Liar, liar, liar.

"I never said they weren't coming tonight," Caroline whispered for Regan's ears only as she walked by.

"I think you're going to be thrilled with what Sawyer's come up with," Max said after taking a sip of his wine. "You've got a good, solid house here, and we've run it by the producers and they're excited about what we've got planned."

Regan gave a half-hearted smile but knew it didn't reach her eyes. As a matter of fact, nothing much was meeting her eyes except for the meat she was meticulously placing on the skewers. She wasn't ready to face Sawyer and his confident smile that screamed *I can win you over with a fancy presentation*.

"Can I help with anything?" Max asked, taking a tray of cheese and crackers from Caroline and placing it on the table.

Caroline was about to tell him no, but Regan took that opportunity to do what she could to remove the Bennett men from the room. "If you wouldn't mind lighting the grill, that would be great." Max went to leave when Regan added, "Actually, Sawyer, I think the tank may be a little low on gas. Maybe you can check it for me? There's a second tank in the garage if you need it." She pasted on a fake smile and thanked them both as they walked out.

Then she rounded on her mother.

"What the hell were you thinking?"

"Oh, for crying out loud. If I had told you they were coming, you would have found an excuse not to be here. This is going to happen, Regan, so you need to get used to it."

"I knew they'd be coming back, Mom, but did you have to invite them to dinner? Isn't that a little unprofessional of them?"

"They have to eat, don't they?"

"Well then, let the network pay for them to eat," she snapped. "Or better yet, maybe let the network pay to take us out to eat! You knew how I felt about this and now you've trapped me into being here."

"Stop with the theatrics, please, and try to have an open mind," Caroline begged. "Please, Regan, this means a lot to me."

"Fine. But if I don't like something about his stupid design, I'm going to speak up."

There was the sound of a male clearing his throat and both women turned to see Sawyer standing in the doorway. "As long as you're keeping an open mind, how can I go wrong?"

"Oh, Sawyer," Caroline gushed, "don't mind Regan. She's a tough sell, but I know you're going to win her over."

"That's the plan," Sawyer said confidently.

Chasing thoughts of Regan from his mind wasn't easy, but somehow Sawyer managed to get through dinner without embarrassing himself and before he knew it, Caroline was looking at him expectantly.

"I am so excited to see what you came up with," she said with a big smile. "Max says it's some of your best work!"

Sawyer looked a little uncomfortable at Caroline's words, but he quickly recovered. With a smile, he said, "Well, if you're ready, I can grab my computer, and we'll tour the house and do a walk-through of what I have planned. You'll be able to see on the screen how it's all going to look."

"Oh, just like on the TV! I love it!"

Regan rolled her eyes at the same moment Sawyer looked over at her. "Open mind," he reminded her as he rose and went to get his stuff. Unable to help herself, Regan watched him leave the room. It didn't matter that she didn't want to like him; the man was one perfect specimen and she couldn't help but appreciate that fact.

Sawyer strode back into the room and held up his full-size tablet. "I was able to program all your rooms in here, so we'll walk around the house while I explain my plans to you, and then you'll see what the finished product will look like on here." When both Caroline and Regan nodded, he continued. "As you know, the main premise of the show is that we do minimal demolition. My plan for your home, Caroline, is to refresh most of what you have. There are minor issues with some cabinetry that I believe can be replaced and there are a couple of windows I'd like to do the same with, but other than that, we're in good shape."

"So you won't be knocking anything down?" Regan asked.

Sawyer shook his head. "I don't plan on it. All the rooms are already good-sized, and I don't see a reason to change that."

"What about if I wanted something changed?" Caroline asked.

"Such as?"

"Well, the fourth bedroom really is too small for any-thing—we always used it as an office, but I was wonder-ing if we could convert it to make the master bathroom larger and maybe do one of those big walk-in closets?"

Both Max and Sawyer nodded in agreement. "It's not normally recommended to eliminate a bedroom because you tend to lose value on the home, but nowa-days everyone is looking for a master suite that really blows you away."

"Wait a minute," Regan interrupted. "Why are we

discussing this?" When three pairs of eyes looked at her like she was crazy, Regan pointed at her mother. "Why are you adding something of that magnitude to this job? I mean, we agreed to a basic makeover."

"Well—" Caroline began, but Sawyer interrupted her.

"If I can add my two cents… Doing a deluxe master suite will add value to the house and therefore, when you sell, you'll be able to list it for a higher price."

Regan wanted someone to love the house as it was; she wanted to be able to walk away and have what she remembered of the house where she grew up remain intact. If everything changed, it would ruin that for her.

"We can come back to this," Sawyer said gently. "Let's walk around and I'll explain the rest of the plans I've come up with."

With every word he spoke and every image he showed them for his design, Regan couldn't help but be impressed. She didn't want to be, but there was no denying that the man had a gift and what he had planned for the house was nothing short of spectacular.

She looked up and caught him watching her and she knew, she just *knew* he was aware of how much she liked what he had presented.

Dammit.

They continued to stare at one another while Caroline and Max talked endlessly about the plans and how wonderful it was all going to be. Regan wished her mother wouldn't gush quite so much; for all she knew the work could come out looking terrible.

And she could sprout wings and fly home.

"So when does all this work begin?" Regan said tiredly. There was no use arguing; this was going to happen. She could only hope now that the whole thing would be quick and painless.

Caroline sat down next to her daughter, squeezed her hand, and smiled. She mouthed "thank you" and then looked expectantly at the Bennetts to hear what their timeline was.

"If we don't have any issues with permits, we've got everything else in place and we'll be able to start the work on Monday," Max replied.

"Monday?" Regan croaked. "That's…that's soon."

Her wide eyes and look of utter shock had him wanting to wrap her in his arms and comfort her.

Only…he couldn't.

Not yet.

He took in the sight of her tonight, wearing a gauzy, sleeveless blouse that hid those phenomenal curves as it landed just below her hips. She'd paired it with white capri pants. She was barefoot and looked more petite than he remembered. Her toes were painted a shade of neon pink, and he noticed the small tattoo on her ankle. *Interesting.*

It must have been covered by her pants the other day and now all Sawyer could think about was what else Regan Amerson was hiding. His mind raced with the possibilities of what he might find the longer he stuck around.

Unfortunately, she was still staring at him, waiting for an answer. His staring at and studying her was starting to become a habit. So rather than say anything right away, Sawyer nodded sympathetically at her. He knew Regan was struggling with this, and he wasn't completely heartless. The network was gunning for the family drama angle, but Sawyer hoped to distract them with plans for the house to give Regan the time she needed.

"And how long will it all take?" she asked.

"The total renovation time should be about four weeks."

He held his breath, waiting to see if Regan had any reaction to that news. Sawyer knew he had to come up with a way to make her a little less annoyed and a whole lot more drawn to him. Unfortunately, his presence in her mother's home represented everything she didn't want.

Good thing he never walked away from a challenge.

Chapter 4

WHEN MONDAY ROLLED AROUND, DEVIN MATTHEWS WAS like a dog with a bone where the conflict between Caroline and Regan was concerned. No matter how Sawyer tried to distract him with new design ideas, Devin kept going back to the mother-daughter angle. When Regan threatened to refuse to sign the paperwork, he had backed down, but Sawyer knew he would have to step in to make sure his show didn't turn into a soap opera.

Sawyer and the crew arrived at 7:00 a.m. on Monday, and Caroline greeted them all in her best work clothes with a great big smile and what seemed like an endless supply of coffee and doughnuts. Introductions were made and soon Sawyer was laying out the plan for what he wanted to accomplish on the first day. Regan was there under protest, but it had been explained to her that there would be times when she was needed for the segment—and the first day of renovations was a key segment.

The scowl on her face told Sawyer how much she was against being there.

Once everyone had their tasks assigned and cameras were set up, Sawyer's opening remarks were filmed. He introduced Caroline and Regan and what the plan was for their home. "Cut!" Devin yelled.

"What's the problem?" Sawyer asked.

"We discussed this. I want you to introduce the project, but I want you to refer to the fact that mother and daughter are not in agreement on this job."

With a low growl of frustration, Sawyer stepped away from the Amersons and pulled Devin aside. "Look, I told you I am not interested in turning this into a damn family drama. If you want to play up that angle, you can find a way to do it during the editing with the voice-overs. I'm not doing it."

Devin glared at him. "I don't see what the big deal is, Sawyer. It's not like I'm asking anyone to play make-believe here—the daughter is clearly ticked off about this." He glanced over at Regan and smirked. "She's sexy as hell, but it doesn't change the fact that she's going to be the villain."

Sawyer could not even begin to understand where the protective instinct came from where Regan was concerned, but before he knew it he had Devin by the collar. "There are no villains here, Dev. If you try to turn this into some kind of freak show, I'll walk."

"You wouldn't dare."

"Watch me," Sawyer snarled and released him. The two men stared one another down, and Sawyer realized they had the attention of most of the crew. "Either we stick to the formula or this is done." A tense moment followed before Devin finally said, "Fine." Sawyer wasn't foolish enough to think this was the end of it, but at least for now they could start filming and begin the renovation.

He led Regan and Caroline into the kitchen. "Okay, ladies," he said, "most of the cabinets in here are in great shape. We're going to take down the doors, paint them, and install new hardware, and then we'll bring in new appliances. This center island, however, does have some issues, so we're going to take it out." They were each handed a large mallet and safety goggles. "Since this is your home," he said with a big grin, "it's only fitting that you get to take the first swing to get this demo going. So when I count to three, I want each of you to take a turn at knocking this island down and then we'll bring the crew in to take over. Ready? One...two...three!"

Caroline took the first swing and knocked off a big chunk of countertop; Regan went next and managed to take down a corner of the cabinet. They each got in a few more swings until the island was gone. Sawyer congratulated them both, and then invited the crew in to take over before ending the segment.

"Great job, ladies!" he said. "We're off to a good start and with the island out of the way, we'll have more room to work in here." He started to tell them what would happen next when Regan handed her mallet and goggles to one of the crew, whispering an apology before fleeing the room. Caroline started to go after her, but Sawyer stopped her. "Let me," he said softly.

It didn't take long to locate Regan in the far corner of the yard. The landscaping was full of beautiful flowers and mature trees, and his heart nearly broke when he found her back there crying with her arms wrapped around her middle. Walking up behind her, he gently put his hands on her shoulders before turning her into his embrace. "What's going on?" he whispered.

It took a moment for Regan to compose herself. When she pulled back and looked up at Sawyer's face she saw genuine concern there, and it just angered her all the more. "You don't get it, do you? To you, that was just a kick start to a demo, but to me, that island was where I did homework for years and had heart-to-heart conversations. That was the place where I would sit and talk on the phone before my father allowed me to have a phone in my room. We prepared meals there, I learned how to cook there, and with a couple of swings of a hammer, it's gone!" She pulled free of his embrace. "So I hope you're satisfied. I hope this earns you ratings, but believe me when I say I will *never* support this idea, nor will I watch your show again. If this is what it takes for you to get your ratings, then I want no part of it."

Regan turned to walk away, but Sawyer reached out and pulled her back. "Believe it or not, this is not how I get ratings. Do you think I want to do this job knowing how much this is hurting you?"

"You don't know anything about me," she said angrily. "I'm nobody to you. This is just a job and you're just jumping through the network's hoops and doing what you're told."

Now he was pissed. "Now, just a minute," he snapped. "You're right, I don't know you, but I was hoping to change that. You'd be surprised if you had any idea of what I've had to go through over this project. They wanted to turn this into a family drama between you and your mother, and I'm doing my best not to let that happen. I've been patient with you and tried to be accommodating, but I don't want to stand here and be insulted on top of everything else."

Unable to resist the hurt look on her face, Sawyer touched her gently on the arm. "I'm sorry this is all so upsetting for you. I'm sorry you have to sell your home, but I am *not* sorry that I'm here or that I've met you." He looked deep into her eyes and saw the exact moment of surprise when she caught his meaning. "I'm not the bad guy here, Regan," he said softly. "If you could look beyond all this and take a little time to get to know me, I think you'll see that for yourself."

Then, because he had nothing to lose, he lowered his head and brushed her lips with his. His first instinct was to take and devour, so long had he been thinking about this moment. But once he felt her soft lips under his and heard her quick intake of breath, he decided on slow and seductive. When Regan leaned into him and lifted her arms to loop them around his neck, Sawyer was lost. No longer was he the one in control. Regan nipped at his bottom lip and tentatively touched her tongue to his. Sawyer's hand glided up into her glorious mane of hair as he anchored Regan to him. Again and again his mouth slanted over hers until he almost couldn't breathe.

With a growl of frustration, he finally broke their kiss, resting his forehead against hers. Sawyer tried to think of something to say, anything that wouldn't break the spell and ruin the moment. Just when he was about to ask if she was okay, Regan's hand snaked into his hair and pulled his mouth back to hers for another searing kiss. It was madness, complete and utter madness as they continued to pull one another closer, until all Sawyer could think about was hauling her behind one of the large oak trees and having her right then and there.

This time it was Regan who pulled away. Her breathing was ragged as she slowly pulled her arms from around him and took a shaky step back. "Wow," she whispered. "What was that?"

Sawyer chuckled. "If you have to ask, then maybe I should try it again." He took a step toward her but Regan held a hand out to stop him.

"No, no—I *know* what that was, it's just…I wasn't expecting it." She looked around the yard, up at the sky, anyplace but at him. "I don't know what came over me," she said shyly. "I'm upset over the house, of course, and—"

Sawyer didn't let her finish. "Don't think this was about the house! I kissed you because I wanted to, because I'm attracted to you. And if you're honest with yourself, you kissed me back because you're just as attracted to me."

Regan crossed her arms over her chest and stared at him in disbelief. "Geez, conceited much?"

"That had nothing to do with conceit, Regan, and you know it. We're both adults and I don't see anything wrong in admitting that there's an attraction here. I want to get to know you better, to spend time with you." He waited to see if she would say anything, but she didn't. "This isn't about the show." Carefully, he reached out and took one of her hands. "We won't even talk about the house or the show. I would like the opportunity to spend some time with you."

Regan eyed him warily.

"Will you at least give me a chance? Can you at least try to separate me from the guy doing work on your house and just see me for me?" he asked solemnly.

"Today is probably not the best day to be asking me this," she admitted. "This is all too much for me, Sawyer. I can't change what just happened between us. I'm not sure I'd even want to, but I can't think beyond this. I need a little time."

Sawyer gently tugged her closer, relieved that she didn't pull back when he kissed her again. "I can spare a little time," he said, then he reluctantly pulled away and smiled at her. "Just not a whole lot of it."

Regan returned his smile, and didn't catch the fact that the camera had been rolling off in the distance.

A week later, Regan was furious. Her mother was out of control with the house and hadn't spent more than a handful of hours at the spa. "This wasn't supposed to be a hands-on project," she reminded Caroline during one of her rare stops at work. "The show is about the work the *crew* does, not the homeowner. Why are you spending so much time there?"

"I'm fascinated by the whole process! It's amazing how much they get done in a day, and Max has let me have a bit of a say in choosing some of the finishes. I think I'm going to High Point with him tomorrow to look at some options for the master bathroom."

"Sawyer had all that designed," she patiently reminded her mother. "You signed off on all his designs. There is no reason to go to High Point, or anywhere else for that matter, because it's a done deal. You jumping in and changing things is just going to drag this job out. Now, in case you've forgotten, we have a business to run here—you have clients you've pawned off on other people all week. Can you please reel it in a bit and give us a hand?"

Caroline sighed dramatically. "Honestly, it's not like I'm needed all that much here. None of my clients have complained—I left them in very capable hands. In case you've forgotten, young lady, there is going to come a time when you will have to run this place without me."

Not this again. "Yes, yes, yes…you're going to retire, I'm going to run the place, blah, blah, blah. While I appreciate not getting the extended disco version of how I can make it on my own, until you retire I would love it if you were here to help me."

Caroline sat down on the office sofa and gave Regan a patient smile. "I don't know if you're aware of this or not, but Sawyer has been getting a lot of grief for not making you appear more on the site. By having me there, at least it's keeping the producer and the network quiet. Now, I'm sorry if you don't like the fact that I'm not helping out here as much, but you have to decide which is more important to you—me being here at the spa or you not having to deal with the home renovations."

Regan rested her head in her hands at her desk and sighed. When had their lives gotten to this point? Things used to be way less complicated, but now it seemed like nothing was the way she wanted it to be. "Fine, go to High Point. Pick out bathroom fixtures and whatnot. I'll handle things here."

Smiling, Caroline stood and walked over to hug Regan. "That's my girl." With a final squeeze, she walked toward the door. "I think you'd really like what they're doing on the house. So far it's much better than I had even imagined. That Sawyer is very talented."

You're telling me. "If you're happy, then I'm happy, Mom." *Just don't ask me to come over there yet.*

"Oh, I forgot to tell you. I made an appointment here for Sawyer for tomorrow morning. He hurt his shoulder on his previous job and it's still giving him trouble. I recommended a deep tissue massage and he was all for it. He'll be here tomorrow at ten." And with that, her mother was gone.

Regan banged her head on her desk. Break time was over. She would be forced to see him and she was certain he was going to ask her about their last conversation, about spending time with one another. Could she go on a date with him? Sure. Could she see herself maybe going out on more than one date with him? Absolutely. Could she see herself having crazy monkey sex with him all over her townhouse?

Oh, yes.

And while yes, all that would be fine and well, the ability to separate Sawyer from his job was going to take a little effort. Not that it was impossible. Regan always hated it when people assumed that all there was to her was a spa owner; she was more than that. She was a woman who enjoyed spending time with her friends or reading a good book, going to the movies, or hiking. When someone only wanted to talk to her about work, it was sort of a turn-off. Couldn't she then take that same attitude with Sawyer and just *not* talk about his work?

If ever there was a time to find out, she guessed it was going to be tomorrow.

<center>~~~</center>

"He's a dude."

"Yes, he is."

"Yeah, that's not gonna happen."

Regan sighed. "Todd is capable of doing this."

"Your mother said you were doing the massage," Sawyer countered mildly.

"Well, since she hasn't been here much, she wasn't aware of my schedule. You need a deep tissue massage and Todd is capable of doing that for you. He has the best hands."

Sawyer clenched his own into fists. "I do not want to be massaged by a guy, Regan," Sawyer said, then looked directly at Todd. "No offense."

"None taken," Todd said, all six-plus feet of him. He turned to face his boss. "It's your call, Rae."

Rae? He has the best hands? What the hell is going on here? Is Regan involved with this guy? Sawyer's mind was spinning. The thought of Regan being involved with another man had never even crossed his mind! He didn't relish the thought of breaking up her and her boyfriend, but neither was he able to deny how much he wanted her. Crossing his arms over his chest, he stared Regan down. "Do you have another client right now?"

"Well, no," she said sheepishly. "But I do have other things to do."

"I can wait until you're done," he said, his lips twitching with a smile because he knew she completely believed him. He would wait all day if he had to if it meant having her be the one to do the massage.

Regan looked from him to Todd and back again. "I've got this, Todd," she said grudgingly. "Why don't you get Mr. Bennett set up in room three, and I'll be in shortly. Thanks." She turned and walked away before Sawyer could see just how uncomfortable she was with this whole situation.

Back in her office, Regan took five minutes to get herself composed. She was a professional, she could do this. She'd massaged her fair share of men since she opened her business and this should be no big deal.

Only it was.

Because it was Sawyer.

Ever since she'd first met him, and especially since their kiss in the yard, Regan had dreamed of touching him. Of course, in her dreams it wasn't in a professional manner; no, those dreams had them alone at her place—or anywhere she could have him—and they were wild for one another just as they'd been last week. Merely the thought of unleashing that kind of passion and have it not be in a public place sent tingles down her spine.

Then again, unleashing that passion in Sawyer any-place was enough to send tingles down her spine.

With a sigh, mentally chanting the alphabet back-ward, Regan headed into spa room three and found Sawyer face down on the table with a blanket draped over his bottom half.

Now, that's a damn shame, she thought and then real-ized she needed to get her professional shield back in place. She went through the questions she asked all her clients—was the temperature in the room okay? Did he want to use an aroma candle? Why was he here?

"I hurt my shoulder last month on a project and it's been acting up again," he said without looking at her. "It's my right shoulder." Regan nodded wordlessly and went to work.

It took less than a minute for her to realize she was in trouble.

He felt even better than she'd imagined, and as soon as she saw her hands on Sawyer's back, all thoughts of professionalism went out the window. It was too easy to imagine her hands on him in a more intimate way, and when he let out a low growl, Regan had to scramble for a way to clear her mind. Unfortunately, her mind wouldn't cooperate.

When she tried to think of her mother's house, she saw the two of them kissing in the yard. When she tried to get angry at what he was doing at her mother's house, she could hear his kind words as he whispered to her. She couldn't remember the damn alphabet—backward or forward—to save her own life. How was she supposed to get through the next...*fifty-five minutes!* Had time simply stopped?

Staring at the clock, Regan worked on Sawyer's shoulder until her fingers started to go numb, and that's when she heard it. Her hands stilled for a moment before she went back to massaging him, and heard it again.

"No sex noises," she hissed.

Sawyer raised his head and sleepily looked at her. "Excuse me?"

"You were just making sex noises. Stop that. It's not allowed."

He flashed her a wicked grin. "Regan, you have no idea what kind of noises I make during sex, but I'm glad to see where your mind is heading."

She stepped away from the table and stared at him. "That is *not* where my mind is heading! I was working on your shoulder and you started...you know, moaning."

"What can I say? You hit the sweet spot."

"The sweet spot?" she croaked and prayed he wouldn't raise himself up anymore. As it was he was braced on his elbows, so now she had a fine view of his chest and yes, it was mouthwateringly good.

Making a *tsking* sound, he shook his head. "Regan, certainly you are aware of sweet spots," he said with a voice that melted over her like butter.

Oh, she was aware of them all right. As a matter of fact, he had several of hers tingling with just the sound of his voice. *This is bad*, she thought. *Bad, bad, bad!* "That's neither here nor there—the fact is that if a massage seems to be getting a client…aroused, then we stop."

"The only one who thinks I'm aroused is you," he said sweetly and put his face back on the pillow. "But if it makes you feel better, I promise not to make a sound."

Regan watched as he got back into position, cursing herself. She should never have agreed to this; it was totally unfair that he seemed unaffected by this while she was practically standing in a puddle of her own drool.

Charming.

With a good mental scolding, she went back to the task. Fifteen minutes later, she needed him to roll over so she could work on the shoulder from the front, and then it was her turn to let out a small sound.

"Excuse me?" Sawyer asked, not opening his eyes. "What was that noise?"

"I don't know… I don't have any idea what you're talking about," Regan lied and went right to work on his shoulder, hoping to distract him.

"Now, I'm no expert in the noises you make during sex, but I'm pretty sure that sounded like a sex noise."

Regan instantly removed her hands from him and stepped back. "I think we're done here."

Slowly, Sawyer sat up, looked at her and then at the clock. "I believe I still have another thirty minutes scheduled."

"Well, if you want to use them, I'll send Todd in to finish," she said tartly. Why was this happening to her? She never made purring or sex noises outside of the bedroom. Why did it have to be here and now with Sawyer?

"Okay, okay," he said, sensing her discomfort. "That was out of line and I'm sorry. I was just kidding with you. It was a little too quiet in here and I just thought I'd say something to break the tension. It was in poor taste and I'm sorry I offended you."

"I just don't think—"

"What you're doing is really helping," he said. "Please, Regan. I won't utter another word until you're done. Scout's honor." He held up his hand and gave her his most innocent smile.

Her lips twitched with the urge to smile back. "How do I know you were a Scout?"

"You can ask my dad, he'll tell you. I went from Cub to Eagle, and he'll be happy to share with you some of the adventures we had." Remembering his promise to stop talking, he lay down and pretended to zip his lips.

And then Regan's soft laugh was the only sound in the room.

―⁕―

The sound of Regan's chuckle made him feel good.

The sensation of her hands on him again left him feeling more than that. As a matter of fact, this position left him rather…vulnerable. If he didn't do something to distract himself, he wouldn't have to worry about sex noises but the tenting of the blanket. His mind scrambled for what to do and he was relieved when Regan chose to talk.

"Speaking of your father, I was wondering why he needed my mother to go with him to High Point today."

"What are you talking about?"

Regan continued to work on Sawyer's shoulder, and then his neck, and up to his temples as she spoke. "Mom said she wasn't coming in today because Max invited her to go to High Point with him to look at bathroom fixtures." Sawyer frowned and Regan removed her hands. "I'm sorry, was that too much pressure?"

"What? No, it's just…well, Caroline called off the crew today because she said she had a migraine. She called late last night and asked if we could take the day off." He opened his eyes and saw the confused look on Regan's face. "Does she normally get migraines?"

She nodded. "They don't happen very often and it's been a while since she's had one, so I guess it's possible. It just seems weird that she would have made the call last night. Normally if one hits at night, she's fine the next morning."

"Maybe she needed a day of no noise in the house just in case," he suggested but could tell Regan wasn't totally convinced. "Do you think she's lying?"

"No, it's not that, I'm just concerned. Normally when she's not feeling well, she calls me. When she was here yesterday, she was pretty excited about looking at bathroom fixtures. If she wasn't feeling well, she should have called to let me know she wasn't going."

"She knows you're busy, Regan. Maybe she didn't want to bother you."

A laugh escaped before she could stop it. "Clearly you don't know my mother very well. She keeps me up to date with everything going on in her life whether

I want to know about it or not. Did your father mention taking her with him to High Point?"

Sawyer thought for a moment. "No, he never mentioned going to High Point because we have all the fixtures ordered. It would be a pointless trip." The look of worry on Regan's face had him sitting up and adjusting the blanket around him. "I don't think you have anything to get upset about, Regan. Dad didn't mention anything to me, but maybe Caroline misunderstood where he was taking her?"

"Something's not right."

"Okay, okay, let's just say something's not right. What exactly are you thinking?"

"I'm thinking your father is hitting on my mother!"

Sawyer laughed. "Are you kidding me? If anything, Caroline has been flirting with Max! And even if they are flirting or whatever, why is it such a big deal?"

"Have you talked to your father today?" she asked instead of answering his question.

"No. After he called me last night to say Caroline wasn't feeling well, he said he was going to take the day to get caught up on paperwork. He knew I was coming here, so there was no reason to talk this morning."

"I don't like it."

Sawyer raked a hand through his hair and sighed. "Look, if it makes you feel better, I'll take a rain check on the rest of the massage and you can go check on Caroline."

The look on her face told him she'd rather do anything *but* give him a rain check. It was really a little amusing how well he was getting to know her, but he knew she'd never admit it out loud. "Fine," she said grudgingly. "Rain check. I recommend you go back to your hotel and soak in a Jacuzzi if they have one. It will help with the muscles. Drink a lot of water and take it easy for the rest of the day. We'll figure out later when to reschedule." She was speaking fast and was about to spin out of the room when Sawyer grabbed her hand and gently pulled her toward him.

"Hey," he said quietly, seriously. "I'm sure everything is fine. You need to relax, okay? I don't like the thought of you driving when you're upset." He gently tugged her hand to get her to step into the space between his blanket-covered thighs. "Do you want me to go with you?"

The sincerity of his words and the silk of his voice were nearly hypnotic, and for a moment Regan forgot what they were talking about. The heat coming off his body combined with the clean, masculine scent of him had her putting a hand on his shoulder—and not for medicinal purposes. He whispered her name as he reached up and cupped the back of her head and brought her lips to his.

There was no hesitation this time; they had been here before and it was everything Regan remembered and more. She stepped in as close to him as she could get and loved the way it felt when his free arm banded around her waist to keep her there. This time she did purr. She didn't care if he heard it or what he thought it was, because she was needy and turned on and hoped he felt the same way.

A quick wiggle of her hips told her he did.

Her hands raked through his hair and it felt glorious.

Sawyer wore it a little longer than conventional style, but it was silky and wonderful and made him look all the more rugged. His name was a breathless sigh as he moved his mouth from hers and traveled the expanse of her throat. The hand at her back began to work its way under her shirt—the feel of his hands on her skin made her knees buckle.

"You never answered my question the other day," he said between kisses.

Question? He could think about questions right now? "Refresh my memory."

He chuckled deep in his throat and continued to torment her with his mouth and his tongue. "Time together. You. Me." He gently bit down on her earlobe and felt her body shiver.

"Oh, that," she said, angling her head back to capture his lips with hers again. It didn't take long for the conversation to come to a halt while they feasted on one another. Sawyer lifted her so she straddled his lap on the massage table, his hand settling on her bottom and gently squeezing.

"I want you," he murmured.

"This is crazy," she whispered back. "I barely know you."

"There's a solution to that." He pulled his head back and did his best to put a little distance between them. "I'm serious, Regan. I can't believe how much I want us to spend some time together, to get to know each other."

She looked at him as if he was speaking a different language. Here she was trying to think of a way to lock the door and have her way with him without her staff hearing and he was talking about generally spending time together. Couldn't they go for the two birds, one stone option? "I kind of like the time we're spending right now," she said in her sexiest tone, and was rewarded when Sawyer pulled her in for a kiss.

"Come back to the hotel with me. It's not far from here." He leaned in and licked a trail down the side of her neck to her collarbone, where he gently sucked. "We can be there in ten minutes. We'll even check in with Max and see what's going on later." Regan stiffened in his arms.

Dammit.

That was the slap of reality right there. Regan scrambled down from his lap and righted her clothing. "What the hell am I doing?" she asked herself out loud, turning and pointing a finger at Sawyer. "You! I cannot believe I forgot about checking on my mother because of you!"

Sawyer stood and pulled the blanket around his waist with one hand while the other reached out to her. "Okay, I think you need to calm down. We can still check on your mother—"

"No, *we* can't. I will. I can't do this with you, Sawyer. Every time I'm around you, I seem to forget myself."

"There's nothing wrong with that. Please, Regan," he said softly as he stroked her arm. "Call Caroline, make sure she's okay, and then…come with me back to the hotel." He leaned his forehead against hers, his eyes searching hers. "Please."

She'd never had a man beg for her before, and while she should have been pleased, she was too distracted. "I can't," she said apologetically. "This just isn't the right time. I need to go and…and do this." And before he could stop her, she fled the room, leaving him standing there wrapped in a blanket, with a raging hard-on and his world turned upside down.

———∿∿∿———

Thirty minutes later, Regan pulled up in front of her mother's house and was relieved not to see any construction vehicles. Her last visit had involved her parking on the street and wading through a sea of power tools and men in hard hats. There are worse things for a single girl to have to wade through, but still.

"Mom?" she called out as she let herself in. Caroline's car was in the driveway, so unless she had gotten over her migraine and gone with Max to High Point after all, she should be home. Regan walked around and marveled at all the work that had been done. As much as she didn't want to like it, things were coming together beautifully. She called out half-heartedly one more time while she ran her hands over the granite countertops in the kitchen. It was stunning, absolutely stunning, and her heart ached that some other family was going to get to enjoy all this.

Off in the distance she heard her mother's voice and let out a sigh of relief. If her mother was talking, then she no longer had a headache. Slowly, Regan made her way to the master bedroom, stopping to admire the new paint colors and the way the hardwood floors were refinished.

Caroline giggled, and Regan smiled as she wondered who her mother must be talking to on the phone. Reaching for the door handle and pushing it open, she said, "Hey, I heard you were down with a—*OH MY GOD!*" Regan didn't know who was more surprised by her appearance—Caroline, herself, or…Max Bennett. "*Mom?*" she said with disbelief.

To their credit, Max and Caroline did their best to cover up as Regan cringed and walked out, hyperventilating. "Ohmygod, ohmygod, ohmygod," she chanted as she made her way quickly back to the kitchen to grab her purse and keys.

"Regan! Wait!" Caroline called as she came into the kitchen. "What are you doing here?"

"What am I doing here?" Regan asked incredulously. "What exactly are *you* doing here?"

"I live here, Regan. And don't be cute."

As much as she wanted to, Regan couldn't bring herself to look directly at her mother. "Believe me, I am not trying to be cute. You told me you were going to High Point today, and then Sawyer comes into the spa and tells me you called off the crew because you had a migraine. So, since I was concerned about you, I decided to stop by and see if you needed anything."

"Well, that was sweet of you," Caroline said calmly and Regan looked at her in shock.

"Yes, I think it was sweet of me to come and check on someone who blatantly lied to me! What are you doing, Mom? What is going on with Max?"

"Regan, please. I may be old but I'm not stupid. You're no virgin, so stop with the outrage. You know exactly what Max and I were doing. I really don't want to have the birds and the bees talk with you again."

Yes, death would be preferable to this, Regan thought. "I'm not looking for the birds and the bees, Mom. I'm wondering when you got...involved with Max and why you were keeping it a secret."

Caroline shrugged. "It wasn't anyone's business. We're both consenting adults and in truth, Regan, it has been a long time since I've had sex." She giggled shyly. "I had forgotten how wonderful it could be."

"Ew, gross, Mom!" Regan slapped her hands over her ears. "I do not want to hear this."

Caroline knocked her hands away. "Cut that out, Regan. You're a grown woman and I think you can handle hearing that your mother had sex!"

"Oh, I not only heard it, I saw it too. Let's not forget that!"

"Well, if you can't be mature about this, then maybe you should leave."

Regan's eyes grew wide. "*Me?* I should leave? How about asking Max to leave? I'm pretty upset here!"

"Yes, yes, poor you," Caroline cooed. "I don't mean to be rude, Regan, but…you really, um…interrupted us and I'd like to go back inside. We'll talk about this tomorrow."

"Talk about what, exactly?" Regan asked, her voice nearing hysteria. "Your sex life?" Caroline guided her daughter to the door. "You can't be serious."

"As a heart attack," Caroline said as she gently shoved Regan out the door.

It was hard to describe which emotion held the top spot at the moment: shock, anger, outrage, disgust, or… jealousy. For crying out loud, was it possible she was jealous because her own mother had a sex life and she didn't? Was that too twisted to consider? And the fact that not only did she have a sex life, but she had one with a Bennett hit a little too close to home.

Regan should be having sex with a Bennett right now, but instead she'd walked away from that possibility to check on her liar-liar-pants-on-fire mother! Storming over to her car, Regan refused to look back at the house.

She climbed into the vehicle and pulled out of the driveway as if the hounds of hell were after her.

Where to go? Where to go? Regan's mind was racing. The responsible thing to do was to go back to the spa and run the business her mother clearly had no interest in. The irresponsible part of her wanted to track Sawyer down and finish what they had started earlier.

Except she was mad.

Really mad.

Really, *really* mad.

Ever since the Bennett men had come into her life, nothing had been the same. Regan liked things simple and predictable. Surprises were never her thing. And yet, ever since Caroline had met Max in the home improvement store, life had been one surprise after another, and not all of them were good. Well, that didn't matter; the fact remained that Regan hated surprises and she wasn't sure if she could take many more. Between the changes at the house, her mother's *affair*, and Regan's own out-of-control feelings for Sawyer, she didn't think she was capable of making any kind of rational decision on anything at the moment.

So instead of following her heart and going to the damn hotel and throwing caution to the wind, she headed toward home. "Well," she said out loud, "it wouldn't hurt to call him and rant a little about what I just saw." Upon all the contract signings, Sawyer had given her his business card with his cell number on it. While stopped at a traffic light, she hit the Bluetooth and dialed his number. His sleepy voice greeted her.

"Hey," he said. "Is Caroline all right?"

Regan debated for all of five seconds on that one.

Hell, if she had to witness what she did, he was damn well going to hear about it. "As a matter of fact, she is," she responded with a hint of sarcasm.

"What's going on, Regan? You don't sound right."

"No? You don't think so?" she asked snappishly.

"Regan…"

"So I got to the house and was all set to make some tea or something light for Mom to eat and I was admiring the granite countertops—"

"They came out great, right?"

Regan ignored his request for praise and continued on with her story. "—when all of a sudden I heard Mom talking. I figured she was on the phone and I took it as a good sign, that maybe she was feeling better."

"And?"

"I had called out to her twice and she didn't answer, but I figured that was because she was on the phone. You know, maybe she didn't hear me. Well, imagine my surprise when I opened the door of the master bedroom and found your father in bed with my mother!"

"*No!*" he said with disbelief. "Oh, geez, Regan, what did you do?"

"What do you think I did? I turned and ran from the room. But not before I got quite the view of naked limbs all wrapped around one another!"

Reagan heard Sawyer sigh in exasperation. "Are you okay?"

"No, I'm not okay. Dammit, Sawyer, I told you something was up! Now I'll have to stab out my own eyes to get that image out of them!" A shudder racked her body and her stomach roiled at the thought of it. "I just cannot believe—"

"That your mother has sex?" he asked.

"Don't say that! She said that too and I just don't want to think about it or hear it because then I start seeing it again!"

"Okay, okay, clearly you're upset. Why don't you come over and we'll grab something to eat and you can calm down?"

Didn't he realize that if she showed up at his hotel, the last thing she'd want to do was calm down? Did earlier today leave no impression on him at all? If she actually did show up, it would be with the sole purpose of stripping him naked and having her way with him!

Hmm... The idea had merit. Maybe that's what she needed: a night of wild, animalistic sex to help her unwind. She could do a more intimate massage than what she'd done earlier, and then she'd let Sawyer have his turn running his hands over her, and maybe then—

"Regan? Are you still there?"

"Huh? What?" *Damn dirty mind.* "No, I think I'll go home and do my best to...forget this day ever happened."

"Look, I really don't think going home and being alone obsessing about it is the answer. If you don't want to come to the hotel, let me come to you. We'll get a pizza, watch a movie...whatever you want to do to distract yourself."

Oh, if only he knew how much she wanted to say yes. Regan had no doubt in her mind that Sawyer could distract her. Hell, he could probably distract her for *days*, but was jumping into bed with him while she was upset the right thing to do? Or would she wake up tomorrow feeling worse than she did right now?

You've seen the man half naked, Regan! There is no way he can leave you feeling worse. While her inner voice no doubt had a point, Regan was not one to do something so wild, so impulsive…so tempting that it was all she could think about! She heard Sawyer clear his throat and realized there had been nothing but dead air for several moments.

The devil in her reminded Regan of how hot they had been this afternoon in the massage room, whereas the practical woman in her reminded her that sex was not a cure-all.

She hated her practical side, because it spoke louder to her.

"I really do appreciate the offer, Sawyer, but I have to pass." There. She'd said it. Now he'd probably be a gentleman and wish her a good night, maybe offer to let her call later on if she needed someone to talk to, yadda, yadda, yadda.

"I guess I understand," he said mildly. "After all, the way you threw yourself at me earlier, you probably don't trust yourself to be alone with me. No worries. I'm sure I'll be seeing you around before the reno is done."

Regan thought that surely she must be hearing things. "Excuse me? What did you just say?"

"You heard me. I don't blame you, really. We're attracted to one another and you tend to…you know, lose control with me whenever we're alone. I'm sure that's not what you need right now after such an upsetting incident at your mom's, so I completely get why you think it's…safer…to be alone."

Regan looked around her car in disbelief and hoped someone else was hearing this, because she certainly couldn't believe what Sawyer was saying! What a conceited, arrogant jackass! Which was exactly what she called him because she couldn't think of anything else to say at the moment.

"You can call me all the names you want if it makes you feel better. I don't mind. But right now, I'm going back to soak in the Jacuzzi like you suggested. It works wonders. I should follow up with a hot shower, too, you said, right?"

Now he wanted professional advice on his injury? Did this man have no decency at all? Did he think everything was about him? Regan was still at a loss for words. "Yeah, sure," she mumbled. "Whatever."

"Have a good night, Regan," he said silkily, and it had Regan's teeth on edge. She may have wished him a good night in return, she couldn't be sure. Once the call ended, she punched the steering wheel. She called him every name in the book and still couldn't believe the ego on him. Did he honestly believe she was the one who couldn't control herself when they were alone? Didn't he realize that he always made the first move? That he was the first one to reach out and find an excuse to touch her?

She drove on, replaying the few short times they had been in one another's company, from the first time when he couldn't take his eyes off her breasts to the way he'd pulled her onto his lap when he was practically naked.

Bastard.

If anything, Regan had no choice but to respond to his…mauling her! Yes, that's what it was. He. Mauled. Her. Repeatedly. And she had no doubt she could easily be in his presence without touching him or kissing him or even wanting to rip his shirt off just so she could marvel at the pure male perfection.

She was better than that.

She was the strong one.

She was…pulling up in front of his hotel.

What??? How had that happened?

Putting the car in park, Regan sat there and contemplated her options. No one had to know she had mistakenly shown up here; Sawyer certainly didn't need to know. It was still a mystery how she had gotten here, when clearly she had wanted to go home to be by herself. That was her plan. It was a good plan.

Well, she thought, *as long as I'm here…*

With a sense of pure determination, Regan got out of the car and walked boldly into the lobby. Without stopping at the front desk, she immediately went in search of the pool. Sawyer had said he was going back to the Jacuzzi, so it made sense she'd find him there.

But she didn't.

Now she had no choice but to go to the desk and ask for his room number. With more bravado than she actually felt, she got the information from the clerk and headed up to the sixth floor. The entire way up in the elevator, Regan reminded herself of Sawyer's cocky words and let herself ride the wave of anger all the way to his room. It would do her good to hold on to that feeling so she wasn't distracted by her attraction to him and find herself doing exactly as he claimed—throwing herself at him.

Sawyer's room was at the end of the hall. She knocked forcefully on the door and nearly fell through into his arms when he opened it up. Luckily she caught herself in time and found herself staring at six-plus feet of wet male in clingy black swim trunks. Her mouth went dry, and she searched her brain for some kind of witty or snarky comment to make to prove she wasn't here to throw herself at him. But she never got the chance. Before she knew what was happening, Sawyer snaked an arm around her waist and pulled her flush up against him, slamming the door behind them.

"It's about damn time you got here," he muttered before covering her mouth with his.

Chapter 5

REGAN WAS TOO SHOCKED TO RESPOND INSTANTLY, BUT once Sawyer had her pinned up against the wall and his tongue licked her bottom lip, she was lost. Dropping her purse to the floor, she wrapped her arms around Sawyer's neck, and managed to pull back enough to say, "How did you know I'd come here?"

He had a dirty comeback for her but didn't dare say it. "Wishful thinking," he panted as he dove back in for another hot, wet kiss. Sawyer knew he hadn't played fair; he'd essentially dared her to show up and be alone with him. It was childish and a huge risk, but he was relieved it had paid off. Regan was here in his arms and he wasn't about to let her run off anytime soon.

She tore her mouth away. "Just for the record, you kissed me first."

Sawyer chuckled. "Just for the record," he said and bit down gently on her earlobe, "I know." He went for her lips again but she ducked her head to the side. "What?" He said a silent prayer she wasn't reconsidering her options or regretting being here, because he didn't think he'd be able to survive if she left again.

"I just…" Regan said. *What?* she screamed to herself. *What could you possibly have to say right now that is better than having Sawyer's hands and mouth all over you?* "I just wanted you to know I didn't come here for this."

Sawyer's smile turned wicked as he leaned into her, resting his forehead on hers. "I know. But I also know I seriously goaded you into being here." Very tenderly, he placed a gentle kiss on the tip of her nose. "I wanted you here that badly."

When his deep green eyes met hers, she was lost. "I wanted to be here, too," she admitted shyly.

"Are we done talking?"

Regan nodded. "Most definitely." She wasn't aware a man could move so quickly. Sawyer bent at the knees and wrapped her legs around his waist as he pressed fully into her so she could feel how glad he was that she was there with him. A soft gasp escaped her lips right before he claimed them again. It was hot and urgent. Regan knew there was nowhere else she'd rather be than right here, right now, with this man.

It all became clear in an instant that this was destined to happen; from the first moment she'd seen him, touched him—even in the most casual of ways—it was all leading up to this moment. Regan had never felt such an instant connection to a man, such an urgent need. She needed Sawyer like she needed her next breath.

And right now, she was gasping for her next breath because of all the wonderfully wicked things he was doing to her. Sawyer's hands skimmed up her sides, her back still braced against the wall. He gently teased the undersides of her breasts and she almost came undone. She gasped his name before uttering, "Bed. Now. Please." Although the whole up-against-the-wall thing could be interesting, right now Regan wanted to feel the weight of Sawyer on top of her.

Naked.

No sooner were the words out of her mouth than she found herself sprawled out on the king-size bed with Sawyer stretched out beside her. "Promise me you're not leaving," he said, staring intently into her eyes. "Tell me what you want." His words were spoken so low and so deep they were nearly a growl.

Regan was never one to be bold, but right now, under the intensity of Sawyer's gaze, she was. Slowly, she lifted her shirt over her head and faced him in her simple black skinny jeans and a hot-pink lace bra.

"You're killing me," he said, entranced by the mere sight of her. His finger lazily traced the outline of the cups of her bra and he hissed when her nipples pebbled as he breathed over them. "From the first time I saw you in the sparkly T-shirt, I wondered what you were wearing underneath." He removed his finger from her breast and reached up to trace her cheek. "This is better than I fantasized."

"You fantasized about my underwear?" she teased.

Sawyer leaned forward to trace the line of one full cup with his tongue. "No," he said simply. "I fantasized about you."

Then they were done talking. Again. Regan lost track of how the rest of her clothes fell away. She couldn't remember how she found the strength to have Sawyer stop touching her while she removed his swim trunks. But the next thing she knew they were both sighing with pleasure at the full skin-on-skin contact from head to toe.

Sawyer's hands were everywhere, his mouth never far behind. Regan found herself on the brink several times, but Sawyer wasn't ready to let her come yet; he seemed content to take his time loving every single inch of her. "Sawyer, please," she begged, needing him more than she'd thought possible and finding she didn't want to wait another moment to feel him inside her.

They were on the same page, because in the next instant he was kneeling between her legs, sheathing himself with a condom. His expression told her he was just as close to the edge as she was. "I'm not making any promises, Regan," he said seriously, dipping his head to suckle on one of her nipples. "I feel like I've waited a lifetime for you. This is going to be fast and it's going to be hard, but I promise you, the next time will be better."

He didn't wait for a response; he surged forward, his eyes locked on Regan's. When hers closed, he commanded her to open them back up and to look at him. He needed to watch her and wanted her to see into his very soul as he loved her. She was wrapped tightly around him, and Sawyer swore when he was buried as deep as he could possibly get.

Perfect.

It didn't take long for Regan to climax once he was inside her, crying out his name over and over as wave after wave of pleasure crashed over her. Never in her life could she remember an orgasm as intense as what she was feeling. The longer he moved inside her, the more sensitized she became, until she wasn't sure the feeling would ever end.

As promised, once Sawyer found his rhythm, he all but lost control. She was too…everything. The feel of her, the sounds she made, the look in her eyes as they glazed over when he drove into her harder and faster… he was on sensory overload. His eyes started to shut. He was so close. Just another thrust—

"Look at me," she whispered, and that was all it took. His gaze shifted to Regan's and he lost the battle for control, filling her with everything he had. Their bodies were sheened with sweat. As soon as the waves of pleasure began to subside, Sawyer leaned down and kissed her and knew it wasn't enough. One time wouldn't be enough; hell, he was pretty certain a lifetime might not be enough.

He settled lightly on top of her and if anything, Regan wrapped herself even more snugly around him. It took a while for their breathing to settle and when Sawyer felt he could move, he rolled over and tucked Regan at his side. She placed a hand over his heart and sighed contentedly. When her breathing returned to normal, she said, "Wow."

Sawyer pulled her close and relished the feel of her beside him. "You were pretty 'wow' yourself." He kissed the top of her head, unsure what else to say. He had played dirty to get her here, but there were certainly no regrets. The fact that Regan was silent had him worrying that she did. Reaching up, he tucked a finger under her chin to force her to look at him. "You're not sorry you're here, are you?"

Regan shook her head. "No," she whispered. "I'm not. I'll admit I've never quite done anything like this, but…"

"Well, you were a natural," he teased, and she pinched him. "Hey!" he yelled with a laugh.

"I don't mean I've never had sex before, I just never…lost control with anyone so entirely. I don't know what you do to me, Sawyer Bennett, but I think I like it." She smiled up at him and Sawyer was lost. She was so beautiful, she fit him so perfectly, and he knew he had finally found that something elusive he hadn't even been aware he was searching for.

"Well," he said silkily, "if you liked that, then you're going to love this." And lightning-quick, he had her on her back again and was ravaging her mouth. "I believe I made some grand statement earlier," he said when he finally released her kiss-swollen lips. "Something about the next time being better."

Regan pretended to have to think about it. "Oh yeah," she said, deep in thought. "I think I remember something about that." She shrugged. "I'm not sure you can do much better than what we just did. After all," she said and had to stop herself from giggling, "I thought it was okay."

"Okay?" he sputtered. Pinning her hands up above her head, Sawyer gave her a devilish grin. "Sweetheart, I can guarantee you by the time I'm done, okay will be a distant memory."

Her legs snaked out to wrap around his waist. "I'm counting on it."

The sun was setting and Sawyer was curled around Regan's back. He wanted to know more about her, so he jumped in at the only place he could think of to start. "So tell me," he said quietly, placing a kiss on the side of her neck, "why won't you buy your mom's house?" Her body stiffened at the mention of the house, but his whispered question had her softening against him.

"I have a place of my own," she said simply.

"Regan…" he said and heard her sigh.

"A lot of men are intimidated by the fact that I own

my own business," she said, and when Sawyer didn't respond, she continued. "I'm an independent woman. I take pride in the fact that I was able to start a business that is successful and thriving."

"As you should."

"Well, you would not believe how many men find that to be a bad thing."

"I don't get it."

"Most men claim they want an independent woman, but if she's successful or more successful than them, it's not such a good thing." She thought briefly about the last guy she had dated and how much he used to complain about all the time she spent at the spa. In the end he had asked her to choose—she chose the business and never looked back. "Then there's the fact that I'm a little old-fashioned."

Sawyer's brow furrowed with the last comment. "What does that have to do with anything?"

"Well, I don't know if that's the right way to put it, but…if a man has a problem with me owning my own business, then he's definitely going to have a problem if I own my own house too."

"You own your townhouse, don't you?"

Regan nodded. "I do, but it's small, perfect for one person, maybe a couple, but not someplace you'd stay long term."

"So you think that's safe? And men don't find it intimidating?"

"Oh, I know they don't. Owning the townhouse shows that I'm practical, possibly good with money. But if I were to own a home the size of my mother's, I don't see a guy feeling good about moving into it. Like maybe I would have more of a say in things since it's *my* house."

"I'm sure there are men out there who wouldn't mind that at all."

"Sure, men who still live at home with their mommies and are looking to skate through life with everyone else taking care of them. I believe a marriage should be a partnership, but the man should be the head of the household."

"Ah, there's the old-fashioned coming through."

Regan nodded. "I know it's silly and maybe an outdated way of living, but…my parents had a great marriage. My mother worked until I was born, and then she was a stay-at-home mom for years. She went back to work part-time once I was in school, and when I got older, she went back full-time. My father passed away when I was sixteen, and from that point on, she and I were a team. The only reason I was able to open the spa was because of my mother. She's my partner. My father's life insurance policy helped us get started. As independent as we both are, I still can see every day that she's not comfortable being in control of everything. She misses my dad."

"Well, of course she does, Regan. She obviously loved him."

"It was more than that—they were one. I want that. I want to find someone who's not in a competition and there's no mine or his—there's simply ours."

"Nothing wrong with that," he said—although it bothered him that she might be telling him all this because he wasn't that person. He automatically hated the man she deemed worthy of being made one with her. Sawyer already knew it could, and should, be him.

He just had to convince Regan of it.

Chapter 6

A WEEK LATER, SAWYER WAS DEEP INTO THE RENOVATION when Devin hovered over him, scowling. "Is there a problem, Dev? We're on schedule and under budget. What's with the face?"

"It's boring."

"Excuse me?"

"You heard me. This is boring. We had it all planned out that there was discord between the mother and daughter, and the daughter has been a no-show through two weeks of renovations. I'm not happy, Sawyer. Get the daughter here and get me some drama to put into this episode or we'll be doing contract negotiations sooner than expected." He turned to walk away but Sawyer stopped him.

"Are you threatening me?"

Devin faced him. "I told you from the get-go what I wanted out of this particular episode."

"And I told you I wasn't doing that."

"Well, you're not in charge—I am. And the network wants to mix things up a little. Everyone likes to see a little family drama. Get the daughter here, because I happen to know for a fact that if anyone can, it's *you*."

Sawyer dropped the hammer he had been holding. "What is that supposed to mean?"

Devin stepped in close so he and Sawyer were nose to nose. "It means I am aware of how you've been spending your spare time. I've got some great B-roll going. Get the daughter here to snap and gripe at her mother or at you. Otherwise the drama we add will have to do with your extracurricular activities. Do I make myself clear?" He didn't wait for an answer before storming off and telling the camera crew they were done for the day.

Sawyer felt pure rage. Max came strolling in and knew immediately something was wrong. "Sawyer? What's going on?" He placed a hand on his son's shoulder, but it was quickly shaken off.

"Nothing," Sawyer said with a near growl and reached for his hammer to get back to work.

Max spun him around. "Dammit, what is going on? What did Devin say to you?"

Sawyer glared at him. "Nothing that concerns you, okay?" When Max went to stop him again, Sawyer snapped. "Look, what do you want from me, Dad?"

"What I want is for you to talk to me. You're clearly upset. I know I haven't been around much this last week and…well, you're probably wondering where I've been."

Now Sawyer had an idea of how Regan must have felt when she walked in on his father and Caroline, because just thinking that his father was going to talk about it had him breaking out in a cold sweat. He held up a hand to stop the words before they came out. "I know where you've been—you've been spending time with Caroline Amerson and that's fine. You don't owe me any explanation."

"How did you know? We've been very careful."

"Regan told me," he said and knew he had just opened up a huge can of worms. Max blushed and Sawyer had no doubt they were both feeling a level of discomfort they had never experienced before. "It's okay, Dad. I'm fine with it."

"I don't think Regan is."

"She was…shocked. But that's probably because of the way she found out."

"Yeah, that was awkward. Caroline was a little embarrassed, to say the least, but once she shooed Regan out the door, she was fine. She's an amazing woman, Sawyer. I—I don't normally get too serious with a woman, but I think I could change with Caroline. If she'd let me."

Sawyer nodded because he completely understood. He felt the same way about Regan. How ironic—was this a case of like mother, like daughter or like father, like son? It was too bizarre for it to be a case of them both. If Devin wanted some drama, they had it going on here in spades!

Max looked at his son. The question was there in his eyes, but he knew he had to voice it out loud. "Does it… does it bother you? The thought of me getting serious with someone?"

With a shake of his head and a chuckle, Sawyer said, "Of course not, Dad. You deserve to be happy, and I think Caroline is great. It's a little fast, sure, but sometimes that's the way it happens, right?" Sawyer knew firsthand that it did because if he had his way, things would be a lot more serious with Regan.

They had spent every night together since she had come to his hotel, but now they spent the time at her place. The first time Sawyer had shown up there, he saw what she meant about it not being practical for more than one person. The space was cozy, and that normally worked in his favor, but the space was too small for him to be in the kitchen and watch Regan cook the way he liked to do. There was a breakfast bar where he had to be content sitting on a stool with a granite-covered island separating them.

He smiled, thinking of some of the things they had done on that granite-covered island.

Max, oblivious to what was going on in his son's mind, kept talking. "I know you weren't happy about doing this job, but the way things have turned out, I can't be sorry. But," he said and then hesitated, "I think the time may be right for me to start easing out of all this."

Sawyer's head snapped in his father's direction. "What?"

"I've been in construction for a long time. I'm not getting any younger, and I'm seeing now that there are a lot of things I'd like to do—I'd like to travel, and not just from job site to job site. I've worked hard all my life, Sawyer. I think it's time to retire."

He almost wished they'd had the sex talk instead. "You've only known Caroline for all of two weeks. I don't get it." Sawyer was thoroughly confused, and this was the last conversation he'd thought he'd be having with his father.

"Like you, I've been a little less than enthusiastic about the direction of the show. Working with Devin has turned into a real chore. I know you're not happy, and it's safe for me to admit I'm not either. Maybe it's time for both of us to move on."

"Great," Sawyer snarled, throwing the hammer down. "That's just freakin' great." He stormed from the house and out into the backyard, because suddenly the walls seemed to be closing in on him. It didn't take long for Max to find him.

"I'm not saying I'm leaving tomorrow, Sawyer. I'll finish out my contract, but I won't be re-signing, that's all. We can still work together from time to time, but, well, I think you are capable of doing this on your own."

Raking a hand through his hair in frustration, Sawyer turned toward his father. "I'm not mad at you, Dad, that's not it. I just feel like I'm at a crossroads here and unlike you, I can't retire. If I don't stay with the show, then what? What am I supposed to do?"

Max reached out and put a reassuring hand on his son's shoulder. "Whatever it is you want to do, Sawyer. You are extremely talented, and I think if this show were to end tomorrow, you would move on to bigger and better things." He stopped and considered his next words. "Maybe with a different schedule, you might even consider finding someone, getting married, and settling down. I don't want you to spend your whole life alone like I did because you're too afraid to put the time into a relationship."

Sawyer desperately wanted to share with his father about the turn in his relationship with Regan, but he would need to discuss that with her first. Between all of the suddenly secret relationships, the show, the renovations, and Devin's threat, he wasn't sure which topic would upset Regan the least.

And if there was one thing Sawyer wanted more than anything, it was to make sure Regan was happy.

Later that night, Sawyer sat across from Regan while she prepared dinner for them. "How can that be a quick sauce when you're starting from scratch?" he asked. "A quick sauce would be opening a jar."

Regan rolled her eyes. "Let me tell you something, the day you find jarred sauce in my pantry, just shoot me. Clearly I'll have lost the will to live."

One of the many things Sawyer was learning about her was that she never did things the easy way. Tonight's dinner was just another example. She didn't use processed foods, she made almost everything from scratch, and where her business was concerned, she took on most of the responsibilities there, as well. Hell, she didn't let him do anything for her, and it was starting to wear on him.

"How about tomorrow night I take you out?" he suggested lightly, taking a pull from the chilled bottle of beer she'd had waiting for him when he arrived.

"Why?" she asked, chopping tomatoes and adding them to the saucepan that was already simmering with fresh garlic and olive oil.

"Because I want to," he said. "I'd like to take you out on a date."

Regan put down the knife and stared at him. "A date?" She made it sound like it was a foreign concept. "Why?"

He stood and walked around the counter into her tiny kitchen. When he was right in front of her, Sawyer placed both hands on her hips and pulled her in close to kiss her. "Because you're an old-fashioned girl and I've been less than old-fashioned with you." His gaze was intense as it held hers. "And for that I am sorry."

Something inside Regan softened, along with her

heart, hearing the sincerity in Sawyer's words. How was this possible? It had only been a matter of weeks and yet she couldn't seem to stop herself from falling hard and fast for him. It was out of her comfort zone and totally out of character for her, but standing here and looking in his eyes, nothing had ever felt more right.

"It's not necessary, you know," she said shyly.

Sawyer placed a finger under her chin, tilting her head to look at him. "To me it is. I should have started by asking you out on a proper date rather than daring you to come to my hotel."

Regan smiled. "I didn't mind."

And in that instant, Sawyer knew she was telling the truth. He glanced over at the stove. "I think we need to take a look at that before it gets ruined. It smells fantastic."

Without leaving the circle of his arms, Regan turned off the stove, moving the pan from the burner before facing him again. "It will keep." Lifting up on tiptoes, she snaked her arms around his neck and kissed him, letting him know without words just how much he meant to her and that dinner wasn't what she wanted right now.

Sawyer smiled against her lips and rocked his body into hers, feeling her returning smile at his arousal. "This won't." Regan shrieked as he lifted her up and carried her from the kitchen toward the bedroom. "We'll discuss date plans later," he promised as he kicked the bedroom door closed.

～～

Sated and exhausted, Sawyer finally felt like he was able to breathe again and kissed the top of Regan's head. She was sprawled out on top of him and if it were possible, they'd stay like this forever. He loved the feel of her, the way her hair always smelled like something tropical, and how her heart felt beating next to his.

He was in deep.

Regan disentangled herself and found a comfortable position beside him. "Forget the sauce on the stove— let's order pizza," she said sleepily.

"Food? You're thinking of food right now?" he teased.

"What can I say…you exhausted me and now I need food but don't have the energy to cook."

"Then pizza it is," he said and reached for his phone. An alert sounded to let him know he had a text message. Regan lifted her head in time to see Devin's name on the screen.

"Is everything okay?" she asked, stretching beside him.

It was now or never. "Devin is a little…peeved, shall we say, that you're not at the house more and making a scene. He was hoping for some big drama."

She pulled back and looked at him. "Why? What's the big deal?"

Sawyer didn't want to pull at this thread right now; things were so perfect, so peaceful, and the thought of bringing up a sensitive subject was not how he hoped to cap off the night. The look on Regan's face, however, told him she wasn't going to let it go. "From the get-go, the network was excited about the fact that they had a story line behind the renovation."

"What do you mean by a story line?"

"They liked the fact that you and your mother were

not in agreement over the house and they wanted to use that angle to boost ratings on the episode." There. He'd said it.

"So...what were they expecting? I would have chained myself to the fireplace so you wouldn't knock it down, or maybe lock myself in the bathroom in protest? Or maybe I'd just be a screaming lunatic?" Each word was said calmly and evenly, but he could tell she was barely holding back.

"Something like that." Sawyer stroked her cheek. "I told them from the very beginning that I wasn't doing it. I didn't want to go that route, and I have done everything I could to keep it from happening."

"Then what's the problem? Why are they still so intent on doing it?"

"Because they say the show has gotten boring and predictable, that my designs aren't enough to hold the audience's attention."

"Oh, Sawyer," she said sympathetically. "They're wrong! What you do, what you create, is magnificent! You know I was against this from the beginning, but now, seeing what you've done with the place? It's blown me away. I never thought the house could look like that. In just a few short weeks you've created a transformation that is beyond my comprehension!" She sat up and pulled the sheet up to cover her breasts, smiling at his boyish pout.

"I'm trying to be serious here," she admonished. "You have an incredible gift, Sawyer. If you never did another episode of *The Bennett Project* there would still be people lined up for miles wanting you to do what you do in their houses! Don't let Devin or the network intimidate you into believing you're not enough—the fans watch your show because of you, not because of some conjured-up drama."

Oh, how he loved how passionate she was about this. He didn't want to tell her about the ultimatum, he didn't want her to be hurt, but now he had to do so.

Regan stared at him when he finished and, for the first time, Sawyer had no idea what she was thinking. With a nod of her head, she leaned forward and kissed him on the cheek. "So, what do I need to do? Come to the house and bitch about paint colors? Point out something you've done and how it's not what I wanted and then tell Mom she's made a mistake?"

"I don't want you to have to do any of that, Regan. You shouldn't have to—"

"Shh…" She placed a finger over his lips to stop his words. "You're not asking me to do anything. If my showing up a couple of times to gripe will keep the network off your back, then I'll do it. Mom and I can come up with a doozy of a fight scene, if that's what you want."

Sawyer shook his head in disbelief. "You're amazing, you know that?"

"Me? What did I do?"

He kissed her with everything he had and maneuvered Regan so she was beneath him. "Everything," he said as he aligned their bodies and entered her. Their lovemaking was normally wild and full of passion; now, though, for what she was willing to do for him, he wanted to show her tenderness.

There were no words for what he felt at that moment. Sawyer's body gently rocked into hers, and the laziness of it did nothing to diminish the feeling behind it. She ran her hands up and down his back, softly panting his name, and he couldn't help but want to keep them like this.

Sunlight began to fade and shadows crossed the room, and still he loved her. Sawyer lost track of time; the only thing he could do was feel. Every time he thought he'd let her jump off the peak, he'd start again. Their breathing and the rustling of the sheets were the only sounds in the room, and it was perfect.

When finally Sawyer had given her all he had, when he felt it would be impossible to go any further, he allowed them both to have their release as he looked at her and whispered, "You're everything."

Chapter 7

SAWYER WASN'T SURE WHAT HE EXPECTED, BUT THE SIGHT OF Regan storming around the house was almost comical. She would touch a wall or test a cabinet door and look at him and say, "Really?" Sarcasm was dripping from her tone and he had to do his best not to laugh.

"Is there a problem?" he asked.

"Well, it's just that when you said 'renovation,' I thought you'd actually be *doing* something. I mean, I could have painted the cabinets. Hell, I think monkeys can be trained to do that. Why aren't you replacing them?"

He had hoped she would have chosen to gripe at her mother; they had more practice. Sawyer wasn't sure how to fake arguing with her. He stared at her defiant stance, arms folded over her chest and one dark brow arched with annoyance. "Well, you see, Regan—" he began.

"It's Ms. Amerson," she corrected tartly.

Sawyer had to turn away and clear his throat so he didn't outright laugh at her tone. When he composed himself he began, in his best contractor voice, to explain the logic behind their project and how they always rehabbed what they could to save time, costs, and labor.

"Seems to me like it's a cheap way to go," she said simply and walked away.

Sawyer watched her leave and figured it was a good stopping point for today. Devin was grinning from ear to ear as Regan stormed from the house, and Sawyer had to fight the need to go after her and make sure she was all right.

"Now, that was what I was looking for," Devin said. "Was that so difficult?"

Sawyer glared at him. "It wasn't a matter of difficulty, Devin, this just isn't what we do. I don't argue with homeowners and I don't like to make a mockery of their lives."

"Well, it's time you got onboard the reality TV train because this is what people want to see." He dismissed the crew before turning back to Sawyer. "Tell her to turn up the bitch factor tomorrow. I'd like to see her unleash on her mom next."

Then he was walking out the door and Sawyer had to do everything in his power to keep from throwing something heavy at him.

What had he gotten himself into?

Within fifteen minutes the house was fairly quiet; there were just a few members of his crew scattered around working on finishing up their projects for the day. Stepping outside, Sawyer reached for his phone and dialed Regan's number. As soon as he heard her voice without any of the animosity of earlier, Sawyer felt himself relax.

"Are you okay?" he asked. "I know you didn't want to be a part of this. I swear I'll do what I can to move things along so maybe we can get done ahead of schedule."

He expected her to agree with him, or to maybe complain about the whole thing. What he didn't expect was her laughter. "I have to admit, I really wanted to ignore the whole process, but that was a little fun."

"Fun? You thought that was fun?"

"Hell yes! The look on your face when I said that it was the cheap way to go was priceless!"

He grimaced at her mirth. "I still don't see what's so funny."

"Oh, lighten up, Sawyer. I did what the network wanted, end of story."

"Well…"

"What? What's the matter?"

"I think we've only managed to poke the bear."

"Meaning what?"

"Devin loved what you did today, but he wants more."

Silence.

"Regan? Are you still there?"

"How much more?"

"He loved how you got in my face, but now he wants the mother/daughter fight."

Regan considered his words. "I really hoped it wouldn't have to come to that."

"Me either. God, Regan, I'm so sorry. I'll tell him no, that you're not coming back. He'll be pissed but—"

"I didn't say I wouldn't do it," she corrected. "I was just hoping to be done with it by now. Contrary to popular belief, I do still have a business to run and I have better things to do than spend my time making a spectacle of myself for the camera."

The words were said lightly but Sawyer knew it was the truth. She did have other things to do that were more important than his show and the renovations. "I'll handle it, Regan. Don't worry about it."

"I'll be there tomorrow," she said. "But after that I've got to get back to work."

Sawyer dropped his chin to his chest. "I don't deserve you," he said quietly and smiled when she chuckled.

"Yeah, but you dared me and now you're stuck with me."

He still felt as if he had come out with the better end of the deal.

———~~~———

"Oh, this could be fun," Caroline said the next morning as she sipped her coffee sitting across from Regan in their office.

"I don't know if we'll be able to do this with a straight face."

Caroline shrugged. "There's always that possibility. We've never been able to have a really down and dirty fight without one of us breaking out in laughter. What does that say about us?"

"That we love each other and we know most arguments are about stupid things."

"Maybe…" She paused and studied Regan. "So, before we decide on what we're going to fake fight about, should we get the real fight out of the way?"

Regan's brow furrowed. "What are you talking about?"

"Me and Max. You walking in on us. Any of this ringing a bell?"

Oh…that. "Are we going to fight about it?" Regan asked while silently praying the situation would just go away.

"Well, I don't know if we have to fight about it, but I think we do need to talk about it at least."

"Why? What is there to talk about? Max is a great

guy, the two of you hit it off, and now you're…" *Doing it!* "Dating."

The look of disbelief and a hint of disappointment said it all. It wasn't going away. "Regan, you and I have always been a team. We talk about everything. You can't sit here and tell me you're fine with what you walked in on. I know you too well. Just say what's on your mind and get it over with."

"Honestly, Mom, there is *nothing* on my mind where that's concerned. I've blocked it out."

"That's not healthy. So you walked in on me and Max while we were making love. You saw us both sweaty and naked! He's got a fine ass though, doesn't he?"

"*Mom!*" Regan threw her hands over her ears. "This is so not the conversation I want to have!"

"Why not? We're both women! I may not be a genius, sweetheart, but I know you've had sex. Why can't we talk about our sex lives? Which reminds me, you haven't been out on a date in a while. Everything okay? Don't you miss the sex?"

"Oh. My. God. You did *not* just ask me that!"

"Yes I did! Gosh, I had forgotten how wonderful sex was! It had been years since I'd had any and now, let me tell you, any opportunity Max and I have to be alone, I just—"

"LA-LA-LA-LA-LA," Regan chanted loudly, hands back over her ears. "I'm not listening, I'm not listening!"

"Oh, for crying out loud." Caroline stood and walked over to her daughter, pulling her hands away from her ears. "Cut that out. I am trying to have a serious conversation with you!"

"Don't you have a friend you can talk about this with? Someone who isn't, I don't know…me?"

"All my friends are married and have been for most of their lives. Sex is pretty much over for them. I'm just discovering it again. I need to talk to someone about it."

"Why? Why would you need to talk about…it?"

Caroline sighed. "Your father was the only man I had ever slept with," she said and reached over to smack Regan on the head when she started to put her fingers back in her ears. "So uptight. I have no idea where you got that from." She hugged Regan. "Loosen up a little. Find yourself a nice man and have a crazy night of sex just for the hell of it!"

"Okay, that's it. I can't talk to you anymore," Regan said as she moved away. "I don't know who you are anymore! What has gotten into you?"

"Max!" Caroline said with a wicked grin.

Regan stopped in her tracks and glared at her mother. "I don't know how to respond to that, so I'm not going to."

"Don't go away all mad like that, Regan. Pouting is not attractive on a grown woman."

"I am not pouting, Mom," she said with an eye roll. "I'm just not ready for us to have this kind of relationship."

Caroline approached and pulled her in for another hug. "I'm always going to love your father, you know. This isn't going to change that."

It was a miracle Regan's eyes didn't simply fall out of her head from the excessive eye-rolling. "I didn't think that. I never thought that, Mom." She pulled back.

"I really am happy for you and Max. I like him a lot. I just don't need all the details of how much you like him, okay?"

With a sigh and a nod, Caroline agreed. "I would totally listen if you wanted to talk about your sex life."

"Yeah, I'll just take your word for it, because I am never going to test that theory."

––––––

As promised, Regan and Caroline put on a good show, and luckily Regan had a little bit of anger left from their earlier discussion to keep from breaking out in laughter. They had argued over moving, and she played the wounded daughter part to the hilt. By the time the cameras stopped rolling, Devin seemed damn near giddy.

"Thank you, ladies," he said with a big grin on his face. "I think that should do it until the big reveal when Sawyer and the crew are all done."

They made small talk until Regan could stand it no longer and excused herself. "I really do need to get back to the spa," she said, shaking his hand— immediately, she wanted to pull hers back and wipe it off. The man was sweaty and smarmy and she didn't get a good vibe from him at all. She managed to smile politely and say goodbye, then asked Caroline to walk her out to her car.

"I don't trust that guy," she said when they were out of earshot. "I can't quite put my finger on it, but he just really rubs me the wrong way."

Caroline nodded. "Max was telling me how both he and Sawyer are thinking about moving on and being done with the show. Max sooner than Sawyer. He hasn't come right out and said it, but I think Devin is a big contributing factor."

"Yeah, that's what Sawyer said too." The words came out so easily she forgot her mother wasn't aware that she was spending time with Sawyer outside of the show.

"When did you talk to Sawyer about the show? I thought you didn't like him?"

"Oh, um…when I was here yesterday to film my dislike of the project, he and I talked for a bit. I guess he sensed my unease, and then he told me he was thinking of moving on from the show." Honestly, Regan didn't know why she didn't just come out and tell her mother about her relationship with Sawyer, but for now she was enjoying having him to herself. With Max and Caroline dating, she suspected they'd find themselves sucked into all kinds of double-dates or family time together.

"You really should get to know him, Regan, he's a very nice man. Single, too."

Great, just what I need, my mother playing matchmaker. "Can we please just get through one traumatic event at a time?"

"How is getting to know Sawyer going to be traumatic?" Caroline asked innocently.

"Mom, please. I know you are all happy and glowy right now and that's wonderful. I don't need you playing matchmaker for me and setting me up on dates. When I want to go out and meet someone, I will."

"I'd like to have grandchildren before I grow senile."

Seriously, Regan was going to need to see the eye doctor for this uncontrollable eye-rolling.

"Grandchildren? Now you're going to play the grand-children card?"

With a frown, Caroline conceded. "You're right. It's just that you know the old saying—when you're in love, you want everyone around you to be in love. It would be wonderful if we both fell in love and found the men of our dreams. I just want you to be happy, Regan."

"I am happy, Mom. Right now I'm focusing on the business and getting this house done and sold."

"I still wish you would reconsider and take it for yourself. I know how much you love this place, and for all my flippant remarks about it, I think it would be wonderful for you to have it."

"We've been over this a million times, Mom. I think I'll take that as my cue to leave. Max is waiting by the door for you. Go and play twenty questions with him." She leaned in and kissed her mother on the cheek. "I love you and I appreciate all your concern for my lack of a love life, but honestly, I'm fine with it." Before Caroline had a chance to make another comment, Regan quickly got into her car and drove off. She wished she had gotten the opportunity to have a minute alone with Sawyer, but she was sure she'd talk to him later.

As if he was there reading her mind, her cell phone rang and she smiled when his name came up. "You ran out of here pretty quick," he said by way of greeting. "Are you all right?"

Regan relayed the conversation she'd had with her mother and was a little annoyed at how much enjoy-ment Sawyer was getting out of all of it. "It's not funny, Sawyer," she said when he finally stopped laughing. "Between having to hear about her sex life and her wanting me to find one, I may have to go into hiding. She's killing me."

"So why didn't you let her set us up? I think it would have been pretty comical having to pretend we hadn't already seen each other naked."

"Really? That's what you're going with?" she asked with mock annoyance. "I simply want her to enjoy being a woman who is dating a man that she's crazy about. And she is crazy about your dad." She hesitated and hated how she was fishing. "I hope the feeling is mutual."

"If you want to know how he feels, Regan, all you had to do was ask."

She sighed. "I'm asking."

"He's crazy about her, too. He talked to me the other day and he wants to retire so he can spend some time with her."

"That's sweet," she said with a smile in her voice. "How do you feel about it? The retiring part, not the spending time together."

"Dad's always worked hard. It's been just the two of us for most of my life, and just like you, I think it's time for him to focus on himself. Don't get me wrong, it will be a bit of an adjustment not to work with him every day, but as long as I know he's doing something that makes him happy, I'm fine with it."

"Wow, you sound way healthier about this than I do." And it was true. She could only hope that what Max and Caroline were experiencing was the real deal and not just a matter of being naive. She shared that thought with Sawyer.

"They're adults, Regan. They've both been in

relationships before. I think they know the difference between love and infatuation."

"I hope you're right, I really do. I don't want her to get hurt." While she knew nothing was guaranteed and they were talking about their parents, Regan couldn't help but compare their relationship to that of their parents. Was she really falling in love with Sawyer, or was she just infatuated? What if it was just a strong case of lust?

"What are you doing now?" he asked, breaking her train of thought.

"I'm heading back to the spa. I have to work a little late because we have a bridal party coming in tomorrow for a morning of pampering. I love doing the whole group thing. Unfortunately, it takes a lot of prep work."

"How so?"

"I make little goody bags for each of the girls. I have a list of items I get from the bride or maid of honor ahead of time that tells me the color scheme for the wedding, and so I make sure the spa is decorated a bit in those colors. I do what I can to really personalize the environment in celebration of the big day."

"Wow, that's impressive. How late will you have to work?"

"I'm not sure." She looked at the dashboard clock and saw it was almost four. "If all goes well, I should be done by nine."

"Do you have anyone available to finish up my shoulder massage? The last couple of days have been rough."

"What if I told you Todd was the only one available?" she teased.

"The way I'm feeling right now, I'd accept it. That's how uncomfortable I am."

Her concern for him was instantaneous. "Tell you what, why don't you come in at eight thirty and I'll take care of you."

"Are you sure? I don't want to take you away from what you need to be doing."

"Are you kidding? This will give me motivation to get through all the preparations."

"We were supposed to go on a date, if memory serves," he reminded her.

"We will, just not tonight. It's not a big deal, Sawyer, you don't need to take me anywhere. I enjoy just spending time with you."

Sawyer felt humbled by Regan's admission and with a promise to see her later, he hung up and did a final walk-through of the house for the day. Along the way he made a mental checklist of what needed to be done, where they were lagging behind, what materials needed to still be ordered...

Designing and building came as naturally to Sawyer as breathing. From the time he was a little boy and Max had helped him build his first birdhouse, there was no doubt of what he wanted to do with his life. His father had always been a carpenter, and Sawyer had apprenticed under him all through his teens before heading off to college to learn the design aspect in more detail. Max would have been capable of teaching his son how to do it all, but he also knew it would only serve to benefit Sawyer's future for him to have a college education.

Locking up the house for the night, Sawyer drove back to the hotel, took a hot shower, and then sank down on the bed to relax before heading over to A Touch of Heaven and to Regan.

Regan.

This whole relationship had hit him like a ton of bricks, and Sawyer was in uncharted territory. He was falling hard and fast and if he was reading things correctly, Regan was too. Every minute they shared together felt…right. The more he got to know about her, the more he wanted to know. In return, Regan seemed just as anxious to get to know him. They had so much in common and no one could argue about their compatibility in bed; they were explosive.

Still, as confident as he felt saying all this in the privacy of his hotel room and to himself, the thought of broaching the subject of a future to Regan terrified him. He didn't want to rush her, nor did he want to be the one to jump in and say "I love you" first only to have her say she didn't feel that way.

Sighing, he glanced over at the clock. It was barely six. His body ached from head to toe. As much as he hated the thought of making Regan work late so he could get a massage, it had nothing to do with the physical aspect of their relationship and everything to do with his overall well-being. He hoped Regan didn't feel like he was taking advantage of her.

He really needed to take her out properly. Standing, he walked across the room, grabbed his laptop, and sat down at the desk. He went online and researched the local restaurants and places of interest. While his initial reaction had been to call Caroline and ask what Regan liked, he knew they weren't ready to share their relationship status with their parents.

So he was on his own to plan this little romantic excursion.

Never in his life had Sawyer put any real effort into wooing a woman. He had dated his share of women, but it always came easily to him and he had been happy to go with the flow, let the women take the lead. Plus, he wasn't really interested in taking anything into the long term. He found whoever he had been dating attractive and they, in turn, felt the same way, enjoying one another's company for as long as it lasted and then amicably moving on.

He didn't want to move on.

He didn't want Regan to move on.

He resumed his internet search. Ideally, he wanted to go big but not too big. A weekend away would be his preference, but before he booked such a thing, he'd need to know Regan's schedule.

Inspiration struck. For now, they would have a night out at a restaurant where they could have a nice dinner, listen to some jazz music, and then do the Art Walk around Raleigh. He'd have all the information he needed regarding a weekend getaway to the coast at the ready so as soon as he confirmed when she had time off, he could book it. It was perfect, and Sawyer reclined back in the chair and high-fived himself.

He, Sawyer Bennett, was going to sweep Regan Amerson off her feet. He couldn't wait to stroll with her in the moonlight, holding her hand and hearing her talk about anything and everything that made her smile.

He was hoping he fit somewhere up high on that list.

―∾―

Regan looked around the spa to make sure she hadn't missed anything.

Dimming the lights and getting the blankets and pillows ready, Regan heated some lavender oil in the diffuser to get the scent just right. In the corner she turned on some soothing music, but would leave it up to Sawyer if he would prefer the sound of the ocean instead. For now the music calmed her. While she knew he was coming to her for medicinal purposes, any time Regan thought about running her hands all over Sawyer's body was enough to get herself worked up. The man was simply magnificent.

Over the last several weeks she had gotten to know Sawyer and the more she learned, the more she liked. Was it possible to fall this quickly? Was Sawyer even thinking about a relationship beyond the job, or was this possibly the way he did relationships? That thought did not sit well with her. From everything she had learned about him, Sawyer did not seem like the type of guy who dated based upon the job he was doing. At least she hoped he wasn't, because otherwise where would that leave her? At the end of the job, was she supposed to thank him for a fabulous home makeover and the orgasms and wave goodbye?

Yikes. That was a depressing thought.

On the other hand, if Sawyer felt for her even a little of what she was feeling for him, how would their relationship work once he moved on? Long-distance relationships were never a good thing and rarely succeeded. Would she be able to stand it if he was on another job and met a woman like herself? Not to say that she didn't trust him, but did she know him well enough to spend a large amount of time apart and not question what he was doing in his spare time and who he was spending it with?

She was pathetic. Pushing all thoughts of Sawyer romancing every female homeowner in the Northeast aside, Regan took one last look at the room before stepping out and grabbing a bottle of water. She was starving; she hadn't taken the time to grab any dinner and if Sawyer was on time, they wouldn't be leaving the spa until after ten. Her stomach growled in protest. She could only hope she would make it that long.

As if reading her mind, Sawyer appeared at the door of A Touch of Heaven with a smile and a bag of take-out and Regan almost wept at the sight of him. Once he stepped in she locked the front door, smiling at the wicked glint in his eyes.

"Everyone gone?" he asked, waggling his eyebrows.

Regan swatted at his arm. "Yes, everyone has gone home for the night and since we'll be in the back, it's for safety purposes that I'm locking the door. I don't need anyone wandering in here to rob me blind while we're in the back."

"Well, that's a whole lot less sexy a reason than I was going for," he teased.

Rather than banter with him, Regan heard her stomach let out an unladylike growl and she asked, "What's in the bag?"

"I figured you worked until you lost track of the time, so I grabbed us some Chinese food. I wasn't sure what you liked, so I stuck to the basics, but I bought a variety."

Regan leaned in and kissed him thoroughly. "My hero."

She led him back to her office and set up a makeshift dining area for them. Sawyer could tell she was tired; he saw the shadows beneath her eyes and felt a pang of guilt that he was going to make her keep working tonight for his sake. They sat on opposite sides of her large desk and he reached across for her hand. "We can do this another time if you'd rather call it a day."

Regan waved him off. "Are you kidding? I've been waiting for this all afternoon," she said with a sexy grin. "It's not very often that I get to kick off my own shoes and relax while I'm giving a massage."

"You can kick off anything you want. You don't have to stop at the shoes." His tone was playful but his mind began to conjure up all the possibilities. Before he got too wrapped up in the fantasy, he pushed it aside and decided to ask about the rest of her day.

Regan told him about the preparations for the bridal party and how busy she expected the next morning to be. "They're scheduled to arrive around ten and there are six of them, including the bride. It will be a four- or five-hour event."

"For manicures and pedicures?" he asked.

"Oh, no," she said, waving a chopstick at him. "By the way, dumplings are my favorite." Reaching into the container, she took another one out and ate it before continuing. "If it was only mani-pedis, we'd have the girls in and out of here in about two hours. I would have enough staff to make that happen. No, besides the mani-pedis, the girls are getting facials and massages. Full-service pampering party."

"Sounds like a lot of work."

"It is, but I've got the entire staff coming in tomorrow,

including my mother, so we'll have a nice rotation going." Regan sat back and sighed with pleasure as she ate. It was the perfect meal, and if he had asked her what she wanted, she would have picked everything Sawyer had bought. "I really can't thank you enough for this. I didn't realize I was so hungry until we opened everything up."

"So how does your mom feel about the house? Have you talked to her about it? She's been around the job site more than I thought she would and I'm curious if she's doing it because of my dad or because she's concerned about the work."

"It's definitely because of Max. You wouldn't believe the fuss she put up over having to come in tomorrow. She was going to miss sharing Max's coffee break." There was that eye roll again. "It's like she's a seventeen-year-old girl."

"And that's a bad thing?"

"No, definitely not a bad thing, but it is taking some getting used to. My mom has always been pretty stable and reliable, and for the most part pretty straitlaced. Since she's met Max, I've heard more about her personal life than I'm comfortable with and she's starting to change her appearance."

"How?"

"It was small at first, a bolder nail color and some jewelry. Then it moved on to a sassier wardrobe. She was never one to fuss with clothes, and now suddenly she's all spunky and wearing things that are trendy. She showed me a push-up bra she bought and I'm not going to lie to you, it was a little racier than what I wear."

One dark brow arched at her.

"Whatever you're thinking, stop it," she said as if reading his mind.

"What? What did I do?" he asked innocently.

"Don't think about my mother's underwear. That's just creepy."

Sawyer dropped his chopsticks, nearly choking on his food. Once he was done coughing, he looked at her with disbelief. "Regan, I was *not* thinking about your mother's underwear. I *was*, however, thinking about yours. I wouldn't mind us sampling a little something from the lingerie store."

"You men are way too easy," she said with a laugh and then called dibs on the last dumpling. "What is the point of spending a fortune on ridiculous scraps of silk and lace when they get tossed aside almost as soon as you see them?"

"Maybe. But let me just say that thinking about you in those ridiculous scraps of silk and lace is enough to make me break out in a sweat." Then he winked at her before picking up his chopsticks again.

"As for the house," Regan said, changing the subject, "she's very pleased. She's excited to see all the potential you found in it. While it's been a little more emotional for her than she expected it to be, she keeps commenting on how some lucky family is going to love all the improvements." With one final bite of fried rice, Regan pushed the food away and sighed with contentment. "She sings your praises daily, if that makes you feel any better."

"It does," he teased. "But seriously, I'm glad she's enjoying what we're doing. It really is a great house and other than being a little outdated, there weren't any lurking issues with the structure or plumbing or anything. Whoever built that house built it to last."

A look of sadness came across Regan's face and Sawyer cursed in a low voice. "Hey," he said softly, once again reaching for her hand. "I'm sorry, I didn't mean to upset you. I enjoy talking about the job I'm working on and it just sucks that this one has us at odds."

"You don't have to be sorry, Sawyer. I need to let it go and move on. If I were at a different place in my life, I might not feel this way. But it is what it is and I have to deal with it. Hell, who knows? Maybe my mom and Max will move in together and they'll decide to keep it."

"That would be interesting. Dad has a great house on the coast near the Outer Banks he's been working on for ages. He's never had enough time off to spend doing the things there he wants to do. It would be nice for him to finish it and then they could split their time between the two places."

"Look at us planning our parents' future!" Regan said with a laugh and then stood and stretched. "If I sit any longer, I may fall asleep. Let's clean up and get you on the table so we can work the kinks out of your shoulders."

Sawyer pulled Regan into his arms and kissed her, slowly, sweetly. When he raised his head, his expression was full of tenderness. "I meant what I said earlier, if you'd rather call it a day I would understand. You're exhausted and I don't want to be the cause of you not feeling well."

Standing on tiptoes, Regan placed a kiss on his nose, then took him by the hand and led him toward the room she had set up for him. "You go and get yourself ready while I clean up the dinner mess."

"Regan—" he began.

"Oh, shush," she said and gave him a push in the direction of the room. "Give me five minutes and I'll be in there. No arguments." She didn't wait to see if he had moved but went about cleaning up her office and clearing her mind of any talk of business.

When she finished, she walked to the last door on the right and gently knocked before going in.

Sawyer was on the table, face down with the blanket draped over his hips. Without asking, Regan switched the music over to the sounds of the ocean and kicked off her shoes. There was no reason to speak; words weren't necessary. She got everything she needed and poured the scented lotion in her hands and began to work on Sawyer's back. He let out a low moan of approval and she smiled. It would have broken the mood to talk about sex noises as they had the last time, so for now she enjoyed listening to the sounds of the waves and Sawyer's sounds of pleasure.

By the time Regan reached the injured shoulder, she could tell Sawyer was relaxed. The feel of his muscles and the sight of his tanned skin was having the opposite effect on her. She was anything but relaxed. The more she touched him, the more she heard his moans and sighs of pleasure, the more Regan wanted to please him.

Silently, she took a step back and rethought her original plan for the night. Just when he was about to lift his head and ask if everything was okay, Regan was back to running her hands over him as professionally as she could. Leaning in close, she worked her hands from his lean hips all the way up to his scalp. Gently, she scraped her nails along his skin, moved back down, and started again. She did this several times before returning her attention to his shoulder.

"You can roll over now," she said softly and stepped back to give him room to move. Sawyer's expression started out sleepy, but once his eyes focused on her, it changed. "Is something wrong?" she asked, striking a little pose.

"You seem to have lost some of your clothes," he said gruffly.

There she stood, in all her curvy glory, wearing nothing but deep red lace.

"I'm a woman, Sawyer, of course I shop at Victoria's Secret." She stepped forward and with a hand on his chest, gently forced him to lie back on the table. "Now let's work on the shoulder from this side, shall we?"

He nodded and closed his eyes, but every once in a while she caught him peeking. Every time she leaned forward with the massaging motion, her breasts brushed his arm or his chest. "Regan," he said in a low growl.

"No talking," she whispered. "Just relax and enjoy the sounds of the ocean and the feel of your muscles relaxing."

"Darlin', if you keep this up, nothing on me is going to be relaxed. And that isn't a threat, it's a promise."

His tone was deep and sexy and Regan wanted to run her hands and her mouth over him from head to toe. "But your time isn't up yet," she said sweetly, leaning in even further to put a little more pressure on the offending muscle. Sawyer hissed and she wasn't sure if it was in pleasure or pain, but she continued her work. Her hands slowed as she relished the feel of him and all but purred when he whispered her name.

"I think I may need to change the angle in order to get where you seem to need it most." Her words sounded professional enough, but before Sawyer could take a breath, Regan was straddling him on the table. He said her name again and it came out as a plea. "Is there something you need, Sawyer?" she asked softly, seductively, as she leaned forward and placed her lips a breath away from his.

"You," he said, reaching up and cupping the back of her head. "Only you."

Playtime was over.

"I don't know how you do it," he said breathlessly between kisses, "but you make it impossible for me to have any form of self-control." Another kiss. "I could live ten lifetimes and never get enough of your hands on me."

"Good," she said, licking her way down his throat only to rain a trail of kisses across the expanse of his wonderfully muscled chest. "It's good to know I'm not alone in this." Regan flicked her tongue across one flat nipple and when he hissed, she did the same to the other one. "I have done plenty of massages before, and this is the first time I couldn't keep my clothes on."

"Good to know," he said, pulling her back up so he could kiss her again. "I'd hate to have to come in here and kick every guy's ass that you massage." Regan chuckled softly but Sawyer was serious. His grip on her tightened possessively. "The only man you'll strip for is me," he said in a low rumble. "Mine." It was the last word he could utter before reaching around and grasping Regan's bottom in both hands and pulling her snugly against his arousal.

The intensity of his words and the feel of his hands holding on to her had Regan ready to lose control. Every time with Sawyer was exciting and yet something about this moment seemed so much more. "We'll have to be careful," she whispered. "This isn't the sturdiest of tables." She kissed him, trying to calm the beast in both of them.

"Then we'll have to go slow," he said, lifting her slightly so he could kick free the blanket that had been covering him from the waist down.

Regan gasped. Unable to help herself, she reached out and stroked the hard length of him. "That's pretty naughty," she teased before scooting down a little farther on the table and taking him in her mouth. Sawyer gasped out a breath and ran his fingers through her hair.

Suddenly he stopped her. When she looked at him in confusion, he said, "No more. I need to be inside you. Now." Roughly, he pulled her up the length of his body and then groaned.

"What? What's the matter?"

"Condom," he said. "Over on the chair—in the pocket of my jeans."

There was a seductive smile on Regan's face as she climbed off him and pulled two condoms from his pocket. "I guess you really were a Scout," she teased.

He shrugged. "It pays to be prepared."

While Sawyer sheathed himself, Regan shimmied out of her panties. No sooner had they hit the ground than Sawyer had his hands on her hips, positioning her above him. Just when he was about to enter her he stopped and let his hands skim up her body, where he unhooked her bra and tossed it to the floor on top of her panties, and then finished traveling up to her face.

"You are so beautiful, Regan," he said, mesmerized by the sight of her. "So damn beautiful." Tears glistened in her eyes at his words and she wiggled in his lap, letting out a small plea. Sawyer was more than ready to comply. In one swift move he was inside her. Their mingled sigh of pleasure was the only sound in the room for a long time and then Regan slowly began to move. Sawyer guided her movements, his hands gently gripping her hips.

Between the candlelight, the sounds of the ocean, and the sensual way she rode him, he knew she wouldn't last long, couldn't last long. Taking one strong hand from her hip, Sawyer reached out to where their bodies were joined and gently used his finger to stroke her. Regan gasped at his touch, picking up her pace slightly but Sawyer kept up with her, stroking her inside and out with an accuracy that was guaranteed to take her over the edge. With his name a cry on her lips, wave after wave of pleasure crashed over her. Her hands were braced on his chest as she rode her orgasm out until she felt as if there wasn't a bone left in her body.

Spent and exhausted, Regan draped her body on his. "My turn," Sawyer whispered as he pumped into her repeatedly until his own orgasm took over—and seemed to go on and on until he, too, was completely spent. Their hearts beat against one another in sync and it took long moments for their breathing to calm.

Regan sleepily lifted her head and smiled dreamily down at him. "I think we'll save that second condom for another time."

Sawyer chuckled and reached up to cup her head and bring her down for a soft, lingering kiss. "Deal."

Chapter 8

BRIDAL PARTY PAMPERING WAS ALWAYS FUN, BUT REGAN found she was equally excited when the group was done and walking out the door. She and her entire staff sat like a platoon of wounded soldiers as the last tiara-wearing bridesmaid left the building.

"That is going to be one wild wedding," Caroline said as she slouched down in one of the massaging pedicure chairs. "I can only imagine the pictures they'll get and the stories they'll tell afterward."

"If I had to hear any more about edible underwear, I think I would have had to leave," Todd said with a grin. "And believe me, nothing makes me happier than talking underwear and lingerie with women, but something about that group just made it seem…wrong."

"Poor baby," Regan laughed. "Did they traumatize you?"

Rising, Todd nodded. "Absolutely. Now if you ladies will excuse me, my shift is over. I am going home to rest up for my date tonight." He grabbed his keys and headed for the door.

"Don't forget the edible underwear," Caroline called out and then broke into laughter at the way the color drained from his face.

Todd turned to Regan. "It's even more traumatizing coming from your mother." And with that, he left.

Caroline was still giggling when Regan sat on the

chair beside her and clicked on the rolling massage setting. "I'm glad you think it's funny to taunt the hired help."

"Oh, please," Caroline said with a smile. "That boy has done plenty of sharing way too much information with all of us about his sexual escapades. It was kind of fun to give him a taste of his own medicine."

Regan looked at her mom and was stunned by the transformation. Caroline looked ten years younger; lately she had been smiling more than Regan could remember her doing in years. Caroline noticed Regan's appraisal of her and squirmed a little. "What? What's the matter? Do I have spinach in my teeth?"

Reaching over, Regan took her mother's hand. "You really are happy, aren't you? With Max, I mean."

Nodding, Caroline squeezed her daughter's hand. "I never imagined something like this would happen for me. I was content with my life and looked forward to the day when you would become a wife and a mother. I hadn't realized I had given up on such a big part of my life until I met Max." She sighed and leaned back in her chair. "It was so unexpected. Men never pay me much attention, so when Max approached me, it scared me to death. I mean, here was this big, burly man and he was talking to me and asking to come to my house!"

Regan laughed. "He had a camera crew with him, Mom, it wasn't as if he approached you in a dark alley."

"To me it was almost the same thing." She faced Regan. "Most of the men I come in contact with are husbands of my friends or clients. I don't know, maybe I gave off some sort of vibe that told men to back off, but Max was genuinely the first man since your father to seem to want to get to know me. It was a little unnerving."

"Maybe you just weren't ready until now. There's nothing wrong with that."

Caroline shrugged. "I don't know. Maybe. Either way, I wake up every morning and think, 'Oh my goodness! I get to see Max today!'" She smiled. "It's a wonderful feeling. I wish you would find someone who makes you feel the same way."

I already have, Regan thought and for a brief moment considered sharing that fact with her mother, then shrugged it off. This was Caroline's time to be in the spotlight, and she wanted to give her a little more time to have the focus on her. "You're very lucky and I know that someday it will happen for me, too. And then we'll make everyone around us sick with how happy we are!"

"That's my girl! Watch out, because it happens when you least expect it and sometimes it's even with who you least expect. Your father was a quiet and conservative businessman. Never in my life would I have imagined myself with someone as big and loud and hands-on as Max Bennett." She fanned herself. "The man certainly has a way with his hands."

Regan sat back and closed her eyes, shaking her head. "TMI, Mom… TMI."

Regan had no idea what Sawyer had planned for their date this evening; he was being very secretive about it. Staring at the contents of her closet, she was clueless about how she was supposed to dress. But somehow tonight felt like a special occasion.

Something about this date seemed like a game changer.

Admiring her curvy form in the silky black lingerie she had purchased for this evening, Regan thought they really didn't need much to attain maximum enjoyment of one another. They never ran out of topics to talk about and they had a lot of common interests—and then there was the sex. She sighed. *Enjoyment* seemed too mild a word for that.

Making her mind move away from that particular topic, Regan slithered into a little black dress and then reached for the stilettos. She didn't often wear such racy shoes, but tonight she would make the sacrifice. She rummaged through her closet for a wrap to use when it cooled down later in the evening, and with one last glance at her reflection, headed down the stairs to wait.

Placing her purse and wrap by the front door, she walked to the kitchen and poured herself a drink of water. She was nervous. It didn't make sense, because being with Sawyer was becoming familiar and something she embraced. Regan tried to put her finger on what it was. Surely she couldn't be nervous because they were going out on an official date, could she? A small giggle escaped before she could stop it.

"For crying out loud," she said with a shake of her head. "You're a grown woman and yet here you are acting like a schoolgirl going on her very first date." Immediately, thoughts of her mother and Max came to mind and Regan knew she wasn't alone in what she was feeling. If she let the cat out of the bag on her relationship with Sawyer, would others see the kind of transformation in Regan that she'd seen in Caroline?

With a smile, Regan put down her glass. "I hope so." Seeing her mother so happy made her happy, so maybe if Caroline saw how happy Regan was with Sawyer, it would have the same effect. *You never can have too much happiness, right?*

At six thirty on the dot, there was a knock at her door. Smoothing her dress and with a quick fluff of her hair, Regan opened the door to the man who was fast becoming as necessary to her as breathing. She saw a massive bouquet of tulips and irises in bold shades of reds and purples. "Oh, my," she gasped as Sawyer walked in, dressed in a suit and tie.

"I wasn't sure what kind of flowers you like, but when I saw these colors, they made me think of you."

"Oh, Sawyer, they're magnificent." Taking them in her hands she leaned in to breathe in their perfume and hummed with pleasure. "They're so beautiful and so perfect. Thank you." Before turning to find a vase, she leaned in and kissed him softly on the lips. "I love them."

Sawyer wanted to deepen the kiss, but knew if he started, he wouldn't want to stop. Tonight was about taking Regan out and showing her he enjoyed spending time with her—and not just in bed. He followed her into the kitchen and watched as she fluttered around in search of a vase. As she stretched to reach one he got a full glimpse of what she was wearing. The simple black dress hugged her every curve and was held up with tiny straps. The neckline wasn't plunging, but it gave him a glorious view of her cleavage, where a small heart pendant on a gold chain nestled lovingly.

His gaze raked over her from the top of her head to the tips of her toes and he almost stopped breathing at the sight of the stilettos. Good gracious! He couldn't imagine how she could walk in them, and wondered if he should possibly change their plans for the night so they skipped the Art Walk. He was frowning when she turned around.

"Is everything okay?"

Sawyer felt ridiculous to voice his concern, but more than anything, he wanted this to be a perfect night for Regan and ending the night with blisters on her feet was not anybody's idea of a perfect evening. He cleared his throat and tried to think of a way to say what he had to without it resulting in her changing her shoes.

They looked really good.

Sexy.

He could easily imagine making love to her later on with her wearing nothing *but* those shoes. "You just look so damn beautiful. You take my breath away every time I see you." Taking the few steps to close the distance between them, Sawyer cupped her face and kissed her tenderly before pulling back. "I have this whole night planned and then I look at you and this incredibly sexy dress and those killer shoes and…well…"

"Am I overdressed? Should I go and change?" That wouldn't make too much sense, she thought, since Sawyer was dressed in a suit and tie.

"No, no, Regan, you're perfect. It's just that I had planned on us doing the Art Walk in Raleigh, but I think that would be cruel to do to you in those shoes."

She let out a throaty laugh and leaned back in to kiss him. "Silly man. We women can handle a little stroll around town even in killer heels. No worries. And if they really start to bother me, I'll walk barefoot and just dangle them from my fingers."

Sawyer couldn't say why but even *that* sounded sexy. He had it bad, that was for sure. "I just wanted you to have a heads-up before we left. I had hoped to surprise you with it after dinner, but once I got a look at you, I wanted to make sure you were okay with the plans."

Regan smiled and reached out to cup the side of his face. "I don't care where we go. I'm just looking forward to going out with you tonight."

Her words warmed him and Sawyer held out his arm. "Ready?"

Shyly, she hooked her arm through his and they walked together out to…a Mercedes? Regan looked from the car to Sawyer and back again. "Where did this come from? You have a truck. Where's the truck?"

Placing a hand on the small of her back, he gently nudged her closer to the car. "I didn't want to take you out in my work vehicle. I rented the car for the weekend. I figured it was much more suitable for a night out on the town and doing whatever else we wanted this weekend."

"Oh, Sawyer," she sighed. "You didn't have to do that. I would have been fine with us using my car and, really, it would not have been an issue going out in the truck. I hate that you went through all this trouble just to take me out." She pouted slightly and Sawyer spun her around in his arms.

"I didn't want to take you out in the truck. I also believe a man should pick a woman up to take her out."

She rolled her eyes at him playfully. "You were still taking me out, Sawyer."

He shook his head. "No. I wanted to come here, pick you up, and take you out in my car. Well, a car that's mine for the weekend."

Regan kissed his cheek as Sawyer reached to open the car door for her. "You are very sweet, and I love the fact that you are old-fashioned, too. We have that in common." Carefully, Regan lowered herself into the luxury car and made herself comfortable as Sawyer closed the door and walked around to the driver's side. Once he was seated and buckled in, he turned to her.

"Ready?"

"Are you kidding? I feel like I've been waiting forever for a night like this." And with that, Sawyer pulled out of the driveway and took them toward a romantic new beginning.

"I am so full that it doesn't matter what shoes I'm wearing, I need to walk," Regan said with a laugh as they strolled hand in hand through downtown Raleigh. There were live bands playing and a variety of shops and art galleries open for them to explore. "I've lived here my entire life and have never once done this. How did you find out about it?"

"I did my research and tried to think of something that would be different—even if you'd done it before. This seemed like a good option."

"It's perfect. And so was dinner." Regan placed a hand on her only slightly overfull belly.

Sawyer noticed and chuckled. "It's refreshing to take out a woman who eats."

She punched him in the arm. "Hey! I did not eat that much."

"I didn't say you did," he bantered back. "It's just

that most women I know go out to eat and then pick at their meal. I was glad you enjoyed yours."

"You will never have to worry about me turning down a meal. I could probably stand to skip a few—that's why I'm a little more, shall we say, full-figured than is trendy right now."

"Your body is perfect," he said sternly, stopping them in their tracks. "There isn't a damn thing wrong with you, and if you wanted to go someplace and eat right now, I'd take you. You name it, what would you like? Cake? Ice cream?"

She was laughing out loud now. "I couldn't eat another bite right now if you paid me." Then she stopped and considered her words. "But don't hold me to that an hour or so from now. I almost never say no to ice cream."

"Good to know," he said with a nod, tucking that little tidbit of information away.

They continued to stroll and explore for what seemed like hours when Regan's pace began to slow. "I know I said I could do this for hours, but I think I was being too optimistic." Reaching down, she gracefully stepped out of the heels and then looped them over her fingers. The cool pavement felt wonderful on her sore feet and before she had gone more than five steps, she let out a shriek as Sawyer scooped her up into his arms. "Sawyer? Are you crazy? What are you doing?"

"I thought that would be obvious."

"I know you're carrying me," she said as if she was speaking to a child. "What I don't know is why."

"I don't want you walking on this pavement, you could hurt yourself. We'll head back to the car."

"That's about four blocks from here!" she cried. "I'm fine, really. You can put me down."

"Are you kidding me?" he asked with disbelief. "This could quite possibly be the single most romantic thing I've ever done and you want me to stop?" He was mocking her and added a small pout for good measure.

"You're crazy," she whispered, kissing him. "Fine, now you can say you swept me off my feet in every sense of the word."

He beamed at her. "That's my girl."

—⁓—

They arrived back at Regan's townhouse, and it was a given Sawyer was coming in with her. Regan would have asked him if he wanted to make sure they hit all the highlights of an official date, but she didn't want to play. Sawyer had created the perfect night. Dinner had been magnificent, the restaurant was beautiful, the conversation had flowed, and strolling through downtown to the sounds of local musicians while admiring local artists' works had been more amazing than she ever could have imagined.

Once inside, Regan didn't turn on more lights. She had left a lamp on in the living room and its glow provided all the lighting she needed. Dropping her purse and wrap to the floor, she stepped in close to Sawyer and wrapped her arms around his neck. "I want to thank you for an amazing evening."

Sawyer wound his arms around her, securing her to him. "The pleasure was all mine."

Regan leaned in for a kiss, but Sawyer pulled back. Taking one of her hands, he led her to the sofa and sat down. "I still feel like we've skipped over some of the more timeless aspects of a date. We jumped ahead and missed out on some of the finer things."

She lowered her eyes and smiled. "Like making out on the couch?"

"It's a classic for a reason," he teased and then pulled her in to cut off any further conversation. He started out just gently nipping at her lips and then kissing her cheek before venturing down the column of her throat. Regan let her head fall back on the sofa and purred his name. "A classic," he repeated before working his way back up to her lips.

This time he was a little bolder. His tongue traced her bottom lip and Regan whimpered as she opened her mouth and let him inside. Their tongues did a slow dance with one another as Sawyer's hand came up and traced lazy circles up Regan's neck. Tentatively, Regan placed a hand on Sawyer's chest and he took his free hand to hold it in place over his heart.

Over and over he kissed her. Her emotions were all over the place—she wanted to move things along, yet wanted time to stand still for them so that this night, this one perfect night, could last forever. Slowly, Regan began to move closer—she could hear the change in his breathing. Sawyer removed his hand from hers and made his way, featherlight, up her arm to her shoulder, gently kneading her there, then her neck, before venturing down to cup her breast. Her nipples were already hard and he played with them through the silky fabric of the dress until Regan was squirming beside him, panting his name.

"Make love to me, Sawyer," she whispered. "Take me upstairs and make love to me."

Without a word, Sawyer stood and scooped Regan up into his arms and strode up the stairs; he was a man on a mission. One small lamp was on next to her bed. Gently, he placed Regan on the bed, where she lay back, arms above her head, and watched as Sawyer first removed his jacket and tie, then his shoes and belt. By the time he placed a knee on the bed and leaned in to kiss her, she was certain she was about to go up in flames.

"I need you," she said quietly.

"You have me." Finally he began to remove her dress. Her heart rate kicked up when she saw the heat in his eyes as he studied the tiny pieces of black lace that barely contained her breasts. "If I had known this was what you had on underneath all night, I would have skipped the Art Walk."

"You haven't seen the rest of it," she said.

Not one to pass up a dare, Sawyer continued to peel the dress down her body and let out a low whistle when he saw the matching lace thong she wore. He threw the dress to the floor and sat back on his heels, taking in the sight of her in black lace and stilettos and he thought his heart might explode in his chest. There were no words, simply none. He had told her she was beautiful, had said she was perfect, and yet right here, right now in this moment, those words were too small.

Reverently, he ran a hand up the length of her from her ankle to her face and looked his fill. He could see Regan's pulse fluttering at her neck, could practically hear her heart beating, for he knew it often matched his own and right now his was roaring in his head.

"Please," she finally said, breaking the silence, and with her hair fanned out on the pillows and her arms up in surrender, Sawyer gave up the fight. There would be plenty of time, years if he had his way, for him to look at her and touch her, but right now he needed to love her. He rose from the bed and removed his clothes, then reached over and removed the black lace that would forever be burned into his memory.

He left the stilettos on.

Regan arched a brow at him. "Indulge me," he said as he took a foil packet from his pants pocket and sheathed himself before returning to the bed to cover her body with his. Her skin felt cool, yet it burned against his; she was smooth as silk and smelled good enough to eat. He smiled at how much he wanted to do just that.

All of her.

From head to toe.

He trailed kisses from her lips to her throat to her breasts, where he stopped and paid homage to them until Regan was writhing beneath him. Her fingers were raking through his hair while he nipped and suckled at each crest, and he could have spent hours there.

But there was so much more waiting to be explored.

Gently, he rained tiny kisses along her belly to her hip bone. Rough, callused hands that were used to hard work softly kneaded her hips and his mouth traveled farther, where he did a most thorough exploration of Regan that left her weeping with need for him. She begged for him, cried out for him, and was left shattered into a million pieces by him. It didn't deter Sawyer; he was singularly focused, and until his mouth had finished feasting on all of her, he wouldn't give her what she wanted most.

His tongue traveled the length of each long, silky leg and stopped briefly to kiss behind each knee and ankle before he began the entire process in reverse.

"Sawyer," Regan panted. "You're killing me."

"Oh, no," he said huskily. "Stay with me, baby. The best is yet to come."

No truer words were ever spoken. As Sawyer traveled back up a body that was sheened with sweat and writhing in ecstasy, he thought he had never seen anything more erotic in his life. Regan naked except for the black stilettos and crying out for him pushed him over the edge. He wanted to see her like this bathed in moonlight. Reaching over, he turned off the bedside lamp and did his best to hold on to his control for another moment to take in the sight before him.

One last plea escaped her lips before Sawyer came down and covered her with all of him, hooking his right arm under her knee to help give him access to the heaven that was waiting for him. One smooth thrust convinced him he'd indeed died and gone to heaven; she was the perfect combination of wetness and tightness. If he didn't reel his mind in, all the preliminaries would have been for nothing.

Slowly, he began to move inside her and Regan eagerly met his every motion. Her hands skimmed up and down his spine, now also sheened with sweat. The intensity of the gaze staring back at him made his breath catch in his throat. Never had a woman looked at him like this, never had he thought a woman could look at him like this. Every emotion Regan was feeling was right there before him and it was both humbling and overwhelming.

Because it matched all of his own.

Time lost all meaning as they continued to move together. There was no rush to a finish line, no need to do more than what they were doing right now—which was giving one another endless pleasure. Sawyer reached out both hands and braced them on Regan's headboard for more leverage. She let out a cry of delight as he seemed to push even farther into her. With both legs wrapped firmly around his hips, he could tell she was close to yet another orgasm.

Sawyer changed his angle ever so slightly and that was all it took. Regan's entire body shook with the intensity of her climax. He rode out each wave with her and when he felt her body calming down, he allowed himself to finally have his own release. Spasm after spasm rocked him as he filled her so completely he couldn't tell where he ended and where she began. All Sawyer knew was that he barely recalled his own name or where he was, because all he could do was feel. Every nerve ending was on high alert and it would take a long time for him to come back down to earth and breathe.

It was a damn shame that he had to.

With as much finesse as he could muster, he collapsed on top of her and sighed with relief when Regan wrapped her arms around him and pulled him close. Their heartbeats raged together in a mindless rhythm and Sawyer could only hope they both survived this. He smiled at the thought and a small chuckle escaped.

Breathlessly, Regan asked, "What's so funny?"

He wanted to pull up and look at her, he sincerely did, but his body wouldn't cooperate. "I'm not sure either of us is quite alive here."

She chuckled too. "I know what you mean but what a way to go."

Carefully, Sawyer rolled to his side and pulled Regan with him. She snuggled in close. Words weren't necessary; it was enough to be in one another's arms as they settled back into themselves. When their breathing finally evened out and Sawyer found the strength to pull the blankets up, he heard Regan sigh before she settled more firmly against him.

What did one say after experiencing what they just had? Sex had always been fun for Sawyer, but no woman had ever transformed him like Regan had. It was both terrifying and exciting, and right now all he wanted to do was tell her what he was feeling. Still, saying "I love you" to someone after a mind-blowing orgasm may not be the best way to go. If he had learned anything in his life, it was that people tended to say stupid things while in bed with one another in the afterglow.

But he sincerely felt it. He was in love with her, and he saw that love mirrored in her eyes. Why shouldn't they be able to say this to each other? Why wait? There weren't always perfect moments to make such a momentous confession, and who was to say that *this* wasn't the right moment for it?

Regan stirred in his arms and he held his breath to see if she was awake or not. Lazily, she lifted her head, looked at him, and smiled. "Mmm," she purred. "Hey, you."

"Hey," he whispered, placing a kiss on the tip of her nose.

"Is it still nighttime or even the same year?"

Sawyer nodded and smiled. "I believe so. It doesn't seem possible, though."

Lowering her head, Regan kissed his shoulder and draped an arm across his chest and hugged him. "That was…amazing, simply amazing."

"It's you," he replied. "You're amazing."

Regan shook her head. "It's us. We're amazing together."

Here it was—this was the moment. Sawyer was ready to lay it all on the line when suddenly Regan released him and stretched. He waited a heartbeat to see what she was going to do, and was mildly surprised when she sat up and looked around the room.

"Are you okay?" he asked casually.

"I was just thinking about our date," she said and turned to look at him. "I was so nervous about tonight."

"Why?"

She shrugged. "I don't know. I've been out on dates before, but something about tonight seemed…like something different. Something more." Scooting back, Regan settled against the pillows. "I agonized over what to wear and what to say, and I can't imagine why I made such a fuss out of it." She looked at him again and smiled a serene smile. "It's us. There's nothing about us that should make me nervous."

Her honest words moved him. Regan was right; there was nothing to be nervous about. In that moment Sawyer knew he could tell her exactly how he felt. If she wasn't ready to say those three little words back to him, then he would be okay with it. Well, honestly—he would be disappointed, but he would survive. He would have to remember not to push, not make her feel pressured to say it back to him. Even though they seemed completely in sync with one another, it didn't mean

Regan was as comfortable telling someone she loved him as he was.

Wait, was he? Was he comfortable? How many times had he said he loved someone? Regan shifted positions, her head on his shoulder and her hand lazily tracing lines on his chest. It felt good. But back to the whole saying-I-love-you thing. When was the last time he had said it? He frowned as he racked his brain. Surely in his lifetime he had to have told *someone* that he loved them. Other than his father. A slight shake of his head had him realizing that in all his short-lived relationships, he had not only never said it to anyone, he had never felt it with anyone.

Was he really feeling it now? His heart rate kicked up and he thought he was going to have a mild panic attack. Why now? Why was he freaking out about this now? Two minutes ago, he was confident in telling Regan that he loved her. It was no big deal, he was ready. And now, because he had gone and overanalyzed it, he was second-guessing himself.

Because you've been waiting for Regan, a small voice inside him said.

But he wasn't sure he was ready to believe that voice. It seemed too simple, too at-the-ready. Was it really possible he had been waiting all his life for just one woman? That subconsciously he was aware of that fact? It seemed a little too much to believe.

Regan lifted her head. "You seem to have quite a lot on your mind over there, Bennett," she teased.

He looked at her as if he had forgotten she was there. "What? What do you mean?"

"I mean I can hear you thinking from here. Are you okay?"

Sawyer kissed her forehead and made a snap decision. "I am more than okay—damn near perfect."

Relief seemed to wash over her. "Oh. Okay. That's good." She nibbled at her bottom lip, and now it was Sawyer's turn to ask if she was okay. She nodded. "Like you, damn near perfect."

"Okay, then."

"But…"

He arched an eyebrow at her. "But…?"

"Okay, don't laugh." He made an X over his heart. "But I was thinking about our walk around downtown earlier…"

"Right…"

"And how wonderful dinner was…"

"Okay."

She looked at him with a worried expression and then blurted out, "And now I want ice cream!"

Sawyer let out a full-body laugh and pulled her in close. She was trembling in his arms and he held her like that until they were both exhausted from mirth. "Well then," he began, "please tell me you have some down in the kitchen."

Breaking free from his embrace, she looked at him with patience. "Please—my freezer is always well-stocked in case of an emergency."

Loving the playful banter, Sawyer kicked the blankets away and pulled her from the bed and into his arms. "I love a woman who is prepared."

Chapter 9

THE SUN ROSE WAY TOO EARLY FOR REGAN'S LIKING, BUT she loved rolling over right into Sawyer's arms, which, even in sleep, were waiting for her. A girl could get very used to this.

After their late-night ice cream binge, they had lain in bed together making plans for a beach getaway the following weekend. Sawyer had it all planned out and had just wanted to make sure Regan would be able to take the time away from the spa.

"Your mother's house will be done by Friday," he had told her. "I figure we'll wrap up filming after lunch and then we can get on the road. What do you think?"

Being with Sawyer seemed to take the sting out of her emotional attachment to her family home. Regan was always going to be sad that they were selling it and she wouldn't be able to bring her own children there to visit their grandmother, but she was coming to realize it really was just a place. To coin a phrase, home really is where the heart is.

"That sounds like a wonderful plan, and I can't wait for the renovations to be done so we can get away." Sawyer's expression showed he wasn't sure he'd heard her correctly. "I know, I know, I haven't been excited about the project, but I see now that it's the right thing to do, and while I'm still a little sad, I'm looking forward to seeing what the future holds." She realized how what she said may have sounded, so she cleared her throat and quickly added, "You know, for my mom and Max."

Sensing her unease, Sawyer had kissed her temple and held her close until they both fell asleep.

Now awake and relishing the feel of his even breathing, Regan had a chance to examine her words more closely. She was excited to see what the future held, but not only for her mother and Max. Truth be known, she was still curious as to what the future held for herself and Sawyer. What was going to happen after the beach? Was that going to be goodbye? Was it going to be the place where they figured out how to have their long-distance relationship?

She frowned. She didn't want long-distance, she wanted the here and now. She wanted to wake up with Sawyer every morning and to fall asleep with him every night. While nothing was certain, Regan knew he had commitments to the network before he would be able to settle in any one place, and she could only hope he wanted to settle here, near her.

Peeking over his shoulder at the bedside clock, she cringed; it was only 7:00 a.m. *Yikes—way too early to be up with such deep thoughts.* Unfortunately, the damage was done; she was wide awake, and as glorious as it felt to be wrapped around one very yummy man, Regan was ready to get up.

Carefully disentangling herself from his muscular form, she tiptoed across the room to grab her robe before heading down the stairs. Once in the kitchen and after a quick glance through the cupboards and refrigerator, Regan found she had plenty of ingredients to make a killer breakfast. Feeling energized, she immediately got to work. Soon coffee was brewing, bacon was frying, and pancakes were being flipped. Making up the plates, she set everything on a tray to carry it all up the stairs and wake Sawyer.

In the bedroom, she found him sleepily stretching and was disappointed that he was already awake. He smiled when he saw her. "I thought I smelled something good."

Holding out the tray for him to see, she smiled back. "I was inspired and decided we needed breakfast in bed."

Sitting up and adjusting the blankets, Sawyer took the tray from her hands and motioned for her to join him in the bed. When she went to climb under the blankets, he stopped her. "Nuh-uh, this is naked breakfast in bed—lose the robe." His tone was light and teasing but his eyes were full of heat, and Regan quickly divested herself of the offensive garment and climbed in beside him. "That's better," he said and leaned in to kiss her. "You didn't need to do all this."

"I know I didn't need to. I just wanted to. That's what made it fun." His expression told her she wasn't making sense. "Making breakfast for you isn't a chore, Sawyer. I wanted to do something nice for you. I had hoped to surprise you, but you were already awake."

"But you did surprise me. No one's ever made me breakfast in bed, so this is…" He stumbled a little on his words. "This means more to me than you can know. Thank you."

They ate in silence, enjoying each other's presence and the food. When they were done, Sawyer took the tray and placed it on the floor before returning to his position reclining against the pillows. "That was delicious."

"I'm glad you enjoyed it," she said, leaning against him. "So what's on the agenda for today?"

Sawyer sighed sadly. "Unfortunately, I have to meet Devin at the house later and finalize the plans for the week so he can schedule the camera crew accordingly. Then I'll meet with my guys and hand out assignments for the week so we can finish on time." Turning his head, he smiled. "And then we can ride off to the coast and into the sunset."

"Mmm…sounds wonderful. Max has a house on the coast, doesn't he?"

Sawyer nodded. "His place is in Wilmington. It's been a work in progress for years. Don't worry, we're not staying there."

She laughed. "I didn't think we were. I was just thinking how nice it must be to live there year-round."

"I wouldn't know, and honestly, I don't think he does either. We spend so much time on the road with the show that I don't even remember what it's like to stay in my place."

"Tell me about your house."

He shrugged. "I never invested in a house. I've been single for so long and I worked such long hours, even before the show came along, that it never made sense to buy one. I have an apartment in New Bern I've lived in for about ten years now. It's essentially a storage closet for me. I rent a place where I keep my tools and things for the job, but the apartment is not much different than the hotels where I stay."

"Well, that's just sad, Sawyer."

"I know. Right when we started your mom's house, Dad and I discussed the future a bit and we're both ready to be done with the show. I'm going to address that with Devin today and start laying the foundation for moving on. I didn't commit beyond this season, but I think they were hoping to take the show in a different direction and I'm just not into it anymore."

"The drama angle?"

Sawyer nodded. "That, and it's just not…fun anymore. I don't get to choose the jobs and it's becoming very routine. Your house was a challenge, but that was mainly because I wanted to impress you."

Regan blushed. "You did not!"

"It's true. I went a little over the top with some of the designs because I was determined to win you over where the house was concerned."

"Only the house?" she fished.

"Well, maybe I was trying to show off a little in hopes of winning you over for me personally, too."

"You succeeded," she said and gave him a smacking kiss on the lips.

"There was a lot more I wanted to do for your mom's house, but the network wouldn't go for it."

"Like what?"

"Oh, I wanted to branch out and do the landscaping—do something wild in the backyard to really make it great for entertaining."

Regan sighed. "I always pictured something great back there. It's fine enough and we never did a lot of entertaining, but it's such a fantastic space that I could envision what would look good there."

"Tell me about your vision," he prompted.

"I always wanted a pool," she began and then laughed self-consciously. "I know it's not very original, but the yard is so big and private. I just always imagined how wonderful it would be to have a big in-ground pool."

"I think the yard is perfect for that. Tell me more."

"A pergola. I would have loved to see a pergola with a wonderful seating area on the back deck. Then a fire pit and another seating area out in the yard. This way when you were entertaining, guests would have places to gather and sit. There would need to be a grilling area or, even better, an outdoor kitchen type of setup. In the summer you could cook outside and not have to heat up the house at all."

"What about greenery? What do you like?"

"I have a black thumb," she said sadly. "I kill everything, so I don't know the names of the things that I like. But I love butterfly bushes. Mom has one out in the front yard that just grows wild. In the summer, it's so picturesque with all the different colors of butterflies all around it."

"They are beautiful. What about color? Did you picture flowers in the yard or just greenery?"

Regan considered his words. "I think a little of both." She faced him excitedly. "I love bold colors, like the ones in the bouquet you brought me last night. The reds and the purples—they are just so amazing. I could never maintain such a thing, so while I'm fantasizing about the perfect yard, I'd have to fantasize about the perfect gardener."

"Wait a minute," he said and pulled her into his arms. "I don't think I like where this is going. No fantasizing about the gardener." Then he kissed her with a thoroughness that took her breath away. When they finally came up for air, he saw the knowing smile on her face. "What?"

"You were jealous."

He shrugged. "So?"

Regan stroked a hand down his cheek. "I like it." She pulled herself free of his arms. "Maybe my perfect gardener looks just like you. What do you think of that?"

Now it was Sawyer's turn to smile. "I think I like the sound of that."

When Sawyer arrived at Caroline's home, he wasn't surprised to see his father's vehicle already there. He said a quick prayer that they remembered Sawyer and the crew were coming over and they were decent.

When Caroline opened the door for him, Sawyer released the breath he was holding.

"So good to see you, Sawyer," she said. "You're the first one to arrive, well, after your father, of course."

As if on cue, Max walked into the room. The two men embraced and made small talk before Caroline excused herself. "I promised Regan I'd go in to the spa today and do some paperwork." She sighed dramatically. "It's a tough job but somebody's got to do it." She collected her keys and purse, then kissed Max senseless before waving to Sawyer and leaving.

Sawyer chuckled softly as his father watched Caroline until she was out of sight, and then reached out and placed a hand on Max's shoulder. "You've got it bad, Dad."

Max smiled. "Don't I know it."

"So how are things going?"

"Great. We were talking this morning about how once this place is sold, Caroline would like to move to

Wilmington with me." He watched his son to gauge his reaction. "How do you feel about that?"

"Dad, seriously? Why would I have a problem with it? You're happy, she's happy…you deserve to have a life of your own."

"I know we haven't talked a lot about the show—"

Sawyer cut him off. "We're going to address that today with Devin."

Max arched a brow at him. "We are?"

Sawyer nodded. "We are. It's time. I don't want to drag this out. I have enjoyed this job, but the added pressure to stir up drama just isn't my thing. I'm sure the network can find someone more suited to that kind of thing, but it's just not me. I'm just a guy who likes to build things. Reality TV with all the drama? That's for somebody else."

"I'm proud of you, Sawyer," Max said, waving a hand when his son tried to interrupt him. "No, I'm serious. You're taking a stand and walking away before things get ugly. Have you given any thought to what you're going to do when it's all said and done?"

"I'm thinking of buying a house."

Those were not the words Max was expecting and his shock left him speechless.

"Say something," Sawyer prompted.

"I…I don't know what to say. I guess I was expecting you to talk about a job or a project. I never thought of you wanting to commit to home ownership."

"I think the time is right," Sawyer said cryptically.

Max suddenly had a ton of questions but was interrupted by Devin's appearance. "Gentlemen!" he boomed as he walked into the house like he owned the place. "Things are looking great as usual, Sawyer. Max, you and your team have done a hell of a job." He looked from father to son. "So tell me what's lined up for the week."

They walked into the kitchen, where Sawyer pulled out his plans and tablet and outlined his schedule for the week. "As you can see, everything will be done and in place by Friday morning. If all goes well, you'll be done shooting by lunchtime and then…we're good to go."

Devin slapped Sawyer on the back. "Perfect! Nothing like ending a job early on a Friday afternoon so everyone can go home and enjoy the weekend. From the looks of things, the budget went well, and that, my friends, makes the network very happy. They're already talking about the next couple of shows and are anxious to look ahead to next season."

Here it was, the moment of truth. "Actually, Dev," Sawyer began, "I'm glad you brought that up."

"Is there a problem?" Devin asked.

Sawyer looked at his father, who simply nodded. "I think my time with the show is done. We've had a good run and I've enjoyed working with you, but honestly, I'm ready to move on to other things and Dad is ready to retire."

Devin looked at the two men as if they were crazy. "Do you hear yourself? The show is at the top of its game. We're going to explore a whole new aspect and you're just going to walk away? Were you hit in the head with something heavy?"

Sawyer couldn't help but chuckle as he shook his head. "Devin, you and the network have been great to work with and I think you can have a lot of success with where you want the show to go. I'm just not the guy to host it."

"Why? Because I made you make the mom and daughter fight? Seriously? You'd walk away from what will be a multimillion-dollar contract because you don't want anyone to feel bad?" He sat back in his chair with disgust. "Get a grip, Sawyer, and think about what you're doing. This is a great opportunity for you. I can understand that it will be different. You'll have to get used to working with someone other than Max, but don't be such a damn baby. Life is full of drama! We're just bringing it out in front of the cameras! You don't think people have argued about the jobs we've done? Wake up! I'm just capitalizing on something that's always been there."

Sawyer held his ground. "Like I said, I'm sure you are going to be successful with it, but it's not my thing. I want to design, I want to build things. I don't want to stand back after handing out boxing gloves to a family. I know there's an audience for it and, sure, maybe someday I'll look back and think differently, but for right now, I just want to be done with it."

"Max, please," Devin said, "talk some sense into your son. Don't you want to see him be successful?"

"He already is," Max said confidently.

Devin stood and looked at the two of them with disbelief. "I thought you were smart, both of you. I thought you wanted to be a success, but at the first signs of change you're running scared. Well, let me tell you, if you walk away from this, Sawyer, I'll make sure you never do another show on the network. Ever."

Sawyer was silent for so long he was sure Devin felt

confident he had used the right tactic to get his way. Finally, Sawyer stood and walked up to Devin and extended his hand. "You do whatever it is you feel you need to do. I'm okay with it."

"What the hell happened to you, Sawyer?" Devin yelled. "We've worked our asses off together to create this and we've got a hit on our hands! You don't just walk away from something like this! Think about it."

"I don't need to, Dev, my mind's made up."

Devin shook his head, refusing to listen. "You have until Friday. I won't tell the network about this conversation. Take the next few days to get your head out of your ass and think about what you're saying." He walked toward the door. "Think long and hard about this, Sawyer, because once it's done, it can't be undone."

And then he was gone.

"Well, that went well," Max said sarcastically.

Sawyer shrugged. "It was about what I expected. Devin doesn't like to be challenged. He forgets that we started together, and we were both naive about the whole thing. We've ridden a good wave of success and now that he knows more about what he's doing, it will only benefit him to start a new show with a new host who's as green as I was when I started. He'll get to play puppet master, and that makes him very happy."

"You know the network isn't going to be pleased."

"I can live with that, Dad. I'm not fishing for another show. I'm done living out of a suitcase. It's hit me lately that I want to stay in one place and have a future."

"What brought on this big revelation, may I ask?"

Sawyer knew he could tell his father anything and

he'd take it to the grave, but with the new addition of Caroline, he wasn't sure it would be fair to ask him to keep a secret from her, so he shrugged again. "I look at what you and Caroline have, and I have to admit, I'm a little envious. I want that. I want to find someone to settle down with and have a life with. A life where we travel for leisure, not for work."

"You're a fine man, Sawyer. And I think this is going to be your time to shine. It's not about the spotlight of fame and fortune. Your greatest success is going to be walking away from all that and finding your true passion and making the future you want."

"I learned from the best."

Max pulled his son into his embrace. When he pulled back, he looked at the man before him and felt tears sting his eyes. "I never knew from one day to the next if I was doing the right thing with you. I always felt guilty that you didn't have a mother around."

"That was her choice, Dad, not yours."

"Doesn't matter," Max said. "Maybe if I had been a different kind of man, she would have stayed. But every day since she left, I did my best to provide for you and to teach you right from wrong. Now I'm standing here and realizing that I'm learning a lot from you, too."

"Me?" Sawyer said with disbelief. "What did I do?"

"You're true to yourself. You're an honest, hard-working man who just wants to be happy."

"No, Dad, I learned that from you."

—◦◦◦—

"So it didn't go well," Regan said later that night when Sawyer returned with a pizza for them to share.

"I didn't think it would. Devin likes to get his own way and to be in control. I'm messing with his plans."

"Well, that's just stupid. Doesn't he realize that if they bring in a new guy, he'll have all the power and control?"

Sawyer stared in amazement. "That's exactly what I thought, too!"

"Great minds," Regan said as she reached for a second slice. "How many more episodes are you committed to?"

"Only two. They're both short gigs and are already scheduled, so once they're done, I'm free of my network obligations."

"Tell me about the jobs?" she asked when she really wanted to ask what his plans were for when he was done. Things had been going so well that Regan hadn't wanted to push her luck. In the past, whenever she pushed for more of a commitment from a man, that was when it ended. For now she was forcing herself to learn to be okay with living in the moment.

"The first one is a workshop makeover, if you can believe it. The family has an old barn on their property that the husband has been using as his workshop for the woodworking he enjoys as a hobby, but he's never had the money to make it into his dream space. We're going to make sure the building is up to code and then design the space to include all the tools he needs, add a bathroom, a sitting room, and studio space to display his work." He reached for a third slice. "It will take about three weeks."

"Wow! That sounds fantastic. Where do they live?"

"Not too far from here. They're in Durham." He

waited a moment to see if Regan would comment on it or ask if he was going to continue to stay at his hotel here in town. But she didn't, and he had to tamp down his disappointment. He'd like to stay here with her and if she'd only ask, he'd pay his tab at the hotel and pack up immediately.

"And what about the second one?"

"It's a master suite makeover for a couple of empty-nesters. They want to knock down the wall between their current bedroom and a guest room to make one master suite with a spa-like bathroom and a sitting area. I haven't had a whole lot of time to look at the specs, but I believe that one can be done in a week if we don't hit any surprises."

"So another month and then you're free," she said with what sounded like forced cheerfulness.

"Looks that way," he said, hoping she'd ask for what was next.

But still she didn't.

Sawyer decided to do his father proud and reach for what made him happy. "I was hoping maybe you wouldn't mind having me around for a while," he said and saw first the shock and then the smile spread across Regan's face.

"What did you have in mind?" she asked, tilting her head as she studied him.

"For starters, I'd like to stop going to my hotel to shower and change every day. Neither of the new jobs are far enough away that I can't handle the commute. What do you say? You up for a roommate?"

Regan was speechless. He wanted to live with her. Her! For the first time ever, a man was asking her about their future. It was a pretty heady experience, and she didn't want to seem overly excited. At the moment, she was kind of enjoying the look of near-panic on Sawyer's face.

"Hmm…I don't know," she said, as if weighing her options. "What's in this for me? I mean, do you clean up after yourself? Seems to me you're pretty spoiled by having housekeeping picking up after you every day. I'm not even going to try to compete with that."

"I'm a big boy, Regan. I promise to pick up after myself and do my own laundry. I certainly don't think of you as housekeeping," he teased.

"Well, that's good. That's very, very good. What about cooking? Do you know how to cook?"

"I whip up a mean macaroni and cheese."

She stared at him in mock horror. "If you even try to feed me stuff out of a box, I'll hurt you."

"Okay, now we're getting someplace. Note to self: no boxed mac and cheese for Regan. Anything else?"

"Sex."

He arched a brow at her. "Sex?"

She nodded. "I mean, if you're going to be staying here for a little while, I don't want you to take it for granted that I'm just going to put out whenever you want." Rising from her spot on the sofa, she walked over and took the paper plate he had been using from his hands and flung it on the coffee table before straddling his lap.

"So, no putting out just because I'm here," he restated and situated her more comfortably in his lap. "Hmm… that could be a definite deal breaker, but then I guess I could counter with the same thing. I'm not going to put out on your every whim either."

She wiggled in his lap. "Seems to me we're at a

stalemate here." Soon she felt his arousal growing and wiggled a little more. "Oh well, at least we gave it a shot."

Sawyer flipped her onto her back so fast that she didn't know what was happening. "You drive a hard bargain, but here's my final offer: sex anytime, anywhere you want it. I'm all yours."

"Ooo…I like that," she purred. "How about right here, right now?"

Sawyer kissed her long and deep. "I think I'm going to like staying with you."

The week flew by once Sawyer moved his meager belongings into Regan's home, and before they knew it, it was Friday. Regan was getting ready for work while simultaneously packing for their weekend. Sawyer had packed up his entire suitcase because they planned on stopping by his place in New Bern on the way to the coast so he could refresh his wardrobe.

"What time do I need to be there?" she asked, tossing a bathing suit into the open suitcase on the bed.

"If you get there by eleven, we should be ready for you. We're moving furniture in this morning"—Sawyer looked at his watch—"or actually, right now, and we told your mother to get there around ten thirty. We want to shoot the reveal with her alone first and then we'll do one with you. How does that sound?"

"Like a tight schedule," she said as she continued to hurry around. "I want to be packed before I leave. But I shouldn't have any problems getting to the house by eleven. Mom promised to go in to the spa this weekend and check on things."

"You told her we were going away?"

"What? Um…no. I just told her I was going to the beach for the weekend with some friends."

"You're going to have to tell her eventually, you know."

"I know, I know. I just wanted to get through the whole renovation thing and let her have her time in the spotlight with the big house reveal and Max, and…well, I didn't want to take the focus off of her right now. She deserves to shine."

Sawyer leaned over the suitcase and kissed her. "You are an amazing woman."

Regan blushed. "Thank you. Now go and play contractor and host so I can finish packing and get to work. I promise to see you at eleven."

Sawyer grabbed his suitcase. "I'll be the one that you're supposed to shoot daggers at but then get all overwhelmed by my craftsmanship. Remember that."

Regan chuckled. "I'll try."

Once she heard the front door close, Regan did a little excited dance. The week had been wonderful. It had seemed natural to come home to one another. On the nights when she had stayed to close the spa, she came home to Sawyer's smiling face and dinner on the table.

And it was never macaroni and cheese.

She knew he was spending a fortune on takeout, and she hoped they'd come to a compromise on that one eventually. For now she was giddy to go in to work, then head over to her mother's and be done with the whole renovation thing, then head off to the coast for what promised to be an amazing weekend.

Sawyer was still being vague about what they were doing, and Regan was happy to let him be. It was nice not to be the one making plans, and it really seemed to make him happy to do it this way.

With one last glance around the bedroom, Regan closed the suitcase and headed down the stairs. Caroline would look in on the place over the weekend, so with a little skip in her step, she walked out the door, locked it, and set off for a fabulous day. The sun was shining, there was a great song on the radio, and Regan thanked her lucky stars that she was so blessed.

―◦―

If one more thing went wrong, Sawyer was going to scream. Jobwise, things were running like clockwork, but it was the little things and Devin's attitude that were really starting to grate on his nerves.

Someone had nicked the wall in the hallway, which required a last-minute coat of mud and paint that they were waiting to dry. The sofa that had been chosen for the living room came, but in the wrong color. It still worked, but he was pissed that there was an error at all. As he walked from room to room making sure everything was in place, Devin dogged his every step.

"You're a natural with this, Sawyer. You can't just walk away."

"Devin, please. We've had this discussion and my decision is final."

"The network is prepared to up your salary by ten percent."

"Not interested."

"Sawyer, be reasonable. They're also willing to give

you a larger cut of the merchandising and more of a say in the jobs we take."

That stopped Sawyer in his tracks. "And the drama shit?"

Devin threw up his hands. "It's freakin' nothing in the grand scheme of things! So we make some people fight on camera. What the hell difference does it make to you? Stop being such a martyr and take the offer, Sawyer!"

Sawyer glanced around to make sure no one on the crew was too close by. "You don't get it, do you? This isn't about being a martyr, Dev, this is about wanting to have a little control over my life and doing something for myself. I don't want to instigate drama and I certainly don't want to perpetuate and benefit from the drama. There are enough freaks on television now. I don't want to contribute to creating any more!"

"They'll be there whether you put them there or not, Sawyer. That's just a fact of life."

Sawyer shook his head sadly. "I don't want any part of it, Dev. Believe me, this isn't a rash decision and I'm not trying to negotiate for more money from the network. I'm just ready to be done with it all. End of story."

"You're a fool, Sawyer. You know that? You're a damn fool. You could be a very wealthy man, and money will buy you whatever it is you think will make you happy. Give us another couple of years and you can retire! Then you'll be free to do whatever you want and I won't try to stop you."

"Dev, listen to me and listen good—I'm done." Sawyer took a step back and watched the rage play all over the producer's face. "You should be happy I'm leaving."

"What?" Devin snapped. "How do you figure that?"

"With a new guy, you'll have all the control. You'll say jump and he'll ask how high. You know I'm never going to do that." In an attempt to ease some of the tension, Sawyer placed a hand on Devin's shoulder. "You're a great producer and you have a great vision for where you want to go. Take this chance to build it to what you want without someone like me holding you back—and believe me, I'm holding you back."

Devin considered his words. "Dammit, Sawyer, we work well together. Why can't you just suck it up for now? What's changed?"

"I have. I need a break."

"So if we gave you like…six months off? Would you come back?"

Sawyer laughed. "No, Dev, I won't come back. I want to do my own thing. Go back to doing jobs that aren't being done for the camera. Working in the private sector always was more appealing to me."

"What happened to you, man? We used to want the same things." No longer angry, Devin's voice was now just filled with disappointment.

"I want a life. I want to sleep in a bed of my own and make my own choices. You can't tell me that on some level that doesn't sound good to you?"

Devin eventually shrugged. "I know the traveling is a bitch, but the money is great. You're going to miss it."

"No," Sawyer said confidently, because what he was gaining was worth so much more. "I'm really not."

—⁂—

An hour later Caroline pulled up in the driveway and the camera crew followed her every step as Sawyer met her at the door and gave her a tour of her newly designed home. Even though she had been there through most of the renovation, it was still a big surprise to see everything put together.

"Oh, Sawyer," she gushed, "it's more beautiful than I ever imagined it. Thank you so much!" And then she wrapped her arms around him before wiping the tears from her face. They were a combination of joy and sadness. This was the home Caroline had before she lost her husband, and since that time, it had never been a priority. "You don't know what you've given me," she said as the tears continued to stream down her face. "This was the first home my late husband and I bought, and we raised our family here, talked about all our hopes and dreams here, and—" She stopped as the emotions clogged her throat.

Sawyer pulled her close and hugged her until she was able to speak again.

"I think Sam would have loved what you did here," she finally said. "It's beautiful, it's just so beautiful. Thank you."

They continued to walk around the house for the B-roll shots until Regan pulled in. Devin positioned Sawyer and Caroline where he wanted them and put the camera crew in place to catch Regan's immediate reaction to what she saw.

Sawyer was more nervous for Regan's response than he had ever been for anyone else's. Beside him, Caroline sensed his tension and squeezed his hand. "Don't worry, she can't possibly have anything bad to say about what you've done."

Sawyer knew that was true. They had talked about

the house often enough that he was confident Regan had come to terms with it all. He wanted her to be proud of him, of what he had created.

"Action!" Devin yelled and Regan was cued to walk in.

She stepped through the door and Sawyer held his breath as he watched all the emotion play over her face. Regan was speechless. She stepped into the living room and looked around. Caroline ran up to her and hugged her. "Do you love it? Can you believe this is our house?"

Regan had to remember her role in this whole silly scenario and went directly into character. "But it's not our house anymore, not really." It didn't feel right to say the words, and anyone who knew her would know she was lying, that it was all just an act.

For the next ten minutes it was Caroline who took Regan on the tour with the cameras rolling behind them. When they finally finished, they met up with Sawyer in the kitchen. He was standing behind the granite-covered island, doing his best to keep his expression neutral when all he wanted to do was kiss her and whisk her away from all this. He caught Devin watching and signaling him to get on with the dialogue.

"So, Regan, you had a chance to tour the house with your mom and I'm sure you can tell she is thrilled with the end results. How about you? Did this meet your expectations?"

She wanted to tell him yes, the house was beautiful and his work was amazing. That he was amazing. But that would have to wait until later. "I think you do very nice work, Sawyer," she said evenly.

"Well, I guess that's a start," he said. "Tell me, if you

had to pick something, and I mean *had* to pick something here that you're most pleased with, what would it be?"

Regan spun and looked around the place. Tears filled her eyes as she turned to him. "It still feels like home," she said tearfully and had to wipe her eyes. "I walked in here and it's still home. You did exactly as you said. You didn't destroy, you enhanced." She took in the entire space and knew she couldn't lie. "It's amazing, Sawyer. So much more than I thought it would be."

The urge to say to hell with everything and kiss her was nearly overwhelming, but Sawyer reminded himself that it was only a few more minutes. If he could just wrap up the filming, everything would be all right. "I'm glad you're pleased, Regan. I know you didn't want us here, but I'm pleased that in the end, you're happy with the results."

Sawyer turned toward the camera and did his ending credits speech to the at-home audience and was relieved when Devin finally yelled, "Cut! That's a wrap, people!"

Everything went into motion at once. There were congratulations, people shaking hands, and Regan and Caroline were laughing and joking with the crew. Yet Sawyer felt a sense of dread coming over him. He couldn't put his finger on it, but he couldn't fight the feeling that something was about to go horribly wrong.

Max walked over and put his arm around Caroline, and Sawyer heard him telling everyone how he found the love of his life on this job. People were toasting them with the beverages that were always kept on hand in a cooler, and although Sawyer lifted his own bottle of water, he kept scanning the room for trouble. Regan was talking to Devin, so Sawyer dropped his water and crossed the room to make sure Devin wasn't saying anything to make her upset.

"We really are pleased you like the house, Regan," Devin was saying. "If you're interested, the network also has a great real estate show where we can showcase the home and really work at getting you top dollar for it."

Regan smiled graciously. "Thank you for the offer, but that decision will be up to my mother. Me, personally? I'm done with the whole reality show thing. I am definitely not comfortable in front of the camera and I'm glad we're done."

"Well, that's a real shame, Regan, because you are a beautiful woman who's a natural in front of the camera."

It sounded like a compliment, but coming from this man it made Regan feel dirty. She smiled and thanked him, making her excuses to go and thank the rest of the crew. Sawyer watched her go and then looked at Devin with disbelief. "What is wrong with you?"

"What?" Devin asked, a smirk on his face.

"Why would you offer her another reality show when she hated this one?"

Devin shrugged. "Hey, I'm a network guy and the network really liked her." Sawyer's eyes narrowed. "As a matter of fact, they really wanted more of Regan in the episode but I told them how she kept her distance."

"Good," Sawyer said, relieved.

"However," Devin said slyly, "I do have an awful lot of B-roll on the two of you. Kissing in the yard, the date where you went strolling downtown. Personally, I liked it when you picked her up and carried her to the car. Classy. I think maybe you romancing her was a nice touch. Sure, it cut down on the drama we could have had, but if you sleeping with her kept her on a leash and made the reno go so smoothly, then I bow to the master." He was smiling when his eyes caught on something right beyond Sawyer's shoulder. "Job well done," he said and walked away.

Sawyer turned and felt as if he had been punched in the gut.

Regan.

The look of utter devastation on her face nearly brought him to his knees. "Regan," he said, reaching for her, but she recoiled.

"Is it true?" she asked softly, not wanting anyone to hear her.

"Nothing Devin says is true, trust me."

She looked around and stepped closer to him. "Did you"—she cleared her throat—"did you seduce me for the sake of the show? To make sure your precious renovation went smoothly?"

"No!" he said a little too loudly, and all heads turned to look at them. Off in the distance, Devin gave a jaunty wave and walked out the door. Sawyer wanted to throttle him. "What happened between us was because of our attraction to one another, not the show. You have to believe me!"

Regan wrapped her arms around her middle. "Did you know he was taping us?" She saw Sawyer's hesitation and felt sick to her stomach. "You bastard," she hissed. "You knew there were cameras on us? You let them tape us? Where did it end, Sawyer? How much did they see? Are there hidden cameras in my house? Is that why you wanted to move in, so you can have extra footage to use?"

"Sawyer moved in with you?" Caroline asked as she suddenly appeared next to her daughter.

"Not now, Mom," Regan said carefully, her eyes never leaving Sawyer's. "Tell me, you son of a bitch—how long did you know they were filming us?"

"Regan, please," he began, "let's go someplace and talk in private." He reached out for her but she stepped back.

"Why? The cameras are still here!" She turned and faced the crew who were silently scattered around the house. "You can turn the cameras on! Big fight scene coming! The network will love it!"

"Regan, stop it!" Sawyer demanded. "It's not what you think, dammit. We need to calm down and talk. Privately."

Max got everyone in motion to gather their things and go. When they were gone, he came to stand behind Caroline. "Is everything okay?" he asked, not sure who exactly he was asking.

"Not now, Dad," Sawyer said harshly.

"I think now is the perfect time," Max snapped back at him. "What the hell did you do, Sawyer?"

Sawyer's eyes went wide at his father's tone and words. "Seriously? You too? I didn't do a damn thing!"

"Really?" Regan cried. "Then explain to me how Devin knew about us? How he happened to know about us kissing in the yard and our date last weekend?"

"You kissed in the backyard?" Caroline asked.

"Not now!" both Regan and Sawyer shouted.

Max put his hands on Caroline's shoulders and squeezed. "Sawyer," Max began, "I think you better explain yourself. Did Devin make you romance Regan for the sake of the show?"

"Oh, for crying out loud!" Sawyer threw his hands up in the air and began to pace. "First of all, who talks like that, Dad? No, I didn't *romance* Regan for the sake of the show. What the hell's the matter with you?" He stalked across the room until he was standing toe to toe with Regan. "And you! How dare you question what we have! I've shared everything of myself with you, and you just immediately believe what Devin says? After everything we've shared, you think I did all that for this damn show?"

"Then tell me how you knew he had taped us!" Regan screamed, her voice cracking on the last word.

Rubbing a hand over his face, Sawyer walked to the sofa and sat down. "I didn't know he was still taping," he said wearily. "When you stopped coming around, he told me I needed to get you here to tape a couple of shots where you were pissed off. I said I wasn't going to make you do that, and he told me he knew I could because he'd seen us kissing in the yard." He looked up at Regan, his eyes filled with remorse. "I tried, Regan, I really tried not to make you get involved with any of it."

"Why didn't you tell me this?" she asked. "I don't understand how it went from that conversation to all this."

"When I told him I wouldn't do it, that's when he told me he had footage of the kiss. He said if I didn't get you here to film he would make *that* the drama—me and you. I figured you would freak out, so I made a snap decision. But you have to believe me, Regan, I swear I didn't know he was still following us! I don't know how we missed it!" He went to her, but she still wouldn't allow him to touch her.

Regan turned to her mother. "This damn renovation,"

she muttered. "All this over a stupid home makeover. I hope it was worth it, Mom, because it's just about ruined everything." Turning, Regan calmly walked to the kitchen to grab her purse before heading toward the door. When she was about to leave, she faced Sawyer. "I don't want any part of this. I should have stuck to my original opinion of it all. I can't trust you. How do I know that Devin isn't going to use the footage anyway? You had me sign like a dozen documents that gave the network the right to use any footage they filmed while on this job."

Tears streamed down her face. "And the thing is, Sawyer, I was able to forget all this, the renovation, my disappointment at losing my family home, and that was all because of you. You helped me to see that it was just a house. I watched Mom and Max and saw she was happy, so I was happy. But all along, you had this secret you kept to yourself. So don't talk to me about all you shared with me, because when something directly involved me, you lied and let that jackass make a joke out of what we had."

"Regan, let's just go home and—"

"No!" she snapped. "Don't you dare think you can come to my home. You can give Mom the key." She looked at Caroline and saw her nod. "I don't want to see you again. I just…I can't."

And she was gone.

Sawyer was shocked. What the hell had just happened? His knees felt like they were about to give out and he barely made it back to the couch before collapsing. With his elbows braced on his knees, he dropped his face into his hands. He couldn't speak, didn't know what to say. It took a minute for him to realize his father was beside him. Slowly, he raised his head and looked at his father sadly. "I love her."

Max nodded. "I know you do. I've never seen you like this with a woman. Watching you these last weeks? Well, it was nice to see. You smiled more. There was a spark in your eyes that wasn't there before. I didn't realize why."

"What am I going to do?"

Max looked toward Caroline, who had gone and busied herself in the kitchen to give them privacy. "You need to let her calm down a little. This all came as a shock to her, so I'm sure she needs some time to think it over and then she'll see you didn't do anything wrong."

"But I did, Dad. She's right. I lied to her."

"No," Max said gently, "you omitted the truth about something you knew was going to upset her."

"It's the same thing. And now? She'll always wonder if what we had was real or if it started because of the show. I can tell her I love her until I'm blue in the face, but the beginning of our relationship is ruined thanks to Devin and his bullshit."

Caroline came to sit beside him and handed him a fresh bottle of water. "She'll get over this, Sawyer," she said softly. "Regan is a passionate woman. Sometimes it takes some time for her to calm down and see things rationally."

"I told him to give her some time," Max said. "It's not like he really lied to her."

Stiffening her spine, Caroline looked at him. "Actually, he did. He told her Devin wanted her here to shoot those scenes or he'd be in trouble with the network—not once did he mention there was a damn near blackmail situation going on."

Sawyer sat between the two of them in stunned silence. They kept arguing back and forth—it was like watching a tennis match.

"Blackmail is a little strong, Caroline, don't you think?" Max said with a snap in his voice. "And if it was that, then it's all the more admirable how Sawyer was trying to protect her."

"Regan had a right to know what was going on so *she* could have confronted Devin and the network and threatened them if they tried to use footage taken on her personal time that had nothing to do with the stupid show!"

"Stupid show? And just for the record, it *did* have to do with the show! She was out with Sawyer—who, FYI, is the *host* of that stupid show!"

Caroline leapt to her feet. "Are you defending him?"

Max stood up too. "Yes, I am. He's my son, and I still say he didn't do anything wrong. I agree that Regan has a right to be upset, but she needs to get over it."

Sawyer knew this was going to end badly, so he stood as well. "Guys, look, I don't want you fighting about this—"

"Not now, Sawyer!" they both yelled and Sawyer threw up his hands, stepping around them to gather his belongings. While the couple continued to argue, he sadly took Regan's key off his key ring and placed it on the dining room table. He looked around at all he had created. An hour ago he had been filled with pride. Funny how it could all go to hell in such a short time.

"Well, if that's the way you really feel, then you can leave and go to hell, Max Bennett!" he heard Caroline yell, and to Sawyer's surprise, his father stormed from the house.

He walked over to Caroline and did his best not to step back when she glared at him. "For what it's worth, Caroline, I honestly did enjoy working with you. Thank you for letting me help you with your home."

She continued to glare, so Sawyer nodded his head and walked out of Caroline Amerson's home and out of both Amerson women's lives.

Chapter 10

"OH, FOR THE LOVE OF IT. YOU HAVE A PROBLEM, YOU know that?"

Regan looked up from the cocoon she had made herself on the sofa and glared at her mother. "Why are you still here? Don't you have someplace else to be? Who's running the spa today?"

"That should be you," Caroline gently reminded her. "But you don't seem to be able to stop playing Solitaire on your tablet while listening to music to slash your wrists by."

"That's a good one, Mom. Ve-ry funny."

"Regan, it's been almost a month now. You rarely leave the house, and we really need you at the spa. Now, enough is enough. I know your heart is broken, but you need to move on. I mean, look at me! I lost Max. I waited ten years to give my heart to someone, and he turned out to be a big jerk."

Regan put the tablet down and looked at her mother, her expression bored. "Max wasn't a jerk, Mom. He was defending his son, which was no different from what you were doing for me. Either way, it wasn't a fight for the two of you to have."

"Well, we did and now it's over and so…there."

"Do you feel better now?" Regan asked sarcastically.

Caroline sighed and shoved her daughter's legs off the sofa so she could sit down. "The pity party is officially over. You have a business to run and a life to live. I can't keep covering for you. I'll be out of town for ten days, so it's your turn now."

"Wait. What? What do you mean you're going out of town for ten days? Where are you going?"

"On a cruise." Caroline shrugged. "I've never been on one and a couple of girlfriends invited me. It's a seniors cruise, so maybe I'll meet a nice man."

"You're hardly a senior, Mom. Sheesh."

"It's for those of us who are fifty and older, and I am definitely in that category. So, I'm cruising the Caribbean. I leave on Monday."

"But…that's in, like, three days! Why didn't you say anything until now?"

"Would it have mattered? Regan, I have to move on with my life. I fell in love with Max Bennett and it didn't work out. Am I sad? Yes. Do I miss him? Yes. Am I going to stop living because of it? No. You need to do the same. I'm not saying you need to go on a singles cruise—"

"I'm not fifty and over," Regan deadpanned and pulled back at the look on her mother's face.

"As I was saying, you don't have to go on a cruise, but you do need to leave this house. Now, I brought over some groceries to restock your kitchen with something other than junk food, but tomorrow, you need to open the spa. I'm done covering for you." She leaned down and kissed her daughter on the head. "And it wouldn't kill you to do a little something with yourself. Let one of the girls give you a mani-pedi at least. And maybe do something with your hair." She took in the rumpled flannel pajamas and quilt covering Regan, the empty bags of assorted snacks surrounding her. "And maybe eat a vegetable or two."

Regan sighed with relief when the front door closed. "I'll eat a vegetable when I damn well want to," she said to the now-empty room. "I don't need my mother telling me what to do. I'm a grown woman." It would have felt a lot more freeing if she wasn't saying it to herself.

Deep down, Regan knew her mother was right. It was enough. She needed to move on from the whole Sawyer thing and go back to living her life. She had been fine before she met him, happy and successful and enjoying her life, and she would be again.

Right after she finished watching the thirty-six episodes of *The Bennett Project* that she had recorded on her DVR. Hearing it helped her go to sleep at night. The sound of Sawyer's voice suggested he was in the room with her and that made Regan feel better.

⁓

Monday morning, Regan opened the spa. She'd finished her last episode of Sawyer's show the night before, then erased them all off the DVR with a promise to herself that she was over him.

Maybe.

Well, almost.

Caroline was leaving for her big trip today and promised to stop by A Touch of Heaven on her way out of town. Although Regan did *not* want to go on a seniors cruise, she envied the fact that her mom was going out and taking a vacation. The closest thing Regan would have to a vacation was her weekend at the beach with Sawyer and, well…

Nope, not going to go there.

Not today.

Well, maybe a little.

The beach would have been glorious. She still had no idea what beach he had booked for them or what they were going to do, but Regan was sure it would have been pure bliss. She could only hope that her mother had a good time on her trip, good enough for both of them.

The bell over the front door jingled and Regan turned to find Caroline walking in wearing turquoise capris, a white cami, and big, dangly turquoise earrings. There was a white straw hat in her hand, and she looked like she was definitely ready for her vacation.

"You look almost tropical, Mom," she said when Caroline kissed her hello.

"I'm feeling pretty tropical. Oh, I cannot wait to have that first drink out at sea. I'm going to have something big and fruity that comes with an umbrella in it."

"You're a rebel, Mom. Remember, baby steps."

"Oh, stop." Caroline looked around the spa and waved to the clients who were in the midst of their pedicures. "So, are you going to be okay? Because if you really need me, I'll cancel the trip and stay and help you."

"Mom! Are you crazy? I would never ask you to do that!"

"Whew! Thank goodness! I really didn't want to cancel my trip!"

"Then why did you say you would?"

"Because you're my daughter and I love you and I worry."

The bell above the front door jingled again and Regan

almost fainted when Max Bennett walked in. "Caroline? If we don't get going, we'll miss our flight."

"Mom?" Regan prompted. "Is there something you'd like to tell me?"

"What? Oh, yes… Max called. We talked and, um… he's coming on the cruise with me. I hope you don't mind."

"Mind? How could I mind? The two of you never should have broken up in the first place. I'm glad things are working out for you, Mom."

Max walked over and kissed Caroline, then leaned in and kissed Regan on the cheek. "How are you, Regan?"

"I'm doing well, Max, thank you. Better now that I see you and Mom back together and looking so happy. I hope you have a wonderful time on the cruise."

"I have to admit," Max began, "I've never been on a cruise ship. I've gone out on fishing boats, but never on something like a luxury liner. But that's where Caroline was going and so that's where I wanted to be." He smiled down at the woman who had stolen his heart and kissed her once again. "I missed you so much."

"Me too," Caroline said and then reached up to bring his lips back to hers for a more intimate kiss.

Regan felt a little ill. "Okay, you two. You need to get going so you don't miss your flight." She was gently nudging them toward the door and was relieved when the kissing stopped.

"I'm going to bring you back something tropical," Caroline promised.

"I'm looking forward to it. Is there anything else you need from me? Everything squared away with the house?"

The house sold practically before Caroline had a chance to put it on the market, with an offer the day she put the sign out. She had packed up all her belongings and put them in storage and spent the last couple of nights at Regan's. "Everything is signed, sealed, and delivered. I did leave your name and number with both the Realtor and the lawyer just in case. The new owners are moving in this week."

"I can't believe it happened so fast," Regan said with just a hint of sadness.

"It was better this way, sweetheart. There wasn't time to linger over old pictures or knickknacks, and really, I think it's time for a new beginning for all of us."

Regan wanted to cry, but didn't want that to be the way her mother saw her as she was leaving to take a dream vacation with the man she loved. Forcing a smile and some cheer into her voice, she wished them both "bon voyage" and sent them off with a hug. She stood at the front window and watched them drive away, but couldn't help the pang of envy. Life certainly could be cruel sometimes.

Her mother had Max.

Some new family had her house.

And she had a week's worth of TV dinners to look forward to.

Something had to give.

―――∿∿―――

The week had flown by and Regan had made the schedule so she could have the weekend off. It wasn't that she had anything in particular to do, but it was time to sit down and think about what she was going to do with her life.

Once her mother got back from the cruise, she would most likely move to Wilmington to be with Max. That would leave a huge gap in Regan's life. She and Caroline were more than mother and daughter—they were friends and business partners. Regan knew she'd be okay running the business alone; she had a great staff and already had someone in mind to promote to assistant manager. No, the problem would be going about her everyday life without seeing Caroline. Wilmington was only three hours away, but it was too far to make a trip there on a whim.

So this weekend Regan decided she was going to truly be done with the pity party and erase that one last episode of Sawyer's show where he walked around without a shirt for most of it that she accidentally forgot to erase, then make some calls and set up plans with friends.

If only she could work up some genuine enthusiasm for any of it.

Sitting at her desk in the office, Regan was finishing entering in all their banking information for the week when her cell phone rang. The screen showed that it was Caroline's Realtor, Jackie, calling.

"Hello?"

"Hey, Regan, it's Jackie from GFN Realty. How are you?"

"Fine, Jackie. What can I do for you?"

"Well, I know your mom is out cruising the Caribbean—and I am so jealous of her—but I got a call from the new owners. They found some boxes in the attic and there's some mail that came in before the post office processed the change of address."

"Oh, okay. Do you have the stuff at the office? I can stop by on my way home tonight and pick it up."

"No, no, it's all at the house. They don't mind holding it until Caroline gets back, but I just thought you might want to go get it. It's a box of photographs and a couple of boxes of Christmas decorations. Do you want me to tell them you'll swing by or do you want to let your mom do it?"

Caroline had hired movers to pack up the house to spare her and Regan the emotional task. In her current state of mind, Regan welcomed going to the house for their belongings. "Tell them I'll be by tonight after six, if that's okay. They can leave the boxes on the front porch if they're not going to be home. There's no rain in the forecast, so they should be fine."

"Sounds good, Regan. Thank you for taking care of this. I was glad the sale went so quickly and you were spared having to show the house repeatedly."

"Thanks. I have to admit I was shocked that it happened the way it did. It seemed as though the sign hadn't been up in the yard for more than an hour and the house was sold."

"The buyer said they had friends in the neighborhood. So when the house went on the market, they called them and let them know. It worked out perfectly for everyone."

"I'll say," Regan said and truly meant it. "I'm sure they'll love it, especially with all the renovations."

"They plan on doing a lot of work to it. I was kind of surprised."

That made Regan mad. "Seriously? That house was like a show home after the Bennetts were through. What more could these people possibly do to it?"

"Honestly, I didn't ask. When we closed on the

house, they mentioned they had a lot of ideas on how they wanted to add to it, so who knows what they'll do."

"Some people don't recognize a great home when they see it," she muttered. "Okay, either way, not my problem and I promise to keep my opinions to myself when I stop by later."

"Good girl," Jackie said. "I really appreciate you going by there, Regan. I'm sure you're anxious to get your family's things back, as well."

"Absolutely. I can't believe Mom missed this stuff."

"They said it was tucked away in the back of the attic so I'm sure it was just an oversight."

They hung up and Regan rethought her plan for the night. There was a great Chinese takeout place near the house, and the thought of some of Lin's famous dumplings made her tummy smile. "I'll get the boxes, pick up the food, then go home and eat and go through some pictures. Not an altogether pathetic Friday night. Close, but not completely."

At six o'clock, Regan said good night to her staff and wished them all a good weekend. "I'll be around if you need me," she assured them, "so don't hesitate to call."

"Go, relax," Todd said. "And for goodness' sake, do something that makes you smile. We miss seeing you smile around here."

Unable to help herself, Regan walked over and hugged him. "People like you make me smile. I'm sorry I've been such a mess lately. I promise to do better."

Todd took both her hands in his. "You don't have to promise anything. We all love you, Rae, and we just want to see you be happy again."

Emotion threatened to overwhelm her. "I want that

too." She gave him another quick hug and headed for the door. "I'll see you all on Monday!"

The drive to the house didn't take long. When she pulled into the driveway, she had to calm herself. The house already looked different: the landscaping in the front had been manicured and the front door and garage door had been painted.

"Certainly didn't waste any time, did they?" she muttered as she exited the car. Regan had to remind herself to be polite no matter what they were doing to her beautiful and perfect family home. It wasn't her place to point out if they were ruining everything. There were no cars in the driveway, but when she reached the front door, the boxes weren't there and the door was ajar. She knocked on the screen door and waited.

And waited.

And waited.

"Hello?" she called out and heard the sound of a power saw off in the distance. "Great, now I have to witness the work." Lord knew she'd had enough of renovations and power tools to last a lifetime.

She called out one more time and then cautiously opened the screen door to let herself in. "Hello? Um, it's Regan Amerson. Jackie from GFN called and told me you had some boxes for me." As she walked further into the house, Regan saw the boxes on the dining room table along with a small pile of mail. She contemplated simply grabbing the stuff and going, but that didn't seem right.

For the most part, the interior looked exactly the same. There wasn't a lot of furniture to be found, but she supposed they were still in the process of moving in and getting settled. With a huff of frustration, she headed to the French doors leading out to the yard. The saw was still buzzing but the person working it was well out of sight. "For real?" she muttered.

Pushing open the door with more force than she intended, Regan stepped out onto the deck and went in search of the homeowner. "Like I have nothing else better to do than chase these people around. There are dumplings waiting to be ordered."

Looking around, Regan immediately noticed the new stainless-steel grill and the nice table and chairs set up under a big adjustable umbrella. "At least they didn't ruin the deck area," she said under her breath as she walked toward the steps that led down to the yard. "Hello?" she called out again.

"Around the side," a male voice called out, and as Regan made her way over, she noticed some new plants and flowers lining one side of the tall wooden fence. She shrugged, refusing to be impressed with their selection of colors or how neat and perfect it all looked.

The man had his back to her—he was shirtless.

She knew that back.

She'd run her hands over it dozens of times.

She'd even bitten it a time or two.

What the hell is Sawyer doing here?

Chapter 11

"I DON'T UNDERSTAND," REGAN SAID. "WHAT ARE YOU doing here? Did the new owners ask you to do more work on the house?"

Sawyer drank in the sight of her. She looked better than anything had in a long time. There was a sadness to her and he knew he was the cause of that. Hated himself for it. "Jackie said you'd be stopping by. I have everything on the dining room table for you." He gestured toward the house, but Regan didn't budge.

"You didn't answer my question. Were you hired to do more renovations on the house?"

Reaching for the towel he had nearby, Sawyer wiped the sweat from his brow before reaching for his jug of ice water and taking a long drink. "You could say that," he finally answered.

Regan huffed and rolled her eyes. "Okay, fine. Whatever." She was quiet for a moment, and he would have sworn she was going to argue with him, but instead she waved him off. "Look, I've got plans, so I'll just get the boxes and go." She turned to walk away but Sawyer stepped in front of her, blocking her path.

"How have you been?"

Crossing her arms over her chest, Regan looked at him with disbelief. "Seriously? You think I want to stand here and do the small talk thing with you?"

"What do you want?" he asked softly, his gaze

lingering on her face, his eyes telling her how much he missed her.

Her expressive face—he could almost hear the snarky retorts she wanted to throw at him—nearly made him smile. She wasn't going to give him an inch, he knew that. He didn't expect her to. Although, right now? He almost wished she'd lash out at him so they could go back to the way things were.

"I want to get my things and go," she said and almost pulled off sounding confident, but her breath hitched a bit and she watched as Sawyer's features softened even more.

Unable to help himself, he reached out and touched her face. Regan closed her eyes as his fingers skimmed down her cheek, her jaw. "I've missed you, Regan. It's been hell without you."

She slowly took a step back. "I'm sorry you've had a hard time, Sawyer," she said carefully and then looked around the yard with longing. "I really need to go."

He nodded. Wordlessly, he led her back into the dining room. "I'll help you load the boxes in your car. The mail's right there. It wasn't much, but I wasn't sure what was important and what wasn't, and I didn't want Caroline to miss anything."

Regan reached for the pile, which was right next to another one with an envelope on top that was addressed to Sawyer Bennett. While Sawyer carried the first box out to her car, she quickly went through the rest of the pile and noticed they were all addressed to him. When he came back in for the next box, Regan held up an envelope and waved it at him. "What the hell, Sawyer? What's going on? I thought you were just doing more renovations for the new owner."

"I never said that," he said blandly. "You did."

"Well, you didn't disagree with me. What gives?"

"I bought the house. So I guess, technically, I am doing work for the new homeowner, who just happens to be me."

She looked ready to spit nails. "And you didn't think that was pertinent information? If Jackie had told me you were the owner, I would have asked her to pick these things up. I knew I couldn't trust you, Sawyer, but I didn't expect you to be cruel."

"Cruel?" he repeated. "How am I being cruel?" He was completely confused. Did she not see where he was going with all this? They had always been able to read each other so clearly and now it seemed like they were strangers.

"After all I went through emotionally with this house and then with you, you swoop in and buy the place? And then make me come here so you can rub my nose in it? You don't think that's being cruel?"

He'd had enough. With great purpose, Sawyer strode over to her and took her in his arms and kissed her like he'd been dreaming of doing ever since she'd walked out on him. Regan fought him for just a moment, but then seemed to melt against him. When her arms went up around his neck, Sawyer finally felt like there was hope.

He slanted his mouth over hers again and again, reacquainting himself with the feel of her, the taste of her. "I missed you so damn much," he said against her throat as he kissed his way down to her collarbone and then back again. There was so much more he wanted to say, but she pulled his mouth back to hers for another hungry kiss. It didn't take long for her to align her body to his and she seemed to be doing her best to get as close to him as she possibly could without stripping.

With more strength than Sawyer actually felt, he broke the kiss and held Regan away from him. "I didn't do this to be cruel to you, Regan. I did this *for* you. For us."

She looked at him with confusion. "I...I don't understand."

"You once said to me that you couldn't buy this house because you were old-fashioned and most men were intimidated by a woman who not only owned her own business but her own home. Well, I'm old-fashioned, too. I believe a man should provide for his wife by putting food on the table, taking care of the bills, making sure she knows she is loved and provided for and...gives her a roof over her head." He pointed upward. "I wanted to provide you with this particular roof."

It took a moment for his words to sink in. "You bought this house...for...me? For us?"

"Regan, from the moment I met you, I knew you were everything I ever wanted and yet never dreamed I'd have. You've made me laugh, you've made me happy, and you've made me mad as hell, but most of all, you made me feel loved. I never thought I'd fall in love with anybody, but one look at you? One touch of your hand and I was lost. I've loved you for a long time, and I know I should have said it way before now, but I didn't want to scare you off. There never seemed to be the right time, and I see now that there were hundreds of times that would have been the right time, but I was too stupid to see them. I love you. I pray that you love me too, because I don't think I can keep going without you being back in my life."

"I've loved you for a long time, too," she finally said. "That's why what Devin said hurt so much. He made me doubt what we had. I kept thinking you were a guy who hosted a TV show who had to act a lot as part of your job. I was afraid that seducing me was part of the act."

Sawyer cupped her face in his hands. "Sweetheart, what I felt for you from the moment you walked in the room in that spangly black T-shirt and shook my hand was one hundred percent real. If I could have taken you back to my hotel that night, I would have. I was ready to walk away from this job, but the thought of doing that and never seeing you again was something I was not prepared to do. I wanted to get to know you and for you to see me as who I am and not as the host of a TV show or the guy who was tearing up your family home. I just wanted you to see me as a man."

"Oh, believe me, I did," she admitted with a shy smile. "I didn't want to like you, but I couldn't seem to stay away from you." Regan stepped back into his embrace and held on tight. "I've missed you, too."

"I know you said you had plans tonight, but maybe, if it's possible, you can cancel them and we can order some takeout and just talk. I'd like to talk about our future, Regan. I finally realized what I want to do with the rest of my life and I want it to start now. I don't want to rush you, but I need you to know that I'm serious and I'm not looking for a roommate or someone to sleep with. I want a wife, a lover, someone to have children with, and I want that with you."

"Well then, this is your lucky day. I happen to be off all weekend because I'm trying to put into motion the plans for my future, and a husband, a lover, and someone to have babies with are on my wish list."

Sawyer smiled down at her, his eyes shining bright with love for her. "We've always been on the same page."

Regan nodded. "Then we *must* be meant to be."

"You know it." Taking her by the hand, Sawyer walked them back to the yard so he could show her his plans for a pergola and a fire pit area, before pulling out his cell phone to order Chinese food.

Epilogue

Three months later…

"WHAT WAS YOUR FAVORITE PART OF THE DAY?"

"When everyone left."

Sawyer laughed and pulled Regan close. "No, seriously. I watched you fluttering around all over the place today and always with a smile on your face, but I want to know what your best part of the day was."

Regan snuggled in. The day had been long and it was late. Although she always loved their late-night chats, she was completely exhausted. "Well…if I *had* to choose, I would have to say that it was the location."

"We could have had the same thing," he reminded her, but Regan shook her head.

"I didn't want the same thing. No, it was wonderful to see the look on Mom's face as she saw the way the yard she's always loved was transformed for her wedding. She's never had much of a green thumb either, and with everything looking the way that it did—her smile was priceless."

"I'm glad she was happy."

"Did you see her face as she walked toward your dad? I hope the photographer was able to capture that because it was the stuff of fairy tales."

"You told me to hang those *twinkly* lights," he said with a little disgust at himself for even using the word.

"There had to be a million of those things around the yard so that it would look like a fairyland."

"Magical. I said it would look *magical*," she reminded him. "And it did." Regan placed a gentle kiss on his chest as she rested her hand over his heart. "Thank you for making it all look so amazing. You have a real gift for that sort of thing. Have you ever considered doing it professionally?"

Sawyer chuckled and tickled her ribs until she was squirming and laughing. He rolled her beneath him. "Very funny." His expression turned serious. "It was their wedding, and I wanted everything to be perfect. They've both waited a long time to get married again, so I wanted to make sure that everything went beyond their expectations. But I do have to admit, I outdid myself."

Regan slapped his arm and he rolled off her but immediately pulled her back to his side. "The yard did look amazing. It's a good thing we put off doing the pool until next year. We would have had to eliminate about fifty people."

"Nah, we just would have had to get creative with the seating. Not that it matters—it's not like we're going to host another wedding back there."

"No," she said absently. "It's not."

"Are you sad that we didn't have our wedding back there?"

Regan shook her head. "No, our wedding was perfect. The beach at sunset? I still think you must have made a pact with God to make it so colorful that night." Just thinking back to their wedding two months earlier had Regan feeling all dreamy. They hadn't wanted to wait and neither wanted anything big. Sawyer had decided to take her to the coast. They'd discussed it over coffee a few days before that, told Max and Caroline of their plans, and decided to go for it.

"You looked like an angel walking toward me barefoot in that white dress, which was one of the sexiest things I'd ever seen. That knot in the front had my hands twitching to undo it the entire time we were saying our vows."

That made her smile. "Good. You were pretty sexy yourself standing there with the sun setting behind your back." She sighed.

"So you're not disappointed that we did something small?"

"Sawyer, we've been over this a million times. I didn't want anything big, plus we had a big party here a few weeks later so that we could celebrate with all our family and friends. It was perfect."

"We do throw a good party."

"That we do," she said and snuggled down a little more into the blankets. Sawyer's arm tightened around her. "That we do." Sleep was calling and she softly kissed his chest one last time.

"I wonder what we'll celebrate back there next," he said, unaware that Regan was just about out cold.

"A christening," she said quietly before yawning.

Sawyer jerked up, effectively knocking his wife from his arms. "What?"

Regan pulled herself up to get her head onto her pillow before facing him. "A christening. You know what they are, right?"

He nodded, but his expression was pure confusion. "Whose christening?"

"Oh, that," she said around another yawn. "I wanted to wait until after the wedding—you know, didn't want to take the focus off of Mom and Max." She rolled onto her side to get more comfortable and was finally about to drift off when Sawyer shook her awake.

"Regan? Stay with me here," he said a little frantically. "What are you saying?"

With a huff of irritation, she rolled onto her back and looked at him. "We're having a baby." Another yawn. "Good night."

When she made to roll over again, Sawyer's hand on her arm stopped her. "What? When?" he stammered. "How?"

Regan opened her eyes and looked at him with disbelief. "We are not having the birds and the bees talk now, Sawyer. It's late and I'm very tired. It's a lot of work hosting a wedding in your home while growing a tiny human being inside you."

"Why didn't you tell me sooner?"

"Because you would have gotten all goofy and not let me do anything and then everyone would have known that I was pregnant. Besides, I'm kind of enjoying your reaction right now. I don't think I would have gotten this at some other point in time." She giggled at his indignation. "This really wasn't how I planned on telling you. I was hoping that after the wedding when everything was cleared away and we were back to normal around here, I'd surprise you with the news over dinner or something."

"Oh, you surprised me all right," he said, his expression turning to one of wonder as he placed his large hand over her flat tummy. "There's a baby in there."

Regan nodded. "Sure is."

"When? When are we due?"

"I haven't seen a doctor yet, but—"

"Then are you sure? How can you be sure if you haven't been to the doctor?"

"I took eight pregnancy tests, Sawyer. Honestly, I don't know how you missed the fact that I was taking out the bathroom trash on a daily basis."

He shrugged. "I figured you were a bit of a neat freak." He looked up at his wife's face and saw his whole future there. Them, children, and a lifetime of love. "I can't believe how lucky I am. That I have you. I don't know what I ever did to deserve you."

"I feel the same way," she said softly.

Leaving one hand on her belly, the other cupped her face. "I know that you hated me when we met, but I'm so glad you changed your mind."

"It wasn't you that I hated, Sawyer, it was the situation. And now, looking back, I am so thankful for it. If Max had never approached my mom that day, none of us would be here right now experiencing all this happiness."

"So the show was good for something," he teased, laughing when Regan rolled her eyes.

"Yes, for something. I'm still annoyed that they snuck in some private footage of us, but it all worked out for the best."

Nodding, Sawyer shifted and reclined next to her. "I heard from the head of the network the other day, and he offered me another show."

Regan turned and looked at him. "Why didn't you say anything?"

"Because it meant nothing. They can keep waving the salary increase and the merchandising shares, but they don't seem to understand that it's not about the money. It was never about the money for me. I do what I do because I love it. I love the craft. Plus, I don't want to have to travel and be away from home for such long periods of time again. And if I had known then what I know now, I could have driven that point home even more."

"What did he say?"

"What could he say? I told him that I'm enjoying being back to regular carpentry work and small renovation projects that let me work more closely with the homeowners. He wished me well but said that he's still hoping to find a project to bring me back."

Regan smiled with pride. "That's because you're amazing and they probably lost a large part of their viewing audience when you left."

"I don't think so."

"I do. That one episode where you were shirtless for most of it kept me going while we were apart." Regan had shared with him all about her marathon of episode-watching.

Laughing, he pulled her in close and turned out the bedside lamp. "Well, lucky for you that you don't need to watch it on TV, you've got the live show right here."

Regan giggled at his cocky tone, but was willing to agree. "I am indeed a very lucky woman."

Sawyer kissed the top of her head and sighed. "I'm the lucky one. You changed my whole world and showed me all that I was missing. And now? I have even more to look forward to and it's all because of you. I love you."

"Love you, too," she said sleepily, and this time, she really did get to go to sleep.

*Keep reading for a sneak peek of the next book
in the Montgomery Brothers series from
bestselling author Samantha Chase*

Suddenly
Mine

Chapter 1

"DON'T THESE PEOPLE HAVE JOBS?" CHRISTIAN MONTGOMERY murmured to himself as he sipped his morning coffee.

For a while now, he had taken to having his coffee out on his deck before going into work. It was a chance to breathe in the fresh air and have some peace before the craziness of his day. People-watching had become his favorite hobby, and as odd as it sounded, he found it relaxing and therapeutic.

Scanning the sand, he smiled at the small circle of people doing yoga off to his left. Every day they were out there stretching and holding their poses, and it was almost hypnotic to watch. At times, he even found himself deep breathing along with them, as he imagined they were doing.

Not far from them was a trio of fishermen. Not once had Christian ever seen them catch anything, but they were out there religiously every morning—rain or shine. That was one hobby he had never had an interest in. It looked boring. Those guys were there before Christian came out on his deck, and he imagined they stayed out there long after he left for work. He could only hope they caught some fish.

Then there were the surfers. They were also hypnotic to watch but offered a bit more excitement. There was no way he could even imagine himself doing what those people did, but it was cool as hell to watch. Some of them were amazing at it, while others sort of…well, they tried.

Which reminded him…

"Oh, this is glorious! I could totally get used to this!"

Great. His mother was awake and encroaching on his peaceful time.

Looking out at the waves crashing on the shore, he took another sip of his coffee before turning to look at his mother. "You're up early."

She took a long sip of her own steaming coffee before answering. "Well, as much as I complain about your father's snoring, it appears I can't sleep without him." With a serene smile, she added, "Besides, I was hoping to have a few minutes with you before you left for the office."

He'd been avoiding this sort of thing. After getting ambushed at Megan and Alex's engagement party with the news that his mother and aunt would be coming home with him, Christian had been doing his best to stay out of their way. But apparently, his reprieve was up.

He almost jumped at the feel of his mother's hand covering his. She looked so sweet, yet he had a feeling there was more to this trip to San Diego than starting some sort of wellness program.

"You work too hard," she said, point blank. "Monica and I tried waiting up for you, but we were both exhausted and couldn't wait any longer. What time did you finally come home?"

"I don't know. Sometime around eleven."

She made a disapproving sound. "Were you working all that time or did you happen to have a date?"

It was a challenge not to roll his eyes. "I was working,

Mom. I wouldn't have blown you and Aunt Monica off for a date."

"Well…you should," she argued lightly. "It wouldn't kill you to get out and date more."

"Mom…"

Placing her mug on the deck railing, she faced him. "Christian, you remind me so much of your father." Then she paused. "And that's not a compliment."

Okay, this was new.

"I don't know everything that happened in London and I don't want to know," she stated. "What I do know is that it's gone on long enough. You work too much, you spend far too much time alone, and I can't ignore it anymore."

Christian sighed wearily and drank the rest of his coffee before putting his mug beside hers.

"I get that you're disappointed in me—"

Her soft gasp stopped him.

"Christian, I could never be disappointed in you. Ever," she said vehemently. "But I look at you and I can see you're not happy." Reaching up, she cupped his cheek. "No mother wants to see her child unhappy. You need a life outside of work."

"That's not what Dad thinks," he mumbled.

"You know you don't have to do everything your father says, don't you?" Her words were soft and firm and when Christian looked at her, he saw a hint of a smirk on her face. "Your father is a very intelligent man, but not everything he says is the gospel truth. As a matter of fact, I think it's safe to say that where anything outside of work is concerned, your father doesn't know what he's talking about."

Christian couldn't help but chuckle. "You're pretty feisty early in the morning," he teased.

She waved him off. "I'm feisty all the time, but no one seems to pay attention."

So many thoughts were racing through his mind. It was easy to stand here and say he didn't have to listen to his father—or anyone for that matter—but actually doing it without letting the guilt eat away at him were two different things. And it didn't matter how old he was or how independent he was, for some reason his father could make him feel like an incompetent child with a few choice words.

"Christian," she went on, interrupting his thoughts. "If you're not happy in this career, you know you can change that, right? Just because you have the Montgomery name doesn't mean you have to work for the company."

"Everyone else does."

This time her smile was patient and loving and so completely a mom look. "Your brother doesn't, and for years your sister didn't."

"And now she does," he gently reminded.

"But she turned down the opportunity for a big promotion because she realized she wanted more out of her life. And from what I understand, you helped her realize that."

He felt himself blush. Clearing his throat, Christian turned and leaned on the railing. "Yeah, well… I hated the thought of Megan getting trapped like I am."

He realized a little too late what he'd just admitted.

"Sweetheart, you're not trapped," his mother said quietly, her hand covering his again. "If there's something you want to change, you should! Life is too short to stay in a place that makes you miserable."

"I wouldn't say I'm miserable—"

"But are you happy?" she quickly interrupted.

That question gave him pause. "Sometimes I think I am."

Beside him, she sighed. "Do you like living in San Diego?"

"What's not to like? I've got a great house right on the beach. The view alone makes it pretty spectacular."

"Christian, you've been living here for five years and this isn't even your house. If you like it here so much, why not find a place of your own and settle down?"

It was way too early in the morning for this conversation.

"Mom, Ryder and I have an agreement on the house. He's fine with me living here, and he knows if he wants to sell, I'm the first one who'll put an offer in."

"You're avoiding making any commitment here," she gently chided. "It's your cousin's house and your father's company, and I would love to see you pick something that was yours and enjoy it."

"*Bollocks*," he muttered, raking a hand through his hair.

With a small laugh, his mother scolded him. "No need for that language."

He almost laughed with her. After spending so many years living in London, Christian had picked up a lot of the lingo and every once in a while, it came out.

Usually when he was annoyed.

"Mom," he said with a huff of frustration. "This is not how I want to start the day—arguing with you about my life choices."

"I'm not arguing—"

"You are," he corrected.

"I'm concerned, Christian. There's a difference."

As much as he didn't doubt that, the truth was that he just wasn't in the mood for this particular discussion, so as a distraction, he hugged her. "And I love you for it." He placed a kiss on the top of her head. "Now, tell me how your search for a wellness provider is going."

If she knew why he was changing the subject, she kept it to herself. "I've been pleasantly surprised at how well things are falling into place. Patricia in human resources has been amazing!" She stepped out of his embrace and sat on the nearby chaise. "We're going to be holding more interviews—but it's a formality. Monica and I met the perfect applicant already."

"So then why keep interviewing?"

"This particular applicant we haven't formally interviewed yet, so we're covering our bases."

"Mom," he admonished. "That's not a great way to handle this."

"Oh, hush. Trust me on this one. I want to have backups, but I am confident that once we do the formal interview, everything will fall into place."

He studied his mother for a long moment and realized he didn't want to get too involved in this. Just admitting that to himself let him relax. With a smile, he said, "I do trust you. You've done great things with this program, so who am I to tell you how you should be doing things?"

"Thank you." She smiled proudly. "But the best part of the whole thing was how Patricia was able to secure office space that would require little to no work to modify."

He nodded, thankful for that little bit of news. The last thing he wanted was to deal with the headache of office renovations.

"Basically, you won't have to worry about a thing," she continued. "All you need to do is be pleasant and greet whoever we hire in a way that won't scare them away."

Christian laughed. "I'm hardly scary, Mom."

"You could smile more." She was about to say something else but instead glanced toward the house. "I promised your father I'd call him this morning and you know he'll worry if I don't." Walking over, she gave him a quick kiss on the cheek before heading back inside.

The whoosh of relief at being alone came out before he knew it. As much as he loved his mother, she could be a bit exhausting.

Especially this early in the morning.

Turning his attention to the beach, a slow smile spread across his face. "There you are," he said quietly.

With a quick glance over his shoulder to make sure his mother wasn't coming out, Christian immediately returned his attention to the shore. Every morning, dozens of surfers came out and started their day by riding the waves. When he'd first moved to San Diego and into his cousin Ryder's house, he'd been a bit annoyed at the constant sea of bodies practically right outside his door. It didn't take long for him to realize they weren't the least bit interested in him, they were here for the ocean. Nothing more, nothing less. And the longer he lived here, the more he appreciated all of the activity on the beach—particularly the surfing.

Surfing had never been something that interested him before, but one morning he'd come out on the deck with his cup of coffee and noticed one surfer in particular. Christian didn't know any of them personally, but had named them each based on what he'd observed. For instance, there was Surfer Dude—a young guy with sunbleached blond hair and a tan who embodied exactly what Christian has always envisioned a surfer would look like. Then there was Older Surfer Dude, who was exactly as described. After that the names were a little more random: Tie-Dye Guy, Too-Tan Girl, and Burly Guy. They were the regulars, but if someone new caught his attention, he usually gave them a name while he watched them.

Seriously, this had been his greatest form of entertainment.

Then there was *her*.

No nickname would do her justice.

With long red hair pulled up into a ponytail and skin that was far too fair to be out in the sun for long, she stood out in a sea of blond surfers. From this distance, Christian couldn't be certain how tall she was, but if he had to guess, he'd say she was on the petite side. Dressed in long-sleeved black Lycra that encased an incredibly curvy body, she was completely captivating. Today's bikini bottoms were neon pink. Her legs were just as spectacular without the fabric as they were with. If he was a bolder guy, he'd head to the water and pretend he was a surfer to get a closer look at her and maybe introduce himself.

But…he wasn't.

And he couldn't.

Duty called.

But not before he watched her attempt at surfing awhile longer.

For all her gear and apparent enthusiasm, she wasn't a good surfer. Even without any real knowledge of the sport, Christian could tell she was a novice. He'd watched her stand and fall off her board more times than he cared to count, yet every time she fell, she got up and tried again.

He had to admire her perseverance.

And the way she looked soaking wet.

In his mind, he imagined being able to walk down to the water and right into it with her. He'd put his hands on her waist and help her onto her board. His touch would linger just a bit, and he knew his fingers would twitch with the need to feel her skin—to know if it was as soft as he imagined. In the suit she had on today, he could be bold and run a hand along her leg, skim her thigh before watching her swim into the current.

From there, he'd stay in the water to cool his own skin. He'd watch her catch a wave and ride it successfully until she was back at his side—exuberant at the thought of finally making it. She'd jump into his arms, wrap those magnificent legs around him, and kiss him.

Licking his lips, he could almost taste the salt, along with the softness of her. He almost groaned at the image.

From there he'd invite her up to the house and finally see how she looked without the Lycra.

No doubt it would be fantastic.

Behind him, he heard his mother and aunt laughing and boy, didn't that kill the fantasy. Which was just as well—it wasn't as if he could do anything about it. There was no way he was going down to the beach or into the water or…inviting his surfer girl back to the house.

The thought was more than a little disappointing.

He had to get ready for work. Just like he always did. There hadn't been a day since he was fifteen when he hadn't been responsible or gone to the office. Even all through college Christian had held a job with Montgomerys. Back then it was in his father's New York office, then later he'd jumped at the opportunity to move to London—partly for the change of scenery and partly to have a little independence. That hadn't gone quite as planned and now he was in San Diego, still making sure he never gave anyone a reason to question his dedication to the job.

Although…he was starting to question his own dedication. Lately, no matter how much he tried to tell himself otherwise, there was a growing discontent within himself. Maybe it was the job, or maybe it was just his life in general, he couldn't be sure. All Christian knew was that there were a lot of people counting on him and he couldn't sit out on his deck looking out at the ocean all day. He had a full day of appointments, and no matter how badly he'd like to—for once—play hooky and enjoy a day for himself, he couldn't.

Joseph Montgomery wouldn't allow him to.

And whose fault is that?

Yeah, yeah, yeah. He knew he was responsible for the position he was in now by refusing to stand up for himself early on and letting his father get away with calling the shots. They'd butted heads a lot—particularly in the past five years—but it didn't change anything. Every time they fought, Christian would cave out of respect to his father, because if nothing else, he was a good son. This was their pattern of behavior and it was too late to change the dynamic.

Or was it?

He caught sight of his surfer girl flying off her board and smiled. That made four times in the short time he'd been watching. She came up laughing—as she often did—and in that instant, he envied her. Did she ever feel discouraged? Did she ever break through the water after a fall and scream *bloody hell* and just want to give up? She was clearly failing and yet…she was still smiling and finding joy in it. How was that possible? If it were him and he was the one out there constantly falling off his board, he would have given up by now. Sometimes you had to admit defeat and realize there would be some skills you simply couldn't master. Didn't she realize that?

Now wasn't the time to find out, unfortunately. He had responsibilities and commitments and none of them made him feel joyful. If anything, he could already feel his body tensing up. It felt as if it began at the tip of his toes and was working its way up through his entire being—the muscles growing tighter until it felt constricting, like he couldn't breathe.

It wasn't the first time he'd felt that way, but it was happening with more and more frequency.

Rubbing a hand over his chest, Christian tried to calm down and clear his mind. *Deep breaths*, he reminded himself. *Just take some deep breaths*.

And for several minutes he did. It helped. Sort of. Either way, he felt well enough to grab his coffee mug and give one last look at the beach before heading into the house and preparing for another full day of…nothingness.

Sophie Bennington breathed through the pain as she made her way out of the ocean and onto the shore. That last wave had hit her hard and she knew she'd be feeling the effects of it for the rest of the day.

"So not the day for this," she murmured, walking slowly to her stuff. It was still a bit surprising that she could leave her things in the sand and they'd go undisturbed, but right now she was thankful for it.

The beach wasn't particularly crowded—just folks like her who were interested in catching some waves before they had to head off to their real jobs and responsibilities.

She dropped her board on the sand and sat on her towel. She inhaled the fresh air before letting the breath out slowly. If it were up to her, she'd stay here all day and enjoy the sunshine and sounds of the waves crashing on the beach. Unfortunately, that was no longer an option.

Sure, she'd been pretty much doing that for the last several weeks—not that she spent entire days on the beach, but she also hadn't had any reason to rush off.

Not like today.

Today she had a job interview and almost broke out in a hallelujah chorus over it. Moving to a new state on a whim had been completely out of her comfort zone, but a healthy savings account had meant that she didn't need to stress about finding a job right away. Part of her had felt like being a bit more rebellious and shirking some responsibility for a little while. But fun time was over, and her more practical side was coming out to remind her that she needed to find a job. She just hadn't realized it might take longer than she wanted.

But…she was feeling extremely optimistic about this

interview and she had more than enough credentials and experience, and by all accounts, she should be a shoo-in.

"Don't go getting ahead of yourself," she quietly reminded herself. "Just because you think you're all that and a bag of chips doesn't mean everyone else will."

A girl could hope though, right?

All around her people were moving and laughing and doing their thing, while Sophie contemplated the day ahead. It had been a long time since she'd gone on a job interview. Having lived her entire life in a small town, she knew everyone. Add to that having gone to college in the next town over and living at home, getting a job had been handled over Sunday dinner or at the potluck after church. Dealing with strangers was going to be a bit of a challenge.

"But I'm up for it," she said confidently. "I moved a thousand miles on my own, I can do this."

Daily pep talks were becoming the norm for her and she wasn't quite so sure that was a good thing. Basically, she was talking to herself.

A lot.

Refusing to let herself believe she was going crazy, Sophie stood and stretched. The sky was definitely getting brighter, the morning clouds had moved on, and she noticed a mini mass exodus to the parking lot. That meant it had to be around eight o'clock. Her interview was at eleven, so she had plenty of time, but she had a feeling it was going to take every one of those hours and minutes to get her nerves under control.

With a final look at the ocean, she collected her things. She'd gotten it down to a science—towel rolled and put in her backpack, sunglasses on, flip-flops in her hand, and board under her arm. It only weighed ten pounds, but it was awkward as hell to maneuver: the board was close to seven feet long and she was barely five foot three, but she was stronger than she looked. Most people tended to underestimate her—in just about every way—based on her size. What they didn't know was that she had enough determination to do whatever she put her mind to and was willing to do the work to get it done.

Athletics came easy to her and at times, her size worked to her advantage. Where surfing was concerned, however, she had been encouraged to get a larger board until she gained some skills. That wasn't happening nearly as fast as she'd hoped, and by now Sophie was seriously hoping that she could trade out for a smaller board.

"Soon," she said, making her way back to the parking lot. "I just need to practice a little more."

Or a lot, she corrected.

Walking across the lot, Sophie smiled at fellow beachgoers and said a word of thanks to the kind gentleman holding the door open for her at the surf shop. Renting her board made a lot more sense than going out and buying one outright—especially if she came to the conclusion that surfing wasn't her thing.

"How'd it go today, Soph?" Randy, the owner of the surf shop, asked. He was in his mid-thirties and had the look of the perpetual surfer—tanned, shaggy hair, and puka-shell necklace included.

"I think I'm getting better," she said optimistically. "But that last wave knocked the wind out of me and the board hit me pretty hard as I flipped." Absently, she rubbed her hip. "No doubt I'll have a nice bruise to show for it by lunchtime."

"It goes with the territory," he said, taking the board from her and giving her a receipt. "Do you want to try a different board tomorrow? Maybe something a little lighter?"

"You said this was the size I should be using, since I'm a beginner," she reminded him. "And besides, I think I'm getting used to it. I need to work on my confidence and maybe my concentration."

He grinned at her. "You should have taken more than one lesson. And while I can appreciate your enthusiasm, it never hurts to get a little help with your technique."

Placing the receipt in her bag, she smiled. "I'll think about it. Right now I've got to go and get ready for my job interview."

His blue eyes widened. "Hey, that's great! Did you finally opt to go with an agency?"

"I did," she said, with just a touch of sadness. "They're sending me today to meet with my first client company. It's not exactly what I had planned, but...I'm sure it's going to be great."

It was important to stay optimistic.

Over the past several weeks, she'd shared a little about her job search with pretty much anyone who would listen in hopes of getting some recommendations. She'd begun to lose hope until she'd been talking to a couple of older ladies on the beach and they'd shared with her a lead on a potential position. That morning she had signed on with an agency and had mentioned the job opportunity to her contact. After some negotiation, Sophie had managed to secure the position—even though there were others at the agency who had senior-ity over her.

"Fingers crossed," she said cheerily, walking toward the door. "If you don't see me tomorrow, that means I'm starting a new job!"

"Good luck, Soph! I'm sure you're going to do great!"

"Thanks, Ran!"

Pulling her keys out, she was in her car and on her way home in no time. Her studio apartment was only a mile from the beach, but traffic was already congesting the roads. It was nearing nine o'clock when she walked through her front door. Tossing her backpack on the sofa, Sophie immediately went to the refrigerator and poured herself a glass of orange juice. She was about to take a shower when her cell phone rang.

Taking the phone from her pack, she smiled and sighed at the same time.

"Hey, Nana," she said, kicking off her flip-flops. "How are you this morning?"

"Oh, you know me. Can't complain. How's California treating you? Ready to come home yet?"

They had this conversation several times a week since Sophie moved away. "Nope. I'm enjoying the beach and the sunshine. I think I can see myself living here permanently."

"Now, Soph, you know California is one of the most expensive places in the country to live. Why would you put all that extra stress on yourself, especially when you know the cost of living is so much more reasonable here in Kansas."

"Not everything is about being cost-effective, Nana.

Sometimes you have to leave your comfort zone to find what makes you happy. And worrying about the cost of living does not make me happy."

"I'm sure it won't—if you keep living there, the stress of it will make you downright miserable."

I walked right into that one, she thought.

"I don't think I'll be worrying for too much longer."

"Oh?"

"I have a job interview today!" she said excitedly.

Nana snorted softly.

"Oh, stop," she chided. "I think it's going to be perfect. It's exactly what I was looking for—practically as if the job was created just for me!"

"Probably a scam."

"Thanks for the vote of confidence."

For her entire life, Nana had been her biggest champion—always telling Sophie there wasn't anything she couldn't do. She was the only parent Sophie had ever known, and Sophie knew that right now, Nana was lashing out like this because she missed her.

At least, she hoped that was why.

A weary sigh came over the phone before Nana spoke again. "I worry about you, that's all. This whole thing— you moving away in a show of defiance, well…it's hard for me. I thought you'd go and see that California wasn't for you and just come home."

Resting her head against the sofa cushion, Sophie let out her own sigh. "We've been over this. You know why I needed to do this."

"I know, I know. And…I hope you find what you're looking for, sweetheart. But I hate that you felt the need to do it so far away from me."

For a moment, her heart hurt. "It was time for a change. I couldn't stay there knowing—"

"I know," Nana quickly said, and Sophie was thankful they weren't going into details again. She couldn't handle that right now. Not when she needed to focus on positive things.

"I went surfing again this morning," she said, abruptly changing the subject.

"And? How did you do?" Nana asked, with her first hint of encouragement.

"Still not getting far, but I'm having fun!"

"That's my girl." She paused. "Tell me about this job you're interviewing for. Is it really what you're looking for, or are you settling because you need to find a job? Because if you're going to settle, you know I can help you out financially until you find the right one."

It would be easy to accept the financial help. And right now, with her bank account balance dwindling, a little padding wouldn't hurt. But she'd sworn to herself that she'd make it on her own no matter what. She wasn't broke, and today's meeting was a done deal. They were going to be her first clients, and once she proved herself to the agency, no doubt she'd get a few more assignments.

"I'm fine, Nana. I promise. I have a good feeling about today." For the next several minutes she talked about the position and all it would entail and could barely contain her excitement. By the time she was done explaining, Sophie was almost breathless. "So now I have to shower and find something to wear and do something with my hair so I don't look crazy—"

"Your hair is beautiful. If you use one of those silver

clips I gave you, it will be perfect." Nana was silent for a moment before adding, "You're perfect. And don't you ever forget it."

And just like that, Sophie relaxed.

To most people, she might come off as being confident, but sometimes she needed a few words of encouragement from the one person who loved her.

"Thanks, Nana."

"Go and show these people why they are lucky to have you! And promise you'll call me later and tell me all about it."

Smiling, Sophie replied, "I will."

Placing the phone on the cushion next to her, she wondered why life wasn't always as simple as it used to be. There was a time when she never would have considered leaving her hometown. She knew everyone, and everyone knew her. Life was uncomplicated.

Until it wasn't.

Secrets had a way of ruining everything.

"So not the time to be thinking about this," she murmured, forcing herself to stand up and grab another glass of juice.

One of the reasons Sophie had hopped in her car and driven a thousand-plus miles for a change of scenery was to help her forget. The other was to start over—as someone nobody knew, and people could choose to either love her or hate her for herself, not because of her family history.

So far, it had been working.

Sometimes, however, her mind was her own worst enemy.

"Not now and not today," she stated firmly, drinking

her juice and walking determinedly toward the bath-room. "I have to kick butt on this interview, so only happy thoughts!" With that, she turned on her shower and then immediately reached over and turned on her iPod, cranking up some of her most motivating music.

Under the spray, she sang—badly—at the top of her lungs while she washed her hair. One song led to another and by the time she shut the water off, she'd gone through at least a half dozen of them. Clearing her throat, she realized she may have been a little overzeal-ous in her singing.

"Not smart, Soph. Definitely not smart."

Opting to *listen* to the rest of the playlist, she went about carefully applying her makeup before starting the lengthy process of drying her hair. How many times had she considered cutting her long tresses, only to back out at the last minute? It was a love-hate relationship, basically—she loved how it looked when it was styled and behaving but hated it every time she had to dry and style it.

Studying her reflection as she combed through the wet tangles, she said, "Clearly, I have issues."

Issues or not, she finished getting herself ready—hair, makeup, and a kick-ass outfit with a jade-green pencil skirt that matched her eyes and a white blouse. It was simple but crisp and professional, and when she walked out her front door a little later, she felt like she could take on the world!

About the Author

Samantha Chase is a *New York Times* and *USA Today* bestseller of contemporary romance. She released her debut novel in 2011 and currently has more than forty titles under her belt! When she's not working on a new story, she spends her time reading romances, playing way too many games of Scrabble or Solitaire on Facebook, wearing a tiara while playing with her sassy pug, Maylene…oh, and spending time with her husband of twenty-five years and their two sons in North Carolina.

Also by Samantha Chase